PATH OF THE PALADIN

THE FOURTH BOOK OF THE DARK GODDESS

MELISSA MCSHANE

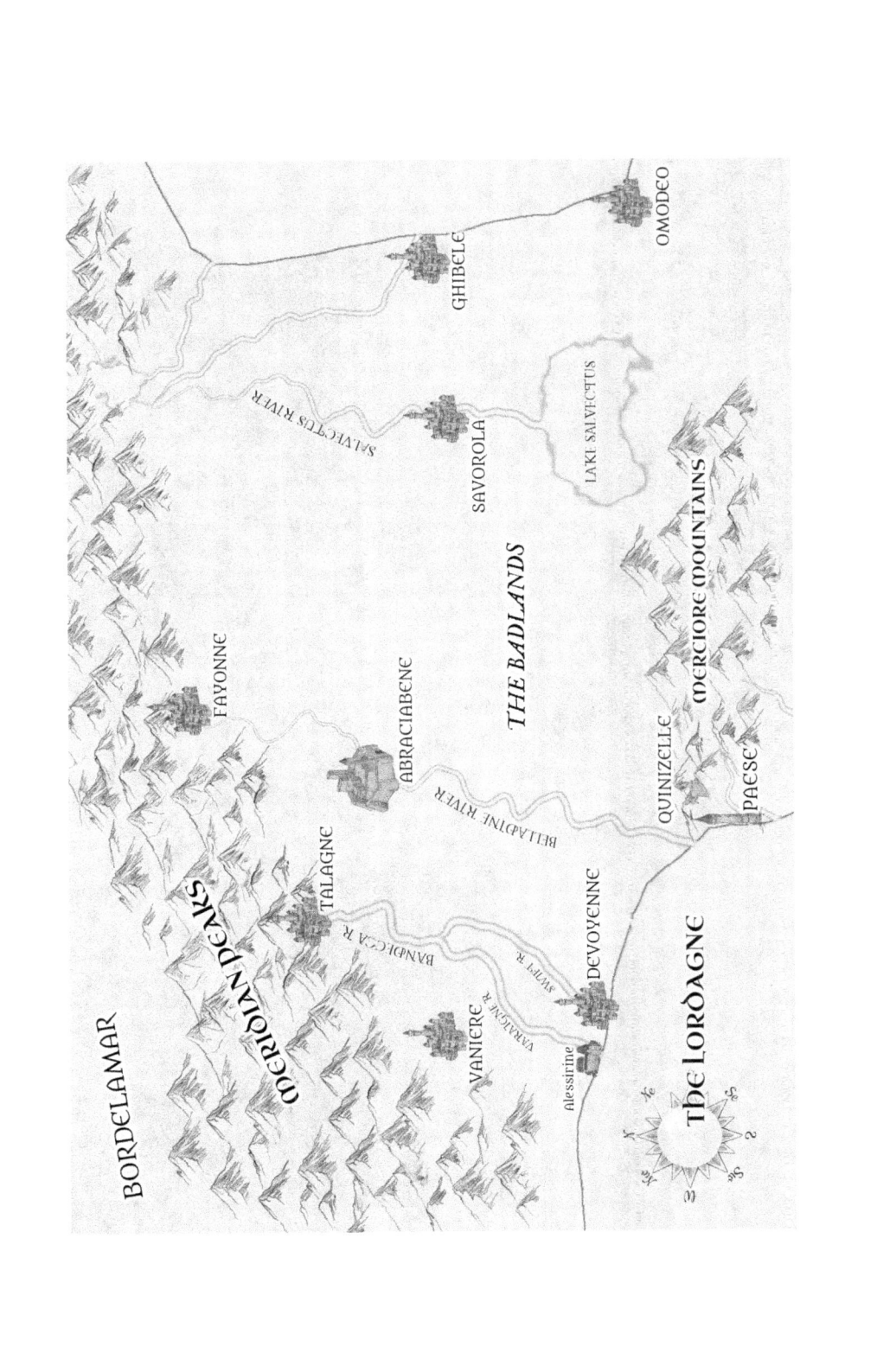

S mell was an odd thing. Some smells took Gunnevra back to her childhood, like hot metal at the forge or the way horses smelled when they came into the paddock after a long day's riding. Other smells were only good at times. Just that morning she'd woken to the scent of honeyed pastries filling the air through the streets of the city of Ghibele. That had been pleasant for the first hour, and then it was cloying and awful.

At the moment, with her face crushed firmly into the turf, all she smelled was damp earth and the nose-tickling scent of grass gone dormant for the winter. Her hand curled more tightly around the handle of the silver mirror. This was not at all the way she'd meant to spend her morning.

She pushed herself to her knees, groaning with effort. Goddess-enhanced reflexes and stamina didn't make her invulnerable, and half an hour of fighting this monster had started to wear on her. Even without armor, just her padded red gambeson and coif to keep stray locks of hair out of her eyes, she had raised a sweat in the autumn chill.

Two feet away, a cow regarded her placidly, its jaw working as it chewed its cud. It showed no sign it knew it was in danger. Ginnevra groaned again and got to her feet. That was how the monstrous catoblepas hunted: it could walk right up to a cow because it looked and smelled just like its prey, save for the serpentine neck four feet long and the permanently drooping, oversized head. A catoblepas looked so harmless—right up until an animal or human caught the creature's gaze and dropped dead.

She angled the mirror to look over her shoulder. She and Eodan had managed to herd the catoblepas away from the other animals, but it kept drifting back in an aimless yet eerily malevolent way, drawn there like water funneling down a drain. There it was, taking another step closer to the unsuspecting cows. And there was Eodan, hovering behind it, black woven sack in hand. His hair was tangled in windblown hanks, and he looked as weary as she felt.

"This isn't working," Ginnevra shouted over her shoulder, hoping the wind would not blow her words too far away. "The damn thing doesn't care what we do to it. I swear it's as stupid as the cows."

Eodan lowered the sack. "We need different bait."

Ginnevra's gaze shifted to the cow. It let out a sound somewhere between "moo" and "blart." "I promised the farmer I would save his cows."

"Sacrifice one for the survival of the rest," Eodan said. "And if the man doesn't butcher us a few steaks after this, I'm going to feel very ill-used."

Ginnevra sighed. "I can't argue with that logic. Besides, with two dead workers along with more than a handful of cows, I'm sure the farmer will see sense."

She lowered the mirror and walked toward the cow, who

continued to eye her in a dull, uncomprehending way. "Go on, you," she said, smacking the cow's rump with the flat of her gloved hand. "Over that way."

She heard the catoblepas take a few more heavy steps, rustling the dry grass. Eodan said, "I almost feel sorry for it."

"Cows are too stupid to understand death," Ginnevra said. "At least, so I've heard. Before this I'd never come closer to a cow than at the supper table."

"I meant the catoblepas. For a monster, it's not so bad."

Ginnevra started to turn around, remembered the monster's deadly gaze, and raised the mirror so she could see Eodan's face. "You can't be serious. One look and people drop dead. That's pretty bad."

"Yes, but it's not malevolent. It kills people mostly by accident." Eodan followed the monster as it walked. "It's dangerous, true, but more in the way a falling tree or a blizzard is dangerous."

"And that's why I will kill it without animosity." Ginnevra smacked the cow's rump again, this time angling the mirror so she could see how close the catoblepas was. "Taking it somewhere far from people is impractical. It would eventually find a settlement or a city."

"I know. I'm not saying don't kill it. I'm saying it's a shame there isn't another option. Blinding it would be cruel."

"I wouldn't do that even if it were possible." The catoblepas had nearly reached the cow. Ginnevra braced herself for its attack.

Then it stopped moving. Its large, bovine head, nose down as if it weighed a hundred pounds, swiveled. It lifted its head, a slow, ponderous motion. Its reflection stared at Ginnevra, its solid white eyes the only truly malicious thing about it. Despite the protection of the mirror, Ginnevra shuddered as if the gaze had gone straight through her.

"Ginnevra," Eodan said, sounding alarmed.

The catoblepas took another step, then another, not toward the cow but toward Ginnevra. She slowly stepped away, never letting the mirror waver. "Eodan, take it," she said just as the wind across the pasture buffeted her words away. "Take it, Eodan!"

Lowering its head, the catoblepas charged. Ginnevra sprinted for the fences.

She knew from the morning's exertions she could outrun the monster over short distances. It took time for the catoblepas' limbs to sort themselves out into a run. But once it got going, it built up speed until it could outrace a horse. Ginnevra ran faster. The one thing she was sure it was incapable of was vaulting a fence.

She didn't bother looking behind her with the mirror; that would only slow her down. She couldn't hear Eodan over the sound of the monster's pounding feet and heavy breathing. With luck, that meant he was in position.

The wind gusted again, bringing her the warm, ripe scent of the catoblepas, just like all the cows except for the smell of rancid meat from the monster's carnivorous diet. The catoblepas was closer than Ginnevra liked, almost breathing down her neck. Even as she reminded herself it couldn't kill her with its gaze if she didn't turn around, she thought of its needle-sharp teeth that had torn into at least seven cows and the farm hands Murria and Piettro.

The fence was mere feet away. Ginnevra reached deep within herself for reserves she hadn't known she had, leaped for the top log of the fence, and sprang over it, rolling as she hit the ground and squeezing her eyes shut. "Eodan?" she shouted. She no longer knew where was safe to look.

There was a pause. Then Eodan said, rather breathlessly, "I caught it. You can look now."

Ginnevra sat up and opened her eyes. The catoblepas stood at the fence, the ground behind it torn up from where it had skidded coming to a rapid halt. The black bag entirely covered its head, and Eodan was just cinching up the ropes that secured the bag to the long neck. His hair was even messier than before, and his face was red with exertion. But he gave her a cheery smile that relaxed her.

"Thank you," Ginnevra said. "I wonder what set it off?"

"Who knows?" Eodan pushed hair out of his face with one hand. The other hand he kept on the ropes, as if he feared them coming undone despite the many knots. Ginnevra sympathized with that fear. "Maybe it didn't like your smell. You *are* rather covered in dirt."

Ginnevra brushed absently at a smear of dirt on her gambeson and succeeded only in making it a larger smear. "I'll be right back."

She was tired, but she pushed herself to run rather than walk to where she had left her paladin's greatsword. Walking meant giving in to weakness, and paladins never let weakness master them. Still, her gait was closer to a trot than a run No sense truly exhausting herself. There might be more monsters around. She examined the broad, grassy fields hemmed in with log fences, the distant glitter of the ocean, and admitted that was unlikely. Even so, vigilance was never wasted.

She hurried back to where she had left Eodan and the cato-blepas. Eodan still hadn't let go of the ropes, but his color had returned to normal and he'd straightened his hair as best as anyone could in this wind. He stepped away as Ginnevra drew her sword. "At least it's a clean death," he said.

"As clean as I can make it," Ginnevra said. She eyed the long, long neck, then brought her sword around for a killing blow. The sharp silvered steel sliced through flesh and bone as neatly as a knife through soft butter. The catoblepas gave out a grunt, its neck slackened, and a few moments later, the body collapsed. Black blood oozed from both sides of the neck. Ginnevra felt a moment's pang she instantly quashed. Her duty was to protect humans from the Bright One's monsters, not to feel sorry for the ones that weren't vicious.

She looked at Eodan, who had his eyes fixed on the cato-blepas' back. Not many months back, she had seen him and all his kind as evil monsters. And then she had learned differently. Her refusal to kill Eodan had led her to a new understanding of her role as paladin of the Goddess, as well as the realization that some few of the Bright One's creations weren't what she had been taught. And she loved Eodan, too. Even though he was a were-wolf. Life was much stranger than she had ever imagined.

"We would have killed a wolf that preyed on the herd, too," she told him. "It's the same thing, killing a monster."

"What? Oh, that. Yes, I agree." Eodan blinked as if rising out of deep water. "I see the necessity." He smiled at her, a tender expression that never failed to make her shiver with delight. "I'd feel sad about killing a wolf, too. I realize that makes me soft."

"I don't think that's true." Ginnevra cleaned her blade on the grass and sheathed it. "It makes you compassionate. Fitting, because I believe a physician should have compassion."

Eodan left the monster's body and put his arms around Ginnevra. "I wasn't always like this," he said. "I used to be ruth-less and completely lacking in compassion. I see that's hard to believe," he added at Ginnevra's skeptical look.

"It's impossible to believe," she said. "What changed?"

Eodan looked past her, his eyes distant. "I realized what I believed about myself, in my pride, was worth nothing. In being humbled, I lost that man and became someone I hope is better. I certainly don't regret the loss."

This was the most Eodan had ever said about himself from the time before he left his werewolf pack to join Ginnevra. Despite her fierce curiosity, she said only, "I love the man you are now, so I'm glad you left the other one behind."

Eodan glanced down at her and smiled. "Someday I'll tell you that story. Right now, we should talk to that farmer. I have no desire to bury that thing, do you?"

Ginnevra shuddered. "We killed it. I think that's enough."

IT WAS WELL into afternoon by the time they settled with the farmer and, laden with a box containing four prime steaks, headed back to the city of Ghibele. Ginnevra removed her coif and ran her fingers through her matted short hair, damp with sweat. Now that they had left the cows behind, the air smelled of sea breezes that had swept away the cloying smell of honeyed pastries. Ginnevra drew in a deep, satisfied breath. "I'm ready for a bath."

"That is an excellent idea," Eodan said. "Then to see about getting the inn's cook to broil these steaks, maybe with some sauteed onions."

Ginnevra's stomach growled. "Maybe I want the bath later."

"We both smell of cow, and I'm sure your gambeson could be cleaner," Eodan pointed out.

"Well, if you want to be logical," Ginnevra said with a pretended scowl.

Ghibele was an old city, nearly as old as the heart of the holy city of Abraciabene, but it looked younger thanks to a populace addicted to building and refurbishing. The streets were all that indicated its age, the cobbles worn down and slick from centuries of feet treading them and the lack of raised walks popular in newer cities across the Lordagne. The bright sunlight dispelled much of the chill in the air, which promised a damp, cold winter.

They turned a corner onto a narrower street where the tall houses, more than twice as tall as they were wide, blocked out that sunlight, casting the street into perpetual twilight. A last breeze chased Ginnevra a few steps in, making her shiver despite the warmth of her clothing. Now that her exertions were over, she felt the chill.

Eodan put an arm around her, hugging her close for a few strides. "You really don't like winter, do you?"

"I really do not." Ginnevra tucked her hands beneath her arms to warm them. "I wish we could go south for the winter. Far south, where it's warm year round. But my duty lies here."

"I love winter," Eodan said. "There's always snow in the mountains where I come from, and I can't imagine anything cozier than a warm den, snuggled up with friends or a mate."

Ginnevra shivered again. "That must be a werewolf thing. Maybe if I had a fur coat, I'd like winter, too."

Eodan laughed and pushed open the door to their inn. "You may have a point."

The small inn they had been staying at for almost a week was always cold, thanks to its unrelieved stone construction, but it more than made up for that by having a bath house on the premises and elegant rooms furnished with thick quilts and mattresses guaranteed vermin-free. Ginnevra didn't even mind climbing the stairs all the way to the fourth floor. She occasionally worried that she had become too accustomed to luxury now that she was a prime of the Blessed, leader of the Goddess's Faith, but at times like that she recalled the many, many nights she had slept cold on the hard ground and decided there was nothing wrong with taking advantage of the comforts of civilization.

She had put her foot on the first step when the front door swung open and a girl dressed in the midnight blue and black indicating the Goddess's service ran in. She startled when she saw Ginnevra. "Oh, my lady, I didn't expect to find you immediately! I'm sent to ask you to attend on Hallowed Riccobene at the sanctuary."

Ginnevra immediately became aware of her grimy condition as she had not been before. "Immediately?"

"She didn't say, my lady." The girl eyed the giant sword in Ginnevra's hand as if she expected it to strike her of its own will. "What may I tell her?"

Ginnevra glanced at Eodan, who shrugged. Granted, the Hallowed would not summon a paladin frivolously, so in a sense all such summons were urgent, but how urgent? "Tell her I need to change my clothes, and I will join her shortly."

The girl nodded and hurried out the door.

"Not a leisurely bath," Eodan said. "But I'm sure the Hallowed will appreciate you not smelling like cattle and sweat."

"I guess the steak can wait," Ginnevra said.

Clean and clad in fresh clothes, Ginnevra and Eodan set out for the Ghibele sanctuary. Ginnevra had gone so far as to put on her plate mail armor, reasoning that for an official request she ought to be garbed in what were essentially a paladin's robes of office. With the sword bouncing over her shoulder, she drew all sorts of attention from the citizenry. Eodan, dressed plainly, drew attention of a different kind. Ginnevra had at first been irritated at how many people admired Eodan's handsome face and powerful build, and then she had realized that bordered on irrational jealousy. Now she reminded herself smugly that *she* was the one who shared his bed, and those people could look all they liked.

Ghibele perched on the cliffside above its harbor, and the Goddess's sanctuary lay at the edge of the cliff, giving anyone who approached it a spectacular view of the harbor and the expanse of the ocean. On a clear morning, with the sun rising over the sea, the water became a reflective sheet of gold, blinding the careless viewer. At this time of day, with the sun dropping lower in the western sky, the glare diminished, and the waves merely glittered like broken crystal. When she had time, Ginnevra enjoyed standing at the tall fence topped with wrought iron curlicues and watching the ships come in. She had no time now, but she still appreciated the sight of the waves until the fence and the sanctuary blocked them from view.

The Ghibele sanctuary was, unlike the city, fairly young, only two hundred and fifty years old, and bore the marks of that era's construction in its perfectly circular shape and uncarved black marble facings. Iron spikes surrounding the roof gave the sanctuary the look of a crown perched atop a giant's head, if the giant were mostly beneath ground. Four people dressed in plain tunics and trousers climbed across the roof, replacing tiles that had been damaged in the last big storm. It was an odd, homely thing to see at one of the Goddess's holiest places, but even holy places needed ordinary upkeep.

There was no door, only an arched entry. Ginnevra said, "I'll see what the Hallowed wants. Sorry to make you wait."

"I don't mind." Eodan kissed her lightly. "The coast is always interesting to watch."

Ginnevra nodded, hoping she looked calmer than she felt. It annoyed her that Eodan couldn't enter the sanctuary—literally couldn't, as they had discovered a few months back when Ginnevra had reported in to the sanctuary at the city of Devoyenne. It had turned out that sanctuaries, protected as they were against evil, did not discriminate based on an "evil" creature's true allegiances, and Eodan had bounced off the entrance in a flash of white light and a loud crack of thunder. If not for the Blessed's word that had gone before them, Ginnevra didn't think she could have kept the anointed at the sanctuary from attacking Eodan.

It was all part of the horrible unfairness that surrounded werewolves, Ginnevra reflected as she entered. Most of them hated and feared their creator and wanted nothing to do with her, and Eodan himself had the Goddess's blessing. But Ginnevra had heard the Dark Lady say She was powerless to accept the were-wolves' allegiance because of oaths She had sworn—oaths She would not elaborate on even to the Blessed. So Ginnevra could do nothing but silently fume and swear to herself she would do whatever it took to see Eodan, at least, was given the respect he deserved.

The arched entrance led to a short corridor that opened almost immediately into the great central dome of the sanctuary. Unlike the Goddess's chapels, which were designed for worship and instruction, the sanctuaries were intended for performing major magical workings sacred to the Goddess. The central dome was entirely empty of furnishings, even an altar, and the walls were blank except for eight doors opening off the room at regular intervals. White lights cast their brilliant radiance over the domed ceiling, dimming the painting of the moon in its many phases. Ginnevra had been unnerved the first time she had entered a sanctuary dome and seen the full moon, emblem of the Bright One, painted on the ceiling. Now she understood the symbolism of never forgetting what their religion stood in opposition to, and it didn't frighten her. Much.

She crossed the floor with its inlaid brass curves for use in rituals and rapped on the door directly opposite the entrance. At a muffled "Come in," she pushed the door open.

The room beyond was nearly as empty as the sanctuary dome, with only a handful of wooden chairs varnished black and a padded prayer stool with a gospel bound in worn, peeling black leather on its lower shelf, easily accessible to anyone kneeling at it. Water sheeted down the face of the round black marble slab mounted on the back wall, collecting in a deep rectangular basin and pouring back into the wall.

The Hallowed Lorrenza Riccobene wheeled herself away from the eternity fountain at Ginnevra's entrance. "Ginnevra, have a seat," she said. Her voice was always so quiet Ginnevra was grateful for her Goddess-enhanced hearing that prevented her asking the holy woman to repeat herself. "I've had a communication from Abraciabene that concerns you."

"A message for me?"

"No, a message about you, in response to a request I made of the Blessed." Hallowed Riccobene ran a hand restlessly over the curve of one wheel of her chair. "I asked the Blessed if she wished to speak to you herself. She said she had complete confidence in your faith being sufficient that you do not need to be commanded directly."

Ginnevra's face warmed briefly. That was either a compliment or a veiled warning. "I am at the Blessed's service, of course."

"My request had to do with providing an escort to one of our Revereds to the holy city for further sanctification. Revered Giulliomocte has achieved the status of Hallowed, and of course this rank can only be conferred by the Blessed herself." Hallowed Riccobene's hand moved again, sliding back and forth over the iron curve of the wheel. "The Blessed would like you to take charge of the Revered's escort."

Ginnevra eyed the woman's restless movements warily. "I thought that was the job of a paladin company, Hallowed. Not that I'm rejecting the Blessed's instructions, but I feel there's something you're not telling me. This Revered, is there something special about her?"

The woman sighed. "There is," she said. "Revered Domenico Giulliomocte is the first man ever to achieve the rank of Hallowed."

TWO

"*A man?*" Ginnevra blurted out. She realized how horrified she'd sounded and quickly added, "That is, of course there's no reason a man shouldn't be Hallowed, but there never has been one before, so I can't help wondering—"

"Why Revered Giulliomocte?" Hallowed Riccobene's lips curved in a rather weary smile. "Who knows why the divine inscrutability does what She does? Domenico has been a Revered for several decades. He is a model anointed, performing all his duties with scrupulous exactness as well as compassion and humility. If he were a woman, I would have expected him to join the ranks of the Hallowed years ago. But there was never any sign that the Goddess had a special role in mind for him, not until a month ago, and that sign was unmistakable."

Ginnevra decided not to pry into what kind of sign the Goddess might give. "So, if the sign was so clear, why is there a problem?"

The smile deepened. "I begin to see why you were made a prime. The sign was manifest only to me and to Domenico, which means everyone else must take it on faith. And I'm afraid even the anointed struggle with their faith sometimes. Your first reaction is the more common one—there are many, anointed and otherwise, who have trouble with the idea of a man becoming Hallowed. Some of them don't like the idea of a man being anointed at all."

"I understand." Ginnevra had grown up believing all anointed were women, and it had been a hard assumption to overcome. "But surely if the Blessed agreed—"

"No one has spoken overtly against Domenico's elevation. But I hear the whisperings. And there are some who believe the Blessed intends to make a political statement in elevating Domenico. That she is taking advantage of Domenico's reputation to make him Hallowed, regardless of the Goddess's wishes."

Ginnevra realized her grip on her sword's hilt was so tight her hand hurt. "I can't believe anyone would think that. That's almost blasphemy. The Blessed would never put politics above the Faith."

"*You* know that. I understand you have heard the Dark Lady's voice yourself. Almost no one living can say the same." Hallowed Riccobene rolled herself within reach of the prayer stool and picked up the gospel. "Not even I. For the rest of us, there is only faith."

She opened the gospel and paged through it. "I've gone back to Blessed Erica Bresail's words often these last few weeks. She faced tremendous opposition for being the first woman born outside the Lordagne to become the Blessed, about a hundred and ten years ago. She wrote, 'The Dark Lady sees all that is hidden, but She makes little of what She sees known to us. When we receive Her knowledge, we should embrace it.'" Hallowed Riccobene closed the book. "I feel we would be rejecting the Goddess's gift of knowledge to elevate our own beliefs and bigotries over what She has proclaimed."

"I agree." Ginnevra's desire to meet this Revered had grown

the longer Hallowed Riccobene spoke. "But I'm still not sure why I've been instructed to escort Revered Giulliomocte. Surely the Blessed doesn't anticipate danger? And if she does, why not send a company? Seventeen paladins can handle things a lone prime can't."

"You will travel with a paladin company, as well as an escort of Revereds and Dedicates." Hallowed Riccobene smiled again, this time bitterly. "The escort is traditional, but I wish for Domenico's sake he could go quietly. He is not a man who enjoys a fuss, certainly not one centered on him. In any case, you are to take charge of the combined group so there is no confusion over authority."

"I understand. Will we take the coastal route?"

"I'm afraid there's not enough time. You'll have to go overland, through the principality of Savorola." The Hallowed's smile disappeared. "Avoiding the city, of course."

Ginnevra managed not to make a face. She had only been to Savorola twice, not recently, and for all the great city was a thriving metropolis with all the benefits of civilization, it was also the center of political and ecclesiastical strife. Even as an ordinary paladin, she had been aware of the conflicts between Savorola's rulers and its anointed. "The strife isn't as bad on the outskirts, is it?"

"Not as bad, but not nonexistent, either," Hallowed Riccobene said. "Some places will consider your presence antagonistic regardless of how you behave. The citizens may not all show you respect." Hallowed Riccobene tapped the gospel against her left hand, making tiny flecks of black leather sift onto her lap. "And not everyone I will send with you is temperate in their reactions to being disrespected. You should expect conflict."

Ginnevra thought about protesting that she wasn't used to being a moderator, remembered what the Blessed had said about her, and held her tongue. "I suppose that means you don't have much choice about who you send."

"There are guidelines when it comes to a journey of this nature. Some of those required to go are those least committed to seeing a man in Hallowed rank." The woman set the gospel back on its shelf. "I'm afraid I haven't given you the most appealing of tasks."

"It's my honor to serve," Ginnevra said. It was the response any paladin made to being thanked, but it fit the moment.

"The party is scheduled to leave day after tomorrow. I'll see you and your companion then."

Ginnevra rose and saluted the Hallowed. But when she turned to leave, the woman said, "Ginnevra. About your companion."

Ginnevra stiffened. The Hallowed's tone of voice promised unpleasantness. "Yes, Hallowed?"

"I feel I should warn you," Hallowed Riccobene said in a slow, contemplative voice, "there are those among the anointed who feel a werewolf is no fit companion for them. Even those who dislike the idea of Domenico's elevation will make common cause with those who disagree with them if it is in opposition to one of the Bright One's creations."

"But the Blessed's message was explicit," Ginnevra protested. "She announced the truth about Eodan and his kind, and said he was to be treated according to his actions and not according to tradition. Would they really act counter to her instructions?"

The woman shrugged. "As I said, even the anointed struggle with their faith. I don't envy you this journey, Ginnevra Cassaline. Nor the longer one your faith has set you on." She gestured, and Ginnevra bowed so the Hallowed could rest her hand on Ginnevra's head. "Go with the Goddess's blessing, and may your journey's path remain clear."

Ginnevra saluted her in silence and let herself out.

She walked to the center of the domed chamber, marked by a foot-wide circle of nacreous black. The shining, iridescent substance harvested from the inner surface of pearl-oysters was called many things throughout the Lordagne. Here in Ghibele, where black pearls were harvested, Ginnevra most often heard the nacre referred to as "Goddess's tears." She ran a booted toe across the disk from one side to the other, marveling at how smooth it was despite its bumpy appearance.

For a moment, she indulged in self-pity. She was expected to shepherd thirty or more people across the Lordagne, all of them at odds with each other when they weren't at odds with her and Eodan. Ginnevra didn't know which was worse, the possibility that some of them might make life hard for Revered Giulliomocte or the possibility they might insult and snub Eodan. In either case, she wasn't allowed to exercise violence to get them to shape up. And if they couldn't avoid conflict, she would have to be diplomatic in Savorola. She wasn't good at diplomacy yet, though she'd been practicing; she still had trouble with the polite lie, and controlling her impatience was harder than she'd expected.

She tilted her head back to look at the ceiling. The slim crescent of the new moon was painted at the exact center of the dome, or—no, it wasn't paint, it was a mosaic of fine black marble and white pearls. Ginnevra assumed they were white pearls, though she'd never seen one before, sacred to her Dark Lady's enemy as they were. They made the surface of the moon ripple beautifully. Ginnevra admired it despite her feeling she should not be drawn by the Bright One even in this indirect way. But Hallowed Riccobene had, again, explained the symbolism—"The Goddess is always at odds with the Bright One, and the new moon reminds us that we must ever be vigilant against evil however and whenever it appears"—and Ginnevra, feeling the message was for her, had looked long and hard at the emblem, committing it to memory.

Now she traced the line of the white crescent with her gaze, tip to tip. The journey would take them across the badlands to the great fertile plains centered on the city-state of Savorola, and from there down the Salvectus River to Lake Salvectus and then through more of the badlands' empty territory to the holy city of Abraciabene. All that uncivilized land meant more opportunities for monsters to attack their party, and Ginnevra was sure even traveling with several of the Goddess's anointed would not make their group immune. It helped that they were approaching the dark of the moon, during which time many monsters were weakened, but Ginnevra saw the wisdom in sending a full company of paladins.

She squeezed her eyes shut briefly, then clasped her hands together at chest level and offered up a brief prayer: *Dark Lady, thank You for your faith in me. Grant me the strength and wisdom to see this challenge through.* Then she walked to the outer door, the sound of her heels echoing in the chamber, and let herself out.

Eodan leaned against the palisade, watching the waves. He glanced at her as she settled beside him, but said nothing. Ginnevra loved how comforting his silences could be. "We have a new mission," she said, and quickly recounted her conversation with the Hallowed. Eodan's neutral expression gave way to a frown that deepened the longer Ginnevra spoke.

When she finished, he said, "That sounds like a guaranteed disaster. Anointed at odds with themselves and at odds with us, a paladin company who may or may not follow the Blessed's instructions—"

"I know, but we can hardly do other than obey." Ginnevra shrugged. "At least, I have to obey. Your decisions are your own."

"I will never leave you, Ginnevra." Eodan put an arm around

her shoulders in emphasis. "You'd have to order me to go, and I might not listen."

Ginnevra put her arm around his waist. "I can't tell you how comforting that knowledge is. Especially given how many women and even men would like your company."

"They'll just have to suffer." Eodan's smile was wickedly amused. "We leave day after tomorrow?"

"Before sunrise. Whenever the moon is at its apex. It will be the half-moon, the world poised exactly between dark and light, and that's considered a good start for new ventures."

Eodan nodded. "Plenty of time to plan a long journey. Or is the planning done for us?"

"I believe the anointed arrange for supplies and housing between here and there. Though we'll be sleeping rough many nights." Ginnevra followed the path of a ship whose sails caught the late afternoon light and carried it in to the harbor, which was in shadow at this hour. "About as often as we did on the way here."

"It was the full moon, so that's just as well." Eodan squeezed a little tighter and then ran his fingers along Ginnevra's upper arm. "And isn't overland the shorter route?"

"It is." Ginnevra assessed her mental map of the area. "It's a three-week trip from here to Abraciabene by way of Savorola, probably longer if we are part of a caravan. Wagons always travel more slowly. Too bad we can't simply provide Revered Giulliomocte with a fast horse and have the two of us escort him."

"It sounded like he might prefer that," Eodan said. "But I imagine for someone who's almost a Hallowed, there are rules."

"Your life certainly isn't your own anymore. I don't envy the anointed at all." Ginnevra released Eodan and stepped away from the palisade fence. "Let's go have those steaks, and enjoy the evening. Tomorrow we'll resupply and see that Ginger and Dauntless are in good health for this kind of trip. And then…"

"No anticipating the worst," Eodan reminded her. "Or the best. There's just the journey, and it's what you make of it."

"You're halfway to being an anointed yourself, with thinking like that," Ginnevra said.

CHAPTER

THREE

I t was still full dark, two mornings later, when Ginnevra and Eodan saddled their horses and settled their gear before proceeding to the sanctuary. Ginnevra had to nudge her horse Dauntless more than a few times to keep him stepping out smartly. Dauntless was well-trained for combat, but he was a little more intelligent than was comfortable for his rider, and he was smart enough to know this was an unusually early hour and he wasn't ready to leave his warm stall yet. Ginnevra prodded his ribs yet again. In a couple of hours, he would be fully alert, and then she would have to rein him in to keep him with their caravan.

Beside her, Ginger trotted along as complacently as ever. Despite his yellow coloring, the big gelding's name did not suit him, given that he was the least excitable horse Ginnevra had ever known. That was fortunate, as he had to carry Eodan, and most horses knew predators when they smelled them regardless of their shape. It was still odd, sometimes, to watch Ginger's lack of reaction to harmless but startling noises other horses shied at.

Lanterns attached to poles glowed at intervals along the street, making pools of light separated by long stretches of darkness. Ginnevra felt the light didn't do much more than draw attention to the darkness. That seemed like a metaphor for something spiritual, but she didn't analyze it further. She was no theologian.

Instead, she kept an eye on the darkened buildings that towered over the two of them. She didn't expect an attack, not in the middle of Ghibele's prosperous merchant district at nearly five o'clock in the morning, but it was when you were complacent that a surprise attack hurt most. In less than an hour, people would ready their shops and stalls for a day of selling, and the dawn's light would dispel the feeling of brooding menace the buildings gave off, but Ginnevra would be well out of the city by then. Well out of the city, surrounded by people who didn't like her and probably didn't like each other. This might be a very long three weeks.

The wide street, which gave plenty of room for sellers to hawk their wares, gradually grew wider until it became the great plaza facing the sanctuary. Despite its size, by day it wasn't much busier than it was by night. People didn't generally hang around the sanctuary, and the plaza was used only for important religious holidays and for major magical workings too big even for the sanctuary dome. At the moment, the space in front of the sanctuary was a dark mass of shifting figures, darker than their surroundings thanks to a dozen white lamps burning beneath the sanctuary's iron crown.

Ginnevra found Dauntless' pace slowing, and this time it wasn't his disinclination to hurry, it was hers. She wished the light were better so she could observe the crowd. Sometimes watching the patterns of movement among a group of people revealed things the individuals preferred hidden. But things were what they were, and Ginnevra would do her best with the opportunity the Goddess gave her.

Eodan came to a stop, slowing Ginnevra further. "Are you worried about this?" he asked.

"No more than is reasonable. I was just—it's not important." Ginnevra nudged Dauntless forward. "No point in delaying longer."

Nobody reacted to Ginnevra and Eodan's approach at first. A group of men and women wearing linen shirts under informal Dedicates' tunics, charcoal gray smocks that in this light looked black, stood chatting in a tight knot, ignoring everyone else. One of them drew Ginnevra's eye; though she wore her hair braided in loops at the back of her head as the other women did, that hair was bright yellow rather than black or dark brown. Someone from Bordelamar to the west, probably. Ginnevra had rarely seen anyone from the country beyond the mountains. She decided to make an excuse to talk to the young Dedicate later.

Three people who were probably Revereds were dressed for travel and wore abbreviated thigh-length black robes with full sleeves as a nod to their usual garb. The Revereds, unlike the Dedicates, did not cluster together and seemed intent on their horses rather than each other or anyone else. Well, they likely knew one another well if they were all from the same sanctuary. Even so, that lack of friendly closeness might become a problem later. Something to keep in mind.

What Ginnevra did not see were any paladins. They would be in plate mail armor just as she was, gleaming silver under the light of the half-moon. She circled around the Dedicates toward the wagons. There were three of them, each bearing the black and silver flag emblematic of the Faith. Two were loaded with the travelers' possessions and supplies for when they would inevitably have to camp in the badlands; the other was ringed with wooden benches. Ginnevra's heart sank. She had hoped everyone could ride, but it seemed they would be tied to the speed of the slowest wagon. She mentally added a week's travel to her calculations.

When she turned to comment on the paladins' absence to Eodan, she realized she at last had an audience. The Dedicates—actually, some of them were acolytes, probably brought along as servants or assistants—all stared at her with the stunned look of people who had just seen a legend descend from the heavens. Ginnevra nodded politely, concealing a feeling of unease. True, the primes of the Blessed were rare, but they weren't so rare as to justify that reaction.

She wheeled Dauntless and paced back around to where the Revered had gathered, wondering if Revered Giulliomocte was one of them. One of the men and the woman were middle-aged, though both looked hearty enough Ginnevra didn't think she needed to worry about their ability to keep up with the undoubtedly slow pace of the wagons. The man's dark hair was thinning on top, while the woman wore hers cut chin-length so it swished around her face when she turned her head.

The other man was younger than his companions, though not by much. His narrow face and slightly protruding front teeth made him look like a hare poised to leap at the first sign of trouble. Ginnevra had to make herself stop staring, even though she really wanted to know if his nose twitched. If that was Revered Giulliomocte, he didn't look like someone who'd achieved the highest rank of the anointed. But, then, hadn't the Hallowed said Revered Giulliomocte had been an anointed for several decades? This man wasn't old enough.

She heard the creaking, rumbling sound of Hallowed Riccobene's chair and dismounted as everyone moved aside to let the Hallowed pass. Eodan followed suit and accepted Dauntless' reins without being prompted so Ginnevra could salute the Hallowed.

"Ginnevra Cassaline, welcome," Hallowed Riccobene said. "What a lovely day to begin a journey."

"It will be clear weather at least until tomorrow," Ginnevra said. "What comes next is in the Goddess's hands."

"Well said." Hallowed Riccobene gestured to the Revereds, who still didn't stand closely together. "My lady Cassaline, may I introduce Revered Orselle, Revered Pratese, and Revered Giulliomocte."

Ginnevra saluted each in turn. Orselle was the younger man, Pratese was the woman, which meant the balding man was Giulliomocte. She examined him curiously for a few moments. He still didn't look unusually holy, though he carried himself calmly enough. Then she realized that although Eodan was at her shoulder, towering over even her height, Giulliomocte was deliberately not looking at him, and the Revered pinched his lips tight together as if he were holding back harsh, critical words. Annoyance flared in Ginnevra's chest, and she dismissed it with an effort. She had a job to do, and Giulliomocte's attitude was irrelevant. Even though she now had doubts about his fitness for the Hallowed rank.

"It's lovely to meet you," Pratese said, saluting Ginnevra in return. "I look forward to getting to know you and your companion better during our journey." The smile she directed at Eodan left Ginnevra with no doubt that one of the Revered, at least, didn't hold Eodan's race against him. The annoyed feeling intensified, in part because of that smile and in part because Ginnevra knew she shouldn't react to a virtual stranger's flirtation.

So she made herself smile in a friendly way and say, "There

will certainly be plenty of time for that. This is not a short journey."

Pratese chuckled. "We're prepared. Aren't we, Domenico?"

Giulliomocte shrugged. "The possibilities are in the Goddess's hands. We show our faith by preparing that which will allow us to meet challenges readily."

"That's so well said," Pratese replied. Ginnevra disliked her tone of voice, too-sweet and smoother than silk. Giulliomocte didn't like it either, judging by how his lips tightened even more. Pratese warranted watching, Ginnevra thought. And it had nothing to do with her obvious attraction to Eodan.

The third Revered, Orselle, watched this interplay with his eyes wide and his mouth slightly open as if he were looking for a way to insert himself into the conversation. When Giulliomocte didn't respond to Pratese's words, Orselle said, "Revered Giulliomocte understands the Goddess's will better than we do, don't you agree, Marsillia? We're sure to have a successful journey."

"That borders on heresy, predicting a chosen future," Marsillia Pratese snapped. Gone were the honeyed words and smooth, sly glances; her voice sounded cut with ice. "You should know better, Tomascio."

Orselle took a step back. "I didn't mean that." He caught Ginnevra's eye, looked once at Eodan with wide eyes, and fixed his gaze on Giulliomocte so overtly Ginnevra had a brief desire to slap him.

"It is hardly heretical to look forward to a desired future, so long as one knows the future is never a given," the Hallowed said mildly. "And I see the escort is arriving. All gather round, please."

Ginnevra had heard the jingle of tack when Pratese was speaking, but she hadn't turned around, not wishing to give offense by seeming uninterested in the Revered's words even though she didn't actually care about Pratese or her interpretation of doctrine. Now, feeling Hallowed Riccobene had released her, she turned to watch the paladin company advance across the plaza. The double column of sixteen mailed women led by their captain sent a pang through her heart. She liked her current assignment, loved being free to travel with Eodan, and yet even now, months after leaving her company, the sight of the sisterhood left her with formless, faint regrets.

The captain brought her mount near and signaled a halt, then dismounted and removed her helmet and coif to reveal tousled, wavy hair cut short to fit easily under a helmet. "Antonnia Buonnane," she said, saluting Hallowed Riccobene. "Your servant, Hallowed."

"We are all grateful for your service," Hallowed Riccobene replied. "Have you met the prime Ginnevra Cassaline?"

Buonnane eyed Ginnevra as if looking her over for flaws. "I have not," she said, and extended her hand. "You are to lead our band, then."

Ginnevra clasped Buonnane's hand, never letting her eyes leave the captain's. "It is my honor to serve," she said. She hadn't liked Buonnane's assessment of her, the more so because Buonnane was older than Ginnevra by at least half a decade and presumably had correspondingly greater experience as a paladin. Ginnevra had plenty of experience in other things, though, and one of those things was recognizing when another warrior considered her a threat. She determined immediately that whatever Buonnane did, she would not draw Ginnevra into a fight for dominance. She also determined not to fall into despair. Four weeks was plenty of time to allow interpersonal conflicts to work themselves out. It was also plenty of time for animosities to fester, but she wasn't going to dwell on that.

"Revereds, to my side. Dedicates and acolytes, clasp hands and circle around us. The rest of you, bare your heads in respect."

Hallowed Riccobene waited for everyone to take their places. Ginnevra removed helmet and coif and ran fingers quickly through her untidy hair. Beside her, Eodan took an easy, relaxed stance she knew he could maintain for hours if necessary. He'd fallen into the habit of giving at least a superficial appearance of participating in such religious rites as he could be present for. How serious he was in his devotion, Ginnevra didn't know, but the Dark Goddess was forbidden by Her own rules from accepting his worship, and Ginnevra didn't know how faithful *she* could remain under those circumstances.

The Hallowed raised both hands to the sky, where the half-moon floated high above. Ginnevra closed her eyes and composed herself for a ritual. But the woman only said, "Goddess, I entreat You who sees all that is done in secret to cast Your watchful eye over Your servants as they travel. Grant them strength of body to endure the demands of the road, and grant them strength of will to withstand the challenges of spirit they will surely encounter, for no journey is ever without peril. We are Your servants. Our lives are in Your careful hand. Bless us to live as You direct, ever in Your name."

The rest of the anointed murmured "Ever in Your name" in a ragged chorus half a breath behind her. Ginnevra said nothing, though she heard a few of the paladins repeat the blessing. She never felt the Goddess cared whether one's prayers were spoken or silent, and she had added a few words to her own unspoken prayer: *Goddess, give me wisdom to keep from failing completely at this task. Give Your peace to those who would otherwise fight each other. And please, please encourage them not to attack Eodan. Ever in Your name.*

"Thank you," she said to Hallowed Riccobene. "I hope we meet again someday."

"So do I. I have a feeling this trip will generate many, many stories," Hallowed Riccobene said with a smile. "If only because any time one is on the road for longer than a day or two, stories come creeping in."

Ginnevra laughed at the Hallowed's gentle humor. "I can't argue with that," she said, taking Dauntless' reins and mounting easily. "Thank you, Hallowed Riccobene."

She cast her gaze on her little party—her little caravan, more like. The Dedicates and acolytes were climbing into the wagon with a minimum of fuss; that was something, anyway. Captain Buonnane had mounted her horse, a gray mare not nearly as nice as Dauntless. Paladins in a company didn't own their own horses, though, so likely the mare wasn't Buonnane's choice. The Revereds all mounted as well. Giulliomocte and Pratese rode well; Orselle rode awkwardly but without giving the impression that he was two breaths away from being dumped out of the saddle. They would handle themselves all right.

Buonnane was staring at Ginnevra with one eyebrow raised. "Prime Cassaline?" she said.

"Yes?" Ginnevra dragged her attention away from the wagons.

"Would you care to lead out?"

Oh. Yes. That was Ginnevra's job now. She managed not to blush and maneuvered Dauntless ahead of Buonnane. Eodan joined her with no sign he found anything about this unusual.

It occurred to Ginnevra that no one had introduced Eodan to anyone. That was either an oversight on the Hallowed's part, or sign of something else, and since Ginnevra had no reason to suspect the worst of Hallowed Riccobene, she had to conclude the woman meant to give Ginnevra the choice for how to bring a werewolf into a group of thirty humans, most of whom worshipped a Goddess antithetical to monsters.

This was going to be a *very long* four weeks.

CHAPTER

FOUR

T hey followed the moon westward through the farmland surrounding Ghibele, most of it given over to cattle. At that early hour, the fields were empty, giving Ginnevra the illusion that they had already passed beyond the reach of civilization and were well into the badlands. The occasional farmhouse comforted her. She wasn't afraid of the badlands, and certainly had no fear of the monsters who lived there, but she had been born and raised in the shadow of the Meridian Peaks, far to the west, and open space left her feeling unsettled. She was never comfortable when she could see all the way to the horizon.

As the sun rose, the moon gradually paled until the fat crescent looked insubstantial against the light blue sky, and Ginnevra's gray shadow pointed the way ahead, long and thin. The cold wind picked up at about that time, blowing them westward as if it wanted to speed them along. Ginnevra huddled into her cloak, heavy dark green twilled cotton that was fur-lined and capable of blunting the edge of all but the worst storms. Eodan laughed whenever she brought it out, saying it made her look like a grumpy bear, but she ignored him. He was a northerner, and their veins all ran with ice water. She was still grateful the lining wasn't wolf fur.

Eodan rode beside her in silence, another comfort; they rarely spoke on long journeys, but when evening came they would huddle together wherever they ended up sleeping and talk about anything and everything for an hour or more. Today, though, she wondered what he was thinking. She knew he worried, as she did, about his presence among all these anointed, and she wished she could talk to him about it. But Antonnia Buonnane's presence on Ginnevra's other side made that impossible.

Buonnane rode as silently as they did, to Ginnevra's right and a little behind. Ginnevra sneaked glances at her occasionally. With her hair tucked inside her helmet, the paladin captain looked older than she had before, hard and stern with no softness to her. That was probably desirable in a paladin, particularly someone responsible for a company, but it made Ginnevra feel awkward about speaking to her. Particularly given Buonnane's thinly-veiled hostility. It would almost be easier if that hostility spilled over onto Eodan, because Ginnevra would then be able to call the woman on her unrighteous behavior, but so far that didn't seem to be the case.

"Have you made this journey before, Captain Buonnane?" she asked. The sound of her own voice, too-loud because of the brisk wind, almost startled herself.

Buonnane glanced her way. "Three times," she said. "Have you?"

"Only once. I'm glad to have your knowledge of the route." Ginnevra felt that was a good, polite gesture toward unity.

"I'm surprised the Blessed assigned a prime to this escort mission. It's a simple enough journey." This time, Buonnane didn't look at Ginnevra, and her chin was tilted high enough she couldn't possibly see clearly ahead. Ginnevra stifled a despairing groan. So Buonnane was annoyed at not leading the caravan. It was no more than Ginnevra had expected, but she'd hoped a paladin captain would be less sensitive to challenges to her authority than, say, a city guard officer. Well, people were people regardless of their callings.

"My understanding is that I am to unify the leadership of the anointed with the paladin company," Ginnevra replied, "and that a prime's authority may be needed while traveling through Savorola." She thought about mentioning her feeling that it would have been better to send Revered Giulliomocte with a small, fast escort, but decided that might come across as pandering if Buonnane felt Ginnevra was trying too hard to get her on Ginnevra's side. Which she almost was.

Buonnane's lips tightened. "I have passed many times through the principality of Savorola. You can see how I might wonder why we suddenly need a different authority."

"I do, actually. But I am sworn to obey the Blessed's command, and she sees farther than either of us. I hope you feel the same way." Ginnevra shot a steely-eyed glare at Buonnane, who didn't flinch.

"Captain Buonnane, what can you tell me about Savorola's capital?" Eodan asked. "I've never been there, but I've heard it's a remarkable city."

Buonnane's horse took a few hasty steps to the right before the captain reined her in. "I'm not sure what you want to know," Buonnane said stiffly. "What does a werewolf care about human cities?"

Ginnevra's hands tightened on Dauntless' reins. Buonnane hadn't sounded disdainful or inclined to mock, but there was an angry edge to her words that worried Ginnevra nonetheless. "Eodan is—" she began.

"Will it upset you too much if I admit werewolves enter human cities on occasion?" Eodan said, overriding her. "I realize that's not something a paladin wants to hear."

Sure enough, Buonnane turned on him sharply, pulling up short as she remembered Ginnevra rode between them. "You *dare*," she said. "Bringing your foul presences into our strong-holds, pretending you're like us when—"

"That's enough, captain," Ginnevra said, bringing Dauntless to a halt between the two. "You received the Blessed's instructions. Eodan is to be treated with the respect due an ally. And I will not put up with fighting among ourselves. You know this journey better than I do—the badlands are crawling with monsters who would love to destroy us. Let's not make it easy on them, shall we?"

Buonnane continued to glare at Eodan, who despite his well-concealed anger at Buonnane's insults was deliberately making himself look as unthreatening as a man his size could be. The paladin captain's shoulders shook with the effort of controlling herself. Finally, she said, "Understood, prime," and jerked her horse around. Ginnevra quietly let out a breath of relief and let her take the lead. It might soothe her angry feelings.

"Sorry," Eodan said in a voice pitched for Ginnevra's ears alone. The blunt, curt word told her he was still reining in his temper.

"It's not your fault," Ginnevra said, and regretted how terse she'd sounded. "I mean—"

"We'll talk later," Eodan said. Now he didn't sound angry, just resigned, and Ginnevra's heart ached for both of them.

Shortly thereafter, their path joined up with a larger one that paralleled a small river, one that would take them gradually south-westward until it joined the Salvectus River. They passed through a couple of villages where the townspeople came outside to cheer them on. Buonnane sat up straighter when this happened, and Ginnevra chose to take it as a good sign. Probably it just meant Buonnane was fonder of praise than she should be, but it might mean she felt the cheering was a sign of the people's respect for the Goddess.

Children ran alongside the procession, waving and shouting excitedly, their hair streaming in the wind and their cheeks rosy with cold. Ginnevra couldn't look back to see how the Revereds reacted to this, but she hoped Giulliomocte, at least, would unbend enough to accept the honor they showed him.

Their first rest to water the horses happened a short time later. Ginnevra didn't think the horses were all that tired yet, but she wanted a chance to get a closer look at the others, and with as early a start as they'd had, food was appealing. So she deliberately waited until they were well out of sight of the last village before calling a halt. That would give the paladins and the anointed no excuse for wandering off.

The acolytes immediately hopped down and hurried to the supply wagons for food. Revered Orselle and Revered Pratese dismounted, while Giulliomocte stayed where he was, wrapped in his own heavy cloak. He looked as cold as Ginnevra felt, and it startled her into an unexpected sympathy for the man.

She walked to his side and said, "Can I do anything for you, Revered?"

Giulliomocte looked startled. "You, Prime Cassaline?"

"Why not? It's my honor to serve. And I was going to see about getting food for myself, so it's not like it's any extra trouble." Ginnevra smiled, inviting him to relax.

For a moment, Giulliomocte's expression was wary. Then he smiled as well. "Thank you, prime, I would appreciate something to eat." He slid down from his horse and patted its neck in thanks.

"But I'll come with you, if you don't mind. Standing still makes me feel in danger of freezing solid."

Ginnevra nodded. "I'm not built for this climate. And the winds on the plains feel like they come straight from the frozen north."

They walked around the caravan to the supply wagon. Dry grass crunched pleasantly beneath Ginnevra's feet. Giulliomocte put up the hood of his cloak and snugged around his neck. "It's been years since I arrived in Ghibele, but I never get used to these winters. Paese's climate is much milder."

"Is that where you were born? It's a beautiful place."

Giulliomocte nodded. "I was sanctified and anointed there, but after I became Revered, I felt a draw to the east. And I do love Ghibele. The ocean is so different from the one near my home."

"I understand that. I'd never seen the ocean before I was a paladin, and the first time I visited Paese, I didn't think I'd ever get enough of it." Ginnevra accepted a short loaf of fine white bread from the wagoner, tore it in half, and handed half to Giulliomocte before remembering what he was. But the Revered said only, "Thank you," and tore off a small piece rather than biting into it.

Ginnevra collected some apples and offered her waterskin to be refilled. While she waited, she took a bite of her half of the loaf. It was the softest bread she'd ever eaten, with a delicate flavor, and although she preferred a robust sourdough or rye, this appealed to her.

She handed an apple to the Revered, who bit into it and murmured with pleasure. "So juicy," he said.

"Shouldn't you pray over your food?" Ginnevra said, again without thinking.

To her surprise, Giulliomocte raised an eyebrow. He finished chewing, swallowed, and said, "Will the food be holier if I do?"

Ginnevra blushed. "It's just something I've always seen the

Revereds do. I thought it was more a matter of giving thanks than, um, consecrating it or anything like that."

"That's certainly an admirable approach. And we are encouraged to give thanks for the Goddess's blessings." Giulliomocte took another bite of apple. "But we're even more encouraged to keep that thanks alive in our hearts at all times," he continued when his mouth was empty. "I don't know that She needs to hear us say the words."

"I've wondered that myself," Ginnevra said. "Sometimes prayer is about community. The prayers we speak at the first of the month, maybe."

"And we pray vocally at those times to join as one," Giulliomocte said with a nod. "But in those times, the words are for our sake, not Hers. The Dark Lady sees everything that is hidden, and that includes the words we keep in our hearts."

"I understand." Ginnevra bit into her own apple. It was a variety she didn't recognize, cold and juicy and tart enough to purse her lips.

Giulliomocte regarded her curiously. "Yours is a strange path. I wonder..."

He looked past her, his voice trailing off. Ginnevra turned to see what he was looking at and saw Eodan approaching. "Ginnevra, the wagon drivers want to know how much farther we'll go today," Eodan said. "They said there are two villages we can reach before nightfall, but one is much farther along than the other." He nodded politely at Giulliomocte, whose face was now rigid.

"I'll talk to them, thanks," Ginnevra said. "Revered, thank you for speaking with me. I appreciate—"

"Yes," Giulliomocte said. Gone was the calm, easy demeanor; his mouth was drawn up in a tight, tense line, and he wasn't looking at Eodan. Ginnevra's momentary feeling of accord vanished. He talked a good line, sounded as wise as someone reaching Hallowed rank should sound, but he clearly objected to Eodan's presence, and Ginnevra didn't have to put up with that. Still, starting a fight before the first day was over would not look good. She walked away without looking back.

The Dedicates and acolytes clustered around the supply wagon chattered like birds, once again ignoring anything that wasn't immediately in front of them. Though none were children, they were all young; Ginnevra guessed all but two of them were adolescents. She spoke with the wagon drivers briefly and established that they were experienced with this part of the route, though none of them had traveled beyond Savorola before. They were large, heavy men who spoke in the slow, ponderous way many large, heavy men have, and it comforted Ginnevra.

When she left the wagon drivers to return to Dauntless, she found two Dedicates and an acolyte waiting for her. One of the Dedicates was the blonde Bordelamarian girl. She stepped forward and said, "Prime Cassaline, can we ask you something?" Her words were heavily accented but intelligible.

"Certainly," Ginnevra replied.

"Is it true werewolves aren't evil?"

Ginnevra almost replied snappishly before she realized the girl looked eager rather than disgusted. "Some werewolves choose to turn their backs on the Bright One," she replied. "They want to live in peace with humans. Like Eodan."

The acolyte looked over his shoulder as if searching for Eodan. "How can you tell the difference if you're not a Revered?" he said.

"The smell is different—but that's something only a paladin would sense. I don't know if there are any other observable differences. Mostly it comes down to speaking to the werewolf."

The acolyte and the second Dedicate frowned. "But wouldn't an evil werewolf tear you apart if you gave him a chance?" the acolyte said. "So it doesn't make sense to not destroy a werewolf on the possibility that he's not evil."

"But we can't destroy creatures who aren't evil just because they scare us," the blonde Dedicate said. "It's not fair."

"You're both right," Ginnevra said. "We have to be vigilant in defending the innocent, and we have to keep an open mind about what seems monstrous. It's not an easy path, but it's the one the Goddess requires of us. I hope someday more werewolves like Eodan will find their way into fellowship with humans."

She hated how pompous she sounded, even though she knew from experience her pomposity was worse in her own head. She'd never been good with instructing the youth, and she was sure these three wished she'd leave so they could make fun of her. But they did a good job concealing it, if those were their true feelings; they were intent on her words, and the Bordelamarian girl looked eager for more.

"It's so romantic, him saving your life, you falling in love with him," the Bordelamarian girl said, and her eagerness came into better focus. Ginnevra managed not to smile. She'd never been one for romantic poems and fables at that age, but she remembered some of her youthful crushes and how powerful those feelings were. And it was such a relief to discover at least one person in the caravan who didn't hate, fear, or despise her or Eodan.

"It took time for me to understand the knowledge the Goddess put in my path," she said. "We're taught werewolves are the pinnacle of the Bright One's creation, and they are, but that's not the whole story. We didn't know how many of them hate and fear her and wish to have nothing to do with her. Those are important truths for everyone." Then she did smile. "Falling in love is optional."

The three young people laughed. "Are all werewolves that big in their human form?" the acolyte asked. He looked impressed, which given how small and weedy he was made sense.

"I don't know," Ginnevra said. "Eodan is the first werewolf I've seen in human form. But in his wolf form, he's about as big as all the other werewolves I've fought."

"That's so strange, hearing you say that," the other Dedicate said. "Does Eodan find it strange that you've fought and killed his kind?"

"Since he's fought and killed his kind as well, no. But it is still a little strange." Ginnevra looked past the three to where the wagoners readied their horses. "We can talk more later, but for now we should get back on the road."

The two Dedicates exchanged glances. "Oh, we're really not anything special, and you shouldn't feel you need to give us your attention," the Bordelamarian said.

"I'm the one the Goddess blessed with this knowledge, and I want to share it as widely as possible," Ginnevra said. "And I don't look for only the wise or titled or wealthy or holy to share it with. Tell your friends they can ask me or Eodan any questions they like, and we'll be happy to give you a moment of our time." She saluted the three the paladin's way, making them all shift in nervous excitement, then returned to Dauntless' side feeling happier than she had all morning.

The rest of the day passed uneventfully, with occasional rest stops and meals. Buonnane remained silent—not only silent, but deliberately avoiding eye contact with Ginnevra. Since on the few occasions Ginnevra looked her way, the woman was scanning the horizon, looking for threats the way a paladin captain should, Ginnevra didn't care about getting the cold shoulder.

She, too, watched the fields, though it was unlikely they would encounter monsters this close to Ghibele. This late in the season, all the crops had been harvested, and the fields were wide expanses of short, pale stubble. They occasionally saw people near the low, thatch-roofed farmhouses, and sometimes those people returned Ginnevra's wave, but all of them without exception bowed to the Goddess's standards flying from the wagons, the flags that signaled the passing of one or more Revered. How much more excited they would have been to know of Giulliomocte's presence, Ginnevra couldn't guess.

They made better time than Ginnevra had feared, and reached the first of the two possible overnight stops well before sunset. Ginnevra weighed the possibilities: stop early and extend their trip that much longer, or push on and risk exhausting people and horses. This was not the sort of decision she usually had to make.

Suppressing a sigh, she said, "Captain Buonnane? Can I ask your advice?"

Buonnane, who had been staring straight ahead at the nearing village, startled. "Excuse me, prime?"

"I would like your opinion on where we should stop for the night. I'm inclined to press on, but I usually have only myself to think of, not the needs of an entire caravan. So, first, do you judge the travel will be too much if we continue to the next village? And, just as importantly, if we stop here for the night, where will that put us tomorrow night?"

Buonnane's eyes narrowed. "Tomorrow night?"

Ginnevra nodded. "We'll be leaving Ghibele at some point tomorrow, and while there are villages here and there in the badlands, mostly we can expect to make camp. I'm as much concerned about our future stops as I am about this one."

For a moment, she wondered if Buonnane's pride would keep her from accepting this peace offering. If it did, to hell with her; Ginnevra would take full command and feel no compunctions about sidelining the prickly captain. Then Buonnane said, "You're right to be concerned about how hard we're pushing ourselves.

But if we can make it to Tesccine tonight—that's the next town on —we'll be within easy reach of Forannine the following night as opposed to either exhausting ourselves to reach it or being forced to make camp."

"That's very sensible. Thank you for your advice, captain. I'll ride back to inform the wagons, if you'll keep watch up here." Ginnevra wheeled Dauntless and trotted to the rear of the caravan to speak to the wagoners.

It wasn't until she was done explaining the situation to the drivers, who didn't look upset at the news that the night's stop was farther away than they might have expected, that Ginnevra realized she'd left Buonnane and Eodan alone together. She refrained from prodding Dauntless into a faster pace. They weren't likely to get into a fight just because she wasn't there. More probably Buonnane would ignore Eodan as pointedly as she'd done Ginnevra all day.

Eodan and Buonnane hadn't closed the distance between themselves at all when Ginnevra returned. Ginnevra cocked an inquiring eyebrow at Eodan and jerked her chin minutely in Buonnane's direction. Eodan just as minutely shook his head. Ginnevra quashed her irrational disappointment. It was extremely unlikely Buonnane would ever come around to liking Eodan, let alone trusting him.

T he last light of the sun was fading past the horizon when they rode into Tesccine, by which point Ginnevra felt numb with weariness from having been awake and in the saddle for most of twelve hours. She steered her horse in the direction of the nearest inn, but was brought up short by Buonnane's addressing her. "What?" she said, too tired for politeness.

"There are only two inns in Tesccine," Buonnane said. She didn't sound annoyed by Ginnevra's curtness. "One of them is accustomed to catering to paladin companies. I suggest we stay there."

"Oh. That's sensible. Yes, I agree." Ginnevra scrubbed her tired eyes. "Will you lead the way, captain?"

Buonnane nodded and urged her horse forward. Ginnevra let her lead. Beside her, Eodan said, "That was unexpectedly helpful."

"She benefits from good shelter as much as any of us," Ginnevra replied. "I'm so exhausted. No more days like this one."

"We're not going to ride out before dawn again, and that will help." Eodan smiled. "I'm looking forward to a warm bed with a lovely companion."

That woke Ginnevra up fully. "You have the best ideas."

The inn was almost at the other side of town, but its size and the warmth and light of its welcome was worth the extra distance. Unlike most of the buildings, it was made of stone and had a slate roof, which told Ginnevra someone had put real effort into constructing an inn that would last for centuries. Its stable yard was accessed at the rear, and Ginnevra gladly followed Buonnane around the side and through the wide gate.

There, however, she had a shock; most of the stalls were occupied, and Ginnevra was sure the inn had enough patrons to be too full to accommodate their whole caravan. As Buonnane dismounted, Ginnevra leaned over to say, "We can't all fit here. Some of us should go to the other inn."

Buonnane looked puzzled. "There's no problem. I'll talk to the innkeeper."

"Excuse me, captain, but how is talking going to create enough rooms for thirty people?"

Buonnane's puzzlement gave way to an amused smile. "They'll send some of their patrons elsewhere. You were with a company once; don't you know how it works?"

Ginnevra's jaw slackened in astonishment. "You mean evict paying guests?"

"We compensate them for the inconvenience. And people are happy to give way to paladins or the anointed."

Buonnane started to walk away. Ginnevra slid down and put her hand on Buonnane's shoulder, bringing her to a halt. "We can't do that. There's no reason we can't split up and take what rooms are available in both places."

Buonnane's smile vanished. "We're meant to stay together, prime. It's my obligation to protect Revered Giulliomocte. I can't do that if half my people are across town. I don't know what kind of strange notions you have, whether you believe you're being humble or self-effacing, but you should keep in mind these people offer respect to the Goddess through us, and what would be arrogance in a king or elector is a holy acceptance of that respect in us." She shrugged off Ginnevra's hand and walked away.

Ginnevra stared after her, fists clenched. She startled when Eodan stepped up beside her. Eodan said, "Is something wrong?"

"I don't know. No. It's fine." She wanted to put her arms around him, but she was still cased in silvered steel. "No. She was right, damn her."

"Right about what?"

Ginnevra watched Buonnane talk to the stable mistress, her plate mail catching the light from the lanterns ringing the yard. "It would be so much easier," she said, "if I could hate her. But she's right. Our mission is more important than other people's comfort, and those people won't begrudge us taking their rooms. It's just not who I am. Not who we are when we're by ourselves. And I need to remember that."

"You're not naturally inclined to seek out preferential treatment," Eodan said. "It makes sense that you would think differently. Let's go inside. We'll have a meal, and get some sleep. And tomorrow—"

"Tomorrow," Ginnevra said with a sigh, "will be the first of many, many days, all alike."

ACCEPTING Buonnane's logic didn't make Ginnevra happy about the necessity. She lingered in the stable yard, giving unnecessary directions about the stabling of the horses and attempting to groom Dauntless herself, until she felt sure she wouldn't encounter any of the men or women or, Goddess forbid, small children evicted by their caravan. Finally, Eodan planted himself between her and her horse and said, "Inside. Now. Before I burn my hands dragging you away."

Ginnevra scowled, but her heart wasn't in it. She tucked her helmet beneath her arm and pulled off her coif, ruffling sweat-dampened hair that chilled her instantly as it was exposed to the night air. Folding her heavy cloak over her arm, she hurried after Eodan.

A short hallway led directly from the stable yard to the tap room. It seemed filled to overflowing with her people—what an odd concept, that they were hers. Her responsibility, certainly, even the paladins who owed their more direct allegiance to Buonnane. Ginnevra stood in the doorway and watched them for a moment. The blonde Bordelamarian Dedicate sat chatting enthusiastically with her fellows. The paladins were scattered throughout the room in twos and threes. All had removed their helmets, and most of them had claimed drinks, though they were on the whole quieter than Ginnevra remembered her own company being.

Orselle had a mug of beer and leaned against the wall by the hearth, looking as though he might never move again. Pratese and Giulliomocte sat near one another without looking or speaking or even touching. Their poses reminded Ginnevra of something she'd seen once, but then Giulliomocte caught sight of her and rose, and the memory vanished.

Ginnevra just had time to realize she didn't see Buonnane anywhere before Giulliomocte approached her and said, "Prime Cassaline, I protest. We shouldn't have sent those people away."

Guilt and embarrassment flashed through her. She shook her head. "I don't like it either, Revered Giulliomocte, but our mission is more important. We can't guarantee everyone's safety if we're spread out throughout the town. And you—"

Giulliomocte raised a hand. "I'm not so obsessed with my own importance as to believe my comfort matters more than theirs."

"Now, Domenico, that's not true, is it?" Revered Pratese appeared at Giulliomocte's side, once more smiling and honey-tongued. "You are, after all, almost a Hallowed. I'm sure every one of those people left here secure in the knowledge that they were in close contact with greatness."

"Marsillia—" Giulliomocte turned on the Revered, his voice sharp and angry. Pratese smiled peacefully at him. Ginnevra's gaze shot from one to the other as she wondered what kind of fight she might have to break up. Laying hands on a Revered was not something she'd ever imagined doing.

Giulliomocte's eyes closed briefly, and he visibly calmed himself. "You are right, prime," he said, turning his back on Pratese. "They show respect not to me, but to the Dark Lady whom I serve. Thank you for the reminder. I would like to sleep now, if that's possible."

"I think Captain Buonnane is arranging things," Ginnevra said. Behind Giulliomocte, Revered Pratese continued to smile as peacefully as if Giulliomocte's moment of anger had never happened. Why Pratese felt the need to needle her religious superior, or at any rate someone who would be her superior in a few weeks, Ginnevra had no idea, but she wished whatever hostility lay between them could go dormant until they reached Abracia-bene. That was an unlikely wish to see come true, even if Ginnevra were inclined to trouble the Goddess for her intervention in that way.

At that moment, Buonnane entered the tap room and crossed to Ginnevra's side. "There will be rooms enough in about half an hour," she said, addressing both Ginnevra and Giulliomocte.

"Most of these rooms are doubles, but they have a common loft at the top of the inn where the Dedicates and acolytes can sleep comfortably. There's a place for you ready now, Revered Giulliomocte, if you'll follow me?"

"And the rest of us?" Ginnevra said.

Buonnane regarded her with a bland, neutral gaze. "You, too," she said, as if Ginnevra had asked some embarrassing personal question and Buonnane was deliberately ignoring her boorishness. Ginnevra glared back, refusing to let the captain get to her.

Ginnevra's room was on the second floor at the far left end, across from Revered Giulliomocte's. Ginnevra made a spiteful guess that whatever room Buonnane had claimed for herself would be as far from Ginnevra and her werewolf lover as possible. She entered the room and wearily began stripping off her armor. Her extraordinary strength combined with clever design made the plate mail easy to wear and easy to remove oneself, but tonight she felt like one of those warriors from before the coming of the Goddess's faith, burdened by iron plates and followed around by servants to remove them.

"It's not that bad," Eodan said.

Ginnevra paused in unbuckling her vambraces. "What do you mean?"

"You look like you've been sentenced to death. Go ahead and get out of that armor and sit here with me." He sat on the edge of the bed, which was wide and had a thick mattress.

Ginnevra arched an eyebrow. "*Sit* with you?"

"Well. We'd start by sitting." Eodan's smile broadened.

"I can't," Ginnevra said, sighing. "I have to go back down and make sure everyone finds a place to sleep. It's my responsibility." She piled her armor on the second bed, for once not being as cautious as she usually was with it. The light from the lantern on the table by the door turned the silvered metal tawny gold like a dragon's treasure. Ginnevra had met a dragon once, but the creature hadn't enlightened her as to whether dragons actually hoarded gold and gems.

"We should eat, too," Eodan pointed out. "Plenty of time for other things after that."

When they returned to the tap room, it was mostly empty. Ginnevra's faint discomfort at not having been there to supervise faded when the serving lad set a plate of fat noodles in olive oil and cracked black pepper in front of her. The young man winked at her when he set down a bottle of wine next to the plate. "Anything for a paladin," he said with a smile that left nothing to the imagination. Beside her, Eodan let out a muffled snort of laughter before digging in to his own meal.

"Can't he tell we're together?" Ginnevra muttered when the young man was gone.

"Probably. That might have been the draw for him. It is for some people," Eodan protested when Ginnevra turned a startled look on him. "Stealing someone's heart away from another is a unique kind of challenge."

"You seem awfully certain of that." Ginnevra forked up a twirl of pasta and ate heartily.

Eodan shrugged. "It's not from personal experience, if that's what you mean. People are people whether they're human or werewolf. At least that's what I've discovered in the last few months." He poured wine for both of them. "And vice and virtue are the same regardless."

Buonnane entered the tap room just then and crossed to stand in front of Ginnevra. "Everyone is settled, and I've told the paladins we will ride out after sunrise. I hope that's acceptable." Her look told Ginnevra that she didn't actually care if it was.

Ginnevra briefly considered letting it go. Then she remembered that she had a responsibility and that four weeks was going to feel like ten if she didn't face this problem head-on. She wiped her lips and stood. "Thank you for correcting me," she said. "You were right, I was not thinking about the respect due this company as representatives of the Goddess. I appreciate your willingness to speak up and I hope you'll continue to do so. But I feel I should remind you that *you* owe respect to *me* for exactly those reasons. I have ultimate responsibility for what this group does and how it travels, and while I value your opinions and advice, I will make the final decisions."

Buonnane's lips twisted in a mocking smile. "If you think we should leave earlier—"

"That's not the point, captain. The point is that if I had decided to house half our party in a second inn, *that is what we would do.*" Ginnevra kept her gaze locked on Buonnane, daring her to look away. "I would, of course, be wrong. But as leader of this group, it's my privilege to take responsibility for decisions both good and bad. My privilege, and my duty. If you have a problem with that, I suggest you take it up with the Goddess. Any of the Revered traveling with us will be happy to hear your complaint."

Buonnane's expression had gradually gone from mocking to uncertain and ended up stunned. Finally, she said, "Prime Cassaline—"

Ginnevra raised both eyebrows, daring her to complete that sentence.

Buonnane swallowed. "Understood," she said. "I —understood."

"I had been thinking we should make a habit of leaving as soon after sunrise as possible, and not traveling well into dark," Ginnevra added. "With the dark moon watching over us, we should be safer, but best not to tempt the Bright One's creatures into attacking us when we're at a disadvantage, yes?"

"That was my thought as well," Buonnane said, regaining

some of her composure. "I can let the anointed know the plan if you want."

"I'll need to talk to the Revereds, but if you'd speak to the Dedicates—you said they were in the common loft?"

"I'll do that now," Buonnane said, and hastily retreated.

Ginnevra resumed her seat and continued eating noodles that had gone a little cold and hard. Beside her, Eodan let out a low whistle. "I didn't know you could do that," he murmured. "I guess you really are a prime."

Ginnevra turned a stricken look on him. Eodan dropped his wooden fork and put an arm around her. "That was a joke," he said, "but it looks like I struck a nerve."

"If I'm the leader, I have to lead," Ginnevra said, "and I can't let anyone believe they can control me or disrespect me. But I don't have to like it."

Eodan kissed the side of her head. "I love you for everything you are. And that includes Ginnevra the prime of the Blessed as much as it does Ginnevra who trusts me enough to sleep beside me. Don't be afraid of who you're becoming, beloved."

"So long as you're with me, I'm not afraid of anything," Ginnevra replied.

She found the other Revereds by way of knocking on each door near hers and waiting for a response. It turned out Buonnane had been serious about clearing the inn; several of the rooms on the second floor were empty. The twinge of guilt Ginnevra felt over this vanished in the much greater relief that she wouldn't have to worry about whether the other guests intended Revered Giulliomocte harm. That probably wasn't likely while they were still within Ghibele, but it wasn't too soon to consider the possibility.

Having spoken to Orselle and Pratese, Ginnevra knocked on the door across from hers. Giulliomocte opened the door immediately, as if he'd been waiting for her. His thinning hair looked thicker in the lantern light, but that same light also deepened the lines across his forehead and at the corners of his eyes. "Prime Cassaline," he said. "I was about to turn in."

"I wanted to let you know we'll be leaving early, just after sunrise."

Giulliomocte nodded. "Thank you. And..."

Ginnevra waited for him to finish his thought, but he merely stood there watching her. She nodded in return. "Good night, Revered."

She had half turned from him when he said, "You play a dangerous game, prime."

"Excuse me?" Ginnevra said, managing not to sound as hostile as his words made her feel.

"That a monster is not evil does not make it less monstrous," Giulliomocte said. "You would not be the first to be seduced by an attractive face."

Ginnevra bit back her first hasty, furious response. Then the second. Finally, she managed, "I'm not sure what your point is. Eodan is no monster, and he's closer to being human than some actual humans are."

"He is still not human, and therefore not a fit companion." Giulliomocte's quiet voice did not sound judgmental, and that infuriated Ginnevra more.

"Thank you for your opinion," she said, trying hard to stay calm. "I'm sure you did not intend to accuse me of bestiality. But the Goddess approves of Eodan, and She approves of our union, so you'll excuse me if I don't privilege your understanding over Hers." She turned on her heel and entered her own room without waiting to hear whatever response the Revered might make. Then she shut the door and leaned against it with her head tilted back, and shook with fury.

With her eyes closed, she was more aware of Eodan's presence than when she could see him. She listened to the bed squeak as he stood, and then to the deeper creaks of the floorboards as he walked barefoot across them toward her. Still with her eyes closed, she put her arms around him, and he drew her into his embrace. He smelled deliciously of the werewolf, but for the first time in months the smell did not comfort her.

"Will it ever stop being difficult?" she whispered in his ear. "Will there ever be a time when we don't have to fight the world to get its approval?"

"I didn't know you cared about approval," Eodan whispered back.

"I don't. And I do. I—damn it. It's just *exhausting*, having to defend my decisions to every single person I encounter." Ginnevra rested her head on his shoulder. "Come to bed with me. I'm too tired for sex, but I want to hold you and forget the world for a few hours."

They snuggled together in bed, not speaking, just holding each other. Ginnevra's weariness had turned into the kind of exhaustion that makes sleep impossible. She watched Eodan sleep, admiring the strong lines of his face, until he startled her by saying, "This isn't anything I ever expected, either."

"I thought you were asleep."

"My thoughts are too busy for sleep." He drew her closer and blew out a breath that stirred the hair across her forehead. "I believed for a long time I would never find a mate, and that led me to rather reckless behavior. Risking myself the way only a person who's given no hostages to fortune can do. And I believed that was a superior way to live."

"Is that why you said you were different now? Why you'd left that other person behind?"

"Some of it, yes." Eodan ran his fingers along the base of her neck, stroking her skin gently. "Someday I'll tell you all about how werewolf packs work—it's late, and we're both too tired for the whole story. But the short version is that males are expected to defend the pack against any threat. Usually those threats are other packs, but we fight for dominance and ranking within the pack as well as against outsiders. And I was committed to being the best. Myself, and my pack. Which means I did things I'm ashamed of to ensure that."

"Don't tell me. I mean, you don't have to if you don't want to, but I'll listen if that's what you need."

"I know. And again, not tonight." He blew out another long, warm breath. "The point is, I thought I was strong because I didn't have anyone depending on me. I believed love made people weak. It was a long time before I realized that wasn't true, and even longer before I met you and discovered how strong two people who love and trust each other can truly be."

Ginnevra's heart felt too full for speech. She cuddled closer and ran her fingers down his chest, through the dark hairs. When she felt more in control of herself, she said, "I don't know who you used to be, but who you are now is more wonderful than I dreamed possible."

He chuckled. "I'm not sure how true that is," he began, and Ginnevra stopped his words with a kiss.

FINALLY, she slept, and rested peacefully and without dreams until she woke to her usual internal alarm. A glance at the dark sky, though, told her she had woken too early. For a few minutes, she lay awake willing herself back into sleep, until she realized sleep was not going to happen again. Sighing, she rose and crossed the room to the window, hoping to get a better look at the sky to see how much time remained before sunrise.

The window looked out over the inn's side yard where the kitchen garden was. Ginnevra hadn't looked at it earlier, though she'd smelled loam under the scent of manure in the stable yard and guessed it was there. It had been put to sleep for the winter, the remaining growth tilled under, the rows ridged and perfect under the light of the half-moon.

Something moved along the rows, something that drifted lazily across the garden. It was white, bone-white, and glowed with more than moonlight. Ginnevra blinked and rubbed her eyes. If she were dreaming...but no, she felt the pressure of her hands against her face, and the floorboards were cold against her bare feet.

The thing was still there. Roughly the size and shape of a pony, it nosed along the barren rows as if it expected to find food there. Then it lifted its head, revealing a horn curved like the scim-itars Ginnevra had seen the royal guard of Paese wield, bright as silver and clearly sharp on both sides.

It looked up at Ginnevra. And it smiled.

Ginnevra snatched up her sword where it was propped against the wall and slammed through the door to race downstairs.

F ear and anger thrilled through Ginnevra, filling her with a readiness to fight. She pelted through the empty tap room to the front door. The entrance was dark even to her enhanced vision, and she fumbled with the latch, cursing her slowness. Finally, she flung the door open and ran, vaulting the short fence surrounding the inn yard rather than going the long way around. She snatched the sheath from her greatsword. Running with a naked blade was dangerous, but so was whatever that creature was.

She rounded the corner of the inn. Dried-up raspberry canes lined the garden fence, still clinging to the last of their leaves and making it impossible to see past. Ginnevra climbed the fence one-handed and dropped to the ground, breathing heavily.

The garden was empty.

Ginnevra drew in a breath and walked forward slowly, scanning the ground for tracks. She saw no horse hoofprints, but a line of perfectly round marks meandered across the hard, cold earth, the marks deeper beneath Ginnevra's window where the creature had stood looking up at her. From there, the tracks led to the garden gate. Ginnevra worked the latch; it was stiff and difficult to manipulate. Probably it hadn't been used since the garden beds were settled for the last time. And the fence was taller than Ginnevra. No horse could jump it. But a creature that only *looked* like a horse?

She surveyed the ground in front of the gate. More little round marks, very deep this time. So it had jumped the fence. Ginnevra hoped it didn't mean the creature could fly. Flying monsters were her least favorite kind.

She pulled the gate open with some effort and took another look. No round marks on the far side, but the garden gate opened directly on the stable yard, whose ground was hard-packed earth tamped down from centuries of patrons and inn workers walking over it. Nothing would leave tracks in it unless there'd been a heavy rain the day before, and the weather had been clear all week. So she still might not be dealing with a flying monster.

She checked the stable yard anyway, just in case. No lanterns burned there at this hour, and the horses drowsed in their stalls. Dauntless was a blue-gray shadow near the middle of the line, and he didn't wake when she neared. Ginnevra didn't need more light to see than the half-moon provided, less than that, but even so, she wished it were daytime. Not for the sake of more light, but because whatever that creature had been, it no doubt drew strength from its mistress's moon.

She paused at the end of the stables, listening. Something had moved nearby, just out of sight. Again she heard it—a faint scraping sound, like stone over wood. Silently, she took a few steps in that direction. The sound stopped. Ginnevra smelled the faintest whiff of something foul. She took a few more silent steps, then ran full-speed for the back of the stables.

Nothing. Not even small round foot marks. The ground there

was as hard as in the stable yard, and whatever the creature was, it had left no trace of itself. Ginnevra scanned the dark, narrow area, listening, smelling, but it was no use. The thing was gone.

Ginnevra returned to the garden gate and put a hand on the latch, but didn't open it. Paladins had a duty to hunt the Bright One's monsters, but Ginnevra had a duty to her company that superseded that. Not to mention she was dressed only in her shirt and drawers. Now that the immediate threat was gone, she felt the night's chill and shivered convulsively. She needed to gather her resources, not fly off madly into the night.

She ran around the garden and the inn yard back to the front door, watching in all directions just in case the monster came back. She saw nothing, heard only the usual night noises of the wind in the tree branches. At the door, she made one last visual sweep, then shut and latched the door behind her.

She sheathed her sword as she hurried up the stairs, still shivering. Indoors with no fire wasn't much warmer than outdoors. To distract herself, she ran through the lists of monsters she'd either seen and fought directly or been taught about in her training. She couldn't remember anything about a small white horse-like creature with a scimitar horn growing out of its head. That seemed so impractical, even by monstrous standards. Even the catoblepas made more sense.

Eodan was sitting up and dressed when she entered their room. "What's wrong?" he asked. "I woke when the door slammed, and you were gone."

"Sorry." She propped the sword against the wall and began dressing. "I need your help."

"Is anyone hurt?"

"Not that. I saw something outside. A monster. I need you to help me track it." She shoved her feet into her boots and stamped to settle them.

"What monster?" Eodan stood and reached for his coat.

"Don't know. But it was whiter than anything I'd ever seen and it looked like a small horse with a damn great blade coming out of its head." Ginnevra gathered up her sword again. "It was in the garden."

"I've never heard of anything like that," Eodan said. "Let's take a look."

This time, Ginnevra headed straight for the stable yard and the garden gate. "It couldn't have leaped the fence," she said, "at least, nothing normal could, but the last footprints end on the garden side of the gate. Please tell me it didn't fly away."

Eodan sniffed, then crouched to smell the hard ground in front of the gate. "I don't smell anything," he said. He opened the gate and examined the small round marks, finally going to his knees to press his nose almost to the earth. "No. Still nothing. That's odd."

"There was something," Ginnevra insisted.

"Of course there was. It left tracks. It just didn't leave a scent." Eodan began removing his clothes. "No scent this form can detect, anyway. Give me a minute."

Ginnevra held Eodan's clothes and boots and watched his naked body shimmer with silver before becoming the black-furred wolf whose shoulders came nearly to her chest. Eodan padded around the footprints, his nose pressed to the ground. He backtracked through the dead garden, following the round marks, until he came to where the creature had stood beneath their window.

"Anything?" Ginnevra asked.

Eodan shook his head. He prowled the fence, following it all the way around the garden, and then returned to Ginnevra's side. With another shimmer of silver, he was human-shaped again. "There's nothing to smell," he said, accepting his clothes and dressing. "It's as if whatever made those marks isn't flesh at all. Except that's not right, either, because even wood and stone and water have scents. This is disturbing."

"I heard it again over here, behind the stables," Ginnevra said, pointing. "At least, I think I heard it. But over there, I did smell something. Something foul."

Eodan followed her to the stables, but his steps slowed as they neared the building. "It's bad," he said. "You can't smell it?"

"I did, but I didn't recognize it."

Eodan stopped at the back corner. "Werewolf," he said with a grimace. "One of the Bright Goddess's creatures."

Ginnevra's hand closed on the hard, reassuring solidity of the wooden wall. "I didn't know. Shouldn't I have known?"

"Werewolves can alter their smell if they work at it hard enough. This one had washed thoroughly before approaching. It definitely wanted to stay concealed. But we can't hide our scents from each other."

"Still—"

"It's gone, Ginnevra. It doesn't matter." Eodan put his hand on her arm. "You went out here alone, unarmored—you might have been killed."

That had occurred to her. She shivered, this time with fear. "So it left rather than attack me," she said. "Why?"

"If it was spying on us..." Eodan's voice faded.

"That means it's part of a pack." Ginnevra stared into the dark space behind the stables. "A pack that has some other plan. How big is a pack, normally?"

"A hunting pack has anywhere from ten to twenty-five members. The full pack is bigger, but that includes non-combatants, children and so forth."

"They almost certainly aren't here in Tesccine, because someone would notice that many strangers." Ginnevra let out a breath. "And then there's the other creature. Two monsters, completely different, on the same night?"

"It could still be coincidence," Eodan said. "Werewolves don't make alliances with other monsters. We keep to ourselves because we are superior to our creator's other children."

"And the creature has no scent, and it leaves almost no tracks."

Eodan nodded. "It concealed its trail better than that werewolf did."

"So it's definitely a monster, as if we needed more proof," Ginnevra said.

"I don't see what else it could be. But this means we really can't locate it unless we discover some other trait it has that can be followed." Eodan turned to survey the street behind them, but it was empty as before. "I thought you hunters in darkness knew all the monsters there are."

Ginnevra frowned. "So did I. I'll have to ask the paladins in the morning. When we're out on missions, we sometimes run into monsters that have been forgotten, or for some reason no one's ever heard of them. Buonnane might recognize it, if she can bring herself to cooperate with me."

"You made your point fairly decisively earlier. She's not going to fight you."

"No, but she's not going to be helpful, either." Ginnevra sighed. "And werewolves. This is turning out to be a more exciting trip than I guessed."

"We just have to continue being watchful. And a pack of werewolves won't be able to conceal itself easily." Eodan smiled. "It will give all those paladins something to do."

Ginnevra smiled back, but wearily. "It's almost sunrise. And here I was hoping for a little more sleep."

"You'll have to settle for an early breakfast," Eodan said.

WHEN GINNEVRA CLIMBED the stairs to roust the others, she discovered the paladins were all awake as she'd expected and the Dedicates and acolytes hadn't yet begun stirring. They woke slowly but without complaint, which was good because Ginnevra's mood hadn't improved and she found herself looking for an excuse to tear into someone. Not the best start to the day.

So she returned to her own room for a little calming meditation before knocking on the Revereds' doors. Pratese didn't answer, but it turned out she was already gone. Orselle was bleary-eyed and morose. Ginnevra didn't understand anyone who wasn't a morning person. Who didn't love greeting the dawn, breathing in the fresh air as if the rising sun created the air anew? Orselle must struggle with the dark of the moon rituals at the beginning of each month.

She didn't want to speak to Giulliomocte at all, but she reminded herself of her duty and politely knocked at his door. "Revered, it's time we were heading out," she said.

Giulliomocte answered the door, fully dressed and groomed and with his belongings neatly packed. "Thank you, prime, I'm ready to go."

Ginnevra stood aside to let him pass. She braced herself for another lecture, but the man didn't even look at her, just walked to the stairwell and descended. Sighing, she returned to her room a final time for her gear. They didn't need to talk, let alone be friends.

In the tap room, she sought out Buonnane, who was tearing into a steak like it was her worst enemy. "Captain, there's something you should know," Ginnevra said, seating herself opposite the woman.

Buonnane eyed her, but said nothing. Ginnevra quickly described the morning's encounter, including Eodan's failed tracking and the disappearing werewolf. Buonnane's eyes hardened the longer Ginnevra talked and narrowed when she mentioned Eodan taking werewolf form. When Ginnevra finished, Buonnane said, "I might have known we'd see trouble."

Ginnevra tamped down on her anger. "You'd better not be implying that Eodan has anything to do with werewolves coming after us."

"I didn't mean that," Buonnane said, rather insincerely to Ginnevra's ears. "This is unique, the first male Hallowed, and maybe it's not so strange that the Bright One's creatures might be interested in interfering."

Ginnevra thought about pushing her harder. She was fairly certain Buonnane did suspect Eodan's presence had something to do with evil werewolves following them. But with Buonnane not making any overt accusations, that would only end in greater animosity. And the captain had a point. "True," she said. "What about the other thing? The horse?"

Buonnane's lips tightened. "Karkadann."

"I've never heard of that."

"It fits the description. I've never seen one, but I had a captain who'd encountered one, and she used to tell the story often." Buonnane pushed her plate away as if she'd lost her appetite. "They're omens of bad luck. Not in the heretical sense, just that a karkadann's appearance is always followed by bad things. Other monsters, or the Bright One's evil influence. My captain said the one her company encountered followed them for miles, appearing here and there but never staying put long enough to be killed. Then it disappeared, and a day later they were ambushed by a fester of malignae no one detected. You know how malignae smell —that ought to be impossible."

"So it could be a harbinger of the werewolves. Since we haven't heard anything about bad luck in Tesccine, it couldn't have been here long."

Buonnane took a long drink of ale before answering. "Whether it's related to the werewolf appearing or not, karkadann are supposed to be creatures of the badlands or wilderness. If it came into the center of civilization, it was certainly looking for something. Us, apparently."

Ginnevra had expected this, but Buonnane's words still sent a chill down her spine. "You're not wrong that the Bright One might have an interest in our group."

"We'll just have to stay vigilant. Karkadann hunt at night, and we've got at least two more days before we're likely to make camp between towns." Buonnane rose. "Though..."

"Though, what?"

Buonnane fixed her gaze on Ginnevra's face as if searching it for flaws. "The karkadann showed itself to you, not anyone else. It might be drawn to us for some other reason than the werewolves."

Ginnevra, confused, was about to ask what she meant when she realized what the captain was getting at. "Eodan turned his back on his creator," she said sharply. "It's not as if he's in league with evil creatures."

"Evil calls to evil," Buonnane said. "It's in their natures. Maybe your lover wants to change, and maybe not, but he's still a monster, and—"

Ginnevra stood in one swift movement. "Enough," she said. "Eodan is one of us, and you'd better remember that. He's not a monster."

Buonnane shrugged. "Then I'd watch your back. If the karkadann showed itself to you, there might be a reason for that." She turned and shouted, "Time to go!"

Ginnevra unclenched her fists and drew in a shaky breath. Buonnane's matter-of-fact words had disturbed her more than if the woman had made threats. Eodan *wasn't* a monster, but Ginnevra couldn't help remembering that flash of white light and clap of thunder at the Devoyenne sanctuary. Suppose there were some aspect of Eodan's nature that called to other of the Bright One's creations? Something inherent that had nothing to do with Eodan's choices?

She shook her head to clear it. She'd traveled with Eodan long enough that if monsters were drawn to him, they would have noticed. Buonnane's theory was plausible, but wrong. But she'd been right about one thing: Ginnevra needed to be alert for the karkadann's return, and for anything it might bring in its wake.

THE DAY's journey was less punishing than the previous one, but more uncomfortable for the awkward silence Ginnevra rode in. Buonnane ignored her completely, speaking only to the paladins at their occasional rest stops. In the face of that silence, Ginnevra felt incapable of speaking to Eodan of anything more serious than comments on their surroundings. So she rode wrapped in her own thoughts, which centered on getting them all to Abraciabene without being attacked and killed.

They left Tesccine behind for the broad highlands, treeless plains where almost nothing grew and the river ran fast and deep. Here at the beginning of winter, the plains were even less appealing than usual, with the scrub grass turned yellow and the broken, dead weeds giving the land the appearance of something long dead. Ginnevra hated this part of the journey. When she and Eodan had traveled from Devoyenne to Ghibele, they'd taken the longer route to the south that ran up along the coast for the last hundred miles. It was beautiful and temperate and almost resigned Ginnevra to the coming of winter. This was nothing but hundreds of miles of tedious, freezing nothing.

She wrapped herself more deeply in her cloak and watched the sky for anything to break the monotony. No birds, no clouds, just an empty ice-blue expanse paler than Eodan's eyes that made her feel even colder.

When her gaze returned to earth, she watched the horizon where the icy sky met the frozen ground, bisected by the fast-moving river. No landmarks gave her something to look forward to, not even a lone tree or a boulder. She envied the paladins and the others in the line of march behind her. At least they had other people's backs to look at. She reminded herself that werewolves would have trouble sneaking up on them in this empty wasteland, and tried to take comfort in the idea.

Movement on the horizon caught Ginnevra's attention. She focused on it, but whatever it was had vanished. She strained to see anything—monsters might prefer to attack in darkness, but that didn't stop them attacking during the daytime as well.

Another flicker of movement, this one to the left. Ginnevra scanned the horizon in that direction. This time, she saw a white shape, moving fast. It looked like a pony or a small horse. Ginnevra blinked, and it was gone.

Cursing, she brought Dauntless to a halt. Eodan stopped as well. "What is it?" he asked.

"There's something out there. I think it's the monster I saw last night." Ginnevra urged Dauntless in that direction.

Eodan brought Ginger around to block her movement. "You're not going after it, are you? Because that could be dangerous. To all of us, not just to you. Just because we can't see werewolves doesn't mean they're not out there, following us."

Ginnevra blinked, bringing her attention back to Eodan. "Yes. You're right. I don't know what I was thinking." Then she saw the creature again, and pointed. "There!"

Eodan and Buonnane both turned to look. "I don't see anything," Buonnane said.

"It's right—no, it's gone again." Ginnevra swore again. "I see what your captain meant about it being elusive. Let's ride on. We might chase that thing all day and accomplish nothing but exhausting ourselves."

Buonnane gave Ginnevra a skeptical look, but said nothing more.

CHAPTER

SEVEN

Ginnevra saw the karkadann half a dozen times throughout the day. Always it appeared at the limits of her vision. No one else ever saw it, though twice it remained in sight long enough for Ginnevra to draw Eodan's attention. By the time they reached Forannine, exhaustion and blurry vision combined to make her long for a bed that didn't move.

Forannine was much smaller than Tesccine, but it still had two inns on the main road, both of them sizable enough to accommodate a company of paladins and anointed. This time, Ginnevra didn't protest when Buonnane spoke to the innkeeper of the smaller inn, resulting in a steady flow of people leaving it for the other one. The encounter with the karkadann, and the near-encounter with the werewolf, had left her feeling wary and less inclined to separate their party. She stayed with their group long enough to establish that they all had rooms, then fell into her own bed and was asleep in minutes.

When she woke before dawn the next morning, she lay there

listening to Eodan breathe and let her mind wander. When this was all over, she intended to take some time for herself. Her family, with the exception of her Aunt Caterrina, had never met Eodan, and it was only a few days' journey from Abraciabene to her family's home in the principality of Talagne. She could justify a few days' holiday.

Beside her, Eodan stirred and then sat partly up, propping himself on one elbow. "You're awake," he said. "We need to talk."

Cold dread filled Ginnevra. "Talk? About what?"

"It's nothing dire. Not yet, anyway." Eodan fixed his blue-eyed gaze on her in what Ginnevra recognized as his you-won't-like-this look. "I stayed in the tap room after you went to bed, talking to people, but mostly listening. I don't like how the party is fracturing."

"Fracturing?" The dread feeling expanded. "I haven't seen anything like that."

"No, because we ride at the head of the caravan—as is proper, that wasn't a criticism. But it was clear, listening to the anointed talk, that there's a schism within that group centered on Revered Giulliomocte. More accurately, less than half of them are supportive of him and are thrilled about his elevation. The others aren't openly disrespectful, but the way they talk about him and refer to him says they don't believe he deserves the new rank."

Ginnevra lay back and closed her eyes. "Which is no more than Hallowed Riccobene suggested would be the case."

"That's not the worst part. None of them came to this conclusion independently. Revered Pratese is the source of their discontent. She praises Revered Giulliomocte in an insincere way that gets her listeners thinking about why he doesn't deserve that praise. And I'm pretty sure every one of those in the opposition secretly believes Revered Pratese is the one who ought to become Hallowed."

"I've noticed she likes to needle him. So, there's bad blood between them, and Pratese wants to weaken him by encouraging the ones who are opposed to his elevation." Ginnevra stared at the ceiling. It was low and not very clean, with wispy gray cobwebs in one corner, drifting in air currents she couldn't feel. "Is it bad that I'm not sure I care? Giulliomocte as much as accused me of deviant behavior in loving you. And it's not like Pratese and her followers can do anything to him. Anointed aren't elevated based on popular vote."

"Ginnevra, I've seen communities divided like this. The hostility weakens them, makes them vulnerable to outside attack. We're going to be on the roads through the badlands for another four weeks, and we will certainly face monsters, even if it turns out there's no werewolf hunting pack after us. We can't let ourselves be weakened when that happens."

Ginnevra sighed. "You're right. And I really can't let those people go on disrespecting the Revered, regardless of how I feel about him. That can lead to disrespecting the Goddess. I'll ride with the anointed this morning and see what I can do."

"I'll join you," Eodan said. "I have no desire to ride in hostile silence with Buonrane. She can't stay vigilant if she's afflicted by fear." He rolled out of bed and reached for his clothes, draped over the room's one chair.

"What is she afraid of?"

"Me." Eodan stood with his trousers in hand, but made no move to put them on. "She hides it well, but the smell of fear is unmistakable even when I'm not the wolf."

Ginnevra sat up. "I didn't realize. It explains so much, between that and her anger at being displaced in authority by me. You know, I almost feel sorry for her? Not a lot, because she irritates me, but I can see her side better now."

Eodan returned to Ginnevra's side. "And that," he said, kissing her lightly, "is one of the many reasons I love you. Now, if you can manage to feel that way about Revered Giulliomocte…"

Ginnevra shuddered and pulled her shirt over her head. "Him, I *don't* understand. He believes the Blessed's edict, but he still thinks it's wrong to give full fellowship to werewolves like you? I thought someone who's almost a Hallowed would have stronger faith than that."

"It's asking a lot to expect anointed to change their views overnight. Give it time." Eodan smiled. "The younger ones, the Dedicates and the acolytes, aren't nearly so rigid. Mostly they wanted to know what it's like traveling with a prime. Only a few of them refused to acknowledge me, but even those were too curious to be truly hostile."

"That's a relief." Ginnevra slid her feet into her boots. "I can only fight so many battles at once."

BUONNANE LOOKED RELIEVED, and a little suspicious, when Ginnevra told her the plan for the day. Ginnevra didn't understand the suspicion, but she decided it wasn't her job to keep Buonnane happy and rode off with Eodan to join the Dedicates at their wagon.

A little careful questioning was enough to reveal what Eodan had described. Ginnevra listened rather than speaking and felt increasingly disturbed. Revered Pratese had done an excellent job swaying these young anointed to her side. Furthermore, she'd done it in a way that wouldn't come back to bite her in the ass if anyone challenged them on their opposition to an anointed. Even in her frustration, Ginnevra had to admire her skill.

But she *was* frustrated, mostly because she didn't know how to counter this. The Dedicates probably believed their opinions were their own and would protest their respect for Giulliomocte if challenged. Which meant Ginnevra ought to deal with the source. She had no desire to chastise a Revered, particularly one as clever as Pratese. But Ginnevra was in charge, and she had to do *something*.

Night fell with no town in sight. Ginnevra called a halt an hour before sunset, and they set about making camp. She didn't like their position, though the openness of the highlands and the river on one side meant nothing could sneak up on them. No, it was the lack of trees, and thus the lack of firewood, that had her concerned. She walked between the tents, shivering in her fur-lined cloak, and contemplated the reality of a cold supper and a colder bed.

"Something wrong, prime?" Revered Giulliomocte said. He looked up from where he had smoothed a patch of ground clear of weedy yellow grass.

"Just cold," Ginnevra said, for once not dwelling on their animosity. She could be polite.

"I can take care of that." Giulliomocte closed his hand into a fist and held it above the cleared spot. *"By Your grace the fire burns bright."*

His fist burst into flame, a golden-yellow flickering glow that made Ginnevra gasp and reach for him. Before she could touch him, he relaxed his fist, and the fire drifted down to settle in the center of the cleared spot, where it burned as steadily as if in a nest of logs. "It will burn as long as we need it," Giulliomocte said.

Ginnevra stretched out her hands toward the fire and flexed her fingers in its warmth. "Thank you. I didn't realize those fires burned without fuel. I've only ever seen them used to attack."

"Interesting. I hadn't thought about them being used for that purpose. I've dedicated my life to preventing conflict." Giulliomocte settled cross-legged beside the fire. "Though I appreciate those who do that more directly. Sometimes conflict is inevitable."

"I'm surprised to hear you say that."

Giulliomocte gave her an ironic look. "You and I have been in conflict since the beginning."

Ginnevra scowled. "And whose fault is that?"

"Prime Cassaline, fault is irrelevant when it is a matter of two people with different goals or different understandings," Giulliomocte said. "Your experiences are your own. I hope only to make you see the matter differently."

"I don't understand you at all," Ginnevra replied. "The Blessed herself says Eodan isn't a monster. How can you reconcile the things you've said to me with that? You who are nearly a Hallowed?"

"Our faith is our own, and the Goddess blesses us with the gift of following Her in our own ways." Giulliomocte looked more severe than ever. "The Blessed instructed us to pray for our own understanding of the knowledge you brought her. And my prayers led me to know that whatever choices some werewolves make, they are still by nature the Bright One's creations and therefore dangerous. I feel no animosity toward your companion—"

"He has a name. Which I notice you never use. That's an excellent way to dehumanize someone," Ginnevra retorted.

"I feel no animosity, and I don't fear him," Giulliomocte continued as if she hadn't spoken. "But he is not human and never will be. I wish you would see the truth of that."

Ginnevra shot to her feet. In that brief moment, she regained control of herself, so instead of shouting at the Revered, she said, more or less calmly, "I understand. You have a path to follow, and your faith and knowledge shape it. It's not the path I choose for myself. Thank you for not turning your bigotry into antagonism toward Eodan, because I *will* defend him, even against a Hallowed. And—stop trying to convince me I'm wrong. You're wasting your breath."

She walked away, not wanting to give him the chance to get in any more digs. The *nerve* of some people—! Stalking through the camp, she saw other fires burning without fuel. She was too angry to appreciate the Goddess's blessing. His prayers couldn't be correct, which meant he wasn't—no, she would not judge his worthiness to be Hallowed. That wasn't her right. But she could certainly resolve to have nothing more to do with him.

She passed beyond the last tent and stood looking eastward, at the darkening sky and at her long gray shadow pointing back toward Ghibele. What angered her, she realized, was that he wasn't entirely wrong. Eodan's people had been created by the Bright One, and abandoning the evil one's worship didn't magically turn Eodan human. He was still a werewolf. It was the conclusion Giulliomocte had drawn that was the problem. Ginnevra didn't believe nature was destiny—didn't believe in destiny at all. You were what your choices made you, day by day, and Eodan had chosen to turn his back on evil. That was what mattered.

She let out a deep breath that steamed in the frigid air. She only had to get Giulliomocte to Abraciabene, and that would be the end of it. Unless he taught his beliefs to others, and they turned against the werewolves, and...

Ginnevra let out another breath, hoping it would carry her worries away with it. Unlikely, but she could always hope.

SHE WOKE in the middle of the night to a sound that in her dream had been a trumpet signaling their entrance to Savorola. She sat up, straining to hear. All was silence. Then another barking yowl pierced the night, followed by another, and a third.

Ginnevra cursed and grabbed her boots. Beside her, Eodan rolled over and got to his feet. "Krokottas," he said. "But there's only a few—"

A massed howl, dozens of voices crying out in challenge, silenced him. "I should remember not to make assumptions," he said.

"That's a full pack," Ginnevra said. She snatched up her greatsword and lunged through the tent flap to find the other paladins emerging from their own tents, dressed haphazardly but all wielding blades. More heads poked out of tents, the Dedicates and Revereds Orselle and Pratese, all looking confused.

"Stay put," Buonnane commanded them. The captain had dragged her chain mail over her head, which was tilted, listening. "That way," she said, pointing with her sword. "You four, to the other side. We can't be caught off guard by a feint. And all of you, stay vigilant. This wouldn't be the first time werewolves used other monsters to cover their own attacks."

Ginnevra waited for Buonnane to direct her, caught in old memories of her last company. But Buonnane trotted away, ignoring her. The next howl brought Ginnevra to herself. Right. She was a prime. Buonnane had no authority over her. Still, it would have been smart to coordinate attacks.

"We need to see what we're facing," she told Eodan, who held her mace firmly in his right hand. "This way."

They ran between the tents, passing Giulliomocte's without seeing the Revered. At least he had the good sense to leave the fighting to the paladins. Nearby, other paladins moved swiftly into position to defend the camp. Ginnevra reached for her pistol only to realize she'd left it in her tent. No time to go back for it now.

On the outskirts of the camp, she came to a halt. The moon was waning toward dark, when Ginnevra's vision would be clearest, but she still saw the landscape almost as clearly as if it were noon. Long grasses, swishing in the frigid breeze; the distant horizon like a line drawn along a ruler; and, between the two, low, hunched shapes that arrowed through the grasses like sharks. The krokottas probably thought they were concealed. They weren't the smartest of the Bright One's creations, but they were cunning and worked well as a pack, and Ginnevra had fought enough of them not to underestimate them.

At the moment, their paths curved and interwove with each other, a technique they used to confuse their prey into believing the pack was larger than it was. Ginnevra watched, counting silently. Twenty-two, with more probably sneaking around the perimeter to attack the far side. She knew better to run at them, screaming a challenge, not while her sister paladins hadn't fired yet.

She shot a glance at Buonnane, who stood near the center of the line of paladins. She and the others held pistols at the ready, but Buonnane hadn't given the order to fire. Ginnevra once again cast her gaze over the pack. They were well within range, so what was Buonnane waiting for?

The krokottas' weaving gait sped up, and they drew nearer. Black spots stippling their tawny fur increased the illusion of many bodies. Ginnevra drew in a breath. Any longer, and the enemy would close with the paladins before they had a chance to shoot.

As one, the krokottas swiveled to lunge at the paladins' line. Buonnane shouted, "*Fire!*"

The night exploded with gunfire and bright flashes of muzzle flare. Krokottas all along the line dropped, but more of them came up behind their fallen packmates, snarling and leaping to the attack. The paladins dropped their pistols and met the charge with swords drawn. Ginnevra ran at the nearest monster, who leaped at her, snapping its powerful jaws and making the high pitched chittering noise that sounded like laughter. It dodged her first blow, but not her second, and Ginnevra impaled it through the stomach, tearing upward with the blade until the thing stopped moving.

She was vaguely aware of Eodan nearby, swinging the mace with a deliberate slowness timed to catch a krokotta mid-air to add its momentum to his blows, but there was no time, in combat, for watching your companions' battles. Not when that inattention could get you killed. She paced the edges of the combat, chasing down monsters that tried to weave their way around the paladins' line to get behind them.

Which was when she saw the karkadann.

Its brilliantly white body stood out against the dark grasses like the full moon fallen to earth. It ran past in the distance, beyond the krokotta pack, and despite the darkness and how far away it was, Ginnevra knew its eyes were fixed on her.

"*Ginnevra!*" Eodan shouted.

His panicked cry brought her back to herself in time to bring her sword up to deflect a krokotta springing at her face. She stepped back, giving herself room to recover, and booted the thing away. It twisted in midair, landed a few feet away, and as rapidly dove at her again. This time, Ginnevra was ready, and with a powerful two-handed swing she took the krokotta's head off.

Breathing heavily with fear as well as exertion, she looked for immediate threats and found nothing within reach of her sword. No larger shapes lurked in the distance, waiting for the krokottas' attack to distract the paladins. "I'm all right," she assured Eodan, though she didn't see him. He was nearby, she was sure. The karkadann had vanished as well.

She was fighting all alone, she realized; her path had taken her well to one side of the battle. With a muttered curse, she ran back toward the paladins. Her pace slowed as she took in the fight. Paladins swung their heavy blades, impaling bodies and severing heads, but it seemed the krokottas were everywhere. And Ginnevra didn't think that was a battle-madness illusion. She had no time to count, but she was sure there were more than the twenty-odd she'd first noticed.

Then the first paladin fell. Three krokottas attacked her instantly and were booted away almost as rapidly by her comrade. Ginnevra pushed herself harder to rejoin the fight, damning the karkadann for its evil influence.

She found Eodan beside her. Blood streaked the side of his face, but he didn't move as if he were injured. "Where did they all come from?" she asked, breathlessly.

"Don't know," Eodan said, and that was all the talk they had time for, because the krokottas had noticed them, and several peeled away from the pack to go after them.

Ginnevra's sword cut a path through the krokottas that drenched the field in blood. Her paladin's reflexes and endurance kept her upright long after any other warrior would have fallen. Yet the krokottas never seemed to stop coming. Another paladin fell, and another. Ginnevra's world narrowed down to one monster after another, or sometimes two at a time. She didn't know where Eodan had gone and didn't have the leisure to worry about him.

A moment of quiet between fights let Ginnevra regain her breath and look around her. To her astonishment, she saw Giulliomocte not twenty feet away, apparently unaware of the krokotta pacing toward him. The krokotta moved with slow deliberation, as if it suspected trickery from the human who might only be pretending to ignorance.

Ginnevra shouted Giulliomocte's name and ran at the monster stalking him. Neither monster nor man reacted to her cries. Giulliomocte appeared to be praying. The krokotta stopped and crouched. Its hindquarters quivered in preparation for a leap.

Giulliomocte's head came up. He raised his hand high above his head. From it dangled a leather thong attached to the jet grace of an anointed. *"By Your grace I smite my foe,"* he declared in a voice that cut across the noise of fighting and echoed even on that grassy, treeless plain.

The sky cracked open with a sound like a whip snapping. Shafts of black lightning streaked through the air to strike at dozens of places around the camp. Ginnevra stumbled to a halt as one of those lightning bolts grounded itself in the krokotta intent on Giulliomocte. Black light illuminated the creature, revealing the skeleton beneath the flesh in one terrifying moment. Then the lightning was gone, and the krokotta slumped to lie dead among the grasses.

Ginnevra spun to survey the rest of the battlefield. All across the field, krokottas fell where they'd stood, with paladins standing over them holding swords that now had no targets. Eodan, who was behind her, lowered his mace. They stared at each other in mute disbelief.

After a moment, Ginnevra turned back to Giulliomocte. "I've never seen anything like that," she said. "I knew anointed had access to graces nobody else does, but—"

"I have never seen the Goddess's power demonstrated so dramatically before," Giulliomocte said. "I am humbled to be the instrument of Her will."

"I'm not sure why the Blessed thought you needed a company's protection." Ginnevra bent to clean her blade off on the grass, then sheathed it. "I don't think anyone could stand against that."

Giulliomocte shrugged. "We do not use that grace against humans, whatever the provocation. There, we must rely on other kinds of protection. Like paladins. And..." He looked unexpectedly uncertain. "And I don't know that this escort is here entirely for my safety."

"I don't understand," Ginnevra said.

Giulliomocte looked past Ginnevra—at nothing, it seemed when she turned to follow the line of his gaze. "Neither do I," he said, and bade her goodnight.

EIGHT

Five of the paladins were injured, two of them seriously. Eodan immediately took over, directing the Dedicates to assist him in bringing the wounded back to camp while the unwounded paladins ensured there were no other enemies. Ginnevra hovered near, ready to help if needed, while Eodan examined their injuries. She didn't like the look of Florra Tionte, whose bloody, shredded shirt clung to her stomach until Eodan peeled the fabric away, revealing terrible claw marks. Florra was pale and breathing rapidly, and she fought Eodan taking a better look until he grabbed her wrists in one large hand and held them away from the wounds.

"That's not good," Eodan muttered to Ginnevra. "They may be deep enough to have reached her abdominal cavity. In which case..." He set about cleaning the area with water fetched by an acolyte and a clean cloth.

At that moment, Pratese approached. Her short hair was disheveled, but she smiled as pleasantly as ever. "May I?" she asked, kneeling beside Florra. She removed her jet grace from around her neck and clasped it in one hand. Pressing her other hand against the terrible bloody gashes, she said, *"By Your grace I knit the wounds."*

Deep red light the color of blood radiated from Florra's torn flesh. Florra let out a deep, satisfied breath, though her eyes remained closed. As Ginnevra watched, the wounds sealed shut, leaving no trace of injury behind, not even the scars that surely should have formed.

Pratese took a wet cloth from the acolyte and washed her bloody hand. "I believe Tomascio is seeing to Paladin Bolgare. I'm sorry, but I'm afraid divine healing is intended only as intervention when someone might otherwise die, or we would help with the others."

"We've seen a grace that was a complete healing," Ginnevra said, not mentioning that it had been performed on Eodan. Pratese already knew Eodan wasn't evil.

"I have never dared attempt that one," Pratese said. "It is granted by the Goddess as a sign to the healed person and those around him or her. Usually the Goddess wants us to remember that Her gifts should not replace what humans already have by nature, such as our bodies' ability to repair themselves."

"That's good, or physicians like me would be useless," Eodan said. "Excuse me, Revered." He had washed the remaining blood from Florra's body and now helped her sit. Florra regarded Revered Pratese with awe.

Revered Orselle had, in fact, healed the other badly wounded paladin, saving her arm. Ginnevra helped Eodan treat and bandage the remaining wounds before going to find Buonnane. The paladin captain was returning from the outskirts of camp, her hands and face smudged with blood too dark to be human.

"We've collected the bodies for a pyre," she told Ginnevra. "The ones not struck down by Revered Giulliomocte, that is.

Those turned to ash without help from us." She shook her head in wonder. "I've never seen the like of that. I guess he really does deserve his new rank."

"I guess so," Ginnevra agreed. "Should we light the pyre now? I don't want to lose travel time by waiting on it to burn itself out all morning."

"That was my thought, yes." Buonnane looked back over her shoulder past the tents. "I'll do that now. We'll watch in shifts until the bodies are burned."

Ginnevra nodded. They couldn't leave the krokottas unburned, since their flesh corrupted any carrion-eater that fed on it, turning them into creatures of the Bright One. "I can take a shift if you want."

"That would be appreciated."

Buonnane's civility unnerved Ginnevra, but it wasn't as if she could accuse the woman of being too polite. She wished she knew what prompted it. "I'll want someone to watch for the karkadann as well," she said.

Buonnane's head jerked back to face Ginnevra. "The karkadann?"

"I saw it during the fight. I think it's why there were multiple packs just now. You said it was an omen of bad luck."

"Yes, but—" Buonnane's mouth snapped shut. "Very well. I'll let you know when it's your turn to watch the pyre." She turned on her heel and strode away.

Ginnevra felt more confused than ever. She had no idea what had prompted Buonnane's strange reaction, but she had the feeling the captain either didn't believe Ginnevra had seen the monster again, or thought Ginnevra had made it up from the start. Neither of which reactions made sense. Ginnevra sighed and continued her path through the camp. She might be the only one who could see the monster, but that didn't make it her imagination. She hoped.

Once she had checked on everyone's condition—she knew it was foolish, but she didn't think she could sleep if she hadn't seen for herself that everyone was still there and hadn't been carried off by krokottas—she returned to her tent and lay down fully clothed. Eodan hadn't returned yet, probably because he felt the same nagging desire she did to check on each individual's health. Ginnevra closed her eyes to sleep.

She discovered immediately that she was so used to Eodan's presence beside her she couldn't sleep without the sound of his breathing. Now what? She needed sleep if she wanted to be functional in the morning.

She lay on her back staring at the tent roof. The memory of that small white horse returned. It had been well away from the battle, far enough even she had trouble making it out, and yet she was sure it had been smiling that impossible smile again. Its taunts infuriated her, the more so because they had yet to meet face to face. It was like discovering you had an enemy you'd never spoken to.

Ginnevra reviewed all the times she'd seen the karkadann that day. There was no reason anyone else shouldn't have seen it, because it had been out in the open every time. And yet no one had, not even Eodan, whose vision was as good as a paladin's. Ginnevra had to conclude the monster was doing it on purpose. If it wanted to make her look unstable for seeing nonexistent creatures, it might be succeeding, based on Buonnane's reaction. Or maybe it had some other intent in only showing itself to Ginnevra.

The tent flap moved, and Eodan entered, ducking low. "I'm sorry, did I wake you?"

"No, I was thinking." She hesitated, then added, "You believe I saw that monster, right?"

"The karkadann? Of course." Eodan removed his shirt and put on a clean one that wasn't bloodstained. "Did Buonnane accuse you of making up stories, or something?"

Ginnevra scooted over to give Eodan more space as he burrowed into the blankets beside her. "She didn't, but she acted so oddly I don't know what to think. It's starting to worry me that I'm the only one who's seen it."

Eodan took her in his arms and kissed the side of her face. "There are any number of monsters who are only visible under certain circumstances. I've heard of spirits—actually, maybe I shouldn't give examples."

"Eodan!"

"Sorry." He hugged her more tightly. "I was going to say there are rumors among my people of a spirit that only reveals itself to someone who's going to die. But I doubt that's something you need to worry about."

"Not unless it's the spirit that kills the person. We don't believe in omens like that," Ginnevra said. "I feel like the karkadann is taunting me. Like it has the ability to conceal itself at will, and it has some purpose in not showing itself to anyone but me. But I have no idea what that purpose is."

"Maybe you should ignore it," Eodan said. "If it enjoys seeing you get angry or frustrated, it might become careless if you pretend not to notice it."

"That's a good idea." Eodan was warm and he smelled so good. Ginnevra realized she had relaxed enough to feel sleepy. "I shouldn't sleep. I have to watch the pyre in a little while."

"You need rest, or you'll be too exhausted to be useful in the morning," Eodan pointed out. "Sleep. They'll wake you when it's time."

She heard his words in a fog of tiredness, and then she was asleep.

BUONNANE DIDN'T CALL her until nearly dawn, when Ginnevra would have roused anyway. Ginnevra stood her watch over the smoking pyre with another of the paladins, both of them standing upwind of the krokotta reek. Even in that position, the bitter smell of krokotta flesh mingled with the more pleasant scent of the crisp, hot fire to make a smell that made Ginnevra's stomach roil and her appetite vanish. When it was time to extinguish the pyre's remains, she made herself stay nearby to ensure there weren't any stray coals that might start the plains blazing, even though the stink was stronger when the remains were doused with water.

She couldn't stand the thought of food, even the sourdough bread they'd bought in Forannine that still looked good a day later, but she accepted a quarter-loaf and a glossy pink apple and stowed them in her saddlebags for later. As she took her place at the head of the line and gave the command to move out, she caught a glimpse of a fast-moving white blur off to the left. Remembering Eodan's comments, she ignored it. Time to see if she could turn the tables on the monster.

She rode in silence beside Buonnane for almost an hour, until the stillness started to get to her. Why Buonnane couldn't talk about things like a normal person, Ginnevra didn't know—except she recalled what Eodan had said about Buonnane being afraid of him. Watching the captain more closely, Ginnevra saw what she had missed before in her irritation with the woman: the way she rode well aside from Ginnevra and Eodan, her tense jaw and narrowed eyes, how she scanned the horizon in all directions except the left where Eodan rode. She was definitely afraid. Ginnevra's earlier sympathy for Buonnane shriveled and died. If she was still afraid of Eodan after he'd fought beside her paladins and treated their injuries, what chance did Ginnevra have of changing her mind?

"Captain, I'm going to fall back for a while," she said. "Do you mind?"

"Do as you like," Buonnane said, not looking Ginnevra's way.

Ginnevra wheeled Dauntless around and, with Eodan beside her, went in search of the other thorn in her side.

She found Revered Pratese riding near the Dedicates' wagon. All of them were laughing heartily as Ginnevra and Eodan approached. "Can I hear the joke?" Ginnevra asked.

"Oh, it's nothing. You'd need to know some of the Revered back at the sanctuary," Pratese said. "What can I do for you, prime?"

Ginnevra glanced swiftly at the wagonful of Dedicates and acolytes, all watching this exchange eagerly. Now was not the time to bring up Pratese's subversion, and Ginnevra didn't think she could gracefully pull the Revered aside. "I wanted to take some time to ride with you, Revered," she said with a cheerful smile. "I'd like to get to know everyone in our group, since we have such a long ride ahead of us."

"How thoughtful," Pratese said, her words once more dripping with honeyed sweetness. She had her gaze fixed firmly on Eodan. "Please, join us."

Ginnevra recalled what Eodan had said about some people enjoying the thrill of stealing someone's affection. Pratese hadn't done anything to try to charm Eodan—yet—and it wasn't as if he was interested in the Revered, but anyone who could think that way was a special kind of dangerous. Too bad Ginnevra hadn't discussed with Eodan the possibility of him using Pratese's interest to dig out her secrets.

"You mentioned the other Revereds at the Ghibele sanctuary," she said. "How many are there?"

"There are fifteen of us," Pratese said, turning her attention on Ginnevra. "I was honored to be chosen to escort Domenico. No other Revered at the sanctuary has achieved the Hallowed rank the whole time I've been there."

"I don't know if that's unusual or not. I'm afraid I don't have much contact with the anointed." Ginnevra nudged Dauntless to walk next to Pratese, while Eodan moved to the far side of the wagon so the two of them bracketed the Revered and the Dedicates. "But I understand there was some sign given that indicated Revered Giulliomocte's elevation in rank."

Pratese's jaw tightened briefly, but when she smiled, it was as cheerful as ever. "That's what I'm told. It wasn't a sign given to anyone but Domenico and Hallowed Riccobene. That's how it works, though. We are expected to exercise faith."

Ginnevra put on a concerned expression, furrowing her brow and narrowing her eyes. "That seems so odd. Not the part about exercising faith, but surely that sign is something everyone should be aware of."

"Oh, I'm sure it's true. Domenico is nothing if not scrupulous in his religious observances. Though..." Pratese's voice lowered dramatically. "I would have thought," she added, "that there would have been some other evidence of his worthiness."

"Revered Giulliomocte isn't any more worthy than the other Revereds," said one of the Dedicates, a young man with bad skin and untidy black hair. "If the Blessed was going to choose someone as Hallowed, it shouldn't have been a man."

"The Blessed doesn't choose, she's the voice of the Goddess," the blonde Dedicate said. "And there's no reason a man shouldn't be Hallowed. I'd think you would be happy about that, for what it says about men as anointed."

"I know my role in the Goddess's plan," the young man said, somewhat primly. "I accept that the Goddess reserves Her highest blessings for women. It's the way things are."

"Now, Federrino, Bidelia, let's not argue," Pratese said, in a voice that Ginnevra couldn't help but hear as insincere. "The Goddess's decisions are Her own. It's true, it can be hard to understand Her words, as she speaks to our hearts and not our ears. But the Blessed is experienced at understanding. I'm sure she wouldn't make a mistake in this respect."

"Actually, the Goddess speaks to her out loud," Ginnevra said.

Everyone's attention was immediately on her. "Impossible," Pratese said sharply.

"No, it's true. I've heard Her voice speak to the Blessed. It was unmistakable." She didn't add that the Goddess had had words for her as well. That was a memory she cherished close to her heart.

"What did She say?" the blond Dedicate, Bidelia, asked.

"It was to do with the werewolves. How She would like to accept their worship, but can't. And the Blessed spoke with Her the way, well, like you and I are speaking now. It felt as if they conversed frequently, by how personal the conversation was.' Ginnevra let memory carry her back to that moment, several months ago. The Goddess's voice was not something she would ever forget.

"How honored you must feel to have been present for such a sacred moment," Pratese said, her voice once more as sweet and rich as honey. Though her words were straightforward enough, her tone made them sound insincere. Irritated, Ginnevra bit back a harsh reply. She would only make herself seem unstable if she reacted to what was, on the surface, a perfectly ordinary comment.

"Of course, the rest of us must make do with what the Goddess tells us in our hearts," Pratese continued, this time looking at the Dedicates and acolytes to make her statement more like religious instruction. "Something all Her followers are entitled to."

"Of course," Ginnevra said. She, too, watched the anointed riding in the wagon, assessing them. Eodan was right; more than half watched Pratese with eager awe the way they would an esteemed mentor. The others looked conflicted, as if they wanted to argue even though Pratese had left them with nothing to argue over. Bidelia was one of the latter.

"I've always believed," Ginnevra added, watching Bidelia out of the corner of her eye, "that one's faith should be bolstered by the faith of others. That is, I believe the Blessed speaks for the Goddess, and that her statements reflect the Goddess's will, so I can accept them as part of the foundation for my faith."

Pratese smiled, a pitying expression. "We anointed are taught to question everything, and to use our minds and our hearts to fathom the divine inscrutability. I'm sure a paladin wouldn't care about such subtleties, fighting evil directly as you do."

That sounded like an insult, but again, it wasn't one Ginnevra could challenge. "What, you have no one whose word you trust implicitly? Someone who, if they told you your food was poisoned, you would believe without needing to question?" Peripherally, she saw Bidelia lean forward, an intent look on her narrow face.

"There is always external confirmation for any assertion. That means it's not necessary to take any one person's word as infallible, whoever they are." Pratese turned to the Dedicates again. "I hope you all understand that. You are entitled to personal confirmation of anything your religious superiors tell you."

"Yes, Revered," some of the murmured.

"Then you've received personal confirmation of Revered Giulliomocte's elevation," Ginnevra said.

Pratese turned her gaze on Ginnevra. "My relationship with my Goddess is private, prime. I would think you of all people would appreciate that."

Ginnevra inclined her head. "Of course. My apologies for prying. I should have said, you wouldn't have taken the Revered's assertion of the sign he received as sufficient proof, yes?"

"Of course not," Pratese said.

"Then I'm glad you've encouraged these anointed to ask for inspiration themselves," Ginnevra said. "Since you wouldn't want them to take your word for it."

The shot hit home. Half the Dedicates shifted uncomfortably on their wooden benches. The other half nodded slowly, as if coming to a realization. Bidelia looked radiant with satisfaction.

Pratese, on the other hand, looked sour. Ginnevra kept a straight face, but pleasure at having turned the tables on Pratese filled her heart. Before Pratese could speak, Ginnevra added, "I seek the Goddess's inspiration all the time, Revered Pratese. I like to think I'm worthy of receiving Her wisdom. But I'm always glad to have the guidance of knowing there are those whose word I trust. Perhaps you should consider it."

Pratese gave a curt nod. Ginnevra chose to take it as a sign of her triumph.

CHAPTER

NINE

F our days later, on the first day of the new month, they saw the first signs of the badlands turning into civiliza- tion. It had been an uneventful four days, with no sign of monsters except Ginnevra's continued glimpses of the karkadann and no attacks by werewolves. Although they had maintained vigilance, Ginnevra was sure they were all weary of staying alert all the time. Civilization would be a welcome respite.

With the memory of saluting the new moon with her sister paladins that morning fresh in mind, Ginnevra observed the scat- tered settlements with pleasure. Whatever else it might be, Savorola certainly proved the tenacity of humans and their ability to carve a living out of the least hospitable places.

On the other hand, the outlying settlements and farmsteads didn't look all that welcoming here at the beginning of winter. The caravan hadn't ridden through any snowstorms, but snow drifted between the furrows of harvested fields bristling with stubble, and the farmhouses, most of them made from local red brick, were small and huddled in on themselves. Ginnevra and

Buonnane didn't need to discuss the possibility of stopping at one of them for fresh food; they would overwhelm any farmer with their demands for hospitality.

But the farther west they traveled, the closer together and more prosperous the farmsteads became. Low stone walls too short to be an actual deterrent divided the properties, giving Ginnevra something to watch for, a visual pause between endless fields. The road became wider, too, wide enough to let other travelers pass in either direction. But it was also deeply rutted and frozen hard, which reminded Ginnevra of Savorola's disagreements with the holy city. All roads leading to Abraciabene, at least the ones in the western Lordagne, were paved with stone, not muddy or frozen. Ginnevra hadn't realized how much she'd taken them for granted until this journey.

They saw their first travelers that afternoon, a man driving a farm wagon with a couple of youths riding in the back, huddled up against the chilly wind. All three stared at the black and silver flags, then at the double column of paladins riding behind. Ginnevra saluted them with a pleasant smile and was disheartened to see them recoil. The driver lashed his horses to move faster. Ginnevra had hoped she was wrong about how ordinary citizens of Savorola felt about the Goddess.

It was also the standard reaction, she soon discovered as they continued westward. Pedestrians veered off the awful road to stay as wide of their procession as possible, and riders on horseback refused to make eye contact. Ginnevra grew gradually more irritated. It wasn't as if they were doing anything to the Savorolans. She didn't even know what those Savorolans feared they might do. Force graces upon them, or require them to instantly drop to their knees to pray? The Goddess didn't work that way. She'd seen hostility against the Faith from believers in the old religion of

Torun, but Savorola rejected that religion, too, and Ginnevra didn't know what to make of their antagonism.

After the fifth or sixth encounter, Buonnane called a halt. "We should lower the banners," she said.

Ginnevra automatically looked behind her to where the black and silver flags snapped in the brisk wind. "Why?"

"They're inflaming sentiment against us. We should be more cautious."

Ginnevra examined Buonnane in her silvered steel that gleamed dully under the pewter overcast, then made a slow and deliberate turn to look at the column of identically-armored paladins following the wagon. "I'm not sure why you think the flags are more of a taunt than eighteen armed and armored women. Or do you suggest we stow our armor as well?"

Buonnane reddened. "It's not about concealing what we are. It's about not cramming that knowledge down people's throats."

Ginnevra's eye once more fell on the flags. "No," she said. "There's nothing wrong with serving the Goddess, not even in Savorola. We're here on private business that has nothing to do with the citizens. And we're going to prove by our example that they have nothing to fear from us—which includes making explicit our loyalties." She nudged Dauntless onward. After a moment, Buonnane joined her. Ginnevra listened to the crack of the flags in the wind until the noise faded in her awareness.

It was barely four o'clock in the afternoon when they reached the first town, but by then Ginnevra was having trouble holding on to her patience. If they were going to be turned away from every inn, better they find that out now and give themselves plenty of time to find a place to camp. She offered up a silent prayer as they filed down the town's main street—*Please, Goddess, grant me understanding, because I sorely need it in dealing with these people*—and watched for signs that any of these buildings hosted travelers.

The town looked as prosperous as the outlying farms, though once again all the buildings were made of red brick. Ginnevra thought of red stone canyons, far to the south, through which white water rushed. The town would have looked terrifyingly uniform if the buildings hadn't each been unique. Four-story edifices with odd, crenellated roofs towered over low, single-story buildings twice their neighbors' width, and every building sported architectural flourishes as if their owners were in competition with each other for who could build the most dramatic structure. Ginnevra had never seen a more youthful and exuberant town.

She identified the inn by its sign depicting a bed and its wide yard, completely clear of snow and circling the three-story red brick building to where the stables lay. The distant scent of horses and manure came to her enhanced senses. Ignoring the stares from passersby, she led the caravan to a halt outside the inn and dismounted.

"Prime Cassaline, take care," Buonnane said. "This could be a mistake."

"If it is, better we find out now," Ginnevra said. She noted that Buonnane made no move to get off her horse and added, "It's not as if there's anything to fear."

Buonnane reddened, but said nothing.

Ginnevra turned and nearly ran into Eodan. "You don't have to come," she said.

"I know, and you don't need protection," Eodan said. He took a step away from her silvered mail. "But I thought it might look less like an armed invasion if I came along."

"You're over six feet tall and you look like you could wrestle a bear into submission," Ginnevra teased. "I'm not sure your presence could exactly be called 'calming'. Seriously, though, I will feel better to have you with me. And you do have a way with words."

"It's not being human that does it," Eodan said. "People sense that I'm genuinely interested in their lives, and that relaxes them."

Ginnevra realized Buonnane was listening to this conversation, though she made a good show of examining the inn's façade. "And they never suspect you're not human," she said, raising her voice. "Let's go."

A silvery tinkle of chimes rang out as she opened the inn's door, startling her into spinning around and grabbing the little cluster of bells. She'd never seen anything like it before, and couldn't imagine the point—draw attention to an arrival, perhaps? Or remind potential patrons that someone was watching them?

"Ginnevra," Eodan said in a low voice, warning her. Ginnevra turned to see a young woman staring at her open-mouthed. The girl wore a full-skirted gown of brown wool with a white wrap-around apron, and black braids pinned in a crown around her head made her look older than Ginnevra guessed she was. She let go of the bells and smiled.

"We're traveling from Ghibele to Abraciabene, and we need shelter for the night," she said. "But I should warn you there are about thirty of us. I'll understand if you don't have room." That was a good, polite way to let the girl save face if she was opposed to hosting servants of the Goddess.

The young woman nodded, her mouth still open in astonishment. "I have to fetch Pa," she said, and pushed through a door opposite the front door, leaving it swinging slowly behind her.

"At least she didn't spit," Ginnevra said quietly.

"Or demand we leave," Eodan replied. "She seemed more startled than afraid."

The swinging door opened again before it came to a full stop. The young woman returned with an older man in tow. He was short and slender, with the same black hair as the girl, though cut very short, and he looked as stunned as his daughter did. "Unbelievable," he said. "I never would have guessed—" Then he startled Ginnevra by sweeping her a graceful bow. "My lady, welcome. The Traveler's Rest welcomes you. How many, did you say?"

"I—you do know who I am?" Ginnevra blurted out.

"I do, and I assume your companions share your Faith." The man bowed again, less deeply but still respectfully. "I take it you've experienced Savorola's hospitality."

"We don't insist others worship as we do." Ginnevra felt as if she'd lost control of the conversation somewhere.

"And an innkeeper can't afford to pick and choose when it comes to custom." The man smiled. "We're on the road that leads to the holy city, and travelers are travelers regardless of the way they pray. Or don't. I'm Actus, the innkeeper. You'll need a night's rest, then?"

"There are thirty-three of us," Eodan said.

Actus' eyes widened. "And isn't that a lot. Very well, I think we can accommodate you, if you don't mind doubling up."

"We'll take whatever you have to offer," Ginnevra said. "Thank you."

"Oh, it's no trouble." Actus' smile fell away. "I don't know that I have to warn you there are those who'd pick a fight regardless of that sword. They know paladins won't use the weapon on humans, and they'll take advantage of your unwillingness."

"We'll keep to ourselves," Ginnevra assured him.

She and Eodan returned outside—this time, Ginnevra was expecting the bells—and crossed the front yard to where Buonnane waited, still mounted, her eyes scanning her surroundings as if she expected an attack. "Are we moving on?" she asked.

"We are not," Ginnevra replied. "Everyone to the stable yard to collect your gear, and then Actus will show you where you'll sleep," she called out. She took Dauntless' reins and led him back down the line of the caravan. "It will be tight quarters, but it's better than a pallet on the cold ground, right? Revered Giulliomocte, a word?"

Giulliomocte dismounted and led his horse to meet her. "Something wrong, prime?"

"Maybe. You don't mind sharing a room, do you?"

With a frown, Giulliomocte said, "That would depend on the person, if I'm allowed to be finicky."

It was not the response she'd expected. "Well, Revered Orselle, obviously. Unless—"

Her memory flashed on seeing Giulliomocte and Pratese sitting near one another, not speaking, both their bodies tense, and realization struck. "I mean," she corrected herself, "you could reasonably expect privacy, you and the other Revereds." What was Hallowed Riccobene thinking, sending Pratese as part of Giulliomocte's escort? Surely the woman knew there was not only bad blood, but a failed relationship between them?

"It's true I prefer privacy, but not to the point of selfishness." Giulliomocte tilted his head back as the first raindrops fell. "Shall we get inside?"

Ginnevra led Dauntless to where the stable hands could care for him. Normally, she would insist on doing that herself, not only because she was perfectly capable but because she relished the calming influence grooming a horse had. Now, however, she had a responsibility that trumped that one. She stood at the inn's back door and shepherded anointed and paladins inside. The young anointed squealed and ducked as the rain fell harder; the paladins walked at an ordinary pace, veterans of much worse weather than this. Once the last of the group was inside, Ginnevra closed the door and stood for a moment just within. Then she removed her helmet and went in search of Eodan, who had gone ahead to help their group find beds. With luck, rain would be the worst of their problems.

GINNEVRA REMOVED HER VAMBRACES, swiped a few last raindrops off them, and laid them atop the pile of armor in the corner. It wasn't the best way to store her plate mail, but she had no other options. She and Eodan had ended up with the smallest room on the third floor by virtue of their needing only one bed, which the room had. The bed was larger than average, but they would still sleep close together, which Ginnevra didn't mind at all.

She buffed the vambraces with the corner of her sleeve, though they were still shiny and perfect from her attentions to the armor that morning. Then she removed her gambeson and hung it on one of two pegs hammered into the wall, draping the coif atop it. She ran her fingers through her short hair flattened by long hours compressed by the coif.

Eodan sat on the bed, watching her. "Feel better?"

"I will once I've been fed." But she sat beside him rather than opening the door. "What are the odds we should come across what is probably the only inn in all of Savorola that will put us up with no complaints?"

"You heard what Actus said. Innkeepers can't afford prejudice." Eodan put an arm around her waist and hugged her briefly. "Or maybe the Goddess is looking out for us."

"Maybe. I'm not going to be complacent, though. Actus may be honorable, but there's no guarantee all his customers will be as well." She kissed his cheek, then rose, bringing him with her. "We just have to stay alert, that's all."

"And be grateful they don't know there's a werewolf present as well," Eodan said, making Ginnevra grimace. It was true— things could be worse.

The stairwell was brightly lit by yellow-tinged lanterns, making the narrow chimney feel warmer with their cheery glow. It was an illusion, because the stairwell was far too large to be adequately warmed by such small fires, but Ginnevra clung to it as she hurried down the stairs behind Eodan. The wind had picked up and was audible even there in the center of the inn, and rain rattled on distant tiles. Winter was *awful*. And summer was months away. The old dream of going somewhere far south returned, and Ginnevra indulged in it for the time it took to reach the ground floor. Then she regretfully pushed it away. Time to be anchored in the present.

The stairs terminated in the little chamber with the front door and a couple of other exits. Eodan was already pushing open the door from which emanated delicious smells and the murmur of dozens of people talking. The tap room, lit by the same lanterns as hung in the stairwell, actually was as warm as it looked, with a fire blazing in a hearth that took up half of one wall and a low ceiling that gave the room a cozy appearance.

Ginnevra scanned the room, looking for potential trouble. All her people had gathered at tables to one side of the room, not the one directly in front of the fire. Someone had realized how potentially contentious it would be for their party to take all the prime spots. The rest of the patrons sat here and there throughout the room, some of them solitary, others in groups of three or four. None of them did more than covertly watch the paladins and the anointed. Of course, none of them sat near enough for conversation, either. Ginnevra decided to call it a victory.

The paladins had all removed their armor, but each wore her sword, as Ginnevra did, strapped to her back in a position she could not easily draw from. To other warriors, paladin and non-paladin alike, it was a sign that the paladin wasn't looking for a fight—though, since a paladin didn't need her sword to beat someone unconscious, it wasn't a guarantee of peace. Ginnevra doubted anyone here understood the significance, but it was worth the effort.

She took a seat at the end of a table farthest from the fire, though curling up in front of it was an appealing thought. She also wasn't happy that every time the door opened, a cold draft brushed her. But she was the leader, and she had to set an example of self-control.

Eodan sat across from her, facing the door. They had perfected this strategy in the months they'd been together, each of them surveying half the room, and although Ginnevra didn't think they were in much danger, complacency would get them killed faster than vigilance would. Eodan's gaze roved the room as hers had. He wrinkled his nose. "That stew has a very strong odor."

Ginnevra sniffed. Her sense of smell wasn't as good as Eodan's, even when he was in human form. "It smells like stew. All right, like stew that's been on the fire for a while. But it's no worse smelling than stew ever is. It's exactly what I expect from wizened vegetables and meat that's almost gone off."

"There's a bite to it. I think the cook added tomato." Eodan leaned back as the young woman from the entrance, presumably the innkeeper's daughter, set a deep plate filled with thick brown lumpy gravy in front of him. She leaned across to give Ginnevra an identical plate.

"There's dried tomato, yes, sir," she said. "I know it's not much of a meal, but there are so many of you."

"It's no problem," Ginnevra assured her. "We're grateful for a hot meal on a night like this." The wind's voice deepened as she spoke as if supporting her words.

The girl wiped her hands on her apron, but instead of walking away, she stood at the end of the table, watching Ginnevra. Ginnevra controlled the unease she felt at being observed so closely and kept it from coming out as anger. "Can I do something for you?" she asked instead.

The girl jumped as if she'd been daydreaming. "I—no, my lady, I was just thinking—I apologize, I shouldn't stare. But I wondered, what's it like?"

Ginnevra managed not to laugh at the girl's innocent curiosity, for fear she'd think Ginnevra was mocking her. In truth, Ginnevra remembered when she'd been that age, how infatuated she'd been with the paladins coming through her father's smithy and how she eagerly hung on every story, every tale of adventure. "Boring, most of the time," she said. "We do a lot of traveling through the Lordagne, sometimes beyond its borders. And not much ever happens on those travels. But sometimes there are monster attacks, and those are terrifying."

"Terrifying?" The girl's brow furrowed. "I didn't think paladins were afraid of anything."

"Courage is not letting fear stop you doing what's right. I've been afraid often, but I don't let fear rule me." It was something one of Ginnevra's first teachers had said, something Ginnevra had stupidly scoffed at until she faced her first maligna and knew what real fear felt like.

"Ginnevra is a prime of the Blessed, so she takes care of other business as well," Eodan said. "Sitting in judgment sometimes, arbitering disputes, carrying messages. We see a lot of different places."

"You mean, like this?" The girl gestured at the half of the room full of their group.

"Like this, sometimes, yes." Ginnevra took a bite of stew. Eodan was right; it had a tang to it, a not unpleasant but definitely unexpected tang.

The girl made a show of looking around, then leaned forward. "Do you have to do something special to become a paladin?" she whispered.

Ginnevra incautiously inhaled and swallowed a bit of potato the wrong way. She coughed it up, wiped her mouth, and said, "What's your name?"

"It's Serenna."

"Serenna. Are you curious, or did you have something in mind?"

Serenna looked around furtively again. "I want to be a paladin, only Pa says it's too dangerous. I was thinking, if you talk to him..."

Ginnevra's eyes met Eodan's. He wore his blandest look, the one he used when a problem came up he was deeply grateful was the paladin's responsibility. Groaning inwardly, she said, "I can't order your Pa to let you train for a paladin."

"No, but you can show him it's not so dangerous as he thinks! And tell him what it was like for you, so he knows what I'd be doing." Serenna's round face was ruddy with excitement.

The last thing Ginnevra wanted was to involve herself in the future of a girl she would be leaving behind in the morning. On the other hand, the Goddess welcomed those whose desires were fervent, and hadn't Ginnevra been just like this only a decade ago? "I can talk to him," she said. "But I won't try to convince him. That's up to you."

"I can do that, but thank you!"

Ginnevra idly stirred her stew with her wooden spoon. "I didn't realize you were of the Faithful. Your Pa gave me the impression that he was, well, agnostic."

Serenna fished an obsidian grace out of the neck of her brown dress. "It's not comfortable worshipping in public, not in Savorola these days. We don't keep our beliefs secret, but we don't flaunt them either." She tucked her grace away again.

"Why is there so much religious turmoil in Savorola?" Eodan asked.

Ginnevra considered that a question with too many answers, few of which she knew. As a paladin with a company, she had had only the vaguest sense of what was going on in the biggest city in the Lordagne. Even now that she was a prime, she didn't know much more.

Serenna shrugged. "The three Hallowed in the city got into a fight with the Princeps and his council. Something to do with owing allegiance, and how the Hallowed wanted to be independent of Savorola's laws. Pa says that's an oversimplification, because the anointed are separate from the law in some ways, but it doesn't mean they can do whatever they want. He says that's all just an excuse for the Princeps to make the Hallowed pay taxes. But now people question whether the Blessed ought to have any authority, and some of them talk about the old ways and how they want to go back to those. But most want not to be governed by any religious authority."

"And people being people, I'm guessing some of those use the disagreement as a justification for harassing anyone who believes differently," Ginnevra said.

"That's right." Serenna smoothed her apron again. "But the Blessed sent word we weren't to stir up trouble, so those of us who are Faithful mostly stay quiet. Or try to. Sometimes—"

"Serenna!"

Serenna jumped at the shout that emerged from the kitchen. "Sorry, I just—you will talk to Pa, won't you?"

"I will," Ginnevra said.

Serenna smiled and hurried away.

"Isn't that interference?" Eodan said. "And I really don't know how you can eat that. The smell is so strong I can't smell anything else." He pushed his plate away.

"Interference, meaning by pleading Serenna's case with her father?" Ginnevra took another bite. "Not really. Becoming a paladin is prestigious, and we're encouraged to watch out for potential candidates as we travel. And she's bright, and interested —I wouldn't push her father hard to get his consent, because I don't know her at all, but there's no reason I can't talk to him and maybe answer some of his questions."

Another cold breeze signaled the entrance of a new patron. Eodan's gaze flicked past her to the door, then settled on her again. "The room's filling up."

"Has anyone approached? Anyone look hostile?" Ginnevra asked without turning around.

"No, not yet, but they're all watching us closely." Eodan rose. "I'm going to see if I can cadge a different meal from the kitchen. I'm not going to starve just because the cook was creative."

Ginnevra watched him cross the room to the kitchen. Then she picked up her plate and turned around on the bench, putting the table at her back so she could watch the entrance. Eodan was right; there weren't a lot of seats free anymore. She surveyed the crowd as she ate, leaning against the table in an attitude of relaxed indifference. Nobody she looked at met her eye for more than a moment. Most of the patrons, almost all of them men, carefully did not let her catch them staring at her or any of her people.

Except one.

The man was slim and looked like he might be tall, but he was sitting and it was impossible to be sure. He was also blond, the only blond man in a crowd of dark-complected, dark-haired men.

And he stared at Ginnevra openly, daring her to make an issue of his regard.

Ginnevra stared back at him, maintaining a look of unconcern that concealed her growing unease. Something about his appearance was wrong, but she couldn't identify it. She didn't think it was his nationality, because Dedicate Bidelia was blonde and she didn't look odd, just unusual. Ginnevra examined him more closely. He was surrounded by other men, but a longer look told her he wasn't attached to any of their groups. His eyes were slanted more than usual, his beard shorter, and when he curled his lips in the appearance of a smile, his canines were more pointed than she'd ever seen on a human.

Ginnevra's heart thumped once, painfully hard, then sped up, filling her with the need to attack. She rose and walked toward the blond man, who watched her approach with no apparent concern. The men surrounding him, on the other hand, edged away while trying not to look like they were afraid of Ginnevra. Ginnevra ignored them.

When she reached the man, the space around him was totally empty. He cocked his head to look up at her and once more bared his teeth in what might have looked like a smile if she couldn't see his eyes. "Can I help you, miss?" he said in heavily accented Lordagni.

"I'm not sure," Ginnevra said, staring him down. "Unless you want to tell me why you're here."

The man spread his hands wide. "I am interested in a warm place for a drink, and are not you the same?"

"You know we're not the same," Ginnevra said. "You're a werewolf."

CHAPTER

TEN

The werewolf raised one blond, bushy eyebrow. "I am an ordinary man," he said. "You paladins all see evil where there is none to be seen."

"You don't move like a human male," Ginnevra said. "And this close, you reek of werewolf. Don't think you can hide from me."

"All right," the werewolf said with a shrug. "Then what are we to do? You will kill me, here in front of all these people who believe I am human?"

Ginnevra had never been so conscious of her sword being out of easy reach. "You know I can't do that. Tell me what you want."

"So direct." The werewolf stood. He was as tall as she'd guessed, not as tall as Eodan, but taller than she, and his slim build made him seem even taller. "I wish only to talk. That is not so bad, yes?"

Ginnevra gestured. "Outside, then."

"You take me for a fool? I will not go where you can kill me privately." He laughed. "And I think you do not want to go out of sight of your friends, since you cannot know what friends *I* have brought."

That chilled Ginnevra more than the draft from the door. She had been so intent on this one monster she hadn't remembered there were certainly more of him outside. "So we'll stay here, and both of us will be safe. For now."

The werewolf laughed again. "You should sit," he said, waving a hand at the nearest bench. "You make the others uncomfortable with your standing."

Ginnevra hooked an unoccupied bench with her ankle and sat, shifting her sword's strap to make it hang more loosely. She still couldn't reach it easily, but its new position eased her mind. "Talk. You're the one who's encroached on us here—tell me why."

The werewolf stretched with a lazy, full-body movement and bared his teeth at her. "We like to know our enemies. You enter this territory, banners flying, and it seems a challenge to us. Do you offer us threat?"

"You know we won't let werewolves prey on humans."

"That is not what I mean. Are you here for us? Or do you have other intent?" The werewolf's false smile disappeared, and his eyes narrowed further.

Instinctively, Ginnevra said, "You know why we're here. Why pretend otherwise? Are you trying to get me to give away information you can use against us?"

For a moment, the werewolf looked stunned. Then he regained his poise and said, "It is true, we have watched long enough to know you are travelers. You protect the ones touched by the Dark One. That man, above all else." He nodded in the direction of the anointed.

Ginnevra didn't want to take her eyes off the creature even to confirm he meant Giulliomocte. "We protect all those in need of protection."

"And yet he is special. We can smell it." The werewolf's gaze shifted, and this time his smile was real. "We can smell *that* one, too. I wonder, do you think you can stop him drawing blood?"

Startled, Ginnevra swiveled around to see Eodan approaching. She stood just as Eodan's pleasant, mildly curious expression changed to one of confusion. "Don't—"

Eodan snarled and lunged. Ginnevra stepped into his path. "We can't start a fight in here!" she exclaimed as all around them cries of fear and consternation sounded.

"We can't let a werewolf roam free," Eodan said, grabbing her shoulders and trying to set her aside. Ginnevra held firm, taking hold of his wrists. She twisted to face the werewolf, but he was gone. The door to the outer room still swung free, back and forth with someone's passage.

Ginnevra exclaimed and released Eodan, who promptly pushed past her and ran for the door. "No!" Ginnevra shouted.

In the next moment, she was surrounded by paladins, all demanding to know what had happened. "Stay here," Ginnevra said. "There's a werewolf."

"We fight werewolves, Prime Cassaline," Buonnane said. Ginnevra heard the unspoken rebuke: *let us do our jobs already.*

"And if that werewolf intends to draw all of us away so the rest of the pack can come after the defenseless anointed?" she said. "We can't let the monsters dictate our reaction. I'm going after Eodan, and the rest of you will *stay here* and watch for more of them." She shoved past the paladins and out the door.

Eodan hadn't gone far. He was standing outside in the heavily falling rain, scanning the dark streets. Nothing moved outside except a cat racing from stoop to stoop, looking for shelter. Ginnevra touched Eodan's shoulder. It was rock-hard with tension. "I'm so glad you didn't run after him."

"I would have run into an ambush, that's sure." Eodan turned and returned inside. Ginnevra sniffed the air once, but the rain washed away any scent of the werewolf.

Once inside, Ginnevra stopped Eodan before he could return to the tap room. "You didn't know him, did you? I realize that's unlikely, but if you did—"

"There are far more werewolves in the world than I'm sure you paladins want to believe. So you're right, it's unlikely. I've never seen him before." Eodan pushed wet hair out of his face.

"He had some nerve, walking into a bar full of paladins and anointed."

"And I didn't smell him. I blame the damn stew." Eodan looked ready to tear into someone.

"It doesn't matter. We couldn't have killed him there, not in front of all those people who wouldn't have known he was a werewolf. That would just have made us look more dangerous and out of control." Ginnevra squeezed Eodan's hand once and then released him. "Werewolves. In Tesccine, and now here. Is that a gigantic coincidence?"

"He wasn't the werewolf I scented outside the inn in Tesccine, but..." Eodan's anger faded. "Coincidence is getting the same meal three days in a row from three different inns. When it's a matter of werewolves showing up, no, I don't think it's coincidence. But we have no proof this is the same pack."

"Let's rejoin the others. We need to talk."

The atmosphere in the tap room had changed noticeably. Now there was an obvious divide between Ginnevra's people and the regular patrons, who had moved as far away from the outsiders as they could manage. The paladins had loosed their swords and taken up positions guarding the anointed. The Dedicates and acolytes huddled together in silence. Revered Orselle was praying, his lips moving soundlessly and his hands clasped in front of him. Pratese stared into the fire. And Giulliomocte continued to eat as placidly as if nothing had happened.

Buonnane walked to the edge of what Ginnevra couldn't help seeing as their territory and stood there, waiting for Ginnevra to cross the rest of the distance. "It escaped," she said, making it a statement.

"We couldn't pursue it," Ginnevra replied.

"I know." To Ginnevra's surprise, Buonnane didn't sound critical. "Damn werewolves. Is it the same pack?"

Eodan, standing beside Ginnevra, said nothing. Ginnevra decided this wasn't the time to correct Buonnane on her overgeneralization. "We're not sure," she said, "but it's safer to assume we've only drawn the attention of one pack. That werewolf acted ignorant, but the way he spoke told me he already knew a lot about us, like they'd been watching for a while."

"And werewolf packs don't cooperate readily," Eodan said. "It's unlikely we encountered a pack in Tesccine that met up with a second pack, told its dominus about us, and sent the second pack to continue following us. It's almost certainly the same one."

Buonnane looked at Eodan for the first time Ginnevra could remember. "I don't know that word."

"It's the name the Bright One chose for the male leader of a pack." Eodan said his creator's name with no self-consciousness. "It's possible you spoke with their dominus, Ginnevra, but it's also likely the dominus sent a lower-ranked male on this errand, on the chance he might have been killed."

"Dominus," Ginnevra said. "I don't know. That werewolf didn't act twitchy the way he would if he were afraid he might die. But it doesn't matter—not now, anyway. We have a worse problem."

"Worse than a hidden pack of werewolves that's been following us for most of a week?" Buonnane said.

Ginnevra nodded. "The werewolves have targeted Revered Giulliomocte."

Buonnane swore under her breath. "So we're not a target of opportunity. Or not *just* a target of opportunity."

"No. They're interested in him. Eodan, can werewolves distinguish humans based on their ecclesiastical status? Does the Revered appear different somehow? That werewolf claimed Revered Giulliomocte smelled different."

Eodan was shaking his head before she finished speaking. "Any human who worships the Goddess—specifically, any human with a grace—smells the same to us. So you're distinct on that level. But there's no further difference between regular humans and anointed, or between anointed and paladins. He wanted to frighten you, make himself and his packmates seem to have more mystical abilities than they do."

Ginnevra didn't look at Buonnane to see what she thought of Eodan's contribution. "Then they couldn't have picked him out based on trailing us and spying on us."

"Right. Something else must have brought him to their attention. But if they were spying on us, well, it's not as if anyone's made a secret of their greater respect for the Revered."

Buonnane said, "That means they're going to keep following us, looking for a moment of weakness to attack. We can't stay hypervigilant for another three weeks."

"And we can't stay here waiting for them to get bored and give up, because that might never happen," Ginnevra said. "We have to move on and pray for the strength to endure."

"I want to post guards tonight," Buonnane said. "Where one werewolf could get in, so could another. And I've already examined the rest of those people in case there's another spy already here."

"That made things worse," Ginnevra exclaimed, glancing at the other patrons sitting closely together, all of them watching this conversation. "We shouldn't make them believe we're the enemy."

"I wasn't rough with them. I had some of the paladins examine them from a distance. They all passed."

"Even so—" Ginnevra pinched the bridge of her nose. "No. It's done, and it's fine. Yes, we should post guards."

"And when the rain lets up," Eodan said, "I'll take a look around and see if I can pick up their trail."

"That's madness," Ginnevra said. "You can't follow them. It will only lead you into a trap."

"There are many things I can learn from their trail that don't include a confrontation," Eodan reminded her. "We need information if we're going to defend against them on the road, starting with the size of their pack. It's worth the risk."

Ginnevra frowned. "I don't like it, but you make sense."

"Then I'll give the others their orders," Buonnane said, and walked away without waiting for Ginnevra's assent.

"She's still afraid," Eodan said in a low voice.

"And she's doing her duty anyway," Ginnevra said. "I admire that, even though she does infuriate me."

She watched the others as Buonnane moved between the small groups of paladins. The Dedicates watched the captain warily, as if she carried bad news. Giulliomocte still ate as if none of this affected him. Curious, Ginnevra crossed the room to where the Revered sat and dropped onto the bench opposite him. "Are you well, Revered?"

"Of course." Giulliomocte set down his spoon and patted his lips with a cloth. "One werewolf is not a threat, not in this situation. And I judged you would handle it well."

"Excuse me, Revered, but at what point did you realize the

man was a werewolf?" Ginnevra knew she sounded accusing, but Giulliomocte's tone, casual and certain, irked her.

"I happened to notice him when he walked in. Don't look like that, prime. I had every confidence you would realize the truth. There was no danger."

"They were looking for you," Ginnevra said.

Giulliomocte's eyes widened. He had picked up his spoon again, and it trembled in his hand. "For me?"

"We don't know how they figured out your importance, but the werewolf pack has a definite interest in you." Ginnevra felt ashamed of frightening the man, but not very much. Fear might have a positive effect on his behavior. "It seems our journey is more dangerous than we believed."

Giulliomocte laid down his spoon again, this time with a deliberate *tock* against the wood of the table. "Are you afraid, Prime Cassaline?"

Ginnevra's eyes narrowed. "That's an odd question. Why should I be afraid?"

"Of course you're not," Giulliomocte said as if she hadn't responded. "And neither am I. If this is the challenge the Goddess has set in our path, I welcome the opportunity to prove my faith."

"That's not the same as not taking precautions," Ginnevra snapped. "Revered, having faith doesn't mean being reckless. And a werewolf pack is no small challenge. You shouldn't be so cavalier about what we face."

Giulliomocte smiled and shook his head. "You've misunderstood me. I meant only to express my confidence in your abilities, yours and those of your sister paladins. I apologize if I sounded brash." His smile disappeared, and he looked past Ginnevra at someone else. "I do worry. So many of my companions are here for the wrong reasons. And while I do not believe one's own faith is affected by that of others, I feel the strain of setting a good example."

His abrupt change of demeanor prompted Ginnevra to ask, "What wrong reasons?"

"The prestige of accompanying a would-be Hallowed," Giulliomocte said, still not looking at Ginnevra. "Or as an assignment they have no heart for. I—" Abruptly, his gaze fell on her, and he blinked. "I beg your pardon, prime, I should not burden you with my concerns. I assure you the faith of the anointed is not a problem, regardless of their motives."

Ginnevra turned in her seat and saw Pratese's gaze flick away from them, rapidly enough that Ginnevra knew the woman had been staring. "And Revered Pratese?" she asked.

Giulliomocte sighed. "A problem for another time." He opened his mouth to say something more, but shut it without speaking. "I believe I will retire now, prime. Thank you for your concern."

Ginnevra watched him go and reflected that they hadn't gotten into an argument about Eodan for once. Maybe Giulliomocte had realized he wasn't going to convince Ginnevra of his point of view.

The paladins had all vanished, most of them to stand watch, no doubt. She listened to the low conversation of the dedicates. They were mostly speculating on the werewolf's presence and where his pack was. Orselle had also gone upstairs, but Pratese sat at the end of the table, silently turning a mug of ale between her hands and occasionally drinking. Ginnevra watched her for a minute or two, but she never looked up or indicated she noticed Ginnevra's regard.

So. Pratese and Giulliomocte had been lovers. And it looked as if the relationship had ended badly, at least for Pratese; Giulliomocte didn't act anything but polite to her. Ginnevra found it difficult to believe a Revered could be motivated by spite or wounded feelings, but Revereds were human, too. Even so, Pratese's actions bordered on insubordinate or even vengeful, and regardless of whether her hurt feelings were justified, she had no business influencing the Dedicates and the acolytes to resent Giulliomocte as well.

Cold air heralded someone's entrance, and Ginnevra looked away from Pratese to see Eodan enter the room. He looked wet and windblown, his cheeks rosy, but his blue eyes were bright and his lips thinned in a frown. He crossed the room and sank heavily onto the bench beside Ginnevra. "There were three of them," he said. "All positioned where they could watch the inn, but not so close we would immediately notice them. They met at the gate and disappeared into the city." He made a disgusted noise. "Disappeared in the sense that I wasn't fool enough to follow them. But that's all I was able to learn, thanks to the storm."

"That's more than enough," Ginnevra said. "We'll post guards, and if they come back, we'll be ready. But I'm guessing, now they know *we* know they're there, they won't return."

"What worries me is what happens after we leave this place." Eodan pushed his wet hair back from his face. "Out on the plains is one thing—we can see threats coming—but most of the route through the badlands takes us through forested country."

"I'll discuss the route with Captain Buonnane tomorrow. Maybe there's another way." Eodan was shivering, Ginnevra noticed, and his coat was soaked through at the shoulders. "Go on upstairs and get dried off, and see if you can get warm."

Eodan grinned. "I can think of an excellent way to get warm."

"You'll have to be patient. I can't leave until our people are out of here." Ginnevra cast her gaze around the room again. "You know, I don't think I want to wait on their inclinations? Go on, I'll be up shortly."

Eodan squeezed her hand once before rising. Ginnevra saw

him take off his coat before she turned her attention on the remaining anointed. "Time to be done," she said.

One of the acolytes groaned, and the Dedicate next to him took a long drink from his mug. "It's not that late," the Dedicate said. "And we're not babies."

Ginnevra crossed her arms over her chest and stared him down, not speaking. The Dedicate reddened and looked away. "With respect, prime," he murmured.

Ginnevra remembered he had been one of Pratese's disciples. Interesting. If Pratese had gone from fomenting discord centered on Giulliomocte to encouraging the anointed to disrespect the Goddess's sworn warriors, Ginnevra was on much firmer ground.

"I accept that you did not mean disrespect, Dedicate," she said. "Let me put it to you another way. I can't go to bed until this room is cleared of our people. Unlike you, I rode all day and then confronted a werewolf, which means I'm tired. So feel free to stay up as late as you want. I'll just sit here and watch you." She straddled the bench near the anointed and propped her elbow on the table, then rested her chin in her hand.

The Dedicate stood and saluted Ginnevra. "I'll just... that is, your words make sense." He hurried away, not looking to see if anyone followed him.

The other anointed didn't look Ginnevra in the eye. Some of them quickly finished their drinks, though there were a few who left half-full mugs on the table. Dedicate Bidelia was the only one who smiled as she left. In less than a minute, only Revered Pratese remained at the table. She caught Ginnevra's eye and smiled, a lopsided, bitter expression that made Ginnevra feel the Revered had wanted to slap her instead.

"Forgive me if I don't leap to my feet," Pratese said. Her words were slightly slurred. "I'm not overcome by a paladin's presence."

"You'd be a poor Revered if that were the case," Ginnevra said, trying for a neutral tone.

"It's what you already think of me, isn't it?" Pratese set her mug down and straightened from her slumped position. "You don't respect my authority."

Wonderful. Ginnevra had exaggerated her tiredness to the anointed, but Pratese's belligerence made her suddenly weary. She stood, resting one hand palm-down on the table. "You should be off to bed, Revered," she said. "You don't want to look back on this evening and regret anything."

"Meaning, regret being honest with you?" Pratese looked up at her, her head tilted so she resembled an inquisitive owl. "I don't appreciate being mocked in front of my subordinates."

Ginnevra gave up. "Then perhaps you should be less deserving of being mocked. *I* don't appreciate seeing the rising generation taught to show disrespect to the Goddess's own chosen servant."

"As if Domenico deserves his elevation," Pratese said bitterly. "He isn't any better than the rest of us. This is all political posturing on the part of the Blessed."

Ginnevra took a step toward Pratese, but stopped herself before she could actually lay hands on the woman. "You're entitled to your opinions, but you're not entitled to spread them where they can hurt others. I don't care if your heart was broken, that's no excuse to tear someone down."

Pratese laughed. The sound was so loud Ginnevra took a step back and looked around to see if it was as noticeable as she'd thought. It had, in fact, drawn all sorts of attention from the remaining drinkers, who stared at Pratese until they caught Ginnevra looking at them.

Pratese stood, wobbling slightly. "My heart's not broken. It's

Domenico who should feel guilty. I don't give a damn about him, and anyone who tells you otherwise is a liar."

"My mistake," Ginnevra said. All she cared about now was getting Pratese out of the tap room. "May I escort you upstairs, Revered?"

Pratese looked very pale and her lips were pinched tight together. Ginnevra worried she might vomit, right there in the tap room. But the Revered shook her head and said, "I wouldn't go as far as the end of the street with you." She pushed away from the bench, got her legs tangled in it, and sat abruptly. Ginnevra offered her a hand that Pratese ignored. The Revered stood, ostentatiously stepped wide of the bench, and staggered for the door.

Ginnevra watched her go, then stared at the door until it finished swinging back and forth and came to rest. Then she signaled Serenna for half a pint of the house brew, dark and rich and delicious. She drank it, still standing, and then put the empty mug down and crossed the room to the outer door.

The little entrance room was brightly lit, and when Ginnevra pushed open the outer door, the lanterns made a warm yellow rectangle on the yard beyond. The rain had stopped, but the air was still dense with moisture that clung to Ginnevra's skin, chilling her instantly. If the temperature dropped much further, snow was likely. The clouds hadn't yet dissipated, and they were low enough to make Ginnevra feel she was in a vast, cloud-topped hall. The dark moon had set some hours before. Ginnevra wished she could see the stars, anything to give her balance after that exchange with Pratese.

She noted the presence of two paladins, one standing guard at the corner, the other walking the inn's perimeter. They were both armored and wore cloaks against the chill. Ginnevra shivered again, but didn't go inside. Instead, she crossed the inn yard and walked down the street, back the way they'd come that afternoon.

It wasn't all that late, but few of the houses—if they were houses and not shops—were lit. Lanterns burned along the street, making puddles of light that brushed one another's edges. Ginnevra stayed outside the illuminated spaces, feeling a need for the comfort darkness gave. No one approached her; no one left the houses or entered them. She stopped once and turned to look back, but saw no movement at the inn. She might well have been the only one alive in the city.

A tiny inner voice shrieked at her to go back, and again she hesitated. There were werewolves in the area, and she had her sword, but no armor. Walking alone at night in a strange city was stupid. But something drew her onward, a strange impulse like the distant voice of a long-lost friend, silencing that warning voice.

She followed the road to where it split into three and turned right. Almost immediately, she smelled blood and entrails and feces and heard the noise of cattle lowing. An abattoir, or more than one, judging by the scent. She walked until she could see the fence shielding the gory work from passersby. She'd never seen such a barrier concealing a slaughterhouse in any other city. Likely it was unnecessary, as anyone who came to this neighborhood knew what they were in for, but in her fey compulsion she was grateful not to see the cows in their last moments.

The road curved past more smelly buildings, a tannery, another abattoir, and then a butcher's, where at least the smell was of fresh meat. Ginnevra's steps slowed as she passed it. There wasn't much city beyond these businesses, and the plains were clearly visible from where she stood.

And so was something else.

The white figure of the karkadann stood where the street ended and the plains began. It was bigger than Ginnevra remembered, though still smaller than a horse. Its two-edged horn shone silver in the darkness, lit not by lanterns or the nonexistent moon but by an inner glow that seduced Ginnevra's eye. It lowered its head as if bowing to her.

Ginnevra put a hand on her sword's hilt. Then she released it. Straightening her back, she walked forward to meet the creature.

ELEVEN

A voice in the back of her head screamed at her that she was mad, that this creature would attack her, or bring werewolves down on her. But she felt too calm for fear or even dread. She didn't even feel as if she were under a compulsion; her head was clear, and she knew the karkadann was a threat. The chilly night, and the smell of rain in the air, heightened all her senses until her skin tingled.

She stopped several feet away from the karkadann and waited, examining it. Even this close, its hide looked as smooth as porcelain rather than anything living, though she could see its sides move as it breathed. Its nose was slim and long, giving its head an elegant, sculptured appearance. The hairs of its mane lifted and tangled in the light wind. It stared her down, its eyes pure deep blue with neither white nor pupil.

"What do you want?" Ginnevra said. She didn't even feel foolish about talking to it the way she would a person. It was all part of the strange, unearthly night.

The karkadann took a single step forward. "That which is

hidden," it said. "The walk, the deeps, the starlit sky. Take the first step."

Ginnevra blinked. Its voice was shrill, discordant, at odds with its ethereal beauty. It echoed as if several creatures had spoken at once. "I don't understand you."

"To know is the first lie," the karkadann said. It dragged its right forefoot across the ground, tearing up dead yellow grass and revealing the dark, wet soil beneath. "Speak, or be spoken to, it is the same."

It took another step forward. Ginnevra's hand fell on her sword's hilt. "Stay back. You summoned me, I know you did. Tell me what you want."

The karkadann shook its head. Its mane flew in the heavy air, fine white hairs tracing paths across the dark sky. "Empty the sea, forsake the land. The birds fly north for the winter." It ducked and scored another line in the weeds, this time with the tip of its savage horn.

Ginnevra opened her mouth to respond—and a thick scent, the sweet-dark odor of decomposition, reached her nose. Werewolves.

In an instant, the fey mood that had propelled her vanished, leaving her sick and cold with more than the night air. She spun around, searching the darkness, but saw nothing. Yet.

When she again turned to face the karkadann, it was gone. No trace of it remained, not a distant vanishing shape or even a white blur rising into the sky. Ginnevra cursed and turned to run. She'd been so stupid, and it might cost her her life.

She pelted back the way she had come, holding her sword so it wouldn't bang against her side. The smells of the abattoirs and tannery weren't enough to block the stench of werewolf that drew ever nearer. She couldn't yet hear them and didn't dare stop to look behind her. It didn't matter whether there were five werewolves or fifty. The smell was strong enough to tell her she was outnumbered.

She reached the branching of the road and kept running. Now she heard footsteps, the light, rapid pattering of four-legged creatures racing along more fleetly even than she could run. She cursed again, this time silently—no breath to spare. Beside her, houses flashed past, none of them lit now. The lanterns offered no help that Ginnevra's enhanced vision didn't already provide.

Her breath sounded harsh and ragged in her ears, her heart pounded rapidly and urged her into faster movement, but her pursuers closed the distance between them with every step. At some point, she would have to turn and fight or be savaged from behind. She just needed that point to come as close to the inn as possible.

The werewolves ran in terrible silence, no howling or barking, but now she heard their breathing. No more time to run. She put on a last burst of speed, taking her to someone's front gate, and turned, putting the wall and the gate behind her. Drawing her greatsword, she shouted, "*Paladins! To me!*" and took a defensive stance.

The werewolves had not been as close as her imagination and acute hearing had believed. They were still a dozen paces behind her. But there were six of them, and they were moving fast. Ginnevra braced herself. If she was going to die here tonight, she would send a few of these monsters to Hell first.

She readied her sword and snarled at the oncoming creatures. Each was a different shade of blond-gray, with the leader almost pure white, and they all stood as tall as Ginnevra's chest at the shoulders. They slowed as they approached rather than rush her all at once the way stupider monsters might. "That's right," Ginnevra said, fixing each with her gaze. "You might be able to take me down, but at least one of you will fall to my blade. Do you like the smell of silver? Come on—which of you wants to be first?"

They spread out, encircling Ginnevra. She pressed back farther into the wall. Keeping them all in sight would soon be impossible, but she held her stance and refused to show fear. "Paladins!" she shouted again. The women guarding the inn could certainly hear her, but she wasn't sure they would leave their posts for the sake of someone shouting in the night. For all Ginnevra knew, they didn't even know she was gone, and her cry was all a trick.

The pack shifted. Then one of them lunged.

Ginnevra turned her back on the moving one and thrust her blade at the werewolf on her other side who had leaped at the other's feint. Her sword plunged deep into the werewolf's chest, making it howl in its death agony. Fur and flesh sizzled as they came in contact with the silvered steel.

She snatched her sword away from the corpse and spun to meet the attack of the first werewolf, bringing the sword up just in time to block its bite. Its foul, stinking breath filled her nostrils, and its jaws snapped shut inches from her face, but the flat of the sword pressed against its throat, driving it back. It howled again and darted out of reach. Ginnevra drew in a shaky breath and gripped her sword more firmly. *That* should draw the paladins.

She swung again, connected with a werewolf's shoulder, thrust and swung and then kicked one in the chest, driving it into its fellow. Her heavy, panting breaths made great pale clouds in the air, mingling with the thinner ones the werewolves breathed out. The creatures fought silently except when she scored a hit, and then they yelped and retreated for a moment or two. Then they surged at her again, weaving back and forth to confuse her.

The heat of battle surged through Ginnevra, humming in her veins. She bared her teeth at the white werewolf, who silently snarled back. He feinted left, but Ginnevra was ready for him. She thrust for his heart. He dodged, crouched, and leaped at her face. Ginnevra brought up the sword in an awkward two-handed block that caught him across the neck and shoved him away without breaking skin. Immediately she turned and slashed another were-wolf, taking a chunk out of its left foreleg. Its howl split the peaceful night, but although it favored its wounded leg, it didn't flee or even retreat.

Then the fighting paused for a moment as both paladin and werewolves fell into defensive stances. Ginnevra gasped for air. She wasn't tired yet, not with her Goddess-given reserves of stamina, but it was still five against one, and so far, she'd been lucky. No. No fear. She raised her sword again. "Come on," she panted. "I'll take you all down."

The werewolves paced in a semicircle before her. The white werewolf alone stood still, sizing her up. Ginnevra focused her attention on him.

Then she heard shouts, and running feet in heavy boots. The werewolves backed up a few steps. The white one looked at the werewolf Ginnevra had killed, then at Ginnevra as if assessing his chances. He let out a low sound somewhere between a howl and a bark, and the remaining werewolves turned and fled.

Ginnevra lowered her bloody sword and caught her breath. Then she turned to face the paladins who ran toward her, swords bobbing over their shoulders. "Prime Cassaline!" the paladin Florra Tionte exclaimed. "What were you doing out here alone?"

That was a good question, and not one Ginnevra had a good answer for. "I wasn't cautious. Thank you for coming to my aid."

"You seemed to be doing all right," the other paladin, Pia Useppe, said. Her close-fitting coif and helmet made her face look perfectly round, almost infant-like, but her expression was stern and serious. "Goddess have mercy. I've never seen anyone take on that many werewolves at once, all alone."

"It was stupid of me to put myself in a position to have to." Ginnevra drew in a deep, calming breath, then bent to wipe her sword on the dead werewolf's fur. "We need to do something about this fellow. There might be a bounty on werewolves, but regardless, we can't leave him in the street."

Pia crouched and got her shoulder under the werewolf's body, hoisting it up across her back with a grunt of effort. "Zana and Usterchia took our places at guard, but we should relieve them," she said, somewhat breathlessly. "Where should I take this?"

"Not the stable yard," Florra said. "There are horses other than our own who will go mad if they smell even a dead werewolf."

"Around the back side," Ginnevra said. "I'll talk to the others."

She strode along behind Pia and Florra with her gaze fixed on the light-furred body streaked with blood. That encounter had not been normal. Fast as she was, she shouldn't have been able to kill the one werewolf and then protect herself against the other coming at her vulnerable side. The werewolves had been holding back, and it was luck and skill that had led to her killing any of them. Which meant their dominus—and she was increasingly inclined to believe the werewolf she'd spoken to, the one who had led the little pack just now, was their dominus—was interested in testing her. Her specifically, or her as a member of the paladin company, she wasn't sure. And maybe it didn't matter, because the werewolves would do whatever it took to get to Domenico Giulliomocte.

Two other paladins, Zana and Usterchia, patrolled the inn and stable yard, but Ginnevra could tell by the tension in their bodies that they'd been all too aware of the fight going on nearby. Ginnevra explained the situation, though she didn't tell them she suspected the werewolves wouldn't try anything again that night. Her instincts shouldn't change their vigilance.

Then she walked around to the far side of the inn, where Pia had deposited her grisly burden. "We can leave it here," Ginnevra said. "In the morning, I'll talk to the innkeeper about disposing of it for good."

Pia nudged the body with the toe of her boot. "I'm glad they don't change to human when they die," she said with a grimace. "Do you know why that is, prime?"

Ginnevra didn't know if Pia had asked her because she was a prime or because of her werewolf lover, but she hadn't sounded judgmental, so she said, "Eodan tells me werewolves aren't more one thing than another. Meaning, they aren't humans who occasionally have to take wolf form, or wolves that can look like people. So whatever form they're in, that's the form they are. If that makes sense."

Pia nodded. She still looked pensive, but Ginnevra didn't care enough to push.

"They do stink something fierce, though," Florra said. "I don't know how you—no offense, prime." She ducked her head to avoid Ginnevra's gaze.

"The ones sworn to the Bright One smell very bad. The others have a more ordinary musk." Ginnevra regarded Florra with a steely expression. She didn't actually mind comments on her relationship with Eodan, who was, after all, unusual, but she took any opportunity to instruct others on the true nature of werewolves, and that was worth seeing Florra discomfited.

"I'm going up to bed," she said, and as if her words were an ancient ritual triggering a grace, weariness swept over her. She nodded politely to each woman and walked to the front door.

Inside, it was so much warmer, even in the drafty entrance unlit by fire or anything but a couple of lanterns on the wall, that Ginnevra didn't know how she hadn't been conscious of the cold before. She ascended the stairs, rubbing her arms for warmth, and trod the hallway to her room without taking care to avoid the creaky floorboards. She might wake someone, but at the moment, she didn't care.

She *did* care about not waking Eodan, so she eased the door open and entered as quietly as she could manage in her heavy boots. There was nowhere to sit but the bed, so she removed her boots while still standing and then took off the rest of her clothes until she was in just her shift and drawers. It was too dark even for her enhanced vision to make out details, so she left her clothes lying in a puddle on the floor and slid into bed beside Eodan.

He was warmer than usual, almost hot, and his body heat relaxed her. She snuggled in closer—and he came awake with a gasp and jerked away. "You're freezing," he exclaimed, and immediately put his arms around her. "Sorry. That was a startling way to wake up."

"No, I'm sorry. I didn't think. Was it really that bad?"

"I was dreaming of chasing the catoblepas, and then it felt like someone shoved a chunk of ice down my shirt." His warm breath sighed across her forehead. "Were you outside?"

"I was. And I did something stupid. Don't yell until you've heard it all, all right?"

Eodan listened while she described her encounters with the karkadann and with the werewolves. His arms tightened around her when she described the battle, but he stayed silent. When she finished, he still said nothing. Ginnevra, afraid, said, "You're angry."

"No." He returned to being silent. Ginnevra held her tongue. Silence usually meant he was working through some strong emotion, or trying to figure out how he felt or thought about something.

Finally, he shifted his weight and let out a deep breath. "Do you think you were compelled? Because I can't think of anything else that would cause you to behave so recklessly."

"I don't know. I didn't think so, because I felt clear-headed and I knew the werewolves might be a danger if I was out alone. But after I spoke to the karkadann, there was a moment when I felt like I was waking from a dream. And then I couldn't believe what I'd done." Ginnevra shivered. "I thought I was immune to mental compulsion. Like a lamia's fascination."

"The karkadann seems to have found a way around that." Eodan raised his hand to her shoulder and rubbed it gently in what felt like absentmindedness. "It's more dangerous than I thought. Suppose it does it again, this time when you're not so close to help?"

"But that's the other thing. Those werewolves had a reason for not tearing me apart, and I want to know what it is. It was like they were testing me for weaknesses."

"That is disturbing, yes." Eodan's hand moved to her back. Ginnevra's muscles weren't sore or tight, but she enjoyed the way his fingers kneaded them. "If it were my pack," Eodan went on, "I'd say they intended to bring a full attack upon us. And that still may be the case. But werewolf packs are sometimes very different, and it's not safe to make assumptions. Aside from how this pack serves the Bright Goddess, based on the smell."

"But what else could it be, aside from determining our weak spots? Or my weak spots, I suppose?" Ginnevra ducked her head so it rested against the curve of his shoulder.

"The dominus might intend to offer you rite of combat," Eodan said. "If you were a werewolf, an attack might be prelude to offering you a place in the pack. Or it could be a warning—stay away, or next time we won't be so generous. But my guess is they're looking for a way to reach Revered Giulliomocte."

"Mine, too." Ginnevra sighed. "We can't stay here another

night, if only because the werewolves will leave when we do. I don't like exposing this town to monsters."

"And yet leaving without more information could be fatal," Eodan pointed out.

"You make good sense." Ginnevra yawned. She was warm again, finally, and her muscles had relaxed like wax warmed over a fire. "We'll discuss it in the morning."

"And hope Buonnane's fear doesn't make her do something foolish," Eodan said.

GINNEVRA WOKE in the pre-dawn hour as usual. She blinked at the ceiling, dim in the strangely-lit room, then rolled out of bed and crossed to the window. There, she stood rooted to the floorboards in astonishment. Snow blanketed the streets and the houses, filling the inn yard nearly to the top of its short wall. The sky was pearl-gray with overcast that dimmed the rising sun. Ginnevra rested her palm flat against the small glass panes and jerked it away from the cold radiating off it.

She turned and saw Eodan was awake, lying on his back and staring at the ceiling as she had done. "Come look at this," she demanded. "This is unbelievable."

Eodan rolled out of bed and joined her at the window. "That is a lot of snow," he said. "Will it comfort you to know it's not the heaviest snowfall I've ever seen?"

"It will not. How are we supposed to travel in this? I doubt the wagons will make it more than a hundred feet."

Eodan put his arm around her shoulders. "We'll have to wait it out. Those clouds look like they're not done unloading their snowy burden on us."

Ginnevra scowled. "I hate delays. Especially when they give our enemies more time to plan an attack."

"They're probably burrowed up somewhere, wishing winter were over." Eodan squeezed lightly and released her. "*You* need to worry about keeping thirty people entertained so they don't accidentally cause trouble with the other patrons."

Ginnevra's scowl deepened. "Thank you for the reminder."

She dressed and slouched down the stairs to the tap room with Eodan following her. Her bad mood subsided at the smell of breakfast, which was much nicer than the stew: steaming, juicy sausages and hot cornbread and sliced tomatoes in oil and vinegar. She washed her meal down with more of the dark ale. Possibly being stuck here for a day wasn't so bad.

The paladins and the anointed gradually trickled in for their meals. The paladins looked fresh and alert; the anointed were bleary-eyed even though it wasn't all that early. Barely past dawn, in fact. Ginnevra took another drink of ale and examined the room. Only a few other patrons were present. She wondered how many of those who'd spent the night here would move on despite the snow to get away from the outsiders.

Another mug of ale landed on the table beside the first. "I hope your stay has been satisfactory," the innkeeper, Actus, said.

"It has. Thank you for your hospitality," Ginnevra said.

"I take it you won't be moving on today." Actus turned his gaze on Eodan. "This snow is too much for a wagon to handle."

"No, and I'm sorry to burden you—"

"It's no burden." Actus waved away Ginnevra's concern. "Though, I hate to bring this up, but there is something."

He sounded concerned, and embarrassed, and Ginnevra said, "Something I can help you with?"

"Possibly," Actus said. "I want you to stop corrupting my daughter."

TWELVE

"Corrupting—" The word came out louder than she'd intended, and paladins and anointed nearby turned to stare. Ginnevra drew in a deep breath and said, "I don't know what you think I've done, but I assure you I haven't corrupted anyone."

"Then you didn't tell Serenna you would take her to Abraciabene to train for a paladin?" Actus' voice was calm, and he sounded only normally interested in this conversation, but one hand was clenched into a fist and tiny lines of anger creased the corners of his eyes.

"I did not tell her that," Ginnevra said, again keeping her voice low. "I told her I'd speak to you and answer any questions you had. We don't take children against their parents' wishes, and Serenna isn't of age."

"You must have said something to encourage her. Serenna isn't prone to lying." Actus leaned over Ginnevra.

Ginnevra tamped down on her irritation. Time to practice diplomacy. "I'm sure it was just a misunderstanding. Serenna was excited about meeting real paladins and is as enthusiastic about becoming one as all of us—" She gestured at the tap room at large — "were at her age. You're right, I didn't discourage her dream. And neither should you, really. Becoming a paladin is a holy desire."

Actus frowned. "She has a place at a prestigious school. She's to inherit the inn someday. She can't do that and become a paladin. You're giving her false hope."

"I said nothing about what she could or couldn't do. If she has a true calling, she'll find a way to live it regardless of what you or I do." Ginnevra rose and immediately regretted it; she'd meant to offer reassurance, but she towered over the man. "Actus, I know you want your daughter to be happy. And for all either of us know, this desire to become a paladin is a passing whim. But you won't help her if you try to force her into a destiny. You know that's not what the Goddess teaches."

Actus' fist relaxed. "I don't want her pining after impossibilities."

"Why is it so impossible? Aside from how you want her to inherit your inn. Which, by the way, isn't incompatible with the paladin life, unless you believe you're going to die soon." Ginnevra hoped she hadn't just flippantly dismissed a concern he actually had. He might have some fatal illness that didn't show on the outside. But Actus didn't react as if she'd hit a nerve. "Lots of paladins serve for five or ten years and then retire to live normal lives."

"Because—" Actus sighed and chewed his lower lip in thought. "There's no way she can train for a paladin in Savorola. She'd have to leave home. I don't want her going so far away."

"I agree, that's a difficulty. No parent wants to see his child leave home forever, or what might as well be forever." Ginnevra put a hand on Actus' shoulder. "But it's ultimately Serenna's choice. And I've known enough paladins whose parents weren't thrilled about their decision to know you will only hurt both of you if you try to force her to act according to your wishes."

Actus frowned. "But you don't have to encourage her," he said. "Bad enough she's got this notion in her head without a paladin telling her glorious stories of battle."

Ginnevra ground her back teeth together. She'd thought she was doing well. "I haven't encouraged her. But it's part of the paladin oath not to discourage potential candidates, either. We don't know which of all the starry-eyed girls will actually make it through training, and we're taught not to try to second-guess their desires. Which means not telling a girl she shouldn't consider it because her father doesn't like the idea."

"I'm not unreasonable," Actus said, scowling. "Serenna has always flitted from one fancy to the next. Last year she wanted to be a fabulist, until she realized it meant she needed good handwriting."

"Then you don't have anything to worry about," Ginnevra replied promptly. "If this is a passing whim, nothing you or I say will have any influence on her."

"I suppose you're right." Actus' lips pressed tightly together, and for a moment he appeared to be seeing some distant memory. Then he added, "I'd still prefer it if you didn't say anything she might misinterpret. I believe you didn't tell her she could come with you, but something put that notion in her head, right?"

"I'll be cautious in what I say," Ginnevra assured him.

She resumed her seat, pushed her plate and mug aside, and propped her elbows on the table and buried her face in her hands. "The day hasn't even fully started yet and already we've had trouble," she muttered. "What next?"

Eodan said nothing. When the silence stretched on too long, Ginnevra said, "What?"

"I was just waiting for someone to slam through the door demanding your head," Eodan said.

Ginnevra choked on a laugh and sat up. "I suppose that would have been the perfect time for it."

Eodan squeezed her shoulder lightly. "I'm going to see if there's anything we can do to occupy our people while we wait. Games, perhaps, or storytelling."

"And I should talk to the wagon drivers. They've made this trip before, and they might know how soon we can safely leave." Ginnevra let Eodan pull her up from the bench and then kissed him. "Why couldn't the Goddess have revealed Giulliomocte's new status in springtime?"

"I thought all you hunters in darkness reveled in challenges," Eodan said with a smile.

"Challenges, yes. Two feet of snow with the promise of more to come—that's not a challenge, that's a nightmare."

Ginnevra crossed the tap room, deliberately paying no attention to the young anointed who stared and whispered. If they'd been watching, and had seen her kiss Eodan, well, it wasn't as if Ginnevra was going to conceal her affection to keep them from being embarrassed. And why should they be embarrassed about a kiss? The paladins Zana and Bartolla were all over each other in the evenings and nobody cared.

The instant she left the tap room for the little entrance hall, she regretted not having her cloak. A persistent whistle of freezing air blew through the crack beneath the outer door, seeking out her vulnerable exposed skin and turning it to ice. Ginnevra hesitated. She could go back to her room for her wonderful fur-lined cloak, but she was here now, and it would take less time to cross the yard and walk—all right, run—around to the stables, where the wagoners had quarters in the mews. Steeling herself, she pulled the outer door open.

The wind nearly took the door out of her hands, gusting wildly. Ginnevra gasped and hurriedly shut it behind her. Snow filled the air, not new snow, but flurries picked up off the snowdrifts by the wind and carried wherever it blew. It was light, powdery snow, not heavy wet flakes, for which Ginnevra was grateful, and it felt like sugar crystals blown against her numb cheeks. The sun was barely visible as a white spot behind the overcast, radiating no heat and very little light.

Someone had dug a path from the door to the street, but it was no more than a foot wide and rapidly filling with snow. Ginnevra ran, ducking her head against the driving snow, and then slowed to trudge through the accumulation clogging the street. Few other pedestrians braved the storm, slogging through the drifts with their heads lowered. All of them were dressed more warmly than Ginnevra. She passed a woman who clutched a covered basket to her chest and didn't do more than glance briefly at Ginnevra. If this was what it took to get the citizens of Savorola to stop running away in fear, Ginnevra would rather be snubbed.

Snow caked her trousers and boots by the time she reached the stable yard. She stepped into the shelter of the stalls and brushed the snow away before it could melt, though she was sure it was too cold for anything out here to melt. Stamping her feet to clean her boots, she walked with a heavy tread along the line of stalls until she reached Dauntless'. Her horse had been fed and watered already, and he came forward to greet her with a whicker of pleasure. She petted his broad nose.

"It's too cold for the likes of us," she murmured. "We should be somewhere warm. Somewhere the sun isn't a frozen disc in the sky and you can have a water trough that doesn't have a skim of ice on it in the mornings." She didn't actually know if the last were true, but it seemed a reasonable assumption.

The sound of horses entering the stable yard drew Ginnevra's attention. She turned, her hand still on Dauntless' face, to watch four riders dismounting at the center of the yard. Their horses were all very fine, glossy chestnut and bay and one pure black with a couple of white markings Ginnevra took for snow. They all had the shaggy look of horses in their full winter coats, and their riders were warmly dressed as well, in heavy cloaks over charcoal-gray twilled cotton coats and trousers.

One of the men, the rider of the black horse, gathered up his reins and strode across the yard to where Ginnevra stood. "Don't dawdle, young lady, our horses need caring for," he said. "We've been riding since dawn."

Ginnevra looked around. None of the stable hands were visible. She could hardly blame them for not wanting to venture out in the snow, except that it was their job. "Of course, but I'm not—"

The man thrust the reins into Ginnevra's hand. "I'm not interested in what you're not," he said. "And you should be ashamed of yourself, wearing your hair so short. A woman's hair is her crowning glory, and cutting it off is indecent." His own hair was closely cropped to his head, revealing an unusually elongated skull and bulging forehead.

Ginnevra blinked. Her hand twitched as she almost touched her hair and then caught herself. "I see," she said. "I didn't realize."

"You didn't realize?" another man said. "Where are you from, that you didn't realize?"

Ginnevra's nerves tingled a warning. "Not from around here," she said. "If you'll wait, I'll fetch the others to help care for your animals." She dropped the black horse's reins and ran for the mews.

The stable hands' quarters were called the mews, she'd been told the night before by the wagon drivers, out of tradition rather than accuracy. They were actually a very sturdy building heated by many small metal stoves, with private rooms not only for the inn's employees but for visiting grooms or footmen. Now, Ginnevra entered and discovered the main door led to a spacious hall with a table surrounded by short three-legged stools. A stove, and many bodies packed into the space, warmed it to where even Ginnevra was comfortable.

The stable hands clustered around the end of the table nearest Ginnevra rose when she entered. She didn't know whether they shared her worship and that of their employer, or if they were just better at politeness than the average Savorolan, but they never snubbed her or the others.

Quickly, she told them of the newcomers, then followed the exodus back to the stable yard. All four newcomers stood in a tight group, apparently unaware of the cold and the blowing snow. They ignored the stable hands who led their horses to shelter. Ginnevra stood in the corner nearest the mews and examined the men. If they had ridden since dawn, they had only been on the road a few hours—not a hard ride even in these conditions. Yet by the way they stood close together, their heads bowed and their conversation intent, they certainly behaved as if they'd done something remarkable.

With the wind howling in her ears, even Ginnevra's keen hearing couldn't make out what they were saying. So she watched their movements instead. Two of the men were tense and kept glancing at the horses, which Ginnevra might have interpreted as uncertainty about the care the horses might receive if she hadn't seen them blithely hand off their reins without looking closely at the stable hands who took them. No, those men wanted to be back on the road, and were unhappy about whatever errand brought them here.

The other two men were arguing with each other—that was

obvious even if she couldn't hear the subject. One of them, the one who'd accused her of being unfeminine, kept shaking his finger in the other man's face past the point where Ginnevra would have broken it in annoyance. But the other man stood his ground, with his arms crossed over his chest. He had pulled his hood far over his face, so Ginnevra couldn't see his expression, but if his opponent's reactions were anything to go by, he looked stubborn.

Finally, the first man stopped waggling his finger at the other and said something that included all his companions. Then he strode past them in the direction of the inn. The others followed him, with the man with the shrouded face bringing up the rear. Ginnevra waited a moment before following them. They might not be here about her people, and Ginnevra didn't want to start a fight if they were. Hanging back to observe couldn't hurt.

At the front door, she brushed herself off again and kicked her boots against the outside wall to knock off the snow rather than track it inside. Once inside, she saw piles of snow that told her the people just before her hadn't been so polite. At least the entrance hall was too cold for the snow to melt immediately.

Through the door to the tap room, she heard raised voices, the sound indistinct as if heard through water. Ginnevra paused at the door, listening. She recognized the voice as belonging to the man who'd insulted her. "—an affront to the people of Savorola," he was saying.

"We intend to pass through Savorola peacefully," Buonnane said. "There won't be a problem unless you make one."

"Typical disingenuity," the man said more loudly. "We expect followers of the Dark Lady to do no less. Or do you deny that those of your faith have challenged the sovereignty of our Princeps?"

"We have no quarrel with your Princeps," Buonnane said. Her

voice was even and free from hostility. "Whatever disagreements the Hallowed of Savorola have with its rulership have nothing to do with us."

"Then you repudiate your own fellows in your faith," the man said. He sounded as if he felt he'd made a killing point in the argument only he wanted to have. "I suppose it's typical that you'd only support each other so long as you felt there was something in it for you. You believe you're above the law, don't you? You carry those swords to intimidate others into doing what you demand. You're nothing but a lot of well-armed bullies."

That sounded like a signal for Ginnevra to intervene, though Buonnane, to her surprise, had handled herself well. She pushed open the door and walked past the first couple of trestle tables to stand behind the four men—not immediately behind, so as to avoid seeming belligerent.

The men appeared not to notice her arrival. Seven or eight paladins, along with Revered Orselle and a couple of Dedicates, sat at the tables behind Buonnane, their attention rapt upon the argument. Buonnane caught Ginnevra's eye immediately. The paladin captain shifted her weight and raised one eyebrow in code for *I think you should take this.*

Ginnevra nodded. For once, she felt in harmony with the captain. "Excuse me, gentlemen," she said.

The four men turned rapidly, one of them with a little jump that said she'd startled him. The speaker, who stood near Buonnane, frowned and said, "What is it? Some nonsense about our horses? Deal with it yourself, and don't bother your betters."

His petulant rudeness amused Ginnevra. "Gentlemen, I am the paladin Ginnevra Cassaline, prime of the Blessed and leader of this company. If you have a complaint, you should direct it to me. But I'll repeat what Captain Buonnane told you—we intend to pass through Savorola peacefully. So there won't be a fight unless you start one."

The speaker pushed past his companions to face Ginnevra. "You deceived me," he snarled, shaking his finger in Ginnevra's face. "You pretended to be a stable hand so you could eavesdrop on me."

"No, sieur, *you* drew assumptions. I tried to tell you the truth, but you overrode me." Ginnevra smiled politely. "And I did arrange for your horses' care. Now, would you care to tell me why you gentlemen are here? Since I failed to eavesdrop to learn that fact."

"You—" The man apparently choked on a dozen different words in his fury. "You *viper*," he finally spat out.

Ginnevra ignored him. She turned her attention on the other men, though her heart was pounding a demand that she snap the man's finger off and make him eat it. She was terrible at diplomacy. "Would someone else enlighten me? Since this gentleman seems incapable of anything but insults."

The hooded man put back his hood. He was clean-shaven where the others wore neatly-trimmed beards, and he was handsome in a lean, angular way. "We are here to inquire about your intentions," he said. "Preaching the gospel of the Dark Lady is frowned on in Savorola."

"Frowned on? Not forbidden?"

"The worship of the Dark Lady is corrupt," the first man said.

Behind Buonnane, every paladin in the tap room stood as one, making benches and stools scrape with a wooden rasp across the floorboards. The man who'd jumped at Ginnevra's appearance made a startled squeak. Buonnane, who hadn't turned her back on the interlopers, signaled, and the paladins relaxed but did not sit.

Ginnevra's heart still beat rapidly, preparing her for a fight.

She drew in a deep breath, released it, and said, "Sieur, I don't believe I've had the pleasure of an introduction."

The man eyed her as if looking for a trap in her words. "Sieur Cagiole," he said finally.

"Sieur Cagiole," Ginnevra repeated. "You are, of course, entitled to your opinion even if it's provably false. But I repeat—we aren't interested in preaching. Savorola is on the route to Abracabene, and diverting to avoid it would mean adding a week to our journey. That's all. Our mere presence here can't possibly corrupt anyone."

She turned her attention to the clean-shaven man. "I ask again, is the worship of the Goddess forbidden, or is it frowned on? Because your party seems not to be in agreement."

Cagiole opened his mouth. The other man said, "Cagiole, that's enough." He stepped forward and inclined his head to Ginnevra. "I'm Sieur Romanone. And I assure you it is not forbidden to worship the way you do."

"Romanone, you traitor," Cagiole spat.

Romanone took a deep breath the way Ginnevra had. "Cagiole, a moment of your time?" He took Cagiole's elbow in a grip that made the man gasp in pain and steered him out of the tap room to the entrance.

The room fell silent, the fire crackling in the hearth loud in the stillness. Ginnevra smiled at the other two men, who looked like they wished they were somewhere far from this inn. Eodan hadn't returned yet, which made her wonder what he was up to. She cast her gaze over the assembled paladins. Their alertness cheered her, though she didn't think they would need to attack these men.

She listened for the conversation Romanone was having with Cagiole and heard snatches of phrases: *not the way to handle* and *better to imply* and *will see what the Councilor says*. When the door opened, she pretended she hadn't been listening and turned a polite, uncomprehending look on the two men. Romanone looked like he'd eaten something bitter. Cagiole's face was twisted in an epic scowl. Ginnevra couldn't tell who'd won.

She waited for them to rejoin their companions before saying, with her attention on a neutral space between Romanone and Cagiole, "Gentlemen, my people have a busy day ahead as we prepare to leave tomorrow morning. Is there something you want of us? Something that isn't an irrational demand that we stop being what we are so the people of Savorola aren't corrupted by the mere sight of us?"

Cagiole's scowl deepened, but he said nothing.

Romanone shook his head. "I apologize for the misunderstanding," he said. "I'm afraid feelings against the worship of the Dark Lady are high at the moment. We had a report of a company of paladins and anointed spreading discord and preaching their faith, contrary to the express decree of the Princeps. We came to investigate."

"Your 'investigation' bears no resemblance to the careful inquiry I was taught," Ginnevra said, turning her gaze on Cagiole. Cagiole glared past her at the wall, his breathing heavy.

"Again, I apologize." Romanone inclined his head again. "I'm afraid I have to ask how long you intend to remain in Savorola."

"We had meant to move on today, but the storm prevented our leaving." He was a little too amiable, Ginnevra decided, just as Cagiole had been unreasonably hostile. That combined with what she'd overheard suggested it might all be an act, a ploy to get Ginnevra to give away—what? "And we have no intention of preaching while we're here."

"Those banners say otherwise," Cagiole muttered.

"Enough," Romanone said. "But Sieur Cagiole has a point. Will you agree to remove the banners while you're in Savorolan territory?"

Ginnevra crossed her arms over her chest. "I will not."

Romanone's eyebrows lifted nearly to his hairline. "It's a reasonable request."

"No, it isn't. Sieur Romanone, there is nothing wrong with worshipping the Goddess, whatever your Princeps says, and we will not stoop to concealing our faith simply to make Savorolans comfortable." Ginnevra's heart was pounding again. She wished it weren't so quick to decide she was in danger. "And frankly, sieur, if your people are so fragile that the mere sight of the Goddess's emblem makes them either lose their own faith or instantly convert to mine, I think you have worse problems than a company of paladins and anointed traveling peacefully through your principality."

"I see," Romanone said. His eyes had narrowed as she spoke until they were nearly closed.

"She refuses because she has an insidious secret plan," Cagiole announced, sounding triumphant again. "We should arrest them all."

Buonnane shifted her weight, the barest movement, but by the way the four men instantly stared at her, she might as well have drawn the sword propped against the table near her. Ginnevra swiftly glanced over the assembled company. None of the paladins wore armor, and only half of them carried swords, but they all looked dangerous, like women capable of taking someone's head off with their bare hands.

But Romanone didn't look afraid of the threat they posed. "Very well," he said. "You would do better to comply, if only to avoid misunderstandings such as the one that brought us here."

"The misunderstanding was all on Savorola's part, sieur." Ginnevra stared him down.

"Nevertheless." Romanone spread both hands in a gesture suggesting he was helpless in the face of fate. "We will be inquiring among the people here and nearby, and if it turns out you *were* teaching others, well, that will warrant further investigation and possible criminal prosecution."

"Because your Princeps has decreed it?"

"Because your so-called faith teaches people to follow blindly and give obedience to leaders who—" Cagiole began hotly.

"*Enough*, sieur," Romanone said. "Lady Cassaline, whatever the source of our laws, they have the full force of our government behind them. I'm sure you respect that."

"Respect" was the wrong word, but Ginnevra nodded. "And I assume you have the right to enforce them. Since you haven't actually said what your position in the Savorolan government is."

"No," Romanone said. "I haven't." He smiled then, a thin twist of his lips that had no humor in it. Ginnevra considered pushing, but it was unlikely four strangers would have ridden since dawn to accuse her people of a crime without having the authority to back it up.

"Then I believe there's nothing left to say," she told Romanone. Behind her, the door opened, and she smelled Eodan's werewolf musk. "Excuse me, gentlemen, I have things to do." She walked past them to where Buonnane stood, not looking to see if they'd left. Instead, she watched Buonnane's eyes, which tracked something behind her. The door opened again, then after a moment shut with a soft thud. Buonnane nodded.

The room erupted into angry shouts and fists slammed on the tables. "Stop," Buonnane said. "They might still hear us."

The shouting stopped. Ginnevra finally turned. Eodan was approaching; the four lawmen, if that's what they were, had gone. She let out a deep sigh. "That was unexpected. Or maybe it wasn't. I don't suppose anyone *has* gotten into an ecclesiastical wrangle with the locals?"

"Unlikely," Buonnane said. Her color was high, and she looked ready to attack someone with her bare hands. "But it wouldn't matter either way."

"No, they'd want to come after us regardless." Ginnevra shook her head, which ached from tension. "And I never did find out when we could safely leave."

"You wouldn't let them drive us away?" Buonnane sounded shocked.

"No, but I was thinking it might be bad for Actus if we're here too long. If they know he worships the Goddess, him hosting us might look like conspiracy, or something. Make him seem more partisan than he is, anyway."

"Actus doesn't mind, or at least that's what he told me a few minutes ago," Eodan said. "I get the feeling he's used to defending his faith."

"We're still not going to repay his hospitality by bringing down the law on him," Ginnevra said. "Captain, will you spread the word that no one is to leave the inn? I don't know that the warning is necessary, given the weather, but I don't want any of our people going off alone."

"I've already done so," Buonnane said. "I didn't like the mood in the tap room last night. There's too much potential for conflict, and I won't tell my paladins they can't defend themselves." She sounded belligerent, but she was looking at the door, after the departed lawmen, and Ginnevra didn't feel attacked. She wouldn't have guessed she'd ever feel in harmony with the prickly captain.

"Actus said word has gotten around about us," Eodan said. "I'd noticed that there were only a few patrons in here this morning, and no one's come from outside for a drink. That might just be the earliness of the hour, but Actus thinks no one's going to come where they might be corrupted. Which is a problem, but in another sense is good, because we can easily keep to ourselves."

"I want guards on the wagons," Ginnevra told Buonnane. "No sense opening ourselves up to vandalism. And I'll—"

The door to the kitchen banged open, and Actus rushed in, steering Serenna before him. The girl's face bore the marks of tears, and she looked frightened. "Prime Cassaline," Actus said. "You have to take Serenna with you when you go."

THIRTEEN

"What happened?" Ginnevra demanded.

Actus was shaking, but his voice was steady. "Those graycoats, they came into the kitchen from the yard. Two of them. They walked around, getting in the way of the workers, making comments about how flammable it all looked."

"Graycoats—does that mean law enforcement?" Eodan asked.

"It does. Not city guard, but the ones who investigate crimes. You don't have graycoats where you come from?"

"Not exactly. Actus, would they burn this place down?" Ginnevra's heart raced again.

Actus shook his head. "It was just noise. Even worshippers of the Goddess are protected under the law. But then the other two came in, and they asked questions. A lot of questions about me and Serenna personally. And then they started asking about her school, and whether she liked it there. I said she did, and the short one, the one with the strangely-shaped head, he said that was a pity, because he was sure they wouldn't want her anymore. Not if she was preaching corruption." His hands closed more tightly on Serenna's shoulders.

Ginnevra and Buonnane looked at each other. "Serenna's just a child," Ginnevra said.

"She's old enough for a grace. They said no school would want someone who practices foul sorceries with her prayers to the Goddess. That Serenna wouldn't find a place anywhere." Actus' cheeks were red with fury. "And the other one, the beardless man, he went on to say if they had proof she'd practiced her religion in public, they'd be within their rights to prosecute."

Ginnevra's jaw clenched. "All right," she said. "What did they want you to do?"

"Kick you out now, obviously," Actus said. "But I'm not going to do that."

"We can leave," Buonnane said. "You shouldn't have to suffer for hosting us."

"I'm not going to be bullied," Actus said. "But Serenna's not safe. Whether or not you leave, they know she worships the Goddess, and that's a whip they can use at their pleasure. If the graycoats have reached a point where they can threaten a child, they'll go on doing it, to manipulate me if nothing else. She has to leave Savorola."

"But I don't want to!" Serenna burst out. "Everyone I know is here. You can't make me leave!"

"You'll do as your father tells you," Actus said, but tears streaked his cheeks. "Serenna, you wanted to train for a paladin. Maybe now you can do that."

"I changed my mind," Serenna said. "I'll just be careful, that's all. I won't use my grace in public, and I won't say anything about the Goddess, but don't make me leave!"

Actus shot Ginnevra a despairing look. Ginnevra took two steps, putting herself in front of the girl. "You shouldn't have to live your life in fear," she said. "Worshipping the Goddess is supposed to bring you joy and peace. And your father is right—if they can think to threaten your position at your school, they'll come up with other threats, and it's just a short step from that to manufacturing accusations that will put you in danger of criminal prosecution."

She looked at Actus. "That applies to you, too. You should both come with us."

Actus shook his head. "I'm not abandoning what's mine. But I'm no fool. I'll see about selling this place, and I'll follow in a few weeks. It's just that Serenna—"

"I know," Ginnevra said. "Those lawmen are looking for excuses. We'll see Serenna safely to Abraciabene, and you can meet her there."

"See?" Actus said to Serenna. "This is the right thing to do."

Serenna swiped an arm across her eyes. "I don't want to," she said, but her voice was weak.

Actus hugged her. "These paladins will be the first to tell you we all have hard things to do. Think of it as an adventure."

Serenna made a choked sound that might have been a laugh and nodded.

SNOW RESUMED FALLING an hour before noon, big fat wet flakes that clumped together and made visibility almost nonexistent. Ginnevra watched the snow fall from her room's window and despaired of ever leaving this awful town. She rested two fingers against the smooth black pearl at her throat, but no prayer came to mind. Instead, she thought about Savorola and its antagonism toward the worship of the Goddess. As widespread as her religion was, there were still some who believed in the old faith in the Lordagne. They mostly kept to themselves and didn't get into religious quarrels over differing beliefs. But this had sounded like Savorolans saw the Goddess's religion as a threat.

Ginnevra had grown up believing in the Goddess. She had been shocked to learn not everyone shared her religious beliefs. It had taken most of a year of paladin training for her to overcome her ingrained, reflexive negative reaction to encountering someone whose faith was different. Even now, she sometimes had to remind herself that worshipping the Goddess was a privilege, not a demand. An ordinary challenge to her faith, she could handle, but outright antagonism and lies about what she believed? That was entirely new, and she wasn't sure how to deal with it except by leaving it behind.

She bowed her head and whispered, "Goddess, whatever is going on in Savorola, please protect those of Your faith. Not all of them are in Actus' and Serenna's position, capable of leaving for more hospitable places. And, if You will, help us leave here without further conflict. We won't start fights, but I won't tell the paladins not to defend themselves or the anointed. Ever in Your name."

The prayer didn't ease her heart the way prayers usually did.

She went downstairs to where Eodan and the Dedicates and acolytes were gathered around the fire, laughing and talking. Ginnevra considered joining them, but the knot of tension in her chest made the thought of joking and telling humorous stories unpleasant. Instead, she sat near the kitchen door and inspected her sword's blade. It was in perfect condition despite her battle with the werewolves the previous night. The sight of it deepened Ginnevra's dissatisfaction. She needed something to accomplish, something to take her mind off her worries about what Romanone and Cagiole might be up to.

Someone settled across the table from her. Ginnevra looked up from her contemplation of her weapon to see Serenna, her eyes still red and puffy from crying, but otherwise looking calm. Ginnevra smiled. "I imagine you didn't think you'd be leaving so soon."

"I didn't know how scared I was of going until I had to," Serenna said. Her apron was crooked, and she wound her fists in its skirt to wrinkle it further. "I—don't know if I want to be a paladin anymore. Is that bad?"

"I think making decisions when your emotions are heightened is a bad idea. You don't have to become a paladin just because we're taking you to Abraciabene. But—" Ginnevra ran her finger down the flat of her blade. "Have you considered that on this journey you'll be in a perfect position to observe a company of paladins up close? That should help you decide what you want."

Serenna brightened. "That's true. And I like the Dedicates. It won't be terrible."

"No, it won't." Ginnevra pushed the sword across the table. "See what you think."

Serenna leaned back. "I shouldn't—I'm not a paladin, so should I touch your sword?"

"It's not a sacred weapon except as we make it so. Go on, lift it. It's not as heavy as it looks."

Serenna hesitated a moment longer. Then she wrapped her hands around the hilt and lifted. "It's still heavy."

"To a paladin, it weighs almost nothing." Ginnevra kept a careful eye on the girl's hands.

Serenna rotated her grip so the sword pointed at the ceiling. "I like it," she said. "It makes me feel powerful."

"That's good. All right, let me take it." Serenna's hands had started to shake. Ginnevra retrieved the sword and sheathed it. "I've defended countless people with my sword, directly or indirectly. But it's still just a reflection of the power granted me by the Goddess. You have some of that power, too, by virtue of your grace."

Serenna touched the lump under the neck of her gown where her grace lay. "But nothing like yours."

"It's not a competition. The Goddess loves us, and she gives us Her power to remind us of that love. That's true of anyone who has a grace, you or me or Revered Giulliomocte." Ginnevra tapped her grace with her forefinger. "The materials are different, but the blessing is the same."

The tap room door banged open, and Ginnevra swiveled on the bench, her hand closing on the sword's scabbard. Dedicate Bidelia stood there, dripping wet. "It's raining!"

The anointed seated by the fire stood, exclaiming over Bidelia's condition. She waved them away and stripped off her coat, shaking it so water scattered everywhere. "The snow was slushy, and then it turned to rain," she said. "The wagon drivers said if it keeps warm like this, we will leave in the morning, no problem. It is melting the snow!"

Ginnevra hurried outside, stopping at the front door. Rain sheeted down, pelting the snowdrifts with soft *plocks* and harder *plinks* on the roof tiles. "Is this real?" she asked Eodan, who had followed her to the door.

"If it freezes again, we'll have a different problem," Eodan replied. "Iced-over roads, particularly ones in the condition Savorola's are, will stop us as surely as snow will."

"Spoken like a true pessimist," Ginnevra scoffed. "I choose to have faith."

"As you should." Eodan put his arms around her and kissed the side of her head. "And I admit this is a fortunate change in the weather. I want away from this place as soon as possible."

Ginnevra turned in his arms and hugged him, resting her head against his shoulder, before stepping away and closing the door on the rain. "I don't suppose the weather will discourage the werewolves?"

"Not if they have a mission and a purpose," Eodan said. "This is just an inconvenience to them, and not a big one."

Ginnevra stopped. "A mission," she said. "Literally a mission?"

Eodan's eyes narrowed. "You mean, someone set them on our path?"

"It would explain how they found us when Revered Giulliomocte doesn't stand out at all, and why they stuck with us all the way from Tesccine. Suppose this wasn't a random encounter? Suppose the Bright One commanded them?" Ginnevra grabbed Eodan's hand. "Is that possible?"

"She does speak to us sometimes," Eodan said. "Tells us our destiny, orders us to obey some command. You're the one who said the Bright One might want to interfere with the first male Hallowed. This is just a more direct interference."

Ginnevra shivered and rubbed her arms. "It doesn't matter," she declared. "Bright One's interference or no, we have a duty to perform. We have to get Revered Giulliomocte to Abraciabene, and it doesn't matter who tries to stop us. We can't let this knowledge frighten us."

"You're not going to conceal this from the others, are you?"

Ginnevra looked at the tap room door as if she could see through the wood. "No," she said, "no, I don't think so. The possibility of it frightening some of those people isn't nearly so dire as not telling everyone what kind of danger we might face. And paladins always prefer to know the truth. It makes us better fighters."

She pushed open the door. Bidelia sat near the fire, leaning forward to tell the other anointed—and Serenna, Ginnevra noted —some story that had them all intent on her. "I'll find Buonnane," Ginnevra said. "You let the rest of them know. Have you seen Revered Giulliomocte at all?"

"He was in here earlier for breakfast, but I didn't see where he went." Eodan stopped Ginnevra with a hand on her shoulder. "Forget what I said about the weather stopping us. If the Bright One has designs on us, we need to reach Abraciabene as soon as possible."

His demeanor was so serious Ginnevra felt an unexpected pang of fear. She nodded and headed off in search of Buonnane.

THE RAIN STOPPED SOMETIME in the late evening, and silence took the place of the endless, welcome tapping on the roof. By morning, the skies were clear, and the sun rose on a cold but not freezing day. Melting piles of snow lay everywhere, and the road, while still rutted and filled with puddles of muddy water, was clear as far as Ginnevra could see from the inn's front door.

She laid two fingers against her grace and bowed her head in silent thanks. The rain had reminded her that sometimes the Goddess came up with blessings better than anything she could think of for herself. Though she wasn't the only one praying for a speedy departure, and maybe this was the result of some other person's prayer. Or it could simply be coincidence. Ginnevra didn't believe the Goddess intervened every single time one of her worshippers prayed for something. Regardless, it didn't hurt to be thankful.

She turned back to where Actus waited behind her with Serenna. The girl's eyes were red once more, but her face was cheerful, and she carried her pack confidently. Actus, too, looked as if he'd wept a few tears. He saluted Ginnevra and said, "Take care of my girl, will you?"

"She'll be safe with us," Ginnevra said. "You take care of yourself. Don't take chances. If those graycoats are really interested in seeing the Goddess's worship suppressed, you could be in danger."

"I don't plan on being more than a week, two at most, behind you." Actus hugged Serenna. "You do as my lady says, understand? Remember what I've taught you, and I'll see you soon."

Serenna clung to her father for a moment, then stepped back and wiped her sleeve across her eyes. "I'll be fine."

Ginnevra saluted the innkeeper and then put a hand on Serenna's shoulder, guiding her through the inn's front yard and around to the stables where the others had gathered. Serenna looked back once, then straightened her shoulders and hefted her pack higher.

Most of the Dedicates and acolytes already waited in the wagon, but Bidelia approached them with an outstretched hand. "It's good you are to come with us," she said to Serenna. "We have fun in the wagon. And you will love Abraciabene. It is the most beautiful city in the world."

Relieved, Ginnevra watched the two young women walk to the wagon. This would be easier if Serenna had a friend to keep her too occupied to feel homesick.

She mounted Dauntless and curbed his first few restless steps. He had energy enough for two horses and didn't like idleness. "You should take advantage of a rest," she told him. "It's going to be hard going once we reach the badlands."

Dauntless snorted and tossed his head. Ginnevra laughed.

Eodan came up beside her on Ginger. "Let me guess," he said. "Dauntless is ready for a race he's not going to get."

"Exactly." Ginnevra wheeled around to survey the rest of their party. All the paladins and Revered Orselle were mounted. "Where is Revered Giulliomocte? And Revered Pratese?"

Eodan scanned the yard. "Their horses are here, but I don't see them."

Ginnevra approached Buonnane, who waited by the gate as if impatient to begin. "Captain, have you see the other Revereds?"

Buonnane looked across the yard the way Eodan had. "They're not here. I don't recall seeing either of them after breakfast."

Grinding her teeth, Ginnevra dismounted and handed Dauntless' reins to Eodan. "I'll check inside. Have them mount up if they return before I do."

She entered by the kitchen door, startling the cooks, and followed her ears to the tap room, where a loud argument was going on. Giulliomocte and Pratese stood by the fireplace, face to face, their bodies rigid with anger. "—is not the way it works!" Giulliomocte shouted.

"Isn't it? I suppose you'd know, Domenico," Pratese shot back. "You have no proof of what you claim. I deny—"

"Proof?" Giulliomocte's voice rose. "You insist on proof—this was always your problem, Marsillia, your insistence on boiling down everything about religion to what you can see and touch. Not a hint of faith—"

Ginnevra cleared her throat loudly, interrupting the Revered and making both Giulliomocte and Pratese turn on her. "I apologize for interrupting your discussion, Revereds, but we're ready to leave, if you'll join us."

"Of course, prime," Pratese said with a smile. All traces of her anger had vanished. "We can finish this later, Domenico."

"I don't think there's anything left to say, Revered Pratese," Giulliomocte said. His voice sounded cut with ice. He stalked out of the room without looking at Ginnevra.

Ginnevra gestured to Pratese to precede her out of the tap room. But Pratese halted at the door and turned to face Ginnevra. "Don't mind Domenico," she said. "I'm sure the strain of his position is hard for him to bear."

Ginnevra raised an eyebrow. "I'm sure," she said. From what she'd seen, it looked more as if the strain of traveling with Pratese was what Giulliomocte found hard to bear. For once she felt sympathy for the man regardless of their disagreements.

As she followed Pratese to the stable yard, Ginnevra considered Giulliomocte's position. He was essentially alone on this journey so far as companionship went. Paladins treated the anointed with respect but not warmth; Revered Orselle was, from Ginnevra's observations, too much of a sycophant to be an equal; and Pratese was antagonistic. Alone, when he was preparing to take on a role he had never imagined for himself. Again, sympathy struck her, followed closely by inappropriate guilt over their arguments. It didn't matter that she wasn't to blame for anything; she might at least try to feel some compassion.

She mounted Dauntless and walked to the front of their procession to stand next to Buonnane. Behind her, the banners snapped in the cold breeze, and she looked at the dark moon emblazoned on them. Such a small thing, and yet these Savorolans saw it as a terrible threat. "Move out," she commanded, and they all set off down the road.

FOURTEEN

They reached the Salvectus River by noon. It flowed, sluggish and cold, from the north where it bisected the city of Savorola. Ginnevra cast her gaze upstream as they waited for the ferry. The great city was no more than a dark blotch on the horizon, weighing down the landscape like the worst monster the Bright One could imagine. Ginnevra shook her head to dispel the image. It was just a city, and not even a dangerous one despite everything they'd heard about the Princeps' dispute with Savorola's Hallowed. No matter how humans fought among themselves, they were still human, not monstrous.

She wrapped her cloak more closely about herself, burrowing into it like some hibernating animal. The fact that it was too warm to snow in no way made the air actually warm, at least as far as Ginnevra was concerned. She watched Eodan, who wore his coat unbuttoned, and Dedicate Bidelia, who had left off her cloak entirely and seemed unbothered by the nip in the air. They were all mad, the lot of them.

The river didn't make things any better. It took the bright, clear blue of the sky and turned it dark and blue-brown and murky. If there were fish in its depths, which Ginnevra doubted, they were invisible if they weren't frozen solid. Looking at the water made Ginnevra shiver again.

She looked instead at the ferry mechanism. A web of ropes crossed the wide river, with the ferries hooked to the web. Complicated pulleys and a series of oars manned by big, silent rowers propelled the ferries across the river, while the rope web kept them from being swept downstream. Using the ferry was expensive, not least because they would need at least four trips to get their whole party across, but it was the only crossing for miles, and the only one between here and Lake Salvectus that didn't mean at least a few of them getting wet.

The first ferry had almost reached the opposite side of the river with its passengers, while the second had cast off the farther shore and was on its way back. Ginnevra stilled her hands so they wouldn't fidget. It was unlikely Romanone and Cagiole would attack them, not with only four graycoats, but she felt exposed out in the open like this, surrounded by potential enemies. Granted, the Savorolans waiting on the ferry stood well away from the party, and none of them were armed, but Ginnevra was still conscious of the potential for conflict.

She turned her horse and rode along the line of their caravan, nodding at the paladins, who'd spread out to surround the wagons. Buonnane herself rode beside Giulliomocte, her eyes restlessly scanning the waiting passengers. Giulliomocte's brows were drawn down in an epic frown, and he looked in every direction except Pratese's. Pratese had her eyes fixed on Giulliomocte and her lips curved in a smug smile. Whatever that argument had been about, Pratese obviously believed she'd won.

Ginnevra reached the back of their group and circled around to the other side. The ferry was about halfway across the river. It was also empty, though there were people massed on the far shore. She suspected they were leery of disembarking where they would be surrounded by worshippers of the Goddess. Ginnevra passed the wagon where the anointed rode and noticed Bidelia and another couple of the female Dedicates in a huddle with Serenna, whispering and giggling. That was something good, anyway.

She stopped near Buonnane and the Revereds and said, "Captain, will you organize us into groups for crossing? We'll need the noncombatants protected."

Buonnane nodded. "Excuse me, Revered," she said to Giulliomocte, and rode to the head of the caravan.

Ginnevra turned to ride away, but Giulliomocte said, "Prime Cassaline, a word?"

She wheeled around to face him. "Yes, Revered?"

Giulliomocte's frown had deepened. "I feel inspired that we should begin our journey today with prayer. But I'm concerned about inciting discontent."

Ginnevra frowned as well. "You're not suggesting we conceal our faith?"

"It's more that we may have to travel alongside some of these people for a time, and I'd rather not frighten them more than we already have just by our presence. I'm asking your opinion on the matter."

Ginnevra surveyed the other travelers on their side of the river. Most of them stared at the caravan in awe or fear. A few ostentatiously ignored them. But Ginnevra didn't get the sense that she was looking at an incipient mob. "I'll gather everyone to the wagon. We can do this without making a scene. And if they're frightened, they'll just have to endure."

It took a minute or two to get everyone close enough to the wagon for a communal prayer. None of the paladins removed their helmets, which Ginnevra thought was sensible. She listened to Giulliomocte's prayer with half her attention. The other half stayed focused on her surroundings. Faith was one thing; letting down your guard in hostile circumstances was cocksure and not something the Goddess approved of.

She noticed Buonnane doing the same. At least the captain was competent, even if Ginnevra had reservations about her character. It was another three weeks to Abraciabene; maybe she would warm up to Eodan. And maybe Ginnevra would grow a pelt and learn to love winter. Well, it was a nice fantasy.

"...Ever in Your name," Giulliomocte said, and the others murmured a response. Ginnevra turned her attention on him. He looked less angry, so maybe that prayer had been as much for his peace of mind as for their party.

The ferry had docked while Giulliomocte was praying, but no one had boarded, not even the Savorolans. They stood huddled to one side, staring at Giulliomocte. Buonnane directed the wagon carrying the anointed to board, along with three paladins who dismounted to lead their horses onto the flat-bottomed ferry. Still no one else came forward. Ginnevra sighed inwardly. At least their open display of religious faith hadn't made anyone actively hostile.

The breeze had picked up, chilling her further. She huddled more deeply into her cloak—and a familiar scent came to her nose, foul and sweetish like decomposition. She wheeled Dauntless around, scanning the crowds. "Werewolves," she muttered to Pia, who was nearest. "Pass the word—but don't shout it out, because that really will start a panic."

Pia nodded and rode past her to the head of the line where Buonnane waited for the approach of the second ferry. Ginnevra put a hand on her sword where it was strapped to Dauntless' saddle. She still couldn't see anyone who might be a werewolf, and the scent came from everywhere.

She turned and rode for Eodan, who had joined the Revereds and was talking to Pratese. "Do you smell that?"

Eodan sniffed. He stiffened, and his expression soured. "There are many," he said. "At least ten, possibly as many as fifteen."

"Fifteen of what?" Pratese said.

Eodan didn't answer her. Instead, he said, "They're not going to attack us in full light where everyone can see. This is a trick."

Ginnevra nodded. "Revereds, can you identify werewolves by sight?"

Giulliomocte shot a glance at Eodan before nodding once.

"Then tell me what you see," Ginnevra added.

Giulliomocte turned his horse as Pratese and Orselle did. "There," he said, pointing. Ginnevra grabbed his arm.

"We don't want them knowing they've been spotted," she said. "They'll know we smell them, but they believe they're still concealed by the crowd." She followed the line of where he'd pointed and saw a fair-haired man who stood out among all the dark-haired Savorolans. He caught her eye and smiled an unpleasant, toothy smile. So much for keeping their advantage.

"Ginnevra," Eodan said in a low voice. A trio of fair-haired men approached from the rear, passing the wagons closely enough that the stolid horses who pulled them shifted restlessly trying to get away. Ginnevra immediately rode to meet them, with Eodan close beside her. The blond werewolf walked at the head of the little group, as confidently as if she and he hadn't tried to kill each other just days before.

When the werewolves were mere feet away, Ginnevra came to a halt and said, "Stop there."

The werewolves hesitated for a moment. Then their leader

said, "And what will you do if we do not? Here, where all these people can see?"

It was Ginnevra's turn to hesitate. The werewolf leader's smile broadened. "I thought as much," he said, and walked forward, passing Dauntless closely enough to make the warhorse step sideways, the closest he would ever come to showing fear. His companions followed close behind. They were both shorter and not as fair-haired as their leader, but they moved with the same easy, loose-limbed grace he had. Dauntless shifted again and let out a snort, tossing his head restlessly. Ginnevra controlled him and wheeled around to follow the werewolves.

She and Eodan paced the three, flanking them—to an outsider, it might have looked like they were herding the creatures. But, then, to an outsider, the werewolves looked like people. Ginnevra kept a hand on the hilt of her sword. If these werewolves tried anything, she would intervene, and to hell with keeping the peace.

The trio of werewolves headed directly for Giulliomocte. Ginnevra opened her mouth to shout a warning, but they stopped several feet from the Revered. Giulliomocte regarded them placidly, with no sign of apprehension aside from how one hand curled over the saddle's pommel to grip it tightly. Then Buonnane was there, putting herself between the two, her sword half-drawn. "That's close enough," she said.

The werewolf leader tilted his head to look up at Buonnane, who had the sun at her back, and raised a hand to shield his eyes. "You paladins always think with your swords," he said. "I have said and done nothing to threaten you. Not even that one." He pointed at Giulliomocte.

Buonnane said nothing more, but she bared her teeth in a silent snarl.

The werewolf leader lowered his hand and regarded Buonnane closely. "You fear me," he said, and laughed. "A brave paladin should fear nothing, but you—you fear my kind."

Buonnane drew her sword and leveled it at the werewolf. "Taunt me again, and we'll see how well you talk when your head is ten feet away from the rest of your body."

The werewolf didn't stop laughing. His companions joined in, their laughter a high-pitched sound almost like a titter that made no sense coming from what appeared to be full-grown men. Ginnevra turned to see what their audience thought. The nearby Savorolans had drawn together in tight groups and were muttering, casting terrified glances at Buonnane's sword. A few of them had broken from the crowd and were running in the direction of the nearest village. It was probably too much to hope that they were just fleeing. No, likely they went in search of someone who could stop the evil paladins from killing an innocent person. Ginnevra felt like screaming.

"Captain," she said, pretending the werewolves weren't there, "we should send off our next group. Revereds, will you join the wagon?"

"You mean you will deny me your blessing?" The werewolf leader took a step forward, avoiding Buonnane, and reached to touch Giulliomocte's knee.

Ginnevra snatched her sword from its scabbard and slid the blade across the werewolf's shoulder, letting the edge rest against the vein in his neck. "Don't," she said as Buonnane moved to intercept the other two. "Touch him, and it will be the last thing you ever do." She had no idea whether the touch of a werewolf intent on evil could harm a Revered, but that wasn't something she wanted to find out.

The werewolf lowered his hand. "You will not kill me. They will see and they will attack."

Ginnevra's blood sang with the need to shed his. She stilled the tremor of fury in her hand and said, "They're already scared of us. Your death won't change anything, except that you'll be dead and your pack will lose its dominus. So I say again, don't."

The werewolf stepped carefully back, away from Giulliomocte and Ginnevra's sword, and turned to face her. But he looked past her to Eodan, who gripped Ginnevra's mace and looked murderously ready to use it. "You traitor," he said, but in the calm tones of one who means no insult. "Standing beside humans as if they are our equals. The Bright Goddess is displeased with you."

"Her displeasure doesn't keep me up at night," Eodan said. "What do you want?"

"Nothing but what we already have done," the werewolf said. "To show you you are helpless against us. We will follow you until you weaken, and then we will attack." He saluted Ginnevra the paladin's way, but with a mocking expression. "You cannot stop us."

"Strong words," Ginnevra said. "You assume we won't attack first."

"You have more to lose than we, and you are outnumbered." The werewolf gestured. More blond men and women emerged from the crowd and approached. Ginnevra gave them one glance before returning her attention to the werewolf leader. He was still smiling that infuriating smile, but Ginnevra had better control than to be goaded by that.

"Captain," she said.

"Onto the ferry," Buonnane said, once more interposing herself between Giulliomocte and the werewolves. Orselle and Pratese urged their horses forward, following the second wagon, but Giulliomocte stayed put. Buonnane glanced once at him. "Revered, please get on the ferry."

Giulliomocte regarded the werewolf closely. "You have a name?" he said.

The werewolf looked taken aback for a moment before his mocking smile returned. "It is Cennfalad."

"I see." The Revered turned his horse so he was looking at the werewolf, Cennfalad, directly. "You were made to mock humans, which you do by taking our shapes and pretending to be other than you are. I warn you, Cennfalad, you tread a dangerous path if you choose to follow us. Stand down now, or the Goddess will not be generous with you."

Cennfalad laughed again, more loudly this time. "Oh, you are so kind to think of this poor creature's welfare! I believe I will do as my Goddess demands, and rend you limb from limb."

Buonnane hissed and drew her sword back for a killing blow.

Behind them, shouts and the sound of pounding hoofbeats rang out. Ginnevra turned in her seat to see a handful of riders bearing down on them. She swore under her breath. "Get them on the ferry *now*," she commanded.

Buonnane sheathed her sword and urged Giulliomocte to follow her. Ginnevra glared at Cennfalad. "Follow us if you want," she said. "Eventually, we'll be where we don't have to worry about observers. That's your only warning, and I suggest you heed it."

Cennfalad bowed his head and gestured to his followers. They gathered in a group near where the other travelers waited to board the ferry, but Cennfalad and the two who had accompanied him first stayed near Ginnevra. Ginnevra cast a quick glance toward the river. The Revereds and the second wagon were all aboard, and the other ferry had cast off from the far shore and was heading back, empty again. Then she turned and smiled at the oncoming riders.

"You think you can threaten people with violence and get away with it?" Cagiole sputtered. "You're nothing but a pack of bullies!"

"Of course not," Ginnevra said, her smile widening. "These gentlemen asked questions about our swords. We were demonstrating. I assure you no one was in any danger."

"You *liar*," Cagiole said. "We have witnesses—"

"I don't think you do," Ginnevra said. She waved at the crowd and drew her sword halfway from its scabbard. "Do any of you want to bear witness against us? No? That's what I thought."

"It's true, sieur," Cennfalad said. He now looked as innocent as a cat who has just drained the cream pot. "There was no threat."

Ginnevra eyed him warily, waiting for the blow to strike. But he and the other two werewolves simply stood there, as amicably as if they were all great friends.

"But you—someone saw her put a blade to your throat!" Cagiole said.

"A trick of the light only," Cennfalad said. "I do not believe the paladin will hurt me, now or ever." He grinned at Ginnevra, daring her to attack.

"I assure you all, I only kill monsters," Ginnevra said, grinning mirthlessly back at Cennfalad. He nodded, acknowledging a telling hit.

"You play a dangerous game, Prime Cassaline," Romanone said. His handsome face was marred by a frown that dragged the corners of his mouth down. "The laws of Savorola are clear. You are not permitted to proselytize, and your remit to pursue justice is void here. And we will not endure strangers threatening our people."

Ginnevra closed her hand tightly on her sword's hilt. "We have threatened no Savorolans," she said, "and we intend to leave peacefully. Taking our trouble with us."

Romanone stared her down. She stared back. Then, to her surprise, he addressed Eodan. "And what are you, then? You are no paladin, and you don't dress the way the servants of your Goddess do."

"I am the prime's companion," Eodan said. He had lowered the mace to rest on his thigh.

Romanone raised an eyebrow. "Companion," he said, giving the word an inflection that made it sound unsavory. "Is that so."

Eodan remained silent. He tapped the mace slowly against his thigh, once, twice. Romanone eyed it, but made no comment.

The third wagon rolled into motion, and Ginnevra realized the ferry had returned again. One more trip, and they would all be across. "Our personal lives are really none of your business, Sieur Romanone," she said. "I'm sorry you were dragged all the way out here for nothing, but I assure you, we mean you and yours no harm."

"I ought to arrest you," Romanone said in a conversational, non-threatening way. "I'm sure I could find a reason. But I find I would rather you leave Savorola and never return."

"I wish I could agree to that," Ginnevra said. "The never-returning, I mean. But I don't believe Savorola's quarrel with the Goddess will last forever. I hope for a resumption of peace between us, sieur. I wish you would as well."

Romanone's brow furrowed again, but this time, he looked puzzled, as if Ginnevra had spoken in riddles. "I defend my country," he said.

"Sieur Romanone, arrest her!" Cagiole demanded. "This instant!"

"I think not." Romanone turned his horse. "Safe journeys, prime, far from here."

Cagiole's face reddened. He looked from Ginnevra to Romanone and back again. Then, with a snort of disgust, he wheeled his horse to follow Romanone.

Ginnevra let out a deep breath. "All right," she said to Cenn-

179

falad. "Why didn't you accuse us? All you had to do was tell the truth, or at least half of it."

Cennfalad shrugged. "I admit it would be easier to reach your Revered if you were gone. But where is the sport in that?" His smile fell away, and for a moment, he looked so vicious it chilled Ginnevra. "And I will not tell my Goddess that I needed the help of humans to do her will. You and I will fight someday, paladin, and you will know I am victorious in the instant before I tear out your throat."

Ginnevra commanded herself not to flinch. "Bold words," she said.

"Indeed." Cennfalad bowed, another mocking gesture, and turned his back on her to stroll in the direction of his pack.

CHAPTER

FIFTEEN

Ginnevra and Eodan waited in silence for the ferry to take them and the last members of their party across. Ginnevra kept her eyes fixed on the werewolf pack, committing faces to memory, though she knew she would likely fight them in their wolf forms. It was something to do that kept her from anticipating the future, which was counter to the Goddess's teachings. The future was what you made it, one moment at a time, but she couldn't help wishing she could make her future right now by slaughtering every werewolf in that pack.

Which was foolish. There was no reason to believe those werewolves represented their entire pack, given that there were only twelve of them. Even Cennfalad's death wouldn't guarantee the rest of the werewolves wouldn't attack later. But Ginnevra stared them down, one at a time, willing them to see her readiness to hurt them. Most of the werewolves were male, but there were three females—she refused to think of them as men and women—who were as tall and blonde as their counterparts. Later, she would ask Eodan if the ratio was typical.

Finally, *finally*, the ferry touched the frozen ground with a crunch of wood against hard earth and stiff, bristly weeds, and Ginnevra guided Dauntless toward it. She made sure she was the last to board, and after dismounting, she again turned to glare at the werewolves, in case any of them got ideas about trying to follow. Cennfalad regarded her with his mocking smile. Ginnevra no longer found it infuriating. She would not be drawn by him again.

As the ferry made its slow progress across the choppy water of the river, the werewolves drifted to positions near the dock, spreading out to circle it as if preparing to attack the ferry when it returned. Ginnevra stood beside Dauntless with her hand on her sword, watching their figures become tiny with distance.

She realized Eodan stood at her left hand just as he said, "They won't attack immediately."

"I imagine they'll wait until we're well into the badlands." Ginnevra's hand closed more tightly on her sword's hilt. "But not because they care about witnesses. They'll harry us for miles, heightening our tension and putting us under strain so we'll be weakened by the constant need for vigilance. They hope."

"My pack never hunted humans, but that sounds like a reasonable strategy. In the absolute sense, not because I approve. If you know what I mean."

"I do." Ginnevra wished she could take his hand, but with the werewolves still watching, she didn't want to do anything that might indicate uncertainty.

They stood together, watching the werewolves, until another soft *crunch* told them they'd arrived. Then they led their horses off the ferry and walked them to where they could join the others. Buonnane, who'd gone across with Giulliomocte and the other Revereds, had gotten their caravan organized and everyone pointed in the right direction. Ginnevra mounted Dauntless and steered him to the captain's side.

"We're going to have company," she said in a low voice. "Let's get down the road a few miles, and then I need to speak to everyone."

Buonnane nodded. She looked like she wanted to ask questions, but refrained. Ginnevra's estimation of her rose again.

They followed the road south, which paralleled the Salvectus without being so close Ginnevra could smell the cold, silty scent that made her feel frozen. The clear, beautiful day seemed less beautiful with the memory of the werewolves fresh in her mind, so she made herself watch her surroundings and appreciate their stark, wintry loveliness. That wasn't easy, because she had memories of this bare landscape during summer, when the tall green grasses touched with yellow where the sun burned them waved in the breeze. Then, the Salvectus ran low and smooth with ripples that gleamed in the sun, and insects chirred in an endless high hum that felt like the earth was singing. Now, it just felt dead.

If there was beauty here, it lay in the stillness and the way the land rose to low hills in the west, far from where they would travel. The sun lit the hills in a way it did not touch the lowlands, turning them warm gold from the winter-yellow grasses and weeds covering their slopes. Since Ginnevra felt permanently in shade where she was despite the brightness of the sunlight, the sight warmed her.

No villages broke the monotony of the landscape, and Ginnevra didn't remember this route well enough to know when they would reach the next one. So after riding a few miles and seeing no one on the road in either direction, she called a halt and brought everyone in to a close huddle.

In a few words, she explained the situation with the werewolves and her suppositions about how they would attack. "We'll have to be on our guard, true, but we can't be so anxious we lose our edge," she said. "This represents a challenge to our faith. If we fear what might happen, that's the same as anticipating a future in which that fear comes true. That's counter to everything we're taught. Instead, we should remember that the Goddess has blessed us with the strength and courage to face our challenges, and that nothing the werewolves bring against us can take that away."

She nodded at Buonnane. "Captain Buonnane will lead our resistance. She has experience fighting werewolves, and between her experience and Eodan's knowledge, we have a tremendous advantage against our enemy. Captain, can you give us some idea of what to expect from the road between here and the holy city?"

Buonnane nodded. "There aren't many villages between here and Lake Salvectus. Most Savorolans are conscious of having carved a settlement out of the badlands, and they cluster as near Savorola as they can. That combined with their general hostility means we will always make camp rather than stay at inns. It means we're more exposed, but we also have more control over our surroundings."

She drew her belt knife and crouched to carve lines in the frozen earth. "We follow the river south to Lake Salvectus. There are some fishing communities there we can trade with—they're not Savorolans, but independents who are fierce about maintaining that independence. From there, we follow the lake shore to the foothills of the Merciore Mountains, skirting the badlands. The forests begin roughly *here*, maybe ten miles west of the lake."

She made an X with the tip of her knife at a point near the western point of Lake Salvectus, which was a long, flattened oval in her sketch. "That's where things get dangerous. The road is an old one, and the forests grew up around it. They're full of monsters, and worse, they'll give cover to anything that wants to attack us. We'll have to be at our most alert for that part of the journey. However—" She stabbed the knife deep into the frozen ground. "The forest ends at the Belladine River, which we'll follow north to Abraciabene. The river runs through the badlands, but the territory is well-known and patrolled by paladin companies. Once we've reached the Belladine... well, I won't say we'll be safe, but we'll be in a much better position to defend against attacks."

"Thank you, captain." Ginnevra swept the group with her gaze, assessing them. The young anointed looked nervous, but none of them appeared ready to panic. Orselle's hare-like nose quivered as he stared at Buonnane's sketch. Pratese and Giulliomocte wore identical frowns that would have amused Ginnevra if she hadn't so clearly remembered their fight that morning. The paladins were all relaxed, but then most of them had made this trip before, though never with a werewolf pack breathing down their necks. The wagon drivers, standing at the edge of the crowd, looked the most worried. Ginnevra reminded herself to have a reassuring word with them later.

"As I said, there's no point giving in to fear," she said. "We will do our best, and that will be enough. And the Goddess is on our side. Now, let's ride. I want to put as much distance between ourselves and Savorola as we can before nightfall."

She surveyed the land behind them as everyone mounted or climbed into the wagon. Nothing moved. There was no sign of travelers, and no furry bodies low to the ground, loping toward them. And so it began.

They continued south along the road, which was not as deeply rutted as the one crossing Savorola. Buonnane's words about how few settlements there were to the south came to mind—fewer settlements, fewer travelers. They saw no one until they neared one of those settlements, which wasn't much more than a cluster of houses spread out on either side of the road. Men and women stopped what they were doing to stare at the caravan, their gazes riveted on the double column of paladins when they weren't fixed on the black and silver banners. Ginnevra ignored them, though normally she would give a polite nod to anyone they passed. She remembered what Giulliomocte had said about not frightening people more than they did by their mere presence.

When they left the settlement behind, the sun was dipping below the distant foothills, but Ginnevra didn't call a halt until they were well past the houses and the sun's rim lit the tops of the hills with a line of gold. "I didn't want to make them feel threatened," she said to Buonnane.

"I agree," the captain said. She still avoided looking at Eodan, but she didn't seem quite as tense in his presence as at first. Ginnevra chose to take it as a hopeful sign.

They made camp in the fields to the west of the road. Ginnevra encouraged the Dedicates and Revereds to make as many magical campfires as they wanted. The party didn't need to hide from anyone—yet—and the warmth would hearten them all. She didn't believe she was the only one who hated the cold.

She paced between the fires, nodding to people but not stopping to speak to anyone. The Dedicates and acolytes clustered around the largest fire with Revered Orselle, who was telling a story that had them all laughing. Ginnevra hadn't thought Orselle capable of anything but awkward comments, but then, Revered Giulliomocte wasn't there, and Ginnevra judged Orselle to be very eager to please the man who would be Hallowed soon.

She walked to the western edge of camp, where Usterchia stood, her unusual gray eyes scanning the western horizon. Usterchia nodded a greeting in silence. "Good visibility," Ginnevra said. "It's going to be a clear night."

"We'll have snow or rain tomorrow afternoon, though," Usterchia said. She was short and compact and gave the impression of someone who might watch, boulder-like and stolid, until some outside force moved her. Ginnevra didn't smell snow in the air, but she didn't ask Usterchia how she knew. Usterchia had a sense for changes in weather that Ginnevra would have called prophetic in anyone but a paladin.

Ginnevra groaned, making Usterchia crack a smile but not abandon her vigilance. "I'll appreciate the clear weather while we have it, then," Ginnevra said.

She returned to her campfire, the one she shared with Eodan, and found a steaming bowl of soup waiting for her. She folded the tail of her cloak under her as protection from the hard, frozen ground, and said, "I didn't realize the wagon drivers were so versatile. Or that they could produce soup so quickly." The broth was savory beef, the carrots and potatoes diced small, and soft grains of barley floated in the soup, little white puffs that turned out to be chewy when she took a bite.

"I asked," Eodan said. "They told me the Revereds bless the casks to preserve the food longer than it would normally last, though in this weather I'm not sure how necessary that is. So there's a barrel of beef broth, and they started soaking the barley and vegetables in it while they were waiting for all of us to cross the river, and in the evening, it's just a matter of heating it up."

"Just so it's not stew," Ginnevra said. "That takes forever, and it's never as good as eating the individual ingredients prepared properly." She ate soup until she was pleasantly full, then set the empty bowl aside and leaned in to warm her face by the fire. "What a lovely evening."

"You're surprisingly relaxed." Eodan set his own bowl down and scooted over to put his arm around her.

"Just taking my own advice. Being wound tight all the time

could get us killed." Ginnevra leaned against his shoulder and breathed in the werewolf musk.

They sat in silence for a while. Ginnevra listened to the sounds of people at the other campfires, the laughter of paladins and anointed, and listened too for the footsteps of the patrollers, crunching softly on the frozen grass. One set of footsteps drew nearer, and Ginnevra raised her head to see Revered Giulliomocte approaching. Annoyance flashed through her before she controlled herself. If he intended to start another fight, she refused to be drawn into it.

"Prime Cassaline," Giulliomocte said, coming to a stop beside her. Ginnevra didn't like being loomed over. She rose to face him. Standing, she was slightly taller than he, but she didn't feel that gave her the advantage.

"Revered Giulliomocte," she replied. "What can I do for you?"

"I wanted to ask about your reaction this afternoon." Giulliomocte sounded as calm as ever, but there were tiny lines of worry at the corners of his eyes. "You seemed afraid of what might happen if that werewolf touched me."

"I was. Contact with the Bright One's creations can be dangerous. Some of them have a corrosive effect, or carry disease."

Giulliomocte's gaze flicked briefly to Eodan, who'd remained sitting. "You can't possibly believe that is true of werewolves."

Hot blood rushed to Ginnevra's cheeks. "Because I'm sleeping with one, is that it?"

"I have already warned you," Giulliomocte said, "of the dangers of the path you take. I see no reason to repeat myself, since you've made it clear you won't abjure the creature you've taken up with."

"I *am* sitting right here, Revered," Eodan said. He sounded amused, but he wasn't smiling, and his hands clasped together on his knees showed his knuckles were white.

Giulliomocte ignored him. "My point is that I don't believe the touch of a werewolf is dangerous, and I don't think you do, either. So I want to know what prompted you to intervene."

Ginnevra unclenched her fist and let out a long, slow breath. "Revered," she said, "those werewolves worship the Bright One, and if their dominus made an effort to reach you, it was surely because he has a plan for your destruction. I don't think it's unreasonable to take precautions."

"So it's not because you believe me so unworthy I am vulnerable to their corruption?" Giulliomocte's eyes narrowed, and his chin lifted in a defiant gesture.

Ginnevra blinked. "I don't believe you are unworthy at all. Why would you say that?"

"And yet you disregard my advice," Giulliomocte shot back. "You don't—"

"Ginnevra doesn't have to obey you blindly, Revered," Eodan said, getting slowly to his feet. "She has her own understanding of the Goddess's word."

"*You* don't speak the Goddess's name," Giulliomocte said. "Whatever your allegiance, you are still the Bright One's creation, and not deserving of her salvation."

Eodan took a step forward, his lips drawn back in a silent snarl. Ginnevra put herself between the two. "Enough," she said. "Revered, I've warned you before. I know how the Goddess feels about the werewolves who turn their backs on Her Bright Sister. You and I disagree about what that means, and I accept that you are acting in accordance with your beliefs. But if you attack Eodan, I *will* defend him, and to hell with your anointed rank."

Giulliomocte's chest heaved with the force of his agitated breathing. "Then it's as I feared," he said. "You don't believe I deserve this rank."

Ginnevra shook her head. "The Goddess gave you and

Hallowed Riccobene a sign revealing your new rank. The Blessed must agree, or she wouldn't have sent for you—or do you think she'd risk all our lives on this journey only to tell you you don't deserve to be Hallowed? And I have faith in the Blessed's word. It's true, I don't understand why the Goddess would elevate someone who disregards Her instructions, but I, unlike you, recognize that my understanding is limited." She drew in another deep breath, calming herself. "I will protect you with my life, Revered. I wouldn't do that if I believed you didn't deserve it."

Giulliomocte glared at Ginnevra. Then he turned on his heel and strode away.

Ginnevra watched him go, then unclenched her fists again and sighed. "It's occurred to me," she said, "that having one of the Hallowed opposed to seeing werewolves living in harmony with humans might postpone that dream indefinitely."

Eodan took her hand and made her look at him. "I don't know how you can treat him civilly."

"Neither do I." She put her arms around Eodan. "You're trembling."

"I'm still angry. I don't like being dismissed or scorned, and I hate seeing your faith challenged." Eodan held her close. "But it's passing. Ginnevra, how can the Goddess put up with his behavior?"

"She doesn't dictate our actions, beloved. She lets us choose, even if that means choosing wrongly. And no, I don't know what that means when it comes to Her highest-ranking servants. I hope the Blessed takes him to task, and that's all I can do." She released Eodan. "I'm going to make the rounds of the camp, and then I want sleep."

"It's a pity tents don't block sound," Eodan said with a smile, "because I can think of better things to do than sleep."

Ginnevra kissed him. "Something to look forward to when this journey is over."

She crossed the camp to the eastern picket line, where the horses were tethered in a makeshift corral and the wagons walled off the southeastern side of camp. She didn't speak to the sentries, just observed their alertness and their patrol pattern before walking the perimeter in a slow, measured path around the south side. The paladins on watch were stationed within sight of one another, and they acknowledged Ginnevra with a nod. It was nice to be part of a company again, however irregularly.

The moonless night sky blazed with stars, sharp-edged in the crisp winter air, and Ginnevra stopped for a moment to watch the distant specks. On this vast plain, with no mountains or forests to obscure the horizon, the sky felt like a bowl turned over on top of her, and she felt simultaneously stifled and on the verge of falling upward into the sky, rushing toward the stars as they grew brighter and larger. She blinked and looked away to dispel the fancy.

She resumed walking until she reached Usterchia at the western edge and paused again. This close to the new moon, her vision in darkness was almost as clear as in full daylight, but there wasn't anything to see, just the plains unrolling before them until they reached the distant hills.

"The stars are so close," Usterchia said, startling Ginnevra out of her reverie. "Close enough to touch."

Ginnevra was about to say it was an illusion when she realized Usterchia was right. Some of the bright specks of light drifted toward them, bobbing as if the air were water and they were floating corks. She took a step toward them. "They're beautiful."

Usterchia sheathed her sword and walked ahead of Ginnevra, who followed after a moment. The specks of light grew larger and brighter the closer Ginnevra came to them. Usterchia was close enough to the first to be able to touch it. Ginnevra hurried her pace. She didn't want to be left out of this encounter with the stars.

This close, it was clear the stars were silver-blue orbs twice the size of Usterchia's head, and they pulsed gently, as if they were breathing. The first one hovered just above Usterchia's shoulders. Slowly, Usterchia reached out to touch it.

As her fingers brushed the orb, it flashed a bright white light that made Ginnevra flinch and close her eyes. When she opened them, the orb had changed. A malevolent face flickered across its surface, its mouth stretching and opening and closing in a terrible, terrifying smile. Then it lunged, expanding in an instant to the size of a man.

Usterchia screamed as it engulfed her.

CHAPTER

SIXTEEN

U sterchia's scream was like a rush of ice water to Ginnevra's face, breaking through the fugue the things had put her in. Blue-white fire that burned cold coursed over the stocky paladin. It clung to her body even as she threw herself to the ground and rolled. Ginnevra batted at the flames and then snatched her hands away from the bone-chilling cold.

She heard shouting from behind her, but she didn't dare look away from the creatures. Several more drifted toward her and Usterchia, their malevolent features flickering through a range of terrible smiles. Ginnevra snarled and drew her sword. She put herself between them and the struggling Usterchia and laid two fingers on her grace. *"By Your grace I call the dark!"*

Flickering tongues of dark flame sprang up all along the length of her blade, making her eyes ache if she looked at them directly. Ginnevra shouted again, a wordless challenge, and sprang at the nearest creature. The orb expanded, stretching wider and taller than she was, and sped to meet her. Ginnevra's sword impaled it left of center, and she stumbled at the lack of resistance as the blade entered the immaterial form.

The creature's light flared bright for a moment, and then the black flame spread like ink across its body, pouring out from the sword to extinguish the blue fire. A high-pitched wail, sharp as a needle, pierced Ginnevra's ears. Then the thing shriveled in on itself and collapsed like a wilted flower, blue-white streaked with black.

Ginnevra had already taken aim at the next creature. This one was cannier, and dodged her blows. It grew thin tendrils of blue-white fire that groped for Ginnevra like a dozen whiplike arms. For every one she cut off, two more grew in its place. She settled into a defensive stance and watched its movements, counting. *One. Two. Three.* On *four* she thrust low in a feint and, when the creature dodged, spun and converted the thrust to a slash that cut diagonally across its body. Once more, the black fire spread, and the thing fell limp to the ground.

Ginnevra stopped to catch her breath. She was no longer fighting alone. Seven more paladins with black-limned swords challenged the creatures, driving their swords into immaterial bodies. She scanned the battlefield. No Eodan. That was good—this wasn't a battle for unarmed combat.

She raced to meet another of the creatures. It shrank in on itself and shot away backwards, away from her and the other paladins. Its companions followed, making streaks across the dark sky like shooting stars. Ginnevra watched, breathing heavily, until she was sure they'd all fled. Then she thrust her sword point-first into the hard ground. The tip penetrated about an inch, which was all she needed. The black fire bled down the length of the sword and flowed harmlessly into the earth until the blade once more shone silver.

She leaned on the sword for a moment after it was clear of the

Goddess's blessing. She had heard of those creatures, though she didn't remember what they were called. Their compulsion wasn't strong enough to override free will, so paladins weren't immune to it, but Ginnevra was angry at being fooled anyway. She and Usterchia—

She snatched up her sword and sheathed it. She'd forgotten Usterchia in the heat of battle. Turning, she surveyed the battlefield once more. Most of the other paladins were extinguishing their swords, but two crouched over a fallen form. Ginnevra ran to join them.

Usterchia's normally darkly tan complexion was frostbitten, pale and dry, the skin puckered around her eyes and mouth. She looked as if something had sucked all the moisture from her body. Pia looked up at Ginnevra, her eyes haunted. But her voice was steady as she said, "The berbenno killed her. I wasn't fast enough."

"None of us were, least of all me, and I was right beside her," Ginnevra said. "Don't take that guilt on yourself."

Pia nodded. "I don't think we lost anyone else. But—"

The howl of a wolf split the night. Ginnevra's head jerked up. "That's Eodan."

The sound had come from the far side of camp. Ginnevra took off running, her heart in her throat.

She came up against a cluster of the anointed at the far side of camp, Dedicates and acolytes clutching each other in mute terror. Past them, the confusion of battle raged, paladins holding their own against wolves whose pale fur gleamed in the starlight. At the center, one black-furred form battled the white wolf, both of them snarling and feinting and snapping.

Someone stepped up beside Ginnevra and raised one fist high in the air. "*By Your grace*—"

Ginnevra grabbed Giulliomocte and put a hand over his

mouth. "Don't you dare," she said. "What if it kills Eodan when he's in wolf form?"

Giulliomocte wrestled away from Ginnevra and turned on her. "If he's not evil, he will be protected."

The memory of a flash of white light at the sanctuary in Devoyenne struck Ginnevra. "Does that grace know the difference?"

Giulliomocte grimaced. "If you have faith—"

Another howl echoed across the plain. It was not Eodan's. Ginnevra turned, terrified that it meant the werewolves had triumphed, but instead the pack had broken away from the combat and was fleeing. Eodan didn't hesitate to follow. Ginnevra shouted his name, once, twice, and the third time put all her fear for him into the cry. That brought him to a halt.

They all watched the wolves run away until even the white wolf vanished into the darkness. Then the paladins sheathed their swords and set about gathering the bodies of the three wolves they'd killed. Eodan returned at a sedate pace, his head drooping as if in tiredness. Ginnevra had a feeling it was more than that.

"It's not about faith," she said, not looking at Giulliomocte. "You said it—he's still a werewolf, no matter what he believes or chooses. Maybe that makes him a monster so far as that grace goes. I'm sure to you that proves something. But what I just saw was a werewolf who turned on his own kind to protect you. And that proves something to *me*."

She walked forward to meet Eodan and ran her fingers through the thick fur of his ruff. "Are you injured?"

Eodan shook his head. He wasn't limping, and she didn't smell blood, so he wasn't pretending to be whole to keep her from coddling him. All around them, the paladins were spreading out through the camp, watching for a surprise second attack, tending to frightened horses. Ginnevra hadn't considered that the werewolves might have struck at the horses, dealing their party a secondary blow. The horses were fine, and nobody seemed injured, at least not severely so.

She walked with Eodan back to their tent, where he resumed his human shape. "That might have been a mistake," he said.

"What might?"

"Fighting in wolf form. I'm not sure I didn't frighten some of our people." He ducked inside the tent, and fabric rustled as he dressed.

"I didn't notice. I was too afraid. You haven't fought other werewolves since we've been together."

Eodan shifted the tent flap so he could look at her. "Afraid for me? I've fought and killed my own kind more times than I care to remember, Ginnevra."

"I know. I suppose it's more that it looks so vicious. And—" Ginnevra stopped speaking. "It's not rational," she added, though she'd been about to say *and it makes you look so much like an animal.*

Eodan sat in the tent doorway to put his boots on. "I'll check on everyone. I don't think there were injuries, but it's true they might fear me now. I want to remind them of who I really am."

"I want to talk to Buonnane. The werewolves almost certainly set the berbennos on us as a distraction." Ginnevra cursed under her breath. "I thought they'd wait a while longer before attacking."

"Which means this was another test." Eodan stood and took Ginnevra's hand. "Did we pass, or fail?"

"I'm not sure which would be worse," Ginnevra said.

BUONNANE MET Ginnevra and Eodan near the center of camp. The anointed, except for Giulliomocte, surrounded them in small groups, huddled together like sheep in a high wind and talking in low, urgent voices. Buonnane gave Eodan only the briefest glance before settling her gaze on Ginnevra.

"Usterchia is our only loss," she said. "We fought off the enemy on both sides, so in the cold, hard sense we had a victory. But losing any one of us is a terrible tragedy."

"I know," Ginnevra said. "I wish—she died right in front of me, and I'm having trouble not revisiting that. Wishing for a different outcome. And yes, I know that's unworthy," she went on as Buonnane opened her mouth to object. "I don't know why I didn't recognize the threat."

"Berbennos have an insidious compulsion. If you're close when you see them, it's already too late to resist." Buonnane let out a deep sigh. "The werewolves must have herded them into position before making their real attack on the far side of camp."

"Werewolves frequently use berbennos to herd animals where we can slaughter them," Eodan said.

"You could have mentioned that," Buonnane said sharply.

"I didn't think of that tactic being used against humans." Eodan sounded calm, not at all affected by Buonnane's aggressive words. "We consider—"

He stopped. When he didn't finish his sentence immediately, Ginnevra said, "What?"

Eodan shook his head. "Forgive my bluntness, Captain Buonnane, but werewolves consider humans the ultimate prey. We don't use anything against them but our own skill and cunning."

Buonnane's lips pursed, whitening around the edges. "Then how do you explain what just happened?" Her voice sounded steady enough, but Ginnevra's sharp hearing picked up the faint tremor in her words.

"In werewolf terms, what they did was dishonorable," Eodan said. "They should have raised a challenge directly rather than drawing some of the paladins away so the others would be more vulnerable. But it's what I saw among my people before I was driven out. The Bright One encourages Her followers to win at any cost, by any method available. She wants us to be perfectly obedient to her, which means turning our backs on our own traditions."

Buonnane's hand gripped her sword so tightly the tendons showed white through her tanned skin. "Werewolves don't stoop to subterfuge, even when it benefits them. They fight as one pack, and they don't leave their wounded behind."

"How do you know?" Ginnevra asked. Buonnane's musing tone of voice puzzled her. The captain sounded as if she were remembering rather than instructing.

Buonnane turned her gaze on Ginnevra. "I've fought were-wolves before," she said. She sounded casual, but her eyes were distant, as if she saw something else where Ginnevra stood.

"That's right," Eodan said. "But it means my knowledge of our enemies' tactics is limited to what I observed before I left. We will have to be on constant alert."

"Which is what they want." Ginnevra flexed her hands, remembering the feel of her sword's hilt and wishing she had an enemy to use the weapon against. "They want us tired and on edge. But it doesn't matter for tonight. We'll bury Usterchia in the morning and continue our travels, and pray for guidance."

Buonnane nodded once, curtly. "I'll see to the care of her body."

"And I'll walk the rounds again, make sure everyone is well."

Buonnane glanced at Eodan. She looked ready to speak, but in the end she just shook her head and walked away.

"I don't know what to make of her," Eodan said, "except she

clearly has first-hand experience with werewolves that probably influences her treatment of me. And explains her fear."

Ginnevra watched Buonnane walk away. "I almost like her, though I doubt that's something she cares about."

"No." Eodan nodded in agreement. "No, I get the sense she doesn't care what other people think of her. She reminds me of you in that way."

"Me?"

"You do what's right regardless of how it makes you look, and you don't let others' opinions of you sway you." Eodan put his arms around her waist and pulled her close. "Even when those opinions hurt."

"*Your* opinion matters," Ginnevra pointed out. She put her arms around him and rested her cheek against his shoulder.

"It matters, but if my opinion was counter to something you knew to be right, you wouldn't let it stop you." He was warm, a barrier against the chill wind rising from the north, and Ginnevra wished more than anything to retreat with him to their tent, not for sex, but for huddling up together for comfort.

"All right, that's true," she said. "So Buonnane and I have something in common. Maybe someday that will make a difference."

"You're the most optimistic person I know," Eodan said.

THERE WAS no time to wait on the rise of the dark moon to bury Usterchia. Instead, two paladins dug a grave in the twilight hour before dawn, and the party gathered at the graveside when the sun rose. Ginnevra listened with half her attention to Revered Giulliomocte's words. It felt wrong for a man to preside over the funeral of a paladin, and yet Ginnevra knew that wrong feeling was all her own. Usterchia's brother back in Fayonne was a Revered, and she would have seen no problem with a male Revered officiating. Ginnevra's disagreement with Giulliomocte was at the heart of her dissatisfaction, and it was an unworthy feeling.

Still, she couldn't help but be distracted by other thoughts, which tugged her attention away every time she wrenched herself back to the present. It wasn't possible that Ginnevra was the only person who wasn't completely comfortable with male anointed performing sacred rites. Probably Giulliomocte faced more prejudice than Ginnevra was aware of, and that could only be worse once he became Hallowed. That ought to inspire sympathy in her. But his treatment of Eodan only made her angry.

She closed her eyes and took a deep, calming breath. This was getting her nowhere. Once more she dragged her attention back to the service.

"...and we commend to You the spirit of Your servant Usterchia Zenarre, paladin in life, paladin in death," Giulliomocte was saying. His voice was calm and restful, with a commanding directness that Ginnevra would have found more soothing if she hadn't disliked him. "We ask that You grant her release from her vows in life, and the grace of Your presence upon her in death. Ever in Your name."

"Ever in Your name," everyone repeated. Ginnevra opened her eyes as the words passed her lips.

"We don't know where Usterchia's spirit is now," Giulliomocte said. "The Goddess teaches us not to aspire to heaven or hell, but to live each moment in a way She will admire in us. She also reminds us that our eternal rest is one of both perfect justice and perfect mercy, and when we pass the threshold of death, we will be content with our souls' disposition, knowing it is right."

Ginnevra focused on the canvas-wrapped bundle lying in the deep grave. The sight angered her. How content could Usterchia be with her paladin's life cut short? Ginnevra had never considered death in that light before, but now she wondered if dying in battle really was how she wanted to go. Granted, if she were protecting the innocent, she didn't think she'd begrudge an early death, but what if—

She clenched her teeth to hold back an angry hiss. Those thoughts verged on blasphemy. Not the wondering about death, but the idea that one fate was superior to another. You did the best you could in the time you had, and faith had to cover the rest. Thinking about "what if" was what the Bright One wanted. It was how she led humans astray. And Ginnevra could afford that kind of thinking even less now than usual.

Giulliomocte lowered himself to one knee at the head of the grave and bowed his head. "The Goddess's blessing through me be upon you, Usterchia. We gathered here today thank you for your service, and witness to hold your memory dear wherever paladins join together." He picked up a clod of earth and broke it apart in his hands, then scattered the dirt across Usterchia's body and the sword laid lengthwise atop it.

One by one, the paladins walked to the foot of the grave, knelt, and tossed in a handful of dirt. Ginnevra took her turn with the others, silently wishing Usterchia well. Finally, Buonnane cast in her handful and rose to her feet. Giulliomocte continued kneeling throughout, his head bowed and his lips moving in soundless prayer. Watching him, Ginnevra found her earlier resentment gone. For once, she wished they were friends enough that she could ask him what he'd prayed for.

Giulliomocte rose to his feet and clasped his hands before him. "May Your guidance work within all of us here today," he prayed, "and may we find the strength to continue this journey, ever in Your name."

Ginnevra again murmured the ritual words. There was a moment of silence. Giulliomocte stepped back from the grave. "Thank you for your participation," he said. "I haven't buried a paladin before, and I hope I won't again."

Buonnane nodded. "Let's finish this," she said, and three paladins picked up shovels and filled in the grave.

"Everyone else, prepare to leave," Ginnevra said.

She walked to Buonnane's side and watched the white bundle disappear under the dark earth. "How long did you serve with her?" she asked.

Buonnane didn't look her way. "Seven years. Two before I became captain. She was a real pain in my ass."

Startled, Ginnevra said, "You seemed amicable enough."

"She was a good friend. But anyone who serves with you before you are their captain—they've seen you at your worst, and they know how to needle you even if they mostly show respect." Buonnane tilted her head back to stare at the sky. Gray clouds hid the rising sun, filling the air with a pearly light that fit the ceremony.

"I've never served under a captain who'd been one of my sisters."

"It's not common. I was given command of this company, and Usterchia and Pia transferred in a few months later. I'm not sure whether the General thought I needed humility, or they did." Buonnane's lips curved in a sideways smile.

Ginnevra chuckled. "That must be an interesting challenge." She gazed at the southern horizon, misty with distance—and there, at the limits of her vision, something white moved. She grabbed Buonnane's arm. "Look there!"

Buonnane wrenched away. "Look at what?"

Ginnevra pointed. "It's right there. The karkadann."

Buonnane shielded her eyes. "Right where?"

"Right *there*." Ginnevra grabbed Buonnane's shoulder and turned her. In the distance, the karkadann stopped running. Ginnevra could feel its attention on her, burning like a coal.

"I don't see anything, Prime Cassaline." Buonnane's voice was as cold as the air. "And I don't think you should stoop to deception—"

"What deception? Captain, what possible benefit is there to me to lie about this?" Ginnevra pointed again. "It's standing right there!"

Buonnane turned to face Ginnevra. "I believe *you* believe you see it," she said, not very sincerely to Ginnevra's ears. "But why would the creature only show itself to you?"

"I don't know," Ginnevra said. Her feeling of accord with the captain vanished. "I'd never even heard of it before this trip. You tell me why."

Buonnane looked again into the distance. The karkadann was still there, motionless, but when Ginnevra looked that way, it started moving again. "I don't know," the captain said. "A warning? Or maybe—"

The karkadann vanished over the horizon. "Maybe, what?" Ginnevra demanded.

"Maybe your association with monsters has made you sensitive to them," Buonnane said. "I don't know. And don't rip up at me about your werewolf lover. I didn't say he was evil, but even you can't deny his nature."

"At least I'm not so terrified of him I'm irrational," Ginnevra shot back.

Buonnane's eyes narrowed. "Are you accusing me of cowardice?"

"No. You don't let your fear rule you. But you also don't let the evidence change your mind. What the hell does Eodan have to do to prove he's an ally?"

Buonnane glared at Ginnevra. "He's a monster. He can't change that." She turned on her heel and walked away.

Ginnevra unclenched her fists and let out a deep breath. When her heart rate returned to normal, she crossed the camp to where Dauntless waited to be saddled. Buonnane. Giulliomocte. She couldn't force anyone to change, and it was wrong to try. But it didn't stop her wanting to grab some people by the ears and shake sense into them.

SEVENTEEN

They traveled all day in silence, even the young anointed in the wagon, whose cheerfulness had been blunted by Usterchia's death. Pearly gray skies threatened snow, but none fell. A few travelers passed them going north, well-bundled against the cold. They eyed the paladins and the banners suspiciously, but otherwise didn't shy away or walk wide around their caravan. Ginnevra ignored them. None of them were armed with anything that could hurt a paladin, and no one could reach the anointed to hurt them.

She didn't speak to Buonnane, either. Her earlier anger had faded, leaving her feeling low in spirits. She would almost have welcomed a monster attack. It would give her something to do that wasn't dwelling on the long, silent road ahead.

By evening, the clouds had grown heavier, and Ginnevra called an early halt. They were halfway through setting up camp when snow started falling, tiny white specks that burned cold where they touched exposed skin. Ginnevra walked the perimeter of the camp, mentally cursing. This snow would give perfect cover to those white wolves.

She neared where Buonnane was giving instructions to a pair of sentries. "Keep moving, and stay alert," she was saying. "We'll have to pull everyone in if the storm grows bad enough, but until then, we stand watch."

Ginnevra saw Giulliomocte approaching from the other direction. Just what she needed, another antagonistic encounter. She put on a pleasant expression and waited for him to draw near.

The sentries saluted and walked away. Buonnane said, "The watches are all set, prime, and—"

"Captain. Prime Cassaline," Giulliomocte said. Specks of snow clung to his thinning hair, and he huddled into his cloak as if the storm were a raging fury. "I believe there is something we Revereds can do to help."

"I thought weather control was the province of the Hallowed," Buonnane said.

"It is. I had something more localized in mind." Giulliomocte turned his attention on Ginnevra. "It is a grace more usually performed for a single person, and with only three of us, it will not be as potent as possible. But we can raise a shield that will protect the camp if something monstrous tries to cross it."

Ginnevra blinked in surprise. "You can do that? Why have we not used that grace every night?"

Giulliomocte grimaced. "It demands perfect harmony among the invokers, and I fear we haven't had that. But I have spoken with Marsillia and Tomascio, and we're enough in accord after last night's attacks that I think it will be possible."

"Then let's do it," Ginnevra said. "What do you need from us?"

"Station the sentries beyond where they would otherwise patrol, but within sight of one another—as much as that's possible in this storm. That will give us a mark to aim for." Giulliomocte wiped snowflakes from his eyes. "And if one of you could identify the center of camp, we will invoke the grace from there."

Ginnevra and Buonnane exchanged glances. "I'll handle the sentries," Buonnane said.

"Revered, come with me," Ginnevra said.

They hurried through the camp, kicking the fine flakes with every step. "How exact do you need me to be?" Ginnevra asked. "I can locate the true center if you're willing to wait."

"It just needs to be close." Giulliomocte ran fingers through his hair, shaking flakes free before they could melt. "You don't have faith in me, do you?"

"That's the second time you've said something like that." Ginnevra came to a stop between two tents. "I believe you are deserving of your rank. Our disagreement doesn't have anything to do with that."

"If you truly believed, you would take my counsel seriously." Giulliomocte faced her, his eyes shadowed. "You would not cling to your own understanding."

Ginnevra ground her back teeth together to keep a hot reply from emerging. When she regained control, she said, "The Goddess teaches us to gain knowledge for ourselves, Revered. You know that. I've heard Her speak, and I believed what She told me. Why should I subordinate my knowledge to yours?"

"Because I have heard Her voice as well," Giulliomocte replied.

Ginnevra's mouth fell open. "That's—" She closed her mouth on the word *impossible*. She was speaking to one of the Goddess's anointed, after all. "Then you're saying She told you to treat Eodan like a monster."

"She instructed me in the truth of his nature, and warned me not to be swayed by his appearance." Giulliomocte's voice was calm, but his eyes were restless, his gaze darting in all directions as if he feared being overheard. "I don't deny he has turned his back on his creator. But the Goddess made it clear to me that this does not make him human, and he does not deserve full fellowship with us."

His words struck Ginnevra like a knife to the belly, a low blow that bypassed all her defenses. Maybe she was wrong; maybe she had misunderstood the Goddess's words. "But I—" She swallowed. "You can't be right. I know what I heard."

"You heard what you wanted to hear." Giulliomocte shook his head. "I understand. You fell in love with someone who appears human, and that's natural. But humans and werewolves are not meant to mix."

Ginnevra shook her head. "No. I don't believe you." She uncurled her fists. "This is the center. I'll get the other Revereds." She turned and ran.

Finding Orselle took some time, but eventually she located him with the Dedicates, laughing and joking as they'd done before the fire—had it really only been a few days ago? It felt like an eternity. Pratese was in her tent, meditating, or sleeping upright, Ginnevra couldn't tell. When she had sent them on their way, she returned to her own tent. With all those paladins, they didn't need her, and Ginnevra didn't care about seeing this grace that required those three Revereds to work in harmony.

The tent was empty. A momentary flash of fear shot through her before she reminded herself that Eodan was in no danger, not from monsters and not from Giulliomocte, no matter what he said about Eodan's race. Ginnevra sat with her arms wrapped around her knees and shook, not from cold but from fear. She couldn't have misunderstood. And if she hadn't, what did that mean about Giulliomocte's revelation?

She heard again in memory the Goddess's words, which she had never forgotten: *You dared much, and in daring, you opened a door even I thought closed forever. Let your compassion guide you, and your choices will be endless.* Loving, encouraging words, but now that Ginnevra considered it, they said nothing about whether her attachment to a werewolf was acceptable. Maybe the Goddess had simply meant her to go on searching for truth. Maybe She had only intended Ginnevra to reveal the true nature of the werewolves. Which meant Ginnevra's love for Eodan might be wrong, after all.

She squeezed her eyes shut and bowed her head. "I thought I understood," she whispered. "The Blessed herself believed You are in favor of my union with Eodan. Now Your voice tells someone else the opposite. And I don't know what to do or who to believe."

No one responded. She hadn't expected a response, so this didn't dishearten her. She felt nothing but the cold, heard only the rising wind that would likely turn into a full-fledged storm by midnight. This grace Giulliomocte and the others were invoking might keep them alive, though Ginnevra couldn't believe the werewolves were immune to the storm either. Probably the night would pass uneventfully.

She sat, hugging her knees, until her shivering stopped. Then she left the tent and walked through the storm to where the pickets stood. Zana saluted her as she approached. "Look at that."

Ginnevra looked. About ten feet from Zana, blue light glowed, radiant against the dark gray of the blowing snow. It spread out like a fence in both directions, disappearing into the night. "It doesn't stop the snow," Zana said, "and nothing's tried to breach it, so I don't know if it does what the Revereds claim. But it sure looks like something a monster would hate."

Ginnevra nodded. "What is it supposed to do?"

"Make a really big noise and a lightning bolt if something monstrous crosses it." Zana grinned a bloodthirsty grin. "Since we'll have to stand down if this mess gets any worse, that will be a blessing."

Ginnevra still wasn't sure they were in any danger that night, but that was no reason to relax their vigilance. "I'll take a shift later. Safe watch to you."

Zana returned her salute, but her gaze scanning the landscape never faltered.

Buonnane turned down Ginnevra's offer to stand watch. "The Revereds' barrier is sufficiently powerful that I don't think it's necessary to post sentries once the storm is on us fully. If that's all right with you."

"You're the captain," Ginnevra snapped. Buonnane's words hadn't been overtly hostile, but being on edge had Ginnevra ready to assume the worst. "I'll see you in the morning."

When she returned to her tent, Eodan was there, removing his boots. "That was an amazing sight," he said. "I don't know if that invocation was more impressive in itself, or because Giulliomocte and Pratese managed not to snap at each other."

"I'm sure it was spectacular."

Eodan stopped with one boot in his hand. "What's wrong?"

"Nothing. I mean, it's not important."

"Ginnevra, you only ever sound like that when it *is* important. Talk to me." Eodan scooted over and put a hand on her shoulder. The gentle gesture brought tears to Ginnevra's eyes. She blinked away the hot wetness and turned so he wouldn't see her face.

"The Goddess has spoken to Revered Giulliomocte," she said. "Everything he's said...it all came from Her."

Eodan's hand closed tightly on her shoulder. "What are you saying?"

"I don't know. I mean, I'm saying I don't know what to think. I don't believe you're a monster. You can't be. And yet—"

"Ginnevra, you're not going to let someone else tell you what to believe, are you? Because I can't believe that's how your religion works." Eodan drew her into his embrace. "Though I don't know what happens when two religious authorities are at odds."

"I would have sworn that couldn't happen." Ginnevra clung to him as if that would stop him being torn from her. "Maybe he's lying. No, I don't believe that."

"Maybe he's mistaken."

"I don't think so. The Goddess's voice is unmistakable." She buried her face in his neck and breathed in the scent of him, the rich werewolf musk she loved. "Maybe *I* was mistaken. The Goddess didn't actually say she approved of our love. Just that I'd followed my sense of what was right, and that my compassion should guide me. But it felt—" She held him tighter. "No. I refuse to believe there's anything wrong with my loving you. Giuliomocte misunderstood somehow, that's all."

Eodan brushed hair away from her forehead and kissed it. "I was afraid you would tell me to leave."

"I will *never* do that."

"Not even if your Goddess commanded it?"

Ginnevra hesitated. "She wouldn't do that," she said, but she wasn't convinced.

Eodan kissed her lips, a warm, firm, comforting kiss. "No, She wouldn't," he said. "Do you know how I can be sure?"

"How?"

"Because that would set you on a chosen path, and that's counter to everything you've taught me about the Dark Lady." He kissed her again, more deeply. "She doesn't command Her servants, she invites and challenges. You follow Her will unflinchingly, and that above all tells me you are worthy in Her sight."

His words filled her heart with peace. "Thank you. I wish everyone saw things as clearly as you do."

"Being on the outside of your faith means my understanding is different." Eodan slipped his hands beneath Ginnevra's shirt. "Fair warning," he said. "This storm's howls block out all other sound, this tent is cold, and I intend to have my way with you. So if you'd rather not, now would be a good time—"

"Shut up," Ginnevra said, and pulled him down to lie beside her.

THE STORM HOWLED itself out sometime before dawn. The lack of noise woke Ginnevra, who rose and dressed, cursing the cold.

"Do you see what I mean about cuddling up with a warm, wonderful mate in winter?" Eodan said as he pulled his shirt over his head.

"You didn't say how awful it was to have to leave the warm nest." Ginnevra shoved her feet into her boots and wrapped herself in her cloak. "I hope the snow isn't too deep. I don't want to have to dig the wagons out."

The snow had blown in drifts against the wagons, but to her surprise, the drifts weren't very deep. "The wind kept them from piling up," Eodan said. "We should be able to leave after dawn."

Ginnevra walked the perimeter, speaking to the sentries. No monsters had attacked in the night. No one had disappeared into the snow, or fallen victim to frostbite. The glowing blue curtain, or fence, hadn't faded, but when Buonnane approached Ginnevra, it vanished as if it had never been.

"Even the horses are fine," Buonnane said by way of greeting. "For all it was snowy, it was a peaceful night. Did you rest well?"

Ginnevra managed not to blush. "I did. We should move on."

"It will take an hour or so to break camp."

Ginnevra nodded. She was about to move on when Buonnane said, "Revered Giulliomocte had a word with me last night."

Her words chilled Ginnevra. "Oh?" she said, trying for a light tone. "About what?"

"About the revelations he's had with regard to your werewolf lover." Buonnane's voice was neutral, but she wouldn't meet Ginnevra's eyes.

Ginnevra pulled her cloak tighter. "And I suppose you want Eodan gone. You could use his name, you know. It's not any harder than yours or mine."

Buonnane shook her head. "I know what the Revered says he's heard from the Goddess. The werewolf is a monster, and nothing will change that."

"Which is what you told me. Forgive me if I'm not thrilled to hear it again."

"It's not like I believe I can change your mind." Buonnane still wasn't looking at Ginnevra. Her gloved fingers flexed in the cold. "But I didn't like what the Revered had to say."

Startled, Ginnevra took a step backward. "I don't understand."

Buonnane's head lifted. "I'm never going to accept a werewolf into my company," she said. "But the Revered all but came right out and asked me to banish him. Eodan." She said Eodan's name quickly, as if it tasted bad and she wanted it gone immediately. "And Revered or no, I don't let any anointed except the Blessed herself tell me what to do."

"Of course not," Ginnevra said. She managed not to add *particularly a man.*

Buonnane sighed. She tilted her head back to look at the sky, where high gray clouds scudded along in a distant wind. "Eodan fought beside us. Fought against his own kind. I'm not saying that's enough to make me love him, but I'm no fool. Either he's playing a very deep game, which I doubt, or he really is committed to leaving the Bright One behind. And I can respect that."

She sounded less antagonistic than Ginnevra had ever heard her. Impulsively, Ginnevra said, "What happened? With the werewolves? Before, I mean."

Still with her chin tilted back, Buonnane said, "Nothing good. And that's all I will ever say on the subject, prime."

"Understood." It was true; she didn't want to intrude on Buonnane's past if it didn't affect her. She might make a case for it actually affecting her, given that Buonnane's experiences with werewolves had a direct impact on the captain's current antagonism toward Eodan. But Ginnevra didn't think that was the case. Buonnane hadn't let fear interfere with doing the right thing, and Ginnevra respected that.

As if the storm had chased the monsters away, they had two days of uneventful travel. The brisk, high wind had blown the last of the clouds away the day after the storm, and from then the sky was as bright and blue as if storms were a thing of myth. The light snow, powder-fine, looked impassable until they stepped into it and discovered it scattered easily. Even the rutted road was less difficult to travel, though the ruts were still deep and frozen hard. Ginnevra still didn't feel warm, but the air on her exposed face didn't cut quite so sharply as it had before.

Ginnevra took her turn at sentry duty the first night, ignoring Buonnane's skeptical glance that said it wasn't something a prime should do. Ginnevra took the opportunity to assess each of the paladins, observe their habits and alertness. She found nothing to complain about, which was what she'd expected. Better, she saw no fear in any of them, something that might have been reasonable after Usterchia's death. Fear was one thing; letting it rule you was another.

That first night, they fought off a pack of krokottas easily, a battle that worried Ginnevra. The monsters were quick to attack, but they didn't conceal their presence well and they fled far sooner than they should have. It was another test by the were-wolves, but Ginnevra couldn't see what Cennfalad could have learned by it. They redoubled their vigilance, but no more attacks came that night.

They came within sight of Lake Salvectus late the following day. It lay at the bottom of a crease in the plains, a broad valley dotted with dark green pine trees that grew more thickly together close to the lake shore. The lake itself was visible only as glints of blue-gray between the trees until the road veered west, away from the river. On the western side of the lake, the trees thinned out, revealing the shoreline. Tiny houses dotted the shore, with docks extending into the water where drab fishing boats were moored.

Buonnane gestured the others to halt, an abrupt motion that startled Ginnevra. "What is it, captain?"

"No smoke," Buonnane said. "And no movement."

Her words jolted Ginnevra out of the dull tiredness she had been riding in. "I'll ride ahead with some of the paladins. If some-thing is wrong—"

"We shouldn't separate the party." Buonnane's gaze was still fixed on the distant settlement.

"We also shouldn't take the Dedicates and acolytes into potential danger. Set outriders to watch the woods, in case some-thing is waiting to attack, and we'll stay within sight." Ginnevra didn't wait for Buonnane's assent.

She and five other paladins rode into the valley, watching for trouble. Either the storm had not struck here with such force, or the constantly blowing winds had carried away most of the light, drifting snow, but the road was clear and unmarked by tracks. If something had come upon this settlement, it had not used the road.

Ginnevra observed the houses as they drew nearer. Despite their small size, they were well-built of pine logs smeared with pitch around the cracks and corners. They even had small glass windows, suggesting the settlers were wealthier than Ginnevra would have assumed of anyone living in the middle of nowhere. The cabins would be snug all winter, warm and secure—except Buonnane was right, and no smoke rose from the compact chimneys.

She slowed Dauntless as they approached, her unease growing. What remained of the snow still showed no footprints or animal tracks, not even the trails that would mean the settlers had all left their homes for... where, exactly?

"Spread out," she commanded, and the paladins all headed in different directions, surrounding the settlement. Ginnevra guided Dauntless toward the nearest house. It was close to the water's edge, where the icy wavelets lapped the shore. A dock extended from near the front of the house, and a fishing boat bobbed at the far end. The scene was so tranquil it set the hair on Ginnevra's neck rising.

Piles of seaweed fetched up around the dock where it met the shore, moving slightly with the water. Ginnevra dismounted and walked toward the house. Its front door was battered with long cuts carved into the wood—no. Scratches. Deep ones.

Ginnevra dropped Dauntless' reins and broke into a run. There in front of the house, the snow was trampled with footprints Ginnevra didn't stop to examine. She rushed up the three steps to the front door and pounded on it, then flung it open without waiting for a response.

The house was a single room with a ladder going up to a loft. No one was there, but something had torn through it, upending furniture, smashing crockery, scattering food across the floor. Ginnevra scanned the room for hiding places, like an overturned table, and saw nowhere anyone might hide. Her gaze fell on the ladder leading up to the loft, which was in shadow.

"Anyone there?" she called out.

No response. She heard no movement from the loft. Cursing silently, she hooked her sword belt over one shoulder and climbed the ladder, then lifted her sword so it extended past where she could see. Nothing attacked.

She climbed the last few rungs and peered over the edge. There was a single thin mattress on the floor, undisturbed. The sight unnerved Ginnevra as the disorder below had not. Again, there was nowhere for anyone to hide. She descended the ladder and left the house.

She again scanned the shoreline. Footprints, leading from the house to the shore. Her gaze landed on the seaweed piled against the dock. The footprints—

Ginnevra gasped and ran to the dock, falling to her knees beside the pile she now recognized not as seaweed—seaweed in a lake?—but as a body. The man lay half in, half out of the water, his face beneath the lake's surface. Ginnevra dragged him out and turned him over. His face was pallid and bloated, but drowning hadn't killed him; something had torn through his chest and stomach, exposing his intestines and staining his shirt black with blood. The water had washed away most of the gore, and his slashed skin looked almost translucent at the edges of the cuts.

Footsteps sounded behind Ginnevra, and she rose, drawing

her sword. But it was Zana, whose blade was also bare. "I found bodies," she said. "Five bodies, in one of the houses."

"This one ran," Ginnevra said, pointing at the dead man. "Did yours look the same?"

Zana nodded. She looked ill.

Ginnevra glanced down at the body again. "Werewolves."

CHAPTER

EIGHTEEN

T hey searched the settlement and the nearby forest thoroughly before summoning the rest of the party. They found no survivors. The werewolves were long gone, judging by how little smell they had left behind. Twenty-two victims, by final count, four of them children. The sight of the small bodies sent two of the acolytes and Serenna out of the wagon to vomit. Ginnevra didn't blame them.

She herself felt nothing but cold fury. She had assumed, wrongly, that their party was Cennfalad's only target. From her own observations and what little Eodan had said about werewolf culture, she had also believed werewolves wouldn't attack helpless human prey. Now she wished she'd cut off Cennfalad's head at the ferry, and to hell with the consequences. He had *dared* to slaughter innocents!

The paladins gathered the bodies and laid them out in rows behind the settlement. Ginnevra watched the grisly parade with her fists clenched. She saw Eodan go past with a body in his arms and said to Buonnane, who stood beside her, "It's not his fault."

Buonnane said nothing. Ginnevra glanced at her and saw tears streaking the grim captain's face. She looked to be in the grip of memory, and Ginnevra decided not to push.

Finally, when the last body had been placed, Buonnane said, "We don't have time to bury them. It will have to be funeral pyres. Goddess have mercy."

"They're past caring what happens to their bodies," Ginnevra said.

"I was thinking of us," Buonnane said. "Our sisters will find a renewed dedication in all this, but the anointed don't see violence on this scale. It concerns me that they might be demoralized or afraid. Which was probably what that bastard had in mind."

"We'll need the funeral service to address that." Ginnevra dug at a frozen tuft of grass with her toe. "I'll discuss it with Revered Giulliomocte."

"I'll do that," Buonnane said. "We don't need increased hostility, and he probably won't pass up the opportunity to remind you werewolves are monsters."

"I wouldn't retaliate," Ginnevra said, stung.

"No, you wouldn't." To her surprise, Buonnane smiled. "You have a prime's discipline in the face of antagonism. I would have punched him days ago."

"He's doing what he believes is right." Ginnevra wasn't sure why she cared about defending Giulliomocte, except that she still had no reason to believe he was lying about hearing the Goddess's words.

"And so are you." The smile disappeared. "I'll talk to the Revered, if you'll arrange for setting up camp."

Ginnevra nodded and walked away. She was sure she would never understand Buonnane, but if the captain's tolerance outweighed her antagonism, Ginnevra would take that as a victory.

The paladins tore apart the cabins with the wagon drivers' help while Ginnevra directed the anointed in setting up camp. They had all been in agreement that the cabins needed to come down, given how many of them had been the site of gruesome murder, and it was easier to use their logs for the funeral pyres than cut down trees. Ginnevra pitched her own tent with Serenna's help. Lost in her own thoughts, she almost didn't hear Serenna say, "Prime Cassaline?"

"Yes? I'm sorry, Serenna, did you say something?"

"I just asked if paladins see a lot of people killed."

Ginnevra observed the girl closely. Her lips were pinched tight as if she were suppressing tears. "No, not really. We kill monsters to prevent human death. But it's true, sometimes we get there too late."

Serenna nodded. "I'm not sure I'm fit to be a paladin. I threw up when I saw the bodies, and now I can't stop crying."

Ginnevra steadied one of the tent poles. "I threw up when I saw my first murdered body, too."

Serenna stared at her. "*You*, prime? But you didn't even flinch when they carried the bodies out."

"You get used to death in this calling. I don't know if that's good or bad. Good, I think, because it means I'm able to endure terrible sights for the sake of helping others." Ginnevra waited for Serenna to look at her, then continued, "How did it make you feel, knowing that those people had been killed by monsters?"

Serenna thought about it. "Angry. It was so unfair, those people dying because werewolves wanted to make us suffer—that's how it went, isn't it?"

"That, and I think their dominus enjoys killing. I think he likes terrifying and hurting humans. And yes, it is unfair. So what do you want to do about it?"

Serenna's chin firmed up. "Stop them ever doing that again."

"And that," Ginnevra said, "is the response of a paladin. Hold to that, and if you still feel that way at the end of this journey, we'll talk again."

"All right." Serenna's worried expression faded, and she smiled.

When camp was set, and the acolytes and Dedicates had begun preparing a meal, Ginnevra checked on the progress of the funeral pyres. Most of the foundations were laid, and more logs lay nearby for the rest. Eodan saw Ginnevra and came to meet her. "We'll be ready in the morning," he said. The setting sun cast his features into shadow, but Ginnevra thought he would have looked weary even without the odd light.

"Are you all right?" she said.

Eodan shook his head minutely. "Maybe I shouldn't have helped. Some of them walk wary around me, and I see the looks the paladins give each other when they think I don't notice. I'm a reminder of what happened here."

"They know you weren't responsible. They're just..." Ginnevra's words trailed off. Reassurances meant nothing when they were surrounded by the werewolves' victims. "They won't blame you," she finished, feeling foolish.

"I wish I'd been able to kill Cennfalad when the werewolves attacked the other night." Eodan's weary look gave way to anger. "He's fast. Vicious. And it's been a while since I fought another of my kind. If I'd won—"

"No dwelling on might-have-beens, right?" Ginnevra squeezed his hand. "I know how you feel. But we can only move forward, and take advantage of the next opportunity."

Eodan shrugged. "That's not as comforting as I'm sure you'd like it to be." He sighed, and put his arms around her. "I'm not even sure things will look better in the morning. Not when the morning promises a mass funeral."

Ginnevra couldn't think of anything to say to that. Teasing him about his innate pessimism felt wrong, and he was right—no reminders of the Goddess's teachings could make this better. So she held him, and prayed silently for the chance to prevent the werewolves from doing this to anyone else.

THEY ROSE before dawn to light the pyres. Giulliomocte led them in the standard service, the one not reserved for paladins or anointed. Ginnevra stood with her sisters and sang the funeral hymn, letting the song fill her chest and fly away into the sky. With seventeen paladins, they had enough voices to perform the full hymn, and the four-part harmony echoed across the lake. The song took nearly ten minutes, but no one said anything about wasting time better spent getting on the road.

When the music died away, Giulliomocte directed Orselle and Pratese to positions on either side of him, facing the ten pyres. "We commend your spirits to the Dark Lady's protection," he said, his voice carrying far in the still air. "May this place once more be one of peace. Goddess, we pray You will welcome these your servants home, ever in Your name."

A ragged murmuring chorus sounded. Giulliomocte raised his grace high. "*By Your grace the fire burns bright,*" he said along with Pratese and Orselle. Brilliant yellow fire streaked from the three Revereds' fists to strike the three nearest pyres. They blazed with columns of bright flame that gave off no smoke, but enough heat that they warmed Ginnevra's face despite her distance from the pyres.

The Revereds repeated their invocations twice more, and then Giulliomocte lit the final pyre. The first pyres were already half-consumed with flame, the bodies obscured by light, but as hot as they were, Ginnevra thought they should have felt much hotter. Certainly Giulliomocte should not have been able to stand as close to the flames as he was. Resentment flashed through her, a brief irritation that she and Giulliomocte were at odds. The first male Hallowed—she had so many questions for him, and no way to ask those questions without getting into yet another argument.

She didn't move when the rest of the paladins dispersed, but stood watching the party members, though she wasn't sure what she expected to see. Eodan stood to one side, his hands clasped loosely behind his back, his head bowed in thought or prayer. Two of the Dedicates walked toward him, deep in conversation. When they drew near where he stood, their steps slowed, and they walked wide around him, shielding their mouths in an attempt to speak privately. Ginnevra's acute hearing, though, picked up the words *He's just biding his time before attacking* and the other's response *I'll wager he told those werewolves where to find this place.*

She was in motion before she made the conscious decision to move. In a few long, angry strides, she had passed the Dedicates and blocked their path. "If you're concerned about the allegiances of any of our group, you bring it to me," she snarled. "You don't whisper allegations and you don't keep your suppositions to yourselves."

The two Dedicates cringed at her sudden attack, but after that first reaction, one of them—Ginnevra recognized him as one of Pratese's toadies—stood up straight and said, "That was a private conversation, Prime Cassaline."

"No, that was slander you didn't have the sense to discuss privately," Ginnevra said. "Because if I could hear it, Eodan certainly could, and I'm damn sure you wanted him to hear those whispers. I am *disgusted* with the two of you. You have no basis for your accusations, and you know it, or you'd have brought it up with Revered Pratese if no one else. Instead you indulged your baser instincts by suggesting that someone who has put his life in danger protecting you is complicit with our enemy because of his race."

The Dedicate recoiled, but defiantly said, "We're not the only ones who think having a werewolf in our group is bad luck. You can't tell us what to think."

"Bad luck?" Ginnevra stepped closer and lowered her voice. "We don't believe in luck, Dedicate. That's the province of the Bright One. Do I need to see you disciplined for spreading false doctrine?"

The Dedicate blanched. "I didn't—not bad luck, I meant—"

"Come with me," Ginnevra said, snapping her fingers in a peremptory gesture and jerking her head in the direction of the Revereds.

The three Revereds stood near one of the pyres, talking quietly. Ginnevra heard enough to establish it was ordinary conversation and not anointed business she shouldn't barge in on, though at the moment she was too angry to care. "Revered Giulliomocte," she said. "What have you told these anointed about Eodan?"

Giullomocte's expression changed from polite to wary. "What I have told you. That the werewolves who turn their backs on their creator may not be our enemies, but are still not equal to humans. I hope you don't intend to challenge me on my right to instruct those in my charge?"

"Our disagreement doesn't mean I disrespect your rank, as I've said." Ginnevra grabbed the Dedicate by the shoulder and towed him forward. "But if you've stooped to suggesting that Eodan betrayed us, or that he is in league with the werewolves—

well, that is paladin business, and you and I are going to have a problem."

The wary look became confused. "Of course not," Giulliomocte said. "Your companion is enemy to the werewolves who killed these people. My opposition to him is not on those grounds." He stepped forward to address the Dedicate, who now looked terrified. "What made you believe such a thing?"

The Dedicate nervously licked his dry lips. "I—it seemed obvious, Revered. Why else would the werewolves have known to attack this settlement?"

"They need no reason other than their desire to hurt and terrorize the Dark Lady's creations." Giulliomocte frowned. "And you came to this idea on your own?"

"I—yes," the Dedicate stammered. "I mean, it's just what you've been saying, that werewolves aren't human. So it makes sense they would side with their own kind."

"That's not what I—" Giulliomocte caught Ginnevra's glare and stopped speaking. He looked like a man wrestling with a problem. "I see I should be clearer in my preaching," he finally ground out. "My apologies, prime, for the misunderstanding."

"I accept your apology. I know how easy it is to make mistakes." Ginnevra released the Dedicate, who cringed from her. "But I think you and I should talk privately."

She walked with Giulliomocte along the lake shore, away from the pyres. When she judged they were outside even the most sensitive paladin's range of hearing, she said, "Is it really necessary for you to harp on Eodan's monstrous nature? Because if one young man came to the wrong conclusion, there have to be others who have as well."

"I'm not going to conceal the truth, prime." Giulliomocte's gaze was fixed on his boots, which kicked small stones out of his path.

"This isn't about concealing truth. It's about choosing what you focus on." Ginnevra came to a stop, forcing Giulliomocte to stop as well. "I have to get you safely to Abraciabene. That can't happen if our party is at odds. We have to trust each other. And you know Eodan won't betray us."

"It's my duty to ensure the anointed aren't led astray. I don't believe in obscuring what the Goddess teaches for the sake of worldly concerns." Now he lifted his head and stared past her at the distant tree line. Ginnevra gritted her teeth.

"I'm sorry, Revered," she said when she had control of her anger, "but I have to ask you to watch what you say about Eodan. There have got to be other things the Goddess wants you to preach. Save your opposition to Eodan until we reach civilization."

"And if I don't?" Now Giulliomocte raised his head. To Ginnevra's surprise, he didn't look belligerent, just resolved. "There isn't anything you can do to me, prime."

"I can ask for a judgment," Ginnevra said. "The Goddess can weigh in on our situation. It will fracture our party more than it already is, and it will call your new rank into question. That will happen even if the Goddess backs you. Is that what you want? Because if you continue to sow dissension, that's what I will do."

"You wouldn't dare."

"Revered Giulliomocte, we are as far from civilization as it's possible to be and still remain in the Lordagne. I am responsible for the safety of thirty-two people, thirty of whom have nothing to do with our argument. I *will* bring all of us to Abraciabene safely and I *will* do this with or without your help." Ginnevra stared him down. "I'm a paladin, Revered. We do the hard things so you don't have to. You can do whatever you like so long as you don't get in my way."

Giulliomocte's chest heaved with his rapid, angry breathing.

"You'll regret this," he said. "The Goddess's word is clear. If you stand in her way, you won't be a paladin for long."

"That's the chance I take every day, Revered. Every day, with every choice." Ginnevra's blood sang with righteous anger. She'd never felt so perfectly in tune with the Goddess in her life.

The Revered looked away. "I will do what I can to keep our party together," he said. "But I won't pretend I don't know what I know. You would be better off casting away the werewolf."

"His name is Eodan," Ginnevra said. She turned on her heel and walked away.

She didn't get so far ahead of Giulliomocte that she wasn't aware of his safety, but she led him by enough that he could feel solitary, if that was what he wanted. She knew she hadn't won that battle—Giulliomocte had the Goddess's voice in his head, after all—but she felt certain of herself in a way she hadn't this whole journey. That was better than winning.

The magical pyres had all but burned out when she returned, and the paladins were stirring the ashes to extinguish the last of the sparks. The anointed were working under the direction of the wagon drivers to load the wagons. Buonnane came to meet Ginnevra at the water's edge. "What was that about?"

"Straightening out some matters of jurisdiction. It was nothing, really."

Buonnane didn't look convinced, but she nodded. "We'll reach the place where the road enters the forest in three days. From there, we'll have to watch carefully. There are hamadryads here and there in the forest, and while they won't attack us unless we attack them, they can have strange ideas about what constitutes an attack. And when they do attack, they're relentless. They enjoy bloodshed, human or animal, it makes no difference."

"I've heard they look exactly like trees."

"That's more or less true. They blend in perfectly, but once they move, you won't mistake them for anything but what they are." Buonnane shielded her eyes. "Are you sure it was nothing? Because Revered Giulliomocte looks angry."

Ginnevra followed the line of her gaze. Giulliomocte was kicking stones into the lake with some force as he walked. "He and I will always be at odds, I think. But I hope I convinced him to see sense."

"I wonder," Buonnane said.

When she didn't immediately elaborate, Ginnevra said, "Wonder what?"

Buonnane shook her head. "It's an unworthy thought."

Ginnevra understood. "I'm convinced he deserves Hallowed rank. But I don't understand it either."

"How he can be Hallowed when he's preaching at odds with the Blessed, you mean?" Buonnane shrugged. "I'm no theologian. I'm sure there are reasons beyond my understanding."

"That's what I think, too." Ginnevra watched Giulliomocte stand at the lake's edge with his hands on his hips and his head tossed back. "Leave the details to the Blessed."

But as she saddled Dauntless and led him to the head of the line, the image of that resolute figure with thinning hair wouldn't leave her memory. Once again, doubt worked its way into her heart. She wished she were more certain the Goddess would be on her side if she asked for a judgment. Giulliomocte was almost Hallowed, and the Goddess spoke to him. If the Goddess was on the Revered's side, supported what the Revered preached, Ginnevra could not say for certain she would have the faith to accept that answer.

CHAPTER

NINETEEN

They were on the road by mid-morning, following its curving path that paralleled the lake shore. No one spoke, and the only sounds were the horses' hooves on the frozen earth and the creaking of the wagon wheels and the rush of wind over the water. The wind brought the scent of the lake to Ginnevra's nose, cool and clean in a different way than the smell of snow or rain. She inhaled deeply and let the smell fill her, easing the tension she felt.

She saw the karkadann at that moment, white against the green-black pines on the far side of the lake. It stood perfectly still, watching her—she was as sure of that as if it were three feet in front of her. She chose to say nothing. Her experience with Buonnane had confirmed the monster had singled Ginnevra out and was concealing itself from everyone else, so drawing attention to it would only continue to make her look unstable to the paladin captain.

Instead, she kept a careful eye on it. If it truly did have the ability to draw other monsters to it, the party was in danger.

Whether it was greater danger than they were already in, what with a werewolf pack stalking them, she didn't know. But she couldn't forget that cold night where she'd faced the karkadann and had an impossible conversation. She hadn't felt a sense of menace from it, and it hadn't attacked her. Granted, she'd encountered monsters before who didn't feel monstrous or terrifying right up until they tried to rip her throat out, but this was different, and she wasn't sure why.

The karkadann appeared to Ginnevra a handful of times that day as they rode. She never saw it move, but every time she inevitably had to look away, when she was addressed by someone, when she looked back it was gone. By nightfall, it had disappeared. Ginnevra didn't think it was gone for good, but she hoped it was gone for the night.

The howling began just after sunset. The first long, terrible cry brought every one of their party to a halt wherever they were in camp, their heads tilted back and turning to identify where the sound had come from. A second howl joined the first. Then a third. Then there were so many it sounded like a great, many-voiced monster, lurking in the forest across the lake.

Ginnevra walked through the camp to the southern side and stared at the forest. Her clear night vision showed the trees distinctly, though darker than in daylight. "They're not close," she said to Eodan, who shrugged.

"That's only half the pack," he replied. "The other half is trying to find a way to sneak up on us while we're supposedly distracted. But this open territory combined with seventeen paladins whose night vision is better than theirs makes that unlikely."

Pia, who stood watch nearby, had her gaze fixed on the lake shore rather than the forest. "Is paladins' night vision better, really?"

"Werewolves' night vision doesn't vary with the phases of the moon the way a paladin's does. That means for the time between half moon and half moon that centers on the new moon, a paladin's senses are superior." Eodan glanced up at the half moon hovering in the western sky. "We won't have that advantage long."

The howl went up again. "They're going to keep that racket up all night, aren't they?" Ginnevra said.

"Wouldn't you?" Eodan said. "If there's even a chance it might demoralize us,, the awareness of how close they are—and then there's the noise. I'm sure they believe it will keep us awake."

"They might be right." Pia sounded alarmed. "What are we supposed to do?"

"It's all right," Eodan said. "They haven't considered that a constant noise ends up fading into the background, and so long as we're not afraid, it will be as a lullaby to our ears."

Pia chuckled. "Do werewolves sing lullabies?"

"We do. But after hearing what you paladins are capable of this morning, with that funeral hymn, I wouldn't dare compare my singing talent to yours." Eodan laughed with Pia. "Ginnevra, you never said you could sing."

"I don't usually," Ginnevra said. "I'm better with harmonies. Not a lot of call for female tenors in the usual run of things."

Another howl echoed across the lake. On a whim, Ginnevra tilted her head back and let out a howl of her own. The werewolves' howl cut off mid-voice. Eodan burst out laughing. "That made them feel stupid," he said. "Do it again."

"Now I'm self-conscious," Ginnevra said. She took his hand and squeezed it. The howling started again, not as loud or as full-voiced as before. "Let's make the rounds. We can warn the sentries, in case the werewolves are stupider than I believe and try an attack."

"With that Cennfalad in charge, I wouldn't count on it," Eodan said.

By the third day, the werewolves were howling during the daytime. Ginnevra watched the moon in its phases, gradually growing fuller, and eyed the forest as they drew nearer to it. She had discussed with Buonnane the possibility of traveling cross-country, avoiding the forest road. The captain had said, "The wagons wouldn't survive the trip, and we need those supplies. And it will add more days to the journey, which will make us run out of food before we get back to civilization." Ginnevra had expected that answer, but it hadn't stopped her hoping for an alternative.

They had rounded the western end of the lake and were following its shore southward. Ginnevra rode up and down their line of march, riding beside the Dedicates' wagon and then next to the Revereds, assessing their mood. The Dedicates weren't as cheerful as they'd been at the outset of the journey, but they talked in low voices among themselves, and since Ginnevra could hear they were telling stories, she wasn't worried about their morale.

Revered Orselle rode less awkwardly than at first, but he still clung to the reins with one hand and the pommel with the other as if he feared his horse might bolt. He smiled at Ginnevra when she passed, a thin, narrow smile that made him look even more like a hare than usual, but didn't respond to her greeting with more than a nod. Ginnevra decided not to press. She didn't need to be friends with the Revereds.

In that spirit, she gave Revered Pratese a polite smile and nod and didn't wait for a verbal response. Revered Giulliomocte ignored her completely. He hadn't spoken to her since that day on the lake shore, for which Ginnevra was both grateful and annoyed. She'd paid close attention to the gossip around the campfires, but hadn't heard anything that suggested Giulliomccte was still spreading dissension centered on Eodan. Since she didn't think he'd given up, this didn't ease her mind much.

The forest loomed ever closer, its dark pines rearing up against the cold blue sky. Under other circumstances, it would have been beautiful, all those trees whose scent Ginnevra smelled even at this distance. Knowing monsters lurked within made it ominous instead, a beast itself that swallowed the road and consumed whoever dared travel it. The mad image persisted even as Ginnevra told herself she was being foolish.

To counter her fears, she made sure she was first to enter the forest. Beneath the shading, spreading branches laden with blue-green needles, a twilight gloom fell over the road. Without the sun's rays, the temperature dropped significantly, and Ginnevra shrank deeper into her cloak, rubbing her fingers through the thick fur lining.

She glanced over her shoulder. The paladins rode ahead and behind the wagons, which creaked along placidly. Maybe she was the only one who felt the oppressive nature of this place. She straightened and nudged Dauntless faster, not by much.

The trees grew close together, enough that they wouldn't be able to make a proper camp. Ginnevra's heart sank further. They would have to spread out, and that would make it harder to secure their camp against attackers, not to mention how exhausting it would be to patrol. For a moment, Ginnevra considered taking the long way regardless. But that would be foolish in a different way, and she'd committed to this venture.

She almost called out a warning, but Buonnane had already

given the paladins their instructions that morning, and an additional warning would be pointless as well as insulting. But the silence beneath the trees was starting to get to her. There were birds, off in the distance rather than nearby, and wind shook the tops of the trees, too far away to feel. It felt as if they traveled in a bubble of quiet, and Ginnevra was on edge waiting for some hostile creature to pop it.

"You warned about hamadryads," she said to break the stillness. "They look like trees, unlike ordinary dryads—dryads are immaterial humanoids, right? How is a hamadryad different from a tree? Visibly, I mean?"

Buonnane didn't stop scanning the area for attackers. "They are a slightly different color, but unless you're in bright sunlight, that difference is hard to distinguish. And sometimes they move, like a..." She made a wiggling wave-like motion with her hand. "A quiver, or heat haze. But mostly, you won't see them until they're on top of us."

"But they won't attack if we don't bother them."

"True, but like I said, they take offense at the strangest things. And no cutting wood, obviously. Those magical fires are going to come in handy, though I think it might be warmer now that we're off the plains and out of the wind."

Ginnevra nodded. "At least the road is clear."

"Let's hope it stays that way," Buonnane said.

Night came early beneath the trees, and Ginnevra called a halt before sunset. She walked through their awkwardly-placed camp, assessing possible dangers. A stream flowed nearby, and when she was finished examining their situation, she led Dauntless to drink and scooped some of the icy, delicious water for herself.

"Prime Cassaline."

She turned to face Giulliomocte. "Yes, Revered?"

"We are prepared to invoke the barrier we used before, if you'd like." Giulliomocte's face was set and rigid, as if he expected an argument.

"Thank you, Revered, that would be appreciated."

Ginnevra tugged on Dauntless' reins, but Giulliomocte held up a hand. "One other thing, prime."

Ginnevra's heart sank, but she maintained a cool, calm demeanor. "Yes, Revered?"

"We will not always be able to maintain that barrier." Giulliomocte's jaw twitched, suppressing a stronger emotion. "If I must defend this group, I can't hold back for the sake of your companion."

"I told you—"

"And *I* told *you* I do not believe him to be evil. You must have faith, prime. The Goddess knows all that is hidden, and that includes the secret hearts of all creatures. Have faith." Giulliomocte turned and walked away, stumbling once or twice over the rough ground. Ginnevra didn't follow.

She made herself breathe in and out without thinking of anything else until she felt calm. It was true, she didn't believe Giulliomocte would deliberately attack Eodan, but she was sure he didn't much care if one of his graces killed the wrong person, if that person was a monster. But, then, what if Ginnevra was wrong, and Eodan wouldn't be affected just because he was technically a monster? After all, the grace hadn't killed him when the Revered invoked it the first time. She hated to admit Giulliomocte had a point about anything, but he was right—she needed to exercise faith.

Muttering curses under her breath, she returned to camp.

THE REVEREDS INVOKED their grace before the sunlight faded entirely. Ginnevra thought the blue glow wasn't as strong as before, but she'd only seen it once and might be mistaken. She was not mistaken that the invocation was not entirely in unison; there was the slightest echo in the words, as if one or more of them were out of harmony. But it couldn't have been too much of a dissonance, or the barrier would not have appeared. Even so, Ginnevra resolved never to depend on that grace. Giulliomocte and Pratese couldn't remain in accord forever.

But it turned out not to matter. Nothing attacked that night. Even the wolf howl was silent. Ginnevra took a turn at watch around midnight, pacing the length of the glowing blue barrier. She saw a fox beneath some bushes, eyeing the barrier speculatively, but it ran away when she drew near. The hoot of a hunting owl sounded overhead and then was gone. If it hadn't been freezing cold, it would have been a perfect night.

When Bartolla took her place a few hours later, she asked Ginnevra, "Everything's well?"

"As peaceful as a farmer's pasture," Ginnevra said. "They won't attack until we're complacent."

"Then we'd better not let our guard down, eh?" Bartolla said with a grin.

Ginnevra nodded, but didn't smile. Staying alert all the time was impossible. At some point, the werewolves would attack.

She walked the perimeter one final time before returning to her tent, which was wedged between a couple of trees. Eodan, to her surprise, was awake. "I've been thinking," he said when she exclaimed over his alertness. "Maybe I need to patrol as well."

"You mean in wolf form. Eodan, it's too dangerous. These paladins may have accepted you for the most part, but they aren't used to you in your other shape. I don't want any accidents." She refused to dwell on the thought of black lightning striking his wolf form.

"Ginnevra, I can avoid being seen. And if I can do that, you can bet the werewolves can, even with that pale fur."

Ginnevra shook her head. "That's worse, you out there alone against twenty-five or more enemies. If anything happened to you, you would be far from allies."

Eodan scowled. "Beloved, we're coming up on the full moon, when my transformation won't be voluntary. Better to get the party used to me before we can't avoid it."

That was a complication she hadn't thought about—or maybe she hadn't wanted to think about it. "I still think it's a bad idea for you to roam far from camp."

"And if it means discovering the werewolves' location?"

"What could we do with that information? It's not as if we can leave the anointed unguarded while we stage a raid on the werewolves. *Please*, Eodan. If you want to patrol, do it here, with the rest of us."

Eodan sighed and reached for her. "You make a good point," he said, drawing her into his arms. "All right. But in wolf shape."

"Tomorrow, when we can warn them. You'd just cause a panic tonight." Ginnevra kissed him. "Now, I'm freezing, and you are warmer than an oven, so if you don't mind, I'd like to sleep close beside you and pretend for the moment we aren't in mortal danger."

"I give it two more days before they attack," Eodan said. He lay down beside Ginnevra, and she snuggled close. "And they'll go for the horses, try to slow us down."

"I wish I could say you were wrong," Ginnevra said.

THEY TRAVELED for three more days without seeing or hearing werewolves. Ginnevra stopped riding at the front and took to riding beside the anointeds' wagon, trying to keep their spirits up. She didn't like their silence, or how frightened they all looked. It was the sort of fear that couldn't last long, but only because it turned into exhaustion and numbness. That was exactly the state the werewolves were after. Ginnevra wasn't worried too much about the paladins, who knew how to handle that emotion. But the anointed had no such experience.

She occasionally rode beside the Revereds as well, striking up conversations she hoped would encourage them. Orselle responded distractedly, like his mind was elsewhere. Pratese had gone back to being sweetly polite, but tension lay beneath her replies, and she never met Ginnevra's eyes, always sweeping the forest with her gaze.

Giulliomocte was the calmest of the three, which annoyed Ginnevra. She should have been grateful that at least one of the Revereds wasn't paralyzed with fear, but Giulliomocte's reaction, or lack thereof, was just one more sign that he had the Goddess's favor. Why else would he be so calm if not because his faith in his purpose was strong? Which meant one more sign that Ginnevra might be wrong. That wasn't the sort of thing she needed now.

She was riding beside Pratese, having an insincere and banal conversation, when Buonnane shouted, "All halt!"

Pratese stopped speaking mid-word and twisted in her seat. "Where? Where are they?"

"It's all right, Revered, I don't see or hear anything." Ginnevra urged Dauntless forward to join Buonnane. "Is something wrong?"

"I saw movement in the trees," Buonnane said. "Low to the ground, and big. Fast."

Ginnevra looked where the captain pointed. "It's gone—no,

there!" Something big darted from tree to tree and vanished into the distance with a rustle of undergrowth.

From behind them, Eodan shouted, "Werewolves! On the left!"

"Form up," Buonnane commanded. "'Ware attack!"

The paladins shifted position, moving to surround the caravan. Cries of dismay erupted from the anointeds' wagon as the Dedicates and acolytes clutched each other in fear. Ginnevra saw Serenna sitting alone, her hands gripping the wagon sides, and then another dark, low shape drew Ginnevra's attention away. She drew her sword, watching for more.

More movement to the left made her shift in that direction. But it wasn't monsters. Revered Pratese had removed her grace from around her neck and now clutched it in one hand, raising it high. Ginnevra suddenly knew what the Revered had in mind. Sick with dread, she called out, "Revered! Don't—"

"*By Your grace the fire burns bright,*" Pratese shouted. A streak of fire flashed from her hand at one of the low, prowling shapes. Whatever it was dodged, and the fire struck a pine tree. With a *whoosh*, its resinous bark went up in flames that licked at the branches.

A scream split the air, too high in pitch to be human. In the next moment, a dozen other screams joined it. "Douse the fire!" Ginnevra shouted, turning Dauntless toward the wagon with the water supplies. "Quickly!"

But as she moved, a figure separated itself from the burning tree. It was roughly human-shaped, but stretched out long and thin and taller than any human. Its thin arms batted at the fire that consumed it, and its mouth opened wide as it screamed in pain. Ginnevra reached the wagon and nearly fell off Dauntless in her haste to dismount. Two of the wagon drivers were struggling with the water cask. Ginnevra lifted it with a groan of effort and staggered under its weight to the burning figure. With another groan, she upended the cask over the figure, sending water cascading everywhere.

A hiss and a cloud of steam rose up. The figure swayed and collapsed. Ginnevra tossed the empty cask away and knelt beside the figure, which wasn't moving. Gingerly, she prodded its shoulder.

"Move back," Eodan said, kneeling next to them. He lifted the thin arm, then laid it down gently.

"Is it..." Ginnevra didn't know how to continue.

"I have no idea. I think it's dead," Eodan said.

With that, a second round of screams pierced the air. Ginnevra scanned the area, but saw nothing, no low, running shapes, no—

Another figure stepped out of the trees, literally out of the bole of a nearby pine. Then another. In moments, the forest was full of them: thin, elongated creatures whose features resembled pine bark, knotted and whorled into faces distorted by anger. Long, skinny arms and legs moved restlessly, like branches in a high wind.

Ginnevra took a step back. "Paladins," she shouted.

With another scream, the hamadryads attacked.

TWENTY

Ginnevra dove for the wagon and the sword she'd dropped when she'd picked up the cask. She brought the weapon around in time to deflect a blow from one of the skinny arms. It felt like hitting an iron bar, reverberating down the blade and up her arms. She snarled and pressed the attack, thrusting the sword at what in a human would be the heart. Her mind gibbered at her, reminding her she knew nothing of this monster's physiognomy, nothing of its strengths or weaknesses. She shut that voice out and focused on what was in front of her.

Her sword connected with the skin—bark?—of the hamadryad and skittered off as if the creature wore armor. It reached for her again, swiping with hands ending in clawed fingers, and scored a hit across her helmet that screeched like rusty iron. She ducked and swung at its midsection, which was shoulder-high on her. Her sword struck its side and sent a chunk of wood flying.

With an anguished scream, the hamadryad advanced on her,

swinging its arms like cudgels. Ginnevra grunted as it caught her across the left arm, sending shooting pain and then a terrible brief numbness through it. She shook it out and changed her grip on her sword. This time, she struck low, at the bend in its legs that was almost a knee. Screaming with effort, she put her whole strength into the blow.

The sword struck the hamadryad's leg and penetrated about halfway to the knee before sticking. Ginnevra jerked hard, but the sword stuck fast. She let go and dodged, not fast enough to avoid a blow to her shoulder. Pain lanced through her left side, and she dropped, rolled, and came up behind the monster. With a roar, she flung herself at its legs and wrapped her arms around them.

The hamadryad fell, barely missing the wagon. More screams, these human, told Ginnevra they were far too close to the anointeds' wagon. Then she heard Pratese's voice again, beginning an invocation. "No!" she shouted, and flung herself away from the hamadryad just as fire struck it. Its screams pierced Ginnevra's heart. She wrenched her sword away before the fire could spread to the monster's legs and rose to her feet, shaking.

"*No more fire*," she said to Pratese, whose darkly tanned face was ashen, and then turned away, surveying the battle. Everything was moving too fast to make sense, but it didn't look like there were more than eight hamadryads. Some of them had fallen, and paladins in twos or threes hacked at them. Eodan had Ginnevra's mace and bludgeoned any hamadryad who approached Revered Giulliomocte. The Revered held his grace in one hand, but hadn't used it as far as Ginnevra could tell. He looked remarkably calm for someone that close to death.

Then Ginnevra remembered. The werewolves. This would be a perfect time for them to attack. She spun around and scanned the forest, looking for those low, dark shapes. Nothing. Breaking into a run, she circled the caravan, prepared to raise the alarm. Still no werewolves appeared.

By the time she reached her original position near Pratese, the fight was all but over. Breathing heavily, she approached Buonnane, who favored her right arm but otherwise looked uninjured. "No werewolves," she said. "I didn't see where they went."

"That makes no sense," Buonnane said. "We were distracted, and they could easily have overwhelmed us." She sheathed her sword, wincing, and put a gloved hand on her right pauldron.

"Are you injured?" Ginnevra asked.

Buonnane shook her head. "Just bruising—ah!" She tried to rotate her shoulder and stopped before she completed the motion.

"We should have Eodan look at that. If you tore a muscle—"

"It's fine," Buonnane said flatly. "I don't need help."

Ginnevra's lips tightened, but she didn't press. Instead, she said, "We certainly pissed the hamadryads off. What are the odds of Revered Pratese hitting a hamadryad rather than an ordinary tree?"

"Even if she had hit a pine, the hamadryads might have attacked anyway." Buonnane made as if to press on her shoulder again, but didn't complete the movement. "They are very protective of the forest and not rational. And with as many of them as there were, they'd been stalking us for a while. Damn—" She shut her mouth. Ginnevra could guess what she'd been about to say.

"It was an accident," she said. "But it could be an accident with consequences. Did any of the hamadryads escape?"

"None. So there's no one to spread the word." Buonnane glanced around as if looking for more enemies. "At least we won't deal with wave after wave of angry hamadryads seeking revenge."

"Unless the hamadryads have other ways of communicating

with each other. They use the trees, right? Trees have roots, and roots can be interconnected."

They both looked at the ground and the nearby trees. "I... don't think it works that way," Buonnane said. "Nobody knows much about hamadryads, not even the paladins who patrol in this direction. But—"

"We're no worse off than we were," Ginnevra said, "and if the hamadryads return, we'll just have to fight them as best we can."

"But none of that explains why the werewolves didn't attack," Buonnane said. "We couldn't have been more vulnerable than we were."

Ginnevra glanced around and saw Eodan approaching. "Maybe he knows. Eodan, why didn't the werewolves come after us?"

Eodan's hair was disordered, and a welt was forming on his cheek, but he moved easily. "I smelled seven werewolves," he said. "Cennfalad wasn't with them. They were likely the outrunners, keeping an eye on us. I doubt they were supposed to let themselves be seen. Which means they wouldn't have had orders to attack on their own."

"But they could have taken advantage of our distraction," Buonnane said. "They could easily have picked off a few of us, or of the anointed. Wear us down, a little at a time."

"I can think of two possibilities," Eodan said. "One is that the leader of their group might not have a lot of initiative. Outrunners generally aren't supposed to make their own decisions. They're intended to obey orders without question and not go running off on their own schemes. But it could also have been Revered Pratese's fire. A lot of werewolves in their wolf forms are superstitious about fire. It's the Bright One's symbol to us, it... that's not important. So werewolves, even the ones who serve Her, avoid fire when they don't have hands to manipulate it. That combined with the typical nature of an outrunner means maybe Revered Pratese did us a favor as well as cause trouble."

Someone shouted Eodan's name, and he turned, grimacing. "It seems I need to perform my trade. Excuse me."

When he was gone, Ginnevra said, "That all makes sense."

"I'll take it," Buonnane said.

Ginnevra shot a sly glance her way. "Good thing we have our own werewolf around, right?"

Buonnane's eyes narrowed. "Don't bother," she said. "I'll put up with him because he's a good physician and he knows our enemy. But we're never going to be friends." She stalked away, once more prodding at her shoulder.

Ginnevra sighed. It had been worth a try.

She helped get the caravan moving again, but only a few hundred yards later became aware of the tension that filled the air like a living thing and decided they'd had enough excitement for one day. She gave the order to make camp despite there being at least another two hours of daylight and then helped the anointed find places to pitch tents. The Dedicates, to her surprise, looked resolute through their fear and ready to face another challenge. Serenna, too, wore an expression of determined resolve. The innkeeper's daughter spoke boldly to her companions and comforted the youngest acolyte, a boy who was likely older than Serenna but was prone to weeping fits. Ginnevra's conviction that Serenna would make a good paladin increased.

Having settled the young anointed, she went in search of the Revereds. She found Giulliomocte in the process of leading his horse to the stream they'd camped near, accompanied by Pia. "A word, Revered?" she said.

Giulliomocte looked weary, far more tired than someone who'd essentially sat that fight out should be. "Yes, Prime Cassaline?" he asked.

His tone of voice, as if she had been badgering him and now had one more unreasonable request, set her back up. She controlled her irritation and said, "I was wondering if you and the others might invoke that barrier tonight."

Giulliomocte's weary expression didn't change. "I'm afraid not, prime. I'm sorry."

"Why not?" That came out more sharply than she had intended, but she didn't regret it. "We are in great danger. Now that the werewolves know that we know how close they are, they will almost certainly press the attack. We could use the extra protection."

"I'm sorry, prime," Giulliomocte repeated. "I'm afraid we are not in harmony enough to invoke that grace, and I—regrettably I'm not able to do it on my own." He let out a deep sigh. "Marsillia and I... no, that's unworthy. We're not in harmony, and that's all I can say."

"Revered Pratese acted rashly," Ginnevra said.

"Yes, and I'm afraid that's in her nature." Giulliomocte looked away from Ginnevra, into the distance. "But don't fear, prime. The Goddess knows our plight, and She is with us. I have heard Her voice assuring me that we are in Her hands."

"That is reassuring," Ginnevra said. "Do you—I beg your pardon if this is presumptuous, but do you hear Her voice in your head, or does She speak so anyone nearby might hear?"

"It is a quiet voice, audible only to me. The voice of someone speaking so as not to be heard by anyone else nearby." Giulliomocte stopped at the stream bed and watched his horse slurp up water. "Her voice is unmistakable. But you've heard her speak, prime, so you know the truth of that."

An uncomfortable feeling filled Ginnevra as Giulliomocte spoke. "I have, and you're right," she said. "But how can you be sure it's the Goddess, if She tells you things counter to what the Blessed teaches?"

Giulliomocte frowned. "So you do question my fitness for this rank."

"I'm not. I don't. I—it's not important. Forget I asked." Ginnevra scanned the trees, searching for enemies, but nothing moved except a gray squirrel scampering up a tree trunk and disappearing into the pine branches. "I suppose I was thinking in the more abstract sense of how anyone can know the difference."

"It's a matter of knowing the Goddess's will, and recognizing when the words you hear are in tune with what the Goddess teaches." Giulliomocte too looked into the distance, between the trees. "And nothing She has said is counter to what the Blessed says, not even with regard to werewolves."

Ginnevra reddened, feeling chastised. If Giulliomocte heard the Goddess's voice, he must have misunderstood Her words, because Ginnevra was certain of what the Goddess had said about Eodan. But that wasn't something she was comfortable arguing. She couldn't tell a Revered he hadn't heard the voice of his Goddess just because he was confused about what it meant.

They fell silent. Ginnevra listened to the sound of the rushing water and the horse lapping it up, and unexpected peace filled her heart. She didn't want it to make her complacent, but one could stay hypervigilant only so long before breaking, and this was a much-needed rest.

She and Giulliomocte and Pia returned to camp, still silent, and Ginnevra left them to find Eodan without another word to the Revered. She stopped Zana, standing watch at the extreme eastern end of their camp. "Have you seen Eodan?"

Zana's lips pinched tight. "He went farther south. I don't know what he had in mind. I told him not to go far, but—I'm sorry, prime, but it's just not natural, him being a werewolf. I know what you and the Blessed said, and I believe you, but all my instincts fight against it."

A dull, unhappy ache gripped Ginnevra's heart. "I understand. If all you can do is not attack him, that's enough."

Zana looked as miserable as Ginnevra felt. "I'm sorry, prime. I thought—but it's different when he's a wolf."

Ginnevra nodded and turned away.

She followed her nose to catch up to Eodan, who was patrolling wide around the camp. His big, black-furred shape usually comforted her. Now it only reminded her of Zana's words. Eodan stopped when she drew near and butted up against her, rubbing his cheek against her hand in greeting. She stroked his head absently. Mentioning what Zana had said was pointless and would only upset him.

"Don't go so far out," she said instead. "Have you smelled any werewolves?"

Eodan shook his head. His form shimmered silver, and then he was human. He rose from a crouch to stand before her. "The farther out I go, the more warning we'll have of an attack. And I can move more quickly than a paladin, so I'll return well ahead of any attackers. Don't worry, Ginnevra. I'm being careful."

"I hate the idea of losing any of us, but losing you would devastate me." Ginnevra put her arms around his neck and held him tightly for a moment before releasing him. "But maybe it's better you patrol out of sight of the others."

Eodan sighed. "I frightened Zana, didn't I? I could smell it, but I hoped I was wrong."

"Unsettled rather than frightened. It's her oaths she's worried about, not the possibility you'll attack her." Ginnevra took his hand. "They trust you, after everything you've done."

"They've reacted more favorably than I expected. It's hard to hang on to pessimism under these conditions." Eodan chuckled.

"Though I don't know that I'm prepared to adopt your optimism instead."

"I don't feel very optimistic now. We're in a terrible situation. The full moon is coming—the werewolves will take advantage of that."

"Nothing we can do about that but keep moving." He kissed her, then added, "Let me patrol. I'll be back soon. You make sure morale stays... all right, 'high' is probably too much to ask."

"At least no one's fallen into despair," Ginnevra said.

Eodan assumed his wolf shape and butted his head against her hand once more before loping off into the trees. Ginnevra returned to camp. The younger anointed had mostly disappeared into their tents. Low but intense voices led Ginnevra to one of the fires burning without fuel, where the Revereds sat. Pratese and Giulliomocte faced one another across the fire. "I won't apologize," Pratese spat. "You wanted to see me humiliated, didn't you, Domenico? Treating me like dirt wasn't enough for you."

"That is not true," Giulliomocte retorted. "You couldn't let go when it was clear—Prime Cassaline." He sat upright and visibly calmed himself. "Is there something we can do for you?"

"Don't think you can weasel out of this, Domenico," Pratese said. "Typical of you to not want to deal with a problem head-on. No, you'd rather just stop talking about it."

"I'm just checking on everyone. I didn't mean to interrupt," Ginnevra said.

"It's no interruption," Giulliomocte said. He stood and brushed damp, clinging dirt off his posterior. "We're done."

"I defended this group against monsters," Pratese said, rising as well. "There's nothing wrong with that."

"Except that your so-called defense started a battle," Giulliomocte said. "If you weren't so hasty—"

"Prime Cassaline, hamadryads are monsters, aren't they?" Pratese said. "They would have attacked us regardless."

Ginnevra briefly considered letting Pratese have the full force of Ginnevra's anger and frustration. It *was* her fault the hamadryads had attacked. But— "Maybe not, not if we didn't disturb them," she said. "But your intent was good, and what happened was an accident."

Orselle cleared his throat. "You attacked a creature that meant us no harm, Marsillia. That was foolish and wrong."

Pratese turned on him. "Shut up, Tomascio, nobody cares what you have to say."

"Revered Orselle, I know it looks like the hamadryads were peaceful," Ginnevra said, "but despite their non-aggressive nature, they really are monsters. That there were so many in one place means they'd been following us, and they were waiting for their moment. Revered Pratese's inadvertent attack only hastened the inevitable fight." She hated defending Pratese, would rather have joined in accusing her, but truth was truth.

"See?" Pratese said triumphantly.

"It's over, and it no longer matters," Giulliomocte said. "Marsillia, you got what you wanted. Let it go." He stalked away before Pratese could respond. Ginnevra saw her face, though, and her expression, mingled fury and longing, made her wish to be far from the Revereds and their conflicts.

She turned her back on the fire and walked away. She'd gotten only five steps when a howl shattered the freezing night. It was immediately followed by two shorter howls, almost barks. Ginnevra stopped. "Eodan," she breathed. Then she roared, *"Paladins! 'Ware attack!"*

As the words left her mouth, a dozen wolves howled. The sounds came from all around the camp. The paladins not on watch surged out of their tents, grabbing their swords. Ginnevra ran south. Eodan was out there somewhere, and if a paladin reacted without thinking—

She reached the southern edge of camp, where two paladins waited, scanning the darkness. The howls were closer now, but Ginnevra still saw no pale-furred bodies. "Spread out," she told the paladins. "We can't let them past." She stabbed her sword into the ground before her for ready access and drew her pistol.

The paladins obeyed without turning their attention from the dark forest. Ginnevra eyed their armor and wished she'd had time to don hers. She remembered the terrible claws and teeth of a werewolf intent on killing her and felt again the raking tear across her thigh. No. No fear. She still hoped the others would take the time to put on their silvered armor.

A ghost of a shape flitted across the extremes of her vision, and she brought her pistol to the ready. "They're coming!" one of the paladins said, stepping forward and then back again as she remembered her discipline.

The white shape drew nearer and was joined by others. "Come on and take us if you're not craven cowards!" Ginnevra shouted. The werewolves continued to advance, slowly at first, then gaining momentum until they were running. Ginnevra counted seven. Seven against three. She hated those odds, but there was nothing she could do.

Then a new voice, a deeper snarl, joined the din. A black figure, running low to the ground, charged the werewolves. Ginnevra shoved her pistol into its holster. "Don't shoot!" she shouted. "Go, go!"

She snatched up her sword and ran after Eodan, who had closed with the werewolves and was snapping and tearing at the lead wolf's throat. She heard the two paladins following, hoped they wouldn't shoot, cursed Eodan for letting his eagerness get in the way of their shots, and screamed a challenge as she lunged at the nearest werewolf.

She was close enough that its stinking breath enveloped her head like a poisonous cloud. Holding her breath, she thrust for the creature's chest. It dodged, but she was ready for that move and converted the thrust into a slash that scored a deep gash across the monster's chest. It howled in pain and swiped at her, forcing her a step back. Then Eodan was there, putting himself between her and the werewolf. His growl, deeper than his enemy's, was loud enough Ginnevra felt it in her bones.

Swiftly she backed away and edged sideways as Eodan and the werewolf circled one another. The werewolf lunged and darted forward, snapping at Eodan's head as Eodan struck back. Its jaws foamed, and it snarled and barked like a maddened dog. With its attention fully on Eodan, it failed to notice Ginnevra circling behind it. With one swing of the greatsword, Ginnevra struck its neck, severing its spine and nearly cutting its head off.

The other two paladins were holding their own, but two were-wolves had dodged their defense and were running toward the camp. Ginnevra ran after them, but Eodan outpaced her. He leaped past the werewolves and rolled, coming to his feet facing them. His body heaved with his labored breathing, but he stood his ground, daring the werewolves to attack.

Ginnevra pounded toward the three, her own breath coming fast and heavy in her chest, her lungs aching with cold. She ran in silence, hoping to catch at least one of the werewolves by surprise. But when she was a dozen feet away, both werewolves gathered themselves and leapt at Eodan, and she screamed, unable to stop herself.

Eodan stood his ground, braced against the impact. One were-wolf came in high; the other dove low. Ginnevra pushed herself harder than she ever had in her life to reach them, knowing it was too late.

The werewolves hadn't attacked at exactly the same time, and the werewolf attacking Eodan from below got there first. It snapped at Eodan's belly, forcing Eodan back. Ginnevra screamed again as Eodan's powerful jaws closed on the werewolf's neck, grabbing it and worrying it like a dog with a hare. Then the second werewolf was on him, aiming its own jaws at Eodan's throat. Eodan dodged without letting go of his prey, who whimpered and clawed at Eodan in its efforts to get free.

The second werewolf backed away and then lunged, a move intended to distract Eodan. But Ginnevra was finally there, and she thrust her blade into the werewolf's side. It howled and backed away from the silvered sword. Eodan bore down on his victim, and bone crunched as he snapped the werewolf's neck.

Ginnevra's attention was all on the second werewolf, though. It backed away from her, snarling, and showed no sign that its wound affected it. Ginnevra bared her teeth at the creature. "It's just a matter of time," she panted. "The silver in that wound will kill you if it's not treated. Better run now, or—"

The werewolf took off running. It took Ginnevra half a breath to realize it was running the wrong way. It was headed for the center of camp.

"I'll follow it," she shouted. "Watch the perimeter." She didn't wait to see Eodan's nod of acknowledgement before she was running after the werewolf.

She cursed, silently, that speed wasn't one of the Goddess's gifts to Her paladins—they were faster than any human, but many monsters were faster than that. No point whingeing about it, not when there was a werewolf to kill.

The creature raced toward camp, and Ginnevra darted after it. The tents were empty, the fires burning low, and she saw no one about. Someone had gathered the anointed somewhere... not safe, nowhere was truly safe, but at least somewhere they could be easily protected. Her momentary relief vanished when she realized the werewolf wasn't stopping to search the tents for prey; it had a target, and it was headed straight there.

The wagons lay at the far northern edge of camp, nearest the road. Ginnevra dodged a tree and saw two paladins standing ready, swords bared and silvered armor glinting in the light of the nearly full moon. The werewolf sprang to the attack, and both paladins met it head-on. The werewolf yelped and then fell to the ground, moving erratically in death. One of the paladins, Pia, impaled its body through the chest in a finishing blow.

Ginnevra slowed to a walk. "Good work," she said.

"It's the only one that's gotten this far," Pia said. She looked past Ginnevra, and her eyes widened. "*Look out!*"

Ginnevra turned just as a werewolf, pure white, launched itself at her face.

TWENTY-ONE

S he brought her sword up to meet his charge. Cennfalad's
leap carried him higher than her sword, over her head and
into the wagon. The acolytes and Dedicates screamed, and
the wagon rocked as they all tried to get away from the werewolf.
Ginnevra hauled herself one-handed over the side of the wagon in
time to see Cennfalad's enormous razor-tipped paw swipe at
Bidelia, who was backed against the side and had nowhere to go.

Serenna appeared out of nowhere and grabbed Bidelia's arm,
yanking her sideways and out of the reach of Cennfalad's attack.
Ginnevra shouted a wordless challenge and lunged for the werewolf dominus. Quick as thought, Cennfalad turned to face her.
The two hovered, each waiting for the other to strike. Ginnevra's
heart hammered in her chest. So close. If any of these anointed
were harmed—

Cennfalad darted forward, and Ginnevra brought her sword
around to block the blow only to discover it was a feint. With a
snarl, the werewolf sprang past Ginnevra, leaping over a couple of
cowering Dedicates and off the wagon. Ginnevra leaped after him.

But the dominus ran away from the wagons, into the trees on the far side of the road. Ginnevra chased him for a few paces before remembering that was stupid.

She ran back to the wagon, where everyone was clustered around Bidelia. The paladins had taken up their watchful stances again. "He's gone," Ginnevra panted. "And—"

A lone howl cut across the night, not Eodan's voice, but one that felt like a command. More howls answered it, fading with distance. "And I wager they're leaving," Ginnevra concluded. "Stay with the anointed. I'll be back soon."

She hurried through camp and circled around to make sure the werewolves were gone. Three white-furred bodies lay dead here and there at the perimeter of camp. Eodan was nowhere in sight. Ginnevra collared Bartolla and said, "Where did Eodan go? And the captain?"

"I haven't seen Eodan," Bartolla said. "The captain is seeing to Erallia."

"What happened to Erallia?" Ginnevra had a sinking feeling she already knew.

Bartolla looked even paler than usual in the light of the moon. "Dead. So is Ranulfia."

Ginnevra felt sick. "We killed six of the bastards. It's not enough."

Bartolla nodded, but said nothing.

Ginnevra found Buonnane standing over Erallia's body. The paladin captain looked grimmer than usual. "I'll have that werewolf's head for making me consider it a blessing that we only lost two," she said.

"I understand." Ginnevra knelt and touched her first two fingers to Erallia's head in farewell. She stood and added, "Was anyone injured?"

"We only lost Erallia and Ranulfia. No one was wounded.

Thank the Goddess." Buonnane herself looked battered, and she continued to hold her right arm as if her shoulder pained her. "Are the anointed all well?"

"Yes, though we almost lost some of them to Cennfalad." Ginnevra cursed and spat to clear her mouth of the foul taste of his name. "He wouldn't stay for a real fight. Went straight for the defenseless anointed. Where are the Revereds?"

"They were with us—I don't know where they ended up." Buonnane looked around in emphasis. "They fought well. We had to defend them, of course, but they are capable of powerful magics."

It occurred to Ginnevra that she hadn't heard Giulliomocte invoke that grace, the one that killed monsters so efficiently. It was probably too much to hope he'd refrained out of a desire to protect Eodan. That reminded her— "I haven't seen Eodan recently."

Buonnane's features tightened, but she said, calmly, "He's coming now."

Ginnevra turned. Eodan limped toward her, favoring his left rear leg. "He fought with us," she said, though she knew the captain wouldn't care.

Buonnane was silent for a moment. Then she said, while Eodan was still out of earshot, "I can't. Don't expect me to change." She walked away without another word.

Ginnevra dropped to her knees and put her arms around Eodan's neck. She buried her face in his fur and said, "This was a disaster. Two more of us dead, and the anointed—Cennfalad nearly killed Dedicate Bicelia in front of me."

Eodan snuffled and rubbed his cheek against her face. Then he put a paw on Erallia's shoulder and bowed his head. The gentle gestures brought tears to Ginnevra's eyes. "There are still so many of them," she whispered. "We can fight them, but at what cost?"

Eodan's form shimmered silver, and then he knelt before her in his human form. "The full moon begins day after tomorrow," he murmured. "We just have to survive until it begins to wane."

Ginnevra nodded. "We can manage that. We're almost out of the forest, and we repulsed them once. We can do it again."

"Bless your optimism," Eodan said with a smile.

He assumed his wolf shape for the walk back to camp. Werewolves didn't have nudity taboos, but humans certainly did, and Ginnevra felt uncomfortable about letting Eodan walk around naked. So she carried Erallia's body to where it would rest in preparation for a funeral and then followed Eodan to the anointeds' wagon.

Bidelia was sitting up, surrounded by the Dedicates and acolytes. "Really, it's nothing," she was saying. "Serenna saved my life."

"I didn't even think," Serenna said. "I saw the werewolf and I grabbed you. I thought I was too late."

"You reacted like a paladin," Ginnevra said. Serenna reddened and ducked her head.

"Anyway, this is just a scratch," Bidelia said.

Ginnevra's blood chilled. "The werewolf scratched you?"

Bidelia looked confused at Ginnevra's sudden intensity. "It would have torn into my chest if Serenna hadn't acted. It only scratched my arm. I think one of the scratches is fairly deep, but it's still not much."

Ginnevra grabbed Eodan's shoulder. In an instant, Eodan was human. He climbed into the wagon and knelt before Bidelia, unconcerned about his nakedness. "Show me," he said. Bidelia, blushing bright red, extended her arm from beneath her cloak. Eodan pushed the bloodstained sleeve up, revealing four scratches beaded along the edges with red. Gently, he prodded the flesh around the scratches. Bidelia winced, but held still.

Eodan released Bidelia, but continued kneeling. "I'll need hot water," he told Ginnevra. "And clothing."

"Pia, get a kettle boiling," Ginnevra said. She leaped down from the wagon. "I'll be back. The rest of you, secure the camp."

She ran to her tent and collected Eodan's clothing. When she returned, only Bidelia and Serenna were still in the wagon with Eodan. Bidelia looked frightened. Serenna had her arm around Bidelia's shoulders and seemed to be supporting her. Eodan accepted his clothing and dressed without any attempt at modesty while the girls averted their eyes. "It might still be nothing," he said.

Ginnevra looked him in the eye. "Sometimes optimism is the wrong approach, beloved."

Eodan nodded. He turned to Bidelia and said, "The werewolf taint fights with your human nature. It's like an illness, and I won't lie to you, it can be fatal."

"But I survived it," Ginnevra said, drawing Bidelia's attention. "Eodan nursed me through it, and he'll get you through it, too."

Bidelia nodded. "I'm not afraid." Her lips were white and pinched, though, and Ginnevra heard the rapid beat of her heart.

"That helps," Eodan said. "I'll go see about that hot water. We can at least clean the wounds. And you're right, they're not much." He climbed out of the wagon and headed for the nearest fire, where Pia crouched beside a kettle.

Bidelia swayed, and Serenna's arm around her tightened. Bidelia blinked. "Everything's hazy, and I feel sick. I—" She jerked away from Serenna's arm, her eyes rolling up in her head, and then more convulsions shook her, making her blonde braids dance and jerk. Ginnevra dove and caught her before she could bash her head against the side of the wagon. After what felt like forever, Bidelia sagged in her arms. Her half-lidded eyes and barely moving lips indicated she was only semi-conscious.

Serenna's own eyes were wide and frightened. "Is she dead?"

Bidelia moved, raising her hand to clutch Ginnevra's arm across her chest. "What happened?" she said in a slurred voice.

"It's as Eodan said, the werewolf's taint is at war with your humanity," Ginnevra said. "Try to relax. There's nothing you can do—let us take care of you."

Bidelia nodded once. It looked as if that gesture took all her strength. "Will I become a werewolf?"

"No. That's a myth. You'll—" Ginnevra couldn't bring herself to promise the girl she would recover. Bidelia was tall for a woman, but slender, and Ginnevra had never been so conscious of the girl's slight frame. Ginnevra had survived a werewolf attack partly because of Eodan's care, which Bidelia had, but also because of the strength and stamina the Goddess gave Her paladins. "You won't remember any of this," she said instead. That, at least, was true no matter what happened.

Bidelia closed her eyes. Her breathing, which had been shallow and rapid, slowed somewhat. Ginnevra's only warning of the next seizure was Bidelia stiffening in her arms, as if all her muscles and bones were drawing in on themselves to protect her. Ginnevra held her tightly while she convulsed. When the seizure passed, Bidelia was unconscious.

"Make a bed for her," Ginnevra told Serenna. "Blankets, cloaks, anything you can find. She needs to stay warm."

She heard someone approaching, and said, "Eodan, are these seizures likely to get worse?"

"I am not your companion," Revered Giulliomocte said. He climbed into the wagon and knelt beside Ginnevra. "But I believe I can help."

Hope bloomed in Ginnevra's heart. "You can invoke a healing grace."

"The Goddess grants Her healing where She will." Giulliomocte removed his jet grace from around his neck. "She will not desert us."

Ginnevra laid Bidelia gently on the makeshift bed. Across from her, Serenna watched wide-eyed as Giulliomocte raised his fist in the air and said, in an unexpectedly quiet voice, "*By Your grace I make all things whole.*"

Ginnevra tensed in anticipation of the brilliant rainbow light she had seen before. But nothing happened. Giulliomocte's other hand on Bidelia's shoulder tensed. "Goddess grant me Your power to save Your servant," he murmured. "*By Your grace I make all things whole!*"

Still nothing. High above, a hunting owl cried out as it flew past. Giulliomocte's breathing was heavy, and he closed his eyes as if in pain. Ginnevra's hope shriveled and died. "The Goddess chooses not to reveal Her sign to us," she said. "Why not?"

"I don't know," Giulliomocte said. "It is a sign of a different nature, one that we should have faith." He released Bidelia's shoulder and stood. "I'm sorry. I will send the others. Perhaps one of them..." His voice trailed off. He climbed down from the wagon and walked away.

"Maybe it was him," Serenna said.

"What?" Ginnevra saw Bidelia shift and snatched the young woman up before her seizure began.

Serenna was silent until Bidelia subsided. "Maybe he's not worthy," she said.

"Serenna, Revered Giulliomocte is about to become Hallowed. His worthiness isn't in question." But she'd been thinking the same thing herself: suppose Giulliomocte's opposition to Ecdan really had put him at odds with the Goddess, and She had withdrawn Her blessing from him?

"If that were so," she went on, "he wouldn't be able to invoke any graces, not just that one." Ginnevra hoped she was right about that. "And I've seen that grace before. The Revered is right that the Goddess grants that petition as a witness to the observer, not just as healing. We have to have faith."

Serenna's face was set in a scowl. "I don't understand. The Goddess loves us. She won't let Bidelia die just because She wants to give us a sign."

"Bidelia's death isn't a given," Ginnevra said. "Eodan will do everything he can to save her."

At that moment, Eodan climbed back into the wagon, holding a steaming pot and with a clean cloth draped over one shoulder. "I'll need more cloth for a bandage," he said. "Ginnevra, you hold her, and Serenna—"

"I'll hurry," Serenna said.

When she was gone, Eodan knelt beside Bidelia and set the pot within easy reach. He pushed Bidelia's sleeve out of the way again, saying, "I'll do what I can, but you know the odds aren't good."

Ginnevra nodded. "I've been thinking. Cennfalad could have killed any number of the anointed before I stopped him. He was very close to Bidelia—she should have been injured far more seriously, even with Serenna's intervention. I wonder if this—" She gestured at Bidelia's arm— "wasn't what he had in mind."

Eodan stopped washing Bidelia's wounds. "It will slow us down. Make us more vulnerable."

"Exactly. A funeral wouldn't have stopped us for more than a few hours, during which we'd be extremely vigilant. Even with the wagon to carry her, we'll need frequent stops to care for her. Didn't you tell me my body temperature rose and fell erratically when I was in her position? I don't know how we'd treat that short of stopping to warm or cool her."

Eodan went back to cleaning the deep scratches. "I'll think of something. The best hope for her is to get through these woods and out of the badlands."

The wagon quivered as Serenna climbed back in, clutching a wad of fabric. She thrust it at Eodan. "I hope this is all right."

"It's fine." Eodan tore the fabric, which looked like someone's undershirt, into strips with the help of his belt knife and bound up the injured arm. Bidelia went into convulsions again as he finished. She was still unconscious, and her mouth hung open, her jaw slack.

"The werewolf bit her," Buonnane said, startling Ginnevra. In her concern for Bidelia, she hadn't heard the captain approach. Now she looked up to discover most of the party gathered nearby. The anointed looked worried, even Giulliomocte, whom Ginnevra was accustomed to seeing remain impassive in the face of catastrophe. The paladins, all of whom showed signs of the fight, looked furious.

"It clawed her, but that's no better," Ginnevra said. "She's a fighter. She'll get through this."

Buonnane gave Ginnevra a measured, appraising look. "Most don't," she said. "Can we travel?"

"We'll need to spread the anointed out through the other two wagons," Eodan said, though she hadn't addressed him. "A few can ride with Bidelia and help me. But controlling her temperature will be difficult. We can keep her warm, but when her fever spikes, we will need to stop to cool her down."

Buonnane turned her attention on him as he spoke. Her rigid jaw and distant gaze told Ginnevra the captain was close to an outburst. But she swallowed, blinked a few times, and said, "We do what we must. You have your orders, paladins—let's get through this night. And I suggest you all pray for Bidelia's strength to be enough... and for the skill of her physician as well." She took a few steps to where the dead werewolf still lay and heaved it over her shoulder without even a grunt of effort, then walked away through the camp.

As the others dispersed, Ginnevra said in a low voice, "That's the most generous she's ever been with you."

"Whatever happened to her at the hands of werewolves, she's not letting it affect what she knows is right," Eodan said. "I wish we could be friends. But I'll settle for this."

"How can I help?" Serenna asked.

Ginnevra had forgotten she was there. The girl looked resolute and pale in the horrible white moonlight. "Let's arrange for a bed for her, Serenna, something that will protect her while she thrashes around. And then you should get some rest."

Serenna shook her head. "I don't think I could sleep knowing she might die. She's my friend."

"I need you to rest so you can take over for me later. I can't stay awake all night and still ride in the morning." Ginnevra tightened her hold on Bidelia, but her seizure wasn't as severe as the last. "Can you do that?"

"Of course!" Serenna hesitated, then said, "You were sick with this once. It wasn't Eodan who hurt you, was it?"

Ginnevra chuckled. "No. He saved me from death at the claws and teeth of the one who wounded me, and then he treated me in the illness that followed."

Serenna looked relieved. Ginnevra chose not to be sarcastic with her about the odds of a werewolf attacking a human and not finishing the job.

They set about arranging blankets in the wagon bed for Bidelia to lie on. The seizures were less frequent now, but Eodan's grim look told Ginnevra this wasn't anything to base optimism on. When Ginnevra moved to put Bidelia down, she felt the girl's hands and said, "Her skin is like ice."

"More blankets." Eodan swore softly under his breath. "I'll be right back."

Ginnevra watched him go, mystified. She sat beside Bidelia while Serenna packed blankets around her, holding the young woman's cold hand and praying silently. With her eyes closed in prayer, the noises of the camp were clearer and louder: low-voiced conversations as the anointed settled in to sleep, the distant noise of paladins pacing the outskirts of the camp on watch, the whisper of the wind that wasn't yet a howl. Ginnevra missed Usterchia and her weather sense. She didn't know if a storm was coming, though the air smelled of snow. She prayed for the strength to endure a storm, though she'd never been so tempted to petition the Goddess for a future in which the storm didn't happen.

Serenna finished folding and spreading blankets, and Ginnevra leaned back to let her climb out. "I'll rouse you after midnight," she told the girl.

"Thank you for letting me help," Serenna said. "I want—I don't think I could bear it if I didn't do something."

Ginnevra watched her go and spared a thought for Serenna's father, who couldn't possibly know the danger his daughter was in. Whether it was worse than the more insidious peril she'd faced back in Savorola, Ginnevra couldn't guess. Personally, she would rather face a danger she could kill.

When she heard Eodan approaching, she also heard a second set of footsteps. Opening her eyes, she saw Eodan climb into the wagon, followed, to her shock, by Revered Giulliomocte. The Revered's thinning hair was disordered, but he didn't look angry or disgusted the way he usually did when he had to interact with Eodan.

"So, is it possible?" Eodan asked.

The Revered examined the wagon bed, then dropped to one

knee beside Bidelia. He took her free hand in his and covered both with his other hand. "How likely is she to survive?" He showed no sign that he felt guilty at failing to invoke the healing grace.

"Likely enough that I won't give up before I've started," Eodan said. His voice was neutral, but Ginnevra saw the way his fists were clenched and knew he was barely controlling his anger. She wasn't sure who he was angry at, Giulliomocte or Cennfalad, and she didn't want to insult him by stepping in to redirect his anger.

Instead, she said, "I survived it. Bidelia has a chance."

Giulliomocte eyed Ginnevra, but said nothing about the difference between a paladin and a sixteen-year-old anointed. Then he turned his attention on Eodan. "It's possible," he said. "I'll have to ride nearby, or in the wagon, to renew the magic after it's been extinguished. But the fires my grace produces won't burn the wagon so long as they're kept well away from the sides."

Ginnevra understood then. "You're going to heat the wagon's interior," she said, "with the fire that burns without fuel. Keep it warm when she freezes, and extinguish the fires when she overheats."

"It is not a perfect solution, but it will keep us moving," Giulliomocte said. "Hold still." Before Ginnevra could ask what he meant, he held out his jet grace and said, *"By Your grace the fire burns bright."* A small fire, no bigger than Ginnevra's doubled fists, kindled in midair, then sank to rest on the wagon bed a little to Ginnevra's right. Ginnevra managed not to flinch. The fire was hot enough to scorch her face, but at a short distance from where Bidelia lay, it would radiate the perfect amount of heat.

Giulliomocte invoked two more little fires, spaced evenly around Bidelia. The air in the wagon began to warm until Ginnevra felt comfortable for the first time in weeks. It felt as if the heat of the fire were pushing back the cold night air, creating an invisible barrier covering the wagon. Bidelia's skin gradually warmed until it felt like flesh and not ice. Then she went into convulsions, and Ginnevra threw herself atop the girl, terrifyingly aware of the possibility of Bidelia falling into one of the fires.

When the seizure passed, Ginnevra sat up, breathing heavily. Giulliomocte regarded her steadily, and for some reason his placid expression angered her. But he'd provided the all-important fire, so she turned away without shouting at him.

"Thank you," Eodan said. "This will make it easier for us to keep moving."

"You should be more worried about the full moon," Giulliomocte said. "That will slow us as well, if we have to wait on your transformation." He still didn't sound critical.

"I'll deal with it." Eodan's short, curt response again sounded as if he were on the verge of anger. "Unless you're worried I'll give in to my nature and attack one of our own."

"A monster is a monster," Giulliomocte said. "Your choices are your own, though, and I don't fear you."

"Revered, you should get some sleep," Ginnevra said quickly. "Eodan, will you tell me if Bidelia's temperature has risen? Thank you again, Revered."

Eodan closed his mouth on whatever retort he would have shot at Giulliomocte and moved to Ginnevra's side. Ginnevra glared at Giulliomocte, willing him to leave without saying anything else. To her relief, he did.

"I can't believe you went to him," she said to Eodan. "I mean, that you didn't ask me to do it."

"I thought he might take the situation more seriously if I approached him. He'd know that meant we are desperate." Eodan sat with his back against the wagon's side and closed his eyes. "But I hate talking to him. All that nonsense about how he doesn't hate me, he just knows I'm not human. As if that weren't a sideways kind of hatred."

"It doesn't matter," Ginnevra said. "We'll get to Abraciabene and leave him behind." She chose not to mention the fears she'd had of a Hallowed in opposition to full fellowship of werewolves. That was close to anticipating a future, and she chose not to blaspheme. No, she refused to worry until she knew for sure what Giulliomocte would do as a Hallowed.

Bidelia twitched, but didn't go into a full seizure. Ginnevra put a hand on the young woman's wrist. "She still feels normal, not too hot or too cold."

"That won't last," Eodan said. "But we can't stop the illness, we can only treat it. So there's no sense worrying."

Ginnevra looked at Bidelia's face, wan and white in the moonlight. "No sense in it," she agreed, "but I think I'll worry anyway."

TWENTY-TWO

The storm had arrived when Ginnevra woke Serenna and then retired to her own tent, fat puffy white flakes that clumped together and turned the black night gray. Ginnevra fell asleep praying for it to pass.

When she woke to the chill hush of falling snow, she lay staring at the tent canvas for a moment or two, calming herself against what she feared seeing. It wasn't enough to prepare her for the snow that blanketed the camp, inches deep where it had drifted. Ginnevra stood outside her tent and stared at the sky. What little she could see of the clouds suggested they weren't going to be done dumping on them any time soon. Her sense of time crawled to a stop. They weren't likely to make much progress that day.

But she hadn't counted on the effect of the previous night's attack. No one wanted to stay where werewolves could attack a second time. With only a little effort, they were on the road before the sun had risen above the treetops.

Ginnevra rode at the head next to Buonnane, scanning the

trees for signs of an attack. Now that she knew what hamadryads looked like, she hoped not to be surprised again, but in the dim light that filtered through the falling snow, all the trees looked peaceful.

"How is the Dedicate?" Buonnane asked.

Ginnevra gripped her reins tighter. "Eodan says she's doing as well as can be expected. Her fever hasn't spiked yet, but she's not fully conscious, and he couldn't get her to eat."

"Starvation might kill her faster than the taint." Buonnane, too, gazed restlessly into the distance. "Damn werewolves."

Ginnevra didn't correct her. "All the Revereds have tried to heal her. None of them succeeded, not even Revered Giulliomocte. We have to endure, and hope and pray she has strength to survive."

"It doesn't matter," Buonnane said. "We'd still be in danger even if Dedicate Bidelia were healed."

A howl cut across her last words. It echoed across the trees, far in the distance. Ginnevra looked at Buonnane, whose lips were white with tension. "How far?" she asked, though she already knew the answer. Buonnane needed something to focus on.

Buonnane drew in a deep breath. "Four miles," she said. "But I doubt that's the only one."

Ginnevra signaled the others. "Don't stop," she shouted. "They want us to be afraid and they want us to slow our progress. They know if they can't get us while we're in the forest, they have no chance in the plains. So keep moving—"

Someone at the back of the line shouted, and deep, terrifying growls filled the air. Ginnevra wheeled Dauntless and raced down the line, shouting, "Hold your positions! Watch for a second attack!" Another howl sounded, this one much closer, and the paladins she passed shifted to face the direction it came from.

The fight was over by the time she reached the back, with a

couple of paladins cleaning their blades and two others helping a third to her feet. That one picked up her sword and said, "They went for the horses. They're both dead. I know I struck one of the bastards, but it wasn't a killing blow. I apologize for failing."

Ginnevra stood over the fallen horses, both of which bore several wounds, all of them mortal. "They know where to hit us."

"Zana and I can walk," the paladin said. "We won't slow us down."

"I know," Ginnevra said. "Stay back here. We need to protect the horses as well as the anointed. And we'll take turns protecting the rear."

She returned to her position and shouted for the caravan to move on. When she explained the situation to Buonnane, the captain said, "There's nothing more we can do except stay alert."

"Yes. I wish—" Ginnevra shut her mouth. No sense wishing for what they couldn't have, such as clear skies or a grace that protected them as they moved.

Buonnane's lips pinched tight shut. "The full moon begins tomorrow."

Ginnevra knew what she meant. "Eodan's not a danger."

"I meant he won't be able to care for Dedicate Bidelia during the night." Buonnane wouldn't look at Ginnevra. "And I don't know what he *does* intend to do."

"He'll fight for us, just as he's done all along. His form doesn't matter."

"I hope not," Buonnane said. For once, Ginnevra didn't hear any suppressed fear in the captain's voice.

The werewolves made two more attacks before nightfall, both at the rear of the caravan. The paladins drove them off with no casualties, human or equine. No one celebrated. They all knew the werewolves had yet to make a serious assault.

When it was almost too dark for an ordinary person to see,

Ginnevra called a halt. They camped closer together than they had before, with the horses gathered where they could be closely guarded and the anointed doubling up in their tents. No one spoke beyond the essentials. Ginnevra paced between the campfires, saying a word or two of reassurance but not pushing further than that. This level of tension could drive some of them to breaking, but trying to cheer everyone up was pointless when they all knew the danger they were in.

She sent Serenna to bed and took her position watching Bidelia. Someone had erected a makeshift canopy over the girl to protect her from the falling snow, made of someone's cloak propped on sticks lashed to the wagon's sides. She was fully unconscious and breathing too rapidly. "What are we going to do?" Ginnevra asked.

"Endure," Eodan said. "If she can make it through the night—"

"I meant about tomorrow," Ginnevra said. "The first night of the full moon."

Eodan looked grim. "Someone else will have to watch her while I'm gone."

Ginnevra said nothing. Eodan hadn't pointed out the obvious —that if something happened to Bidelia while he was involuntarily in wolf form, no one else had a physician's knowledge to treat her.

She ducked out from beneath the canopy and surveyed the sky. The snow fell less heavily now, fine white specks like sugar crystals sifting from the sky, but the clouds still obscured the stars and the moon. "It's too bad the transformation happens regardless of whether or not we can see the moon," she mused.

"Unfortunate," Eodan said. His curtness drew her gaze. He knelt beside Bidelia with a hand on her forehead. "Help me get her out of the wagon."

Ginnevra got her hands beneath Bidelia's shoulders and under her knees. Even through her clothing, the girl's body radiated a dull heat far warmer than human normal. She handed Bidelia down to Eodan, then climbed out and took the girl in her arms again. Eodan patted the nearest snowdrift flat without compacting it fully. "Here."

Bidelia didn't move at all, not even to protest being hauled around. Her jaw hung slack, and her arms dangled loose at her sides. Ginnevra set her on the snowdrift and stepped back. "No, help me," Eodan said. He crouched to heap snow atop Bidelia. Ginnevra joined him, scooping up snow and packing it around her until only her face was visible. A few clumps of snow fell on her forehead and melted instantly.

Eodan sat back, his jaw set and tense. "This might not work. Sometimes a fever is too tenacious for any treatment."

"We can't do *nothing*," Ginnevra said.

"Of course not. I meant we need to be prepared for the worst." Eodan took Ginnevra's hand and drew her to sit close beside him. "Remember how we did this. It may be up to you to do it again later."

Ginnevra nodded. She rested her head on Eodan's shoulder and watched Bidelia, who lay so still she might already be a corpse. Ginnevra closed her eyes and banished that thought. They would do everything in their power to save her, and that was everything the Goddess demanded of Her followers.

When she opened her eyes, the karkadann stood not ten feet past Bidelia, staring straight at Ginnevra.

She gasped and sat up. "What is it?" Eodan asked.

She shook her head. "You don't see it," she said, not making it a question.

"The karkadann again?" Eodan sat up as well and turned his head, looking in all directions. "Where is it?"

Ginnevra pointed. Her hand, to her surprise, was steady.

Eodan stood and walked slowly in the direction she indicated. The karkadann ignored him until he was within touching distance, then took several steps backward.

"You're right on top of it," Ginnevra said. "Maybe you shouldn't—"

The karkadann vanished. Ginnevra took in a deep breath that made her lungs ache with cold. "And now it's gone."

Eodan swiveled in place, once more looking around. "It ran away?"

"No, it disappeared. I wish I knew what it wanted." Ginnevra stood and brushed snow off her posterior, which was damp from sitting. "I'm going to warn Buonnane, and to hell with what she thinks of me. If the karkadann is a harbinger, we might use it to know when the werewolves will attack."

"We'll need to be alert for an attack regardless," Eodan said. "They might not wait for the full moon."

"I wish they would attack." Ginnevra once more looked at the overcast sky. "I want this over with."

SHE WOKE in darkness to the sound of howling. Cursing, she scrambled into her armor, gabbling out *"By Your grace I see clearly."* The interior of the tent sprang into sharp relief, all stark lines and curves. She fumbled with the straps, feeling time rush past out of her control. It was an illusion, she knew, but a compelling one. Every moment was a moment in which the werewolves might kill again.

She settled her helmet in place and crawled out of the tent, dragging her sword behind her. The howling came from everywhere at once, surrounding their camp. Ginnevra tried to count the voices and failed. Surely that was far more than the twenty-five Eodan had said were part of a hunting pack?

Buonnane waited at the southern edge of camp. "They haven't attacked," she said when Ginnevra arrived at her side. "But—you can hear them, they're right on top of us. If not for the dark and the snow, we'd see them."

Ginnevra nodded. "So what are they waiting for?"

She'd meant it rhetorically, but Buonnane said, "The right signal. They wouldn't howl if they didn't want us to know how close they are. They could have surprised us at any time."

Movement in the darkness made Ginnevra grab Buonnane's elbow to silence her. The captain drew her sword, and Ginnevra did the same a moment later. Then the howls ceased as abruptly as they'd begun. Ginnevra held her sword at the ready and waited, listening for the attack.

Nothing happened. The tiny specks of snow swirled in the wind, outlining trees that looked like ink sketches in Ginnevra's enhanced vision. She blinked away snow that blew into her eyes —and a human figure stepped out from beneath the trees, not fifteen feet from Ginnevra and Buonnane. He was tall and blond, with a short beard and pale skin, and despite his nakedness, he seemed unaffected by the cold.

Ginnevra raised her sword. "Come to offer yourself for killing?"

Cennfalad smiled that well-remembered, mocking smile. "I have come to offer you a bargain. It is the only one I will give."

"I don't bargain with monsters," Ginnevra said.

"Not even to save lives?" The smile widened. "Give us the man, and we will leave the rest of you alone." He pointed past Ginnevra. She didn't take her eyes off him, though she wished Giulliomocte had not come to where the werewolves could see him. She still didn't know what an evil werewolf might be capable of beyond rending flesh.

Rather than letting herself become angry, she laughed. "That's not a bargain, that's a joke." She took two steps toward Cennfalad, but stopped when she heard growls coming from behind the werewolf. At least five more there, with however many more there were in his pack nearby.

"He is the only one we want. You can count, paladin. One life in exchange for—" Cennfalad made a show of counting, though the rest of the party couldn't possibly be visible. "Well, you know better than I what this will do for you. Refuse, and we slaughter you all."

"What do—" Ginnevra sucked in a startled breath. The karkadann had walked out of the shadows, its gleaming white hide brighter than the moon. It drew near to Cennfalad, who didn't seem to notice it. Ginnevra swallowed and said, "What do you really want? Because you have to know we won't give up one of our own to be torn to pieces by werewolves."

"A fight will not go well for either of us." Cennfalad's smile disappeared. "We hurt you, you hurt us... it is tedious. Better we come to an accord. My Bright Goddess commands me to take the man, and I will do so. This is a thing that will happen no matter what you do."

Ginnevra's lips peeled back in a snarl. "Then I have a counter-proposal. You fight me. Whoever wins gets to dictate terms. That's fair, don't you think?"

Behind her, Buonnane sucked in a breath. Cennfalad's gaze fell on Ginnevra's greatsword. "Unacceptable."

"You want the Revered? You'll have to defeat me first." Ginnevra took another step forward. The growling redoubled. Beside Cennfalad, the karkadann lowered its head as if its horn were a spear it intended to use.

Cennfalad stared at Ginnevra's sword a moment longer. Then he smiled again. "I am not a fool," he said. "It is that I believe I will kill you, but I am not so certain of myself that I do not also believe you might kill me as well." He saluted Ginnevra, and then his gaze slid past her to focus on something behind her. "Captain," he said, his tone of voice mocking. "How are your scars?"

Buonnane screamed and surged forward, passing Ginnevra so swiftly it startled her. Then she realized the captain wasn't going to stop. Throwing down her sword, she tackled Buonnane and brought her to the ground. Something howled very nearby, and Ginnevra closed her eyes as she wrestled with Buonnane. They were without protection, without the other paladins, and Ginnevra had thrown away her sword. She prayed incoherently for the Goddess's hand to protect them both.

But no jaws closed on her arms or legs. No claws swiped at her exposed face. Ginnevra looked up. Cennfalad was gone. The howls and growling had stopped. The karkadann remained, still with its head lowered, its blue eyes hidden from view. Buonnane squirmed beneath Ginnevra, fighting to get free. "I'll let you up if you promise to stay here," Ginnevra said.

Buonnane stopped moving. After a moment, she said, "All right. Let me up."

Ginnevra rolled off and got to her feet, then extended a hand to Buonnane. Buonnane recovered her sword, which she'd dropped when Ginnevra knocked her down, and sheathed it. She turned her back on the karkadann and walked away.

Ginnevra watched her go, still feeling unsettled by that encounter. When she turned around, to her surprise the karkadann was still there. "Did you bring them to us?" she asked. "Or was that coincidence?"

The karkadann raised its head. Its enormous deep blue eyes

looked nearly black in the low light. "Bound together, fate entwined. They walk where she wills."

"That means nothing," Ginnevra said, frustration surging within her. "Why can't you give me a straight answer, if you're going to talk to me at all?"

The karkadann just stared at her, unblinking. Ginnevra growled in frustration. "Fine," she said. "But don't bother showing yourself again. I'm not interested in discovering whatever mystery you're hiding." She turned her back on the creature and strode away.

Giulliomocte approached her, but she didn't slow, forcing him to hurry to keep up. "That was a foolish risk," he said.

"My risk to take," Ginnevra said. "Would you rather I had turned you over to him?"

"Yes," Giulliomocte said.

Ginnevra jerked to a halt. "That's not funny."

"I'm entirely serious. If we can save the lives of—"

"Revered, I realize you don't have much experience with fighting or subterfuge," Ginnevra said wearily, "but that proposal was a lie. Cennfalad wouldn't have kept his word even if he'd sworn on his foul Goddess. They would tear you apart and then come back for the rest of us. So forget any grand notions you might have of sacrificing yourself for the good of all."

Giulliomocte still looked stubborn. "You can't know that."

"No, but I'm confident enough of my guess that I feel comfortable acting on it." Ginnevra started walking again. "I swore I'd get you to Abraciabene, and I won't be forsworn for any reason."

Giulliomocte followed her. "I can't let these people die for my sake."

"Then let them die for the sake of what they believe in," Ginnevra said, rounding on him. "Everyone here believes the

Goddess has asked great sacrifices of them. You're not the only one with faith."

The Revered's breathing was heavy and angry, and his eyes on her were fierce. Then he turned and walked away. Ginnevra watched him long enough to be sure he wasn't leaving the camp, and then she trod wearily to the wagon. Bidelia slept quietly for once, with Serenna stretched out asleep to one side. Eodan sat cross-legged with his hands folded in his lap and his eyes closed. When Ginnevra said his name, he blinked and rose to his feet. "I heard the howl, but I didn't dare leave her."

"It's just as well. It wasn't a fight." Ginnevra recounted for him what had happened. When she finished, Eodan closed his eyes again and let out a sigh.

"Tomorrow I'm going after Cennfalad," he said. "Don't try to stop me."

"Is it bad that I don't want to? Eodan, if you can kill him, or drive him to where the paladins can kill him, it will save so many lives."

Eodan nodded. "Without their dominus, the hunting pack will have to return to the main body of the pack to choose a new dominus. They won't be able to do that in time to stop us reaching civilization."

"That needs to be our priority, then." Ginnevra kissed Eodan. "Someday, this will be over."

"And when that happens, we will celebrate properly," Eodan said with a meaningful smile.

Ginnevra made the rounds once before returning to her tent. The paladins were all alert; the anointed had gone to their own tents. All was quiet. She settled in to sleep with only the barest feeling of disquiet. If she let her worries disrupt her sleep, she'd be useless.

She woke feeling rested and in better spirits. The snow had

stopped falling, and the sky was clear for once, blue and high and untroubled by human concerns. She put on her armor and walked through the camp, greeting each person while secretly surveying them for signs of fear or despair. The anointed were as sleepy-eyed as they always were in the morning, but not frightened.

She stopped last at the tents where the Revereds slept. Revered Orselle sat at the campfire, waiting for the pot to boil. "Marsillia sleeps late when she has the chance," he said when she asked about the other two. "But Domenico is already awake. I think he went to relieve himself."

Ginnevra's sense of disquiet from the previous night grew. "He rose before you?"

"He usually does." Orselle resumed staring at the pot. Ginnevra walked around him to Giulliomocte's tent and opened the flap. Giulliomocte's bedroll was undisturbed, and his few possessions lay neatly on the ground close at hand to anyone lying there.

Ginnevra ducked back outside. "He hasn't slept in his tent."

Orselle looked up, his hare-like nose quivering. "Of course he has. I saw him enter his tent last night, after the commotion."

"If he'd slept there and rose this morning, he wouldn't have straightened his bedroll, he would have rolled it up so it could be stowed." Ginnevra grabbed Pratese's tent's flap and jerked it open. For the briefest moment, she imagined finding Giulliomocte and Pratese together, reconciled or at least indulging in physical attraction. But Pratese was alone. She blinked up at Ginnevra.

"Revered, when's the last time you saw Revered Giulliomocte?" Ginnevra demanded.

"Saw—" Pratese's jaw hardened. "Last night. And I don't know why you think I keep track of Domenico's movements."

Ginnevra stood without answering. "He's gone," she said to no one. She had a very good idea where.

TWENTY-THREE

S he rushed through the camp to the nearest sentry, on the far western side. "Did either of you see Revered Giulliomocte recently? Maybe a few hours ago?"

Pia exchanged glances with Bartolla. "We only just came on watch about an hour before dawn," Pia said. "He hasn't been here since then."

Ginnevra nodded thanks and set off around the perimeter, loping at a ground-eating pace. Silently, she berated herself. She should have known Giulliomocte wouldn't give in so easily. That damn fool was going to get them all killed.

None of the sentries had seen Giulliomocte. Ginnevra, breathing heavily with exertion, ran for Buonnane's tent. She found the captain speaking with one of the paladins near the supply wagons. "I need everyone gathered where I can speak to them," Ginnevra said. "Revered Giulliomocte is missing."

Buonnane's eyes widened. "See to it," she told the paladin, who hurried off. "You're sure of this?"

"I suppose it's possible he's somewhere in camp, but—yes,

I'm sure. He was talking about giving himself up to the were-wolves last night."

Buonnane swore. "Goddess save me from self-sacrificing idealists. Do you know how long he's been gone?"

"Revered Orselle saw him just after the werewolves made their threat. Call it two o'clock or thereabouts." Ginnevra calmed her breathing and added, "None of the current sentries recall seeing him leave, and the earliest any of them were on duty was six o'clock."

"That's a long time." Buonnane scanned the camp as if she hoped to see Giulliomocte appear. "Someone must have seen *something*."

Ginnevra said nothing. An anointed, particularly a Revered, had access to some of the graces a paladin did in addition to ones reserved for the anointed. And one of those graces shrouded the invoker in darkness—a better concealment than full night. If Giulliomocte had thought to conceal himself that way, they might never find him. Or—

She said, "I'll be back. See what you can learn." With that, she ran for Bidelia's wagon.

Eodan was asleep near Bidelia, who for once didn't look rest-less or over-warm or shivering. She was so peaceful a pang of fear shot through Ginnevra, who quickly knelt beside the girl and felt her forehead. It was normally warm.

Movement nearby drew her attention. Eodan rolled over, blinking. "Ginnevra. She's not feverish again, is she? You look frightened."

"She's fine. Not fine, but—oh, you know what I mean. Eodan, Revered Giulliomocte left camp sometime early this morning. I think he's gone to give himself up to the werewolves."

Eodan sat up. "That fool. They'll kill him and return to attack us."

"Which is what I told him, but he apparently didn't believe me. I need you to track him, if you can."

Eodan nodded. "Keep an eye on Bidelia while I'm gone." He rose and began removing his clothing.

"Oh, no," Ginnevra said. "You're not going alone. I'm coming with you."

"Ginnevra, you can't help me track. I'll find him, I promise."

Ginnevra gripped his wrist. "And do what, then? I'm going with you because I can't let you face the pack alone. Bad enough the rest of the paladins have to stay here in case the werewolves get any ideas about attacking the defenseless anointed while we're all out hunting Giulliomocte. And it's a waste of time for you to locate the Revered and then have to return here to summon us. We're going together."

Eodan smiled, a wry expression. "I suppose I could outrun you."

"Which you would never do, because I would eventually catch up, and then you'd have a hell of a lot worse to deal with than evil werewolves." Ginnevra released him. "I'll wake Serenna."

When she returned with a sleepy-eyed Serenna in tow, Eodan had assumed his wolf form. Serenna gazed at his enormous black-furred shape in wonder. "I didn't realize how big werewolves were as wolves," she said, her voice faint.

"Eodan won't hurt you," Ginnevra said.

Serenna transferred her gaze to Ginnevra. "Of course not. But —he's *really* big."

Her awestruck words made Ginnevra smile. "Watch Bidelia. I'll send someone to help you manage her if her fever spikes. We'll be back soon." She hoped she hadn't just lied to the girl. Well, hopefulness in the face of calamity was a paladin trait; if Serenna intended to join the paladin ranks, she should learn that sooner rather than later.

Ginnevra and Eodan ran to where the rest of the camp gathered. Buonnane watched them approach, but made no gesture at seeing Eodan beyond a tightening of her lips. "No one remembers seeing Revered Giulliomocte," she told Ginnevra, "but two of our sentries reported feeling unexpectedly sleepy for a moment or two around five o'clock. They say it wasn't enough to distract them, and they swear they saw nothing out of the ordinary, but it matches the effect of a concealment grace."

"We weren't careless," Zana insisted. She appeared to be on the verge of tears, which made Ginnevra even angrier with Giulliomocte.

"I don't think you were," she told the paladin. "Don't blame yourselves. None of us thought we had to defend against our own people, or against an attack that came from inside camp. You were on the south, weren't you?"

Zana nodded. "South and a little east."

Ginnevra turned to Buonnane. "We'll start there. Ready the camp against an assault. If we're too late, the werewolves will be on us no later than moonrise."

"You can't go alone. You'll be slaughtered," Buonnane said.

"Yes, and if we are, I swear I'll follow Revered Giulliomocte into the afterlife with some very strong words." Ginnevra settled her helmet on her head. "But I don't intend to go without a fight."

Buonnane looked terribly conflicted, like someone whose available choices were all bad ones. "Take two more paladins, at least."

Ginnevra considered it. She shook her head. "We'll need to move fast, and the more people go with us, the slower we'll be, even if those people are paladins. And I don't want to rob the camp of any of its defenders. Besides, this is ultimately my responsibility."

"I understand." Buonnane signaled the others to close in. "Join with me in prayer."

Ginnevra expected her to ask Revered Pratese or Revered Orselle to pray, but Buonnane clasped her hands near her throat and said, "Goddess, I pray Your watchful eye be upon us this day. Grant us Your strength and courage, and..." She hesitated long enough that Ginnevra started to wonder if she'd forgotten what she meant to ask for. Finally, Buonnane said, "Grant Your servant, and this werewolf, the ability to find Revered Giulliomocte, and if it be Your will, to find him before he is lost to us forever. Ever in Your name."

Ginnevra murmured the final words in a daze. Whether the Goddess would bless a creature She was forbidden from accepting into Her worship, she didn't know. But that Buonnane could bring herself to pray for a creature she feared...

She decided not to say anything to draw attention to Buonnane's humbling of herself. "Thank you," she said. "Please have someone help Serenna with Dedicate Bidelia, and we will return soon." That was a hope for the future she didn't feel superstitious about voicing.

Snow had accumulated in drifts even beneath the pines, making Ginnevra consider how deep the snow must be on the plains. The roads had been bad enough. Now she was grateful for anything that might reveal Giulliomocte's passing. She hung back to let Eodan lead the way. How much of a scent he could pick up in this cold weather, she didn't know, but if Giulliomocte had been clever enough to use a grace that obscured his footprints, Eodan's nose was their only hope.

Eodan stopped and growled, a short, quiet sound that was more of an alert than a warning. Ginnevra stepped up to his side. Footprints marked the snow ahead, boots big enough for a man, with no wear to their soles such as a paladin's would have.

"That's something, anyway," Ginnevra said, curling her fingers into Eodan's fur. "Let's move."

They ran at a slow, jogging gait, watching for where the footprints left the snow to cross the short stretches of open, bare ground. Eodan's path never wavered. Ginnevra left following the trail to him and took to watching their surroundings. Small animals, voles and squirrels and the occasional fox, scurried away as they passed, but she saw nothing larger, certainly nothing that could be a werewolf. The crisp, icy air filled her chest, making her ache with cold, but it smelled fresh and not of sickly sweet-sourness.

Distantly, she heard a howl, and her heart sped up for half a breath before she recognized the sound as that of a real wolf crying out to its pack. Nearer to hand, a branch groaned and cracked in the cold. The sound echoed through the forest. Eodan didn't slow. Ginnevra scanned the trees, though the odds of a branch splitting and falling just as they passed beneath were vanishingly small.

When she returned her gaze to ground level, the karkadann stood in the distance, watching her.

She grabbed Eodan's ruff and said, "Stop. It's the karkadann again."

Eodan came to a halt and looked up at her. She shook her head. "Don't change. It's not doing anything, but it is in our path."

The karkadann regarded Ginnevra with its large blue eyes. Then it turned and trotted away.

Ginnevra watched it go for a moment, then said, "We need to follow it."

Eodan whined, a high-pitched sound that cut off abruptly. "I know," Ginnevra said, "but... I can't explain it, Eodan, but I think it's here for a reason." She ran her fingers through his fur. Eodan lowered his head and shook his head in a gesture Ginnevra recognized as resignation.

Now she took the lead, one eye on the ground and Giulliomocte's tracks, the other on the white flanks of the karkadann. After about a dozen strides, the karkadann's path veered away from Giulliomocte's. Ginnevra slowed briefly, then, with a silent curse, continued to follow the monster. Part of her screamed a warning that she was being a fool and her foolishness was going to get her and Eodan killed along with Giulliomocte, but that fey mood she'd felt while speaking to the karkadann weeks before had returned, and it drew her along in the creature's wake.

Her inner sense of direction, the result of a grace, told her they were traveling in a great curved arc, as if the karkadann were circling something. She lost track of how long they'd been running, and the pines' dark green needles blocked her view of the sun. Surely Giulliomocte couldn't have outpaced a paladin so thoroughly? Ginnevra didn't feel tired at all, not with the relatively slow pace they set, but they were traveling fast enough they should have found the Revered by now. Or would have if they'd stayed in a straight line. At this point, they had no choice but to keep going.

Regardless of how fast they traveled, the karkadann stayed the same distance ahead, close enough to see clearly but far enough that Ginnevra would have had to run at full speed to catch it. And she didn't want to catch it. She felt in her bones that catching it would be a bad idea, either because it was a monster that would turn on her or because that would ruin any chance she had of finding Giulliomocte. So she kept her distance and hoped she hadn't made a mistake.

She looked up from where she'd been searching for the small round marks of the karkadann's hooves to see the creature had stopped. She slowed, grabbing Eodan's ruff again. The karkadann's eyes met hers, blue and fathomless, and she shivered. "What do you want?" she asked. "Why are you here?"

The karkadann turned its head to look in the direction it had been leading them. Ginnevra followed its gaze. There, in the distance, a human figure trudged toward them through the trees, his dark-cloaked shoulders dusted with snow from where he brushed against the pines.

"All right," Ginnevra said, "you brought us the long way around to intercept him. Why couldn't we—"

She looked back at the karkadann, but it was gone. She let out a frustrated breath. "Let's stop him," she said.

She and Eodan ran, not bothering to move quietly, though Ginnevra didn't call out Giulliomocte's name. No sense doing more than they already had to alert the werewolves to their presence.

They reached Giulliomocte in a place where the trees thinned out almost enough to be a clearing. The Revered didn't look up until they were almost on top of him. He looked weary and resigned, for all the world like a child preparing for a lecture. So Ginnevra decided to disappoint him.

"I'm glad we found you, Revered," she said. "We have to go back. The caravan won't go until we're there."

"I already told you what I intend," Giulliomocte said, sounding even wearier than he looked. "You should not have followed me."

"I'm not going to let you be killed. It's my job to get you safely to Abraciabene—"

Giulliomocte's lips pinched tight together in a frown. "Prime Cassaline, this is my duty," he said. "I know what I'm doing. Don't interfere."

"Don't interfere? Revered, how is it your duty to die at the teeth and claws of werewolves?" Ginnevra let out an exasperated breath. "You're to be of the Hallowed. The Goddess requires much of Her chosen servants, but She doesn't send them off to be slaughtered."

"You know nothing of what the Goddess requires." Giulliomocte's frown deepened. "I have faith in Her protection. She has said nothing of protecting anyone else who might get themselves tangled up in this disaster. It's essential that I do this alone."

"Do *what* alone? Revered, you're not making any sense."

Giulliomocte looked down at Eodan. "Werewolves are monsters regardless of their allegiances. I don't believe they deserve full fellowship with humans, and I find your liaison with this one repugnant. But I have sworn never to harm a creature who is not evil. I will find the werewolves and bring destruction down upon them, and if I die in doing that, then I die knowing I served my Goddess."

Ginnevra's thoughts swirled in confusion. She caught hold of the one clear thing she understood of Giulliomocte's words and said, "So you wanted to get away from Eodan so that grace wouldn't kill him? By the Goddess, Revered, I do not understand you! How can you treat Eodan like someone deserving of protection while still thinking of him as monstrous?"

"I won't argue the point with you, prime. We're past that. Go back to the caravan." Giulliomocte turned away. Ginnevra grabbed him by the shoulder and made him face her.

"You selfish, arrogant fool," she said. "You talk of sacrificing your life as casually as if it means nothing to anyone but yourself. Didn't it occur to you how everyone else will be affected if you die?"

Giulliomocte wrenched away from her hand. "You're the one who told me they all have faith. They should understand sacrifice better than the average person."

"Sacrifice, yes, but not blatant stupidity," Ginnevra said. "They look to you as representative of the Goddess's will. If you're killed by the Bright One's creatures, they'll take that as evidence that you weren't what they all believed, and that maybe all those doubts Revered Pratese sowed were legitimate."

Dull redness spread over Giulliomocte's scowling face. "They should know better than to believe Marsillia. Her bitterness is evident."

"Not to those young anointed. Revered, you do have a duty, but it's not to die horribly in the back of beyond. It's to show the world that the Goddess's will is a blessing to us even when we don't understand it. Please, come back with us. We will fight the werewolves our way." Ginnevra wanted to rest her hand on Eodan's head for strength, but she was reluctant to distract Giulliomocte by drawing attention to the werewolf beside her.

Giulliomocte's expression shifted, his complexion returning to its usual pale hue, his frown fading. "I understand," he said. "You haven't heard the Goddess's voice. She commanded me in this course of action. How can I not follow Her instructions?"

His words filled Ginnevra with unease. It was one thing to tell a Revered he was wrong; countering the Goddess's word was a whole new level of audacity. Ginnevra didn't believe the Goddess would ever send any of Her faithful worshippers to their death, but she was keenly aware that she was no theologian and had no understanding of the subtleties of the divine inscrutability. "I don't know," she said. "Maybe She wanted you out here for some other reason. Maybe it was to show me that you really are committed to protecting the innocent, if you were willing to sacrifice yourself so your grace wouldn't kill Eodan. And maybe you're right, and I'm wrong, and this is what the Goddess wants."

She unslung her sword belt from her shoulder and drew her sword. "All I know for sure," she said, holding the sword vertically in front of her face in the salute to the Blessed, "is that I swore to die to protect you. And nothing that's happened can change that. So if you're determined to throw your life away, I'll make sure your sacrifice isn't completely wasted."

Giulliomocte's mouth slackened in astonishment. He looked at Eodan, then back at Ginnevra. "You would," he said, his voice faint. Then he squared his shoulders and tilted his chin high. "I'm not going back."

"Then let's see if we can find the pack." Ginnevra sheathed her sword. "It shouldn't be hard. I'm surprised they haven't found us already."

Eodan sat back on his haunches and whined. Then, in a silver shimmer, he was human. "Maybe that was on purpose," he said.

A chill ran through Ginnevra's veins. "What do you mean?"

"Suppose the Bright One commanded them to stay back until Revered Giulliomocte was too far from the caravan for anyone to help him?" Eodan stood. "She might have more in mind for him than death."

"I don't understand," Giulliomocte said.

The chill deepened. "You're the first male Hallowed," Ginnevra said. "How much better if the Bright One could corrupt you?"

"That's impossible." Giulliomocte frowned again. "I'd never choose to follow the Bright One."

"Maybe not," Eodan said, "but that wouldn't stop her trying to break you." He scanned the trees, then swore under his breath and changed back to his wolf form. He tilted his head as if sniffing the wind.

Ginnevra put a hand on Giulliomocte's shoulder. "We have to get out of here. Now. Whatever the Goddess had in mind, it wasn't for you to be corrupted."

Giulliomocte didn't move. "I have faith—"

"I know you do. But the Goddess tells us that faith won't protect the foolhardy. She gives us reason and understanding so we can make good decisions. And if there is any way this could end with a Hallowed serving the Bright One—" Ginnevra drew in a breath. "I swear by the Goddess I will knock you unconscious and carry you out of here if you refuse to go now."

"You wouldn't dare." Giulliomocte reached into the neck of his thigh-length black robe. Ginnevra reversed her grip on her sword so the round, heavy pommel was uppermost.

"Stop," Eodan said. Ginnevra hadn't noticed him changing shape. "It's too late."

Ginnevra lowered her sword. The sweetish scent of decomposition reached her nose. In the distance, shapes moved, low to the ground and running fast. "This way," she said, grabbing Giulliomocte's free hand and pulling him along despite his protests.

Only a few steps back along the path she and Eodan had made told her running was futile. More werewolves ran toward them from that direction as well. She dropped Giulliomocte's hand. "Time for that grace," she told him.

Giulliomocte's eyes widened. "It may kill your companion."

Ginnevra glanced at Eodan, who was still in his human form. Eodan nodded. "I believe the Goddess knows who the true monsters are," he said. "And it didn't kill me the first time. I'll risk it."

Giulliomocte looked from Eodan to the oncoming werewolves. "I—very well." He fished his jet grace out of his robe and yanked the chain off over his head. Clasping the grace in his right hand, he held it at arm's length high above. Ginnevra moved to stand beside Eodan, taking his hand in hers. Her heart was beating so rapidly it hurt. Eodan had his eyes on Giulliomocte and seemed as calm as if death weren't imminent, one way or another.

When the werewolves were barely fifty feet away, Giulliomocte tilted his head to the unseen sky and shouted, *"By Your grace I smite my foe!"*

Black lightning speared through the pines, cracking open the air with a sound like a million branches snapping under the weight of the snow. The bolts struck the ground in dozens of places around the three of them. The light burned Ginnevra's eyes, and she squeezed them shut and threw up one arm to protect them. The cracking sound was so loud she couldn't even hear her own cry of pain and fear, let alone the howls of the dying werewolves. Her own breath rasped in and out of her chest, making it ache with cold even more than it already did.

The sound faded. Ginnevra uncovered her eyes and blinked. Black rings filled her vision, pulsing like living things. She rubbed her eyes and tried again. Gradually, the rings disappeared, and she realized she was looking at Eodan. He looked just as he always did, and she felt his hand in hers and let out an enormous, grateful breath.

Giulliomocte stood nearby as well. His pupils were the merest pinpricks in his brown eyes, but as she was about to grab him again, the pupils dilated, and he blinked. He looked past her, and his mouth fell open. "Prime," he said, then fell silent.

Ginnevra turned to look at what he'd seen. A line of werewolves faced them, pale and huge and snarling. Not one of them had fallen to Giulliomocte's grace. The line extended in both directions through the trees, curving around them. She spun, confirming that they were surrounded. She didn't have time to count, but she was sure there were more than the twenty-five Eodan had said a hunting pack contained.

To her left, the white wolf approached. He shimmered silver and rose to face her. "Let us see how bold you are now that your Goddess has deserted you," Cennfalad said.

TWENTY-FOUR

G innevra stepped in front of Giulliomocte. Behind her, Eodan was silent, but the scent of his werewolf musk intensified, telling her he had resumed his wolf shape. She brought her greatsword to the ready. "If you know what's good for you, you'll stand aside," she said, her eyes never leaving Cennfalad's.

Cennfalad's smile broadened. "Brave words." He walked forward a few paces, staying well out of her range. "I think you cannot kill us. Not if the man cannot."

"This sword says otherwise," Ginnevra retorted. "Stand aside. Now. Or we'll see how well your pack fights without its dominus."

Every werewolf took a step forward, tightening the circle. Ginnevra didn't twitch. Inside, she frantically cast about for a solution that would get them all out of there safely. Plans rose up and were cast aside as rapidly. She surveyed the ranks of the were-wolves and found a couple of places where there weren't as many heavily-muscled pale wolves as elsewhere. If the three of them ran fast, and focused on attacking just there—

"We all know our destinies," Cennfalad said. "Our Goddess has been very clear. The man will serve her, or die."

"I will never serve the Bright One," Giulliomocte said from behind Ginnevra's right shoulder.

"No? Not when you have been abandoned by your mistress?" Cennfalad's voice was mocking.

"She granted me Her grace," Giulliomocte retorted. "I don't call that abandonment."

"Then what do you call it when we are unharmed?" Cennfalad laughed. "How else can my Bright Lady triumph over her sister than when the Dark Goddess's servant is unworthy?"

Giulliomocte said nothing. His breath rang harsh and heavy in Ginnevra's ear. "Don't listen to him, Revered," she said in a low voice. "He's trying to rattle you."

"I have faith in my Goddess's power," Giulliomocte said in the same low voice. "But I don't understand what happened. I don't know what it means."

"Try again?"

She felt the air move as Giulliomocte shook his head. "I don't dare attempt it a second time if it failed once. The Goddess might see that as me trying to force Her hand."

"Talk all you want," Cennfalad called out. "It changes nothing. The man is the Bright Goddess's prey."

Ginnevra managed not to flinch. She couldn't maintain this stance indefinitely, not because of the physical strain—she could wield her sword for hours without tiring—but because it was spiritually wearying, holding a position on the knife's edge between standing down and attacking. "Then I challenge you as I did before," she said. "You fight me, just the two of us. Defeat me, and you can have whatever you like."

Eodan growled. She ignored him, all her attention on Cennfalad. "What, you don't think you can take me? You need all your friends to fight one woman?"

"You are not the one I want," Cennfalad said, still with that mocking smile.

Ginnevra felt Giulliomocte step out from behind her. Involuntarily, she glanced over her shoulder. In her moment of inattention, Cennfalad rushed her, transforming to the white wolf in midair.

Ginnevra brought her sword back to the ready, but too late; Cennfalad was inside her guard and snapping at her neck. His claws scraped along her cuirass, sending up a terrible shrill *skree* that raised the hairs on the back of Ginnevra's neck. She smelled burnt flesh, but Cennfalad seemed not to care that he was in contact with her silvered armor.

She got her left arm across the werewolf's throat and pushed, regaining her balance. Behind her, Giulliomocte said something Ginnevra couldn't understand. She ignored him and thrust at Cennfalad's heart, forcing him back. He snarled, dodged, and leaped at her face. It was her turn to fall back. She expected to stumble into Giulliomocte, but he wasn't there. Cursing the Revered's stupidity under her breath, she ducked and drove her sword toward Cennfalad's belly. He dodged, but not fast enough, and the tip of her sword scored a line along his stomach.

Cennfalad yelped and backed away. Ginnevra grinned. "Watch yourself," she said.

Then Giulliomocte shouted, *"By Your grace I raise this shield!"*

Blue light flared all around, blinding Ginnevra for a moment. She blinked hard to banish the effect and raised her sword to a defensive position, hoping the werewolves were as blind as she. As her vision was restored, she saw the blue shielding barrier several feet away, surrounding her and Eodan and Giulliomocte, with Cennfalad still nearby, shaking his head as if it hurt, and—

Eodan howled an instant before something heavy struck her from the side. Another werewolf snapped at her face, its jaws foaming. Ginnevra hit the ground and rolled to get away from both her assailants. One of them yelped as Eodan's teeth gripped its ruff, dragging it away. Then Cennfalad was there, his jaws closing over her gloved left hand. She smacked him in the head with the pommel of her sword, stunning him enough that she could wrench away before he bore down hard.

Gasping from fear at nearly losing a hand, Ginnevra rolled again and rose, once more taking a defensive stance. She didn't dare look away from Cennfalad to find Giulliomocte. Maybe the lack of other howls and snarling meant the werewolves hadn't gone after him. She had no idea how many more of the monsters were trapped inside the barrier with them.

Cennfalad paced slowly toward her, his head lowered, his ruff standing on end. She didn't have the breath to taunt him again. Instead, she made a little beckoning motion with her left hand, smiling a predator's smile.

"Dark Lady," Giulliomocte said. By the sound of his voice, he was some distance away and unharmed, or at least wasn't under attack. "I beg of you, hear the voice of Your servant, and save us in our time of need."

Ginnevra waited for him to invoke a grace, any grace, that would defeat these werewolves. The barrier was a temporary solution, one she was grateful for, but when it collapsed, the other werewolves would be upon them. She added her silent prayer to Giulliomocte's that he knew something that would save them. She could kill Cennfalad, probably, but it would take most of her strength and skill, and she now doubted the rest of the pack would leave at the death of their dominus.

Instead, she heard a thunderous voice, rich and deep, that shook her to the marrow of her bones. *Domenico,* it said, *do not let this woman fight your battle for you. Have faith, and invoke My grace again.*

"Goddess, why did it not work before? I don't understand," Giulliomocte said, in a conversational tone as if the voice belonged to any ordinary speaker.

Ginnevra's throat was too dry for speech. Cennfalad had halted outside the reach of her sword and appeared to be listening, which was fortunate because Ginnevra didn't think she could move. She swallowed and moistened her lips. She turned, keeping Cennfalad in her sights, to face Giulliomocte. "Revered," she said. It came out as a croak, and she swallowed again. "Revered, don't do it."

"If the Goddess commands it, even you must obey," Giulliomocte said. His face was turned heavenward, and his expression was far too peaceful for someone facing death.

Ginnevra licked her lips and tried once more. "Revered," she said, *"that is not the Goddess."*

Giulliomocte's head jerked. "Are you so corrupt you don't recognize your own Goddess's voice?"

Out of the corner of her eye, Ginnevra saw Cennfalad take a step toward her. She pointed her sword at him, and he stopped, though he was clearly poised to move if she ignored him for too long. "I do recognize the Goddess's voice when I hear it. It's not something you ever forget. Which is why I know—Revered, is this the voice that's been talking to you?"

Giulliomocte regarded her with a sad, compassionate look. "I know you and I have been at odds, but I didn't believe you would try to deceive me." He turned his face heavenward again and closed his eyes. "Goddess, tell me what to do."

Invoke My grace.

"No!" Ginnevra shouted. "Revered, don't do it. This isn't the Goddess speaking, I swear it."

"You object to me cleansing the world of these werewolves?" Giulliomocte said. "I told you, you must have faith that your werewolf companion is not the enemy of the Goddess—"

"Revered," Ginnevra said, keeping her voice level, "that's the Bright One. If she wants you to do something, it can't be for holy reasons. You can't obey her."

"I know what I believe!" Giulliomocte shouted. "I refuse to listen to someone who's been corrupted by a monster."

Cennfalad lunged. Ginnevra blocked his attack automatically and sliced at the werewolf's neck. Cennfalad backed away again, but remained poised to leap once more. The second werewolf lay a short distance away, its fur slicked with blood. She couldn't take her eyes off Cennfalad to see if any of the other werewolves had attacked. The memory of that deep, rich, horrible voice filled her with sick dread. Whatever the Bright One had in mind for Giulliomocte, it had to mean his destruction.

"Then listen to the Blessed," she said, not looking to see if he was paying attention. "She's the one the Goddess spoke to. I only overheard. Do you think the Blessed wouldn't recognize the Goddess's voice? *Please*, Revered—Domenico. You have faith, I know you do. Now is the time to show it."

Domenico, my beloved. The Bright One's voice resonated within Ginnevra like the thrum of a beating heart, like lifeblood pulsing through her veins. It was close—so similar to the Goddess's voice Ginnevra could understand how someone could be fooled—but this voice lacked the smooth, silken sound Ginnevra had never forgotten. *Domenico, I have commanded you. You have the power to end this. Use My grace to bring the monsters down.*

"Domen—" Ginnevra began, then had to leap away from Cennfalad's attack. Now he bore down on her in earnest, darting in and out with his whole weight behind his attacks, moving fast enough she couldn't go on the offense. She feinted left, swung right, and connected with the werewolf's shoulder. The stink of burnt hair rose up in the freezing cold, and Cennfalad howled and backed away—but only for a moment. Ginnevra took that moment to say, "Domenico, please, you have to believe—"

Cennfalad rushed her again, this time bowling her over in her inattention. Ginnevra hit the hard ground with an *oof* of breath and tried to roll out of the way. Cennfalad bore down on her with all his weight and snapped at her throat. Again, Ginnevra blocked his jaws with her left arm.

Giulliomocte's voice came to her ears again, faintly over the sound of Cennfalad's snarls and her own heavy breathing. "Goddess," he was saying, "prove to me which is truth."

Invoke that grace again. With My blessing, it will work, and you will see the truth of my words.

"No—" Ginnevra gasped. Cennfalad's head drove ever closer to her throat, pressing down on her arm. Where was Eodan? The only reason he wouldn't come to her aid was if he was—she refused to consider the possibilities.

She frantically scanned the woods beyond Cennfalad and saw no werewolves, no Eodan, nothing but the barrier and trees. And then the karkadann was there beyond the barrier, watching her struggle. Its indifferent stance infuriated her. "Get out of here!" she screamed, not caring that this made her seem like a lunatic. "Go on, get! You foul harbinger, you monster—don't you dare stand there like none of this has anything to do with you!"

She struggled to get out from beneath the werewolf, but his weight and leverage were too much even for her Goddess-given strength. With her last burst of strength, she shoved Cennfalad away from her throat and gasped, "What do you have faith in, Domenico?"

Something big and black struck Cennfalad in the side, knocking him away from Ginnevra. Eodan's snarls drowned out

Cennfalad's, and the two werewolves, black and white, rolled and snapped and clawed at each other. Ginnevra rolled to her feet and snatched up her sword. Two other werewolves lay dead nearby, and the rest of the pack had gathered together beyond the barrier to pace restlessly through the trees, every werewolf's attention on the battle between Eodan and their dominus.

Every werewolf but one.

One more werewolf had made it inside the barrier. It was nearly as big as Cennfalad and moved ponderously, slowly, its blue eyes fixed on Giulliomocte. The Revered seemed not to notice it. His head was tilted back, his eyes open and staring at the sky. The chain of his grace dangled from his closed fist. Ginnevra shouted and ran at the werewolf, but came up short when Eodan let out an agonized howl. She turned to see Cennfalad's powerful jaws clamped down on Eodan's shoulder. A shudder ran through Ginnevra. Then she turned her back on them and raced to put herself between the werewolf and Giulliomocte.

The werewolf sprang. With a scream, Ginnevra leaped into its path, hitting its flank and knocking it off course so it missed Giulliomocte by a handspan. Giulliomocte still stood without moving, though his robe fluttered with the wind of the werewolf's passing. Ginnevra recovered her balance and again put herself between the two, sucking in air to keep from falling over.

Domenico, my beloved, the Bright One said. *Have faith in Me and My words. Do as I command, and accept your path.*

The werewolf had also regained its balance and now stood in a wide-legged stance before Ginnevra, poised to leap if she showed the slightest weakness or distraction. Despair flooded through Ginnevra, not for her own sake but for Giulliomocte's. "Domenico," she said, "we've been at odds from the beginning, and I know you think I'm deviant, but I've never lied to you. I swear this voice is the Bright One. Sometimes you have to trust in someone else's word. Let that time be now. Please."

The werewolf rushed Ginnevra. She held her ground and waited for its leap. When it sprang at her, low and fast, she pivoted for a killing blow.

Something else struck her from the side, making her stumble and go to one knee. Cennfalad bore down on her, his maddened eyes and foaming mouth telling her he was too far gone to care that her mail was burning him. She dropped her sword and wrapped her arms around him, wrestling him to the ground. Then Eodan was there, in human form, one arm around the werewolf's throat, pulling him off Ginnevra. She rolled away and came to her feet, searching for her sword.

Ten feet away, Giulliomocte faced the other werewolf, who was poised to leap.

Ginnevra screamed his name and ran toward them. Giulliomocte raised his fist holding his grace high above his head. Then he opened his hand and let the grace fall to the ground. "Let us make an end," he said.

The Bright One screamed, a sound of mingled fury and despair. The werewolf sprang, knocking Giulliomocte back, and raked the Revered's chest with its terrible claws. Giulliomocte made no sound as its second stroke found his throat.

Red haze cloaked Ginnevra's vision. With a burst of strength beyond even what the Goddess granted Her paladins, she lifted the werewolf off Giulliomocte's body and flung it into the barrier. Blue lightning flashed, and the werewolf transformed instantly to its human shape and convulsed violently as if electrified. The werewolves clustered outside the barrier cringed back, and some of them whined in fear. Ginnevra ignored them.

She turned on Cennfalad, who was bleeding from a dozen wounds, and on Eodan, still upright but limping. His head sagged in weariness. Ginnevra retrieved her sword and stalked toward Cennfalad, dragging the sword's tip along the frozen ground. She was too tired to taunt the dominus, and she couldn't think of anything clever to say in any case. Her mind's eye saw nothing but Giulliomocte's bloody body.

Cennfalad walked forward to meet her, his growl low and terrible. Ginnevra stopped a few feet from the werewolf and raised her sword in challenge. Cennfalad took another step, paused, and then with a howl charged her.

Time seemed to slow for everyone but Ginnevra. She watched in a detached, indifferent way as Cennfalad floated toward her, giving her all the time in the world to bring her sword around for a thrust. The blade impaled the dominus through the belly and tore downward as Cennfalad's momentum carried him inexorably to his death.

She stepped back from the body, which twitched once, twice, and then fell still. Time resumed its course, and brought with it all the pains and exhaustion the terror of battle had kept at bay. Ginnevra knelt and cleaned her sword on Cennfalad's fur. Then she stood and looked through the barrier at the werewolf pack. They were motionless, all of them still in wolf shape so their expressions were unreadable. Then two at the rear of the pack broke and ran. A ripple of motion surged through the rest, and they turned to follow those two. In moments, the forest was empty of living werewolves.

Ginnevra sank to the earth as Eodan limped to her side. She almost put her arms around his neck before remembering she was still encased in silvered armor. She wanted so badly to bury her face in his fur, not caring that he was nearly as bloody as Cennfalad. "I failed," she said. "I wasn't fast enough."

Eodan shuddered, and then he was human. He took her hand and said, "Was that really the Bright One's voice?"

"You didn't recognize it?"

"She's never spoken to me." He held Ginnevra's hand tighter. "The Revered didn't obey Her command. He died uncorrupted. Maybe that was the point."

Ginnevra shivered. "I can't believe death was the only alternative, Eodan. He wouldn't have died if I'd been closer." She squeezed her eyes tightly against the hot tears leaking from them.

Eodan said nothing. Ginnevra wept silently, her whole body shaking with sobs. She had seen death before, had caused death herself, but this was the first time she had failed to save someone she was sworn to protect. Guilt and sorrow welled up into more tears she didn't wipe away.

Then Eodan said, "Ginnevra." There was an unfamiliar edge to his voice, warning and uncertainty combined. She raised her head.

The karkadann stood only a dozen feet away, within the barrier, almost on top of Giulliomocte's body.

Ginnevra sucked in a startled breath. "You can see it?"

Eodan nodded. "We have to get it away from the Revered's body. It can't mean anything good."

Ginnevra disentangled herself from his embrace and stood. "Maybe. I wonder."

"Ginnevra. Anything that white has to be the Bright One's creation." Eodan picked up the greatsword, carefully avoiding the blade, and extended it to Ginnevra.

"If it's a monster," Ginnevra said slowly, reaching for understanding, "how did it get inside the barrier?"

She grasped the sword and took a few steps forward. The karkadann didn't move. It looked bigger close up than it had outside Savorola, and its scimitar horn looked even longer and more dangerous than before. Ginnevra stopped within touching distance of the creature, but didn't raise a hand to it. "What are you?" she asked. "What do you want?"

The karkadann bowed its head. "The gift you give. And the gift you take."

Frustration filled Ginnevra, and she said, "You speak in riddles. I don't understand."

"Promises, and your will to be done. Say the word." The karkadann's fathomless gaze made Ginnevra feel dizzy.

She looked from the karkadann to Giulliomocte and lowered her sword. "Do it," she said, without knowing what she meant the creature to do.

The karkadann lowered its head further, until the tip of its horn was scant inches from the terrible gaping wound in Giulliomocte's chest. "Redemption," it said, and rested its horn on Giulliomocte's chest.

A blinding white light engulfed Giulliomocte's body, making Ginnevra and Eodan cry out. Ginnevra threw up her arm to protect her eyes and stepped back. She barely made out the outlines of the karkadann, traced against the light like a pencil drawing. Its eyes were open despite the brilliance, and it didn't flinch.

The light changed. Its sharp, cold brightness warmed to gold, like summer sunlight, though no heat radiated from it. The golden light was thick and heavy, rich enough to be tangible. It flowed over Giulliomocte's body like melted honey, clinging to the edges of his wounds and sparkling there as if it were moving water struck by the sun. Ginnevra realized her vision had returned. She gazed at the karkadann in wonder. The creature, too, looked bathed in light, but as the light flowed over it, its body grew darker, from gold to orange to a deep sunset red, from red to violet and finally to a perfect purply black.

The light faded completely. The karkadann, now black as

night, regarded Ginnevra with its unchanged deep blue eyes. Its scimitar horn remained bright silver. "Redemption," it said, in a rich, melodious voice. "For me and mine. It has been a long time coming."

Ginnevra gaped. "Redemption. Your redemption. Redemption from what?"

At her feet, Giulliomocte shifted. Then he sat up.

Ginnevra jerked away and let out a squeak of surprise, and the karkadann laughed. Its laughter sounded like distant silvery bells. "It was once our gift, bestowing healing on the mortally wounded," it said. "But only a true resurrection could save us."

Ginnevra, still stunned, bent to offer Giulliomocte a hand up. The Revered stood with no sign that he had ever been wounded, no stiffness of motion, no shakiness. His clothes were untorn and no blood showed anywhere on him. "I still don't understand. Revered, are you well? What do you remember?"

"Having my chest and throat torn out," Giulliomocte said. He rubbed his throat as if in memory. "And then feeling more whole than I ever have in my life. Was I dead?" He smiled ruefully. "I suppose the Goddess prefers we not know too much about the ultimate destination of our souls, but a glimpse would have been nice."

Ginnevra released him and turned her attention back to the karkadann. "Thank you. But I have so many questions."

"Some of them I may not answer," the karkadann replied. "Having suffered the Dark Lady's displeasure once, I am reluctant to bring it down upon my people again. It is enough to say that we monokeroi, before we were given the name karkadann by fearful humanity, were beloved of the Goddess and recipients of Her many blessings. Our pride led to our downfall—forgive me for not dwelling on what we did. We lost the Goddess's protection and fell into the hands of the Bright One, our language confused, doomed to be Her slaves and harbingers of Her creations."

"And this was your redemption," Ginnevra said. "How did it work?"

The karkadann—the monokeros—shook its head. "We needed an invitation, and we had heard what you did for a dragon you might have slain. I chose to take a chance on your compassion."

"But I'm no one special," Ginnevra protested, a terrible fear surging through her. "That kind of thinking leads to pride—you ought to know about that, if pride is what lost you the Goddess's goodwill. I don't want to believe I'm the only paladin who thinks this way."

"You are not." The monokeros' gaze held Ginnevra frozen in place. "Change is coming. There are many who follow this path, and the Bright One shrieks in fury to know it. Do what your faith tells you, and you will be guided."

It nodded at Giulliomocte. "You know better now whom you serve," it said. "Faith is only the beginning." It turned and walked away like a patch of midnight, silhouetted against the brilliant blue of the barrier, and then passed through the barrier and disappeared between the trees.

Ginnevra let out a deep breath. She still wasn't happy with the monokeros' answer. It was one thing to be granted special powers by the Blessed and quite another to believe there was something inherently special about her. And yet she couldn't say the monokeros was wrong. Even the Goddess had said Ginnevra had done something in asking a boon for that dragon that no one had ever thought of before.

"Don't let me turn into someone superior and arrogant, all right?" she said to Eodan.

"Not a chance," Eodan said.

"That seems unlikely," Giulliomocte said. "I, on the other hand, was well on the way to becoming such without realizing it."

"I wouldn't say that," Ginnevra said. She concealed the discomfort she felt in talking to the Revered. Nobody had ever come back from the dead before, and if that didn't make someone special, she didn't know what would.

"Because you politely aren't saying 'I told you so.'" Giulliomocte smiled, a self-deprecating expression. "I didn't think of myself as personally important so much as I believed I was the Goddess's token for humanity, but that's a fine line." He shook his head. "Thank you for persisting. I genuinely believed I spoke with the Goddess."

"The voice is very similar," Ginnevra said. "It's understandable that you were fooled."

"I'm not sure that's an excuse," Giulliomocte said. "When we reach Abraciabene, I will confess everything to the Blessed and ask her not to ordain me as Hallowed."

"But you chose right, at the end," Ginnevra protested. "Don't you believe in forgiveness?"

"The Bright One wanted me corrupted so I might work Her evil in my role as Hallowed. I can't risk it." Giulliomocte shivered and rubbed his arms, then bent to retrieve his grace from where he'd dropped it. "We should return. I have many apologies to make—though I should start here."

He bowed to Ginnevra. "I said things to you about your relationship with Eodan that I believed to be true only because the Bright One influenced me. I apologize for whatever injury I caused. And you—" He turned to Eodan. "I believed it was possible to accept your conversion while still denouncing you as a monster, as if that weren't itself a different form of hatred. I hope you will accept my apology."

Eodan put a hand on Giulliomocte's shoulder. "Thank you. That has to have been hard to admit."

"It's surprisingly easy to apologize when your heart is free from conflict." Giulliomocte's smile showed the truth of his words. "Now, we really should move quickly. I feel confident that the Goddess will grant me a healing blessing for Dedicate Bidelia now."

"Because the Bright One's words aren't in the way anymore?" Ginnevra asked.

"Because I'm finally asking for the right reason," Giulliomocte replied.

TWENTY-FIVE

They returned to camp in the early afternoon, with Eodan leading the way and Ginnevra, still alert despite her feeling they were safe from any other predators, bringing up the rear. She and Giulliomocte didn't speak, but it was a pleasant silence, not taut with unspoken anger as their previous silences had been. Ginnevra's weariness had faded with time, her pains subsiding as she healed. She watched Eodan, who stopped limping after about an hour, and hoped that meant his own recuperative powers had taken over as well.

They were met by two paladins, Bartolla and Pia, standing sentry at the southern edge of camp. "Prime Cassaline!" Pia exclaimed. "Are you injured? You look—"

"It's mostly werewolf blood," Ginnevra said. "Don't worry." She saluted Bartolla, whose eyes were wide when they regarded Giulliomocte, and added, "Where's the captain?"

Buonnane stood next to Bidelia's wagon, talking to Serenna. Their conversation cut off as Ginnevra approached. Buonnane's gaze took in Ginnevra's condition and Eodan's gory fur, then went straight to Giulliomocte. "Revered, thank the Goddess you're all right," she said.

"Thank you for not chastising me," Giulliomocte said. "I apologize for leaving and putting this caravan in danger. But if you'll excuse me..." He clambered into the wagon and knelt beside Bidelia.

"I'll explain in a moment," Ginnevra told Buonnane, who looked full to bursting with questions. She made way for Eodan, who leaped into the wagon after the Revered, and then climbed in herself.

Bidelia's face was pale, and she shuddered as if she were freezing despite the warmth of the wagon and the many blankets and cloaks shrouding her. Eodan resumed his human shape and brushed her forehead, then felt her throat for a pulse. "It's bad," he said. "She feels like ice."

Giulliomocte nodded. He clasped Bidelia's hand in one of his and his grace in the other. Quietly, in the same conversational tone he'd addressed the Bright One, he said, *"By Your grace I make all things whole."*

Ginnevra braced herself for an outpouring of rainbow light as she remembered from Eodan's healing months ago. Instead, warm golden light welled up from Bidelia's body, thick and honey-rich as the monokeros' healing had been. Ginnevra smelled wildflowers, and for a moment, the breeze brushing her face was warm and not icy. Giulliomocte's head remained bowed, and he never let go of Bidelia's hand even though the light surged over their joined fists.

After a long moment, the light faded, and Giulliomocte withdrew. Eodan touched Bidelia's skin again. "It's warm. Human-normal warm. Her pulse is steady, she's not breathing shallowly anymore, but she's still asleep."

"I don't know how that healing grace works," Giulliomocte

said. "She may still need rest to fully recover. But the werewolf taint is gone."

"Why did it work now?" Buonnane leaned on the back of the wagon, still watching Giulliomocte.

"It's a long story, captain," Giulliomocte said, glancing at Ginnevra, "and the short version may be even longer. But I believe we were ready for a miracle now in a way we were not before."

Buonnane looked skeptical, but said only, "We should ready the camp for a werewolf attack at moonrise. There's no point traveling on today."

"Ah, about that," Ginnevra said. "The werewolves are gone. Eodan and I killed some of them, including their dominus, and the rest fled."

"As I said, they won't be able to choose a new dominus who could lead them against us before we reach safety," Eodan said. He had removed one of the cloaks that covered Bidelia and wrapped it around his lower body. "We're not out of danger, given that there are other monsters in the forest, but it's not quite so imminent as it was."

Now Buonnane looked like she wanted to shout and didn't have a good target. "Someone had better explain all this," she said.

"We will," Ginnevra said. "But the Revered is right that the short version is even longer than the full story, so we're going to need something to eat first."

After removing her armor, Ginnevra and Eodan settled outside their tent with Giulliomocte and Buonnane to tell the whole story. It took over an hour, because the captain had many, many questions. But eventually, Buonnane said, "Why did you tell me the Bright One spoke to you, Revered Giulliomocte? You know how that sounds."

"Because while the Goddess delights in secrets, She dislikes Her servants concealing truths to deceive others," Giulliomocte said. "And I believe it is a valuable lesson to everyone that no one, not even the Dark Lady's anointed, is immune to the wiles of the Bright One. Besides, it's not as if I will become Hallowed now. I don't think this knowledge will hurt anyone, least of all me. And if it does..." Giulliomocte shrugged. "I endured whispers about my worthiness before, and I can do it again."

"I honor your truthfulness," Buonnane said, bowing her head and saluting him. "I don't know that I'd choose the same, but we all make our own paths. And, Prime Cassaline," she added, "that's quite the story you'll have for the Blessed."

"It's not a story people are likely to believe," Ginnevra said. "The karkadann—the monokeros, I mean—that alone makes everything seem unlikely."

"I wouldn't want to be you," Buonnane said with an uncharacteristic grin. "Strange things happen around you. I'll fight werewolves any day rather than be part of some mysterious monster's redemption."

Ginnevra eyed her. "And will you? Fight werewolves, I mean?"

Buonnane's smile fell away. "If I have to," she said. "I anticipate the possibility of finding more werewolves who've turned their backs on their creator. I'll never forget the past, but I think now I can look to the future instead."

"I'd like to tell you that's more likely, but I don't know," Eodan said. "My pack was divided in its loyalties until the Bright One's followers turned on those like me. There have to be packs that chose a different path. But your willingness to keep an open mind is enough."

"News about the werewolves will spread," Giulliomocte said. "Who knows what effect that will have?" He rose, stretching, and said, "If you'll excuse me, I have amends to make elsewhere."

When he was gone, Buonnane said, "I wonder what the Blessed will do with him? If he's not going to be Hallowed, we made this trip for nothing. People died for nothing."

"I don't know if it was for nothing," Ginnevra said. "The journey changed us. We eliminated a werewolf threat—that pack moved far too freely within Savorola, and I wager they took lives even before we arrived."

"*You* eliminated a werewolf threat," Buonnane said. "I'm grateful to you."

That made Ginnevra feel uncomfortable. "And more people learned the truth about werewolves like Eodan," she said, side-stepping the issue. "From my perspective, that's a blessing."

Buonnane glanced at Eodan, then back at Ginnevra. "I suppose I'd call it a blessing, too." She rose and brushed damp dirt from her posterior. "I'm going to walk the perimeter and let people know we can stand down—to a degree, anyway."

Ginnevra rose as well. She watched Buonnane walk away and said, "I never would have guessed she could change."

"So we've reached the limits of your optimism," Eodan said. He stood and put an arm around Ginnevra's shoulders. "That's reassuring."

"Why, because even I have to face reality sometimes?"

Eodan smiled. "No, because optimism taken too far becomes delusion. And your optimism is always firmly rooted in what's real."

They strolled through the camp, passing tents and sidestepping trees, until they reached the perimeter. "Water," Eodan said. "I'm parched. All that running through the woods left me thirsty."

"I could use a drink," Ginnevra agreed.

But when they neared the stream, Ginnevra slowed her steps. "Someone's there. It sounds like an argument."

Eodan tilted his head. "Not a very heated one, but yes. That's Revered Giulliomocte."

"Then I know who he's talking to," Ginnevra said. She took a few more steps.

"We shouldn't interrupt," Eodan said.

"No, but I am a shameless eavesdropper, and I want to hear this," Ginnevra replied.

Her paladin's hearing was good enough to make out the conversation Giulliomocte was having, though they were far enough away that if the Revered saw them, he would assume they were out of earshot. He and Revered Pratese stood by the riverside, by the tension in their bodies very intent on each other. Ginnevra regretted not arriving sooner, but this would have to do.

"...doesn't matter," Pratese was saying. "You made all the decisions. You ignored me, you avoided me—"

"And I was wrong to do so," Giulliomocte said. "You were right. We should have talked things out. We owed it to ourselves —to what we'd had—not to let it end in recrimination."

"And now?"

Pratese's fear and longing were audible even at this distance. For once, Ginnevra felt sorry for the woman.

Giulliomocte hesitated. "It's over, Marsillia," he finally said. "I don't feel that way about you anymore. And if I'd been able to simply admit that, you wouldn't have hated me. I'm truly sorry."

Pratese was silent. Her back was to Ginnevra, so Ginnevra couldn't see her expression, but Giulliomocte's frown vanished, replaced by a terrible sorrow that made Ginnevra's heart ache.

"I know that's not what you want to hear," Giulliomocte went on. "But I have to be honest with you. I will always care about you, and—"

"Don't," Pratese said. Her voice sounded a little thick. "You can't make this better, Domenico."

"I know. But I don't regret our time together. I hope you won't regret it either." Giulliomocte raised a hand as if he wanted to reach out to Pratese, but lowered it without touching her.

Pratese shook her head. "Maybe someday," she said. "For now —I want you to stay away from me." She turned and walked away, deeper into the woods.

Ginnevra swore under her breath. "She can't be allowed to go off on her own, but—"

"I'll follow her," Eodan said. "Without interfering."

Ginnevra watched him go, then continued on to the stream. Giulliomocte squatted by the water's edge, trailing his fingers in the icy flow. Ginnevra crouched for a drink without saying anything.

"You heard that, didn't you," Giulliomocte said abruptly.

Ginnevra blushed. Her earlier casual attitude about eavesdropping felt childish now. "I did. I'm sorry for intruding."

The Revered shrugged. "Some things can't be mended."

"No." Ginnevra scooped more water. It was cold enough to make her teeth ache.

Giulliomocte sighed. "I have enough regrets for two lifetimes, but that one hurts my soul. Not the fact of our relationship, but that I allowed it to end in the worst possible way. I don't suppose that's something you understand, prime. You strike me as someone who is too forthright to let a romance die a slow, unnecessary death."

"I haven't had a lot of romances. But no, I've never experienced that." Ginnevra wiped her hand on her trousers. "But you did the right thing, in the end."

"Did I?" Giulliomocte laughed, a curt, bitter sound. "Marsillia would not agree with you."

321

"The right thing doesn't always make us happy," Ginnevra said. "It makes us whole."

"That's very wise." Giulliomocte sounded surprised. "I can't give Marsillia what she wants. But maybe I can give her what she ultimately needs."

"You staying in Abraciabene will help," Ginnevra said.

"I don't know—well." Giulliomocte rubbed a hand over his face, which was stubbly from a day's beard growth. "I can ask to remain in the holy city even if I'm not to be Hallowed. You're right, it will ease things for Marsillia if I'm not around."

"You shouldn't assume what the Blessed will do." Ginnevra stood. "Let's go back to camp. I think people need to see you're not gone."

Giulliomocte frowned. "I don't like being a figurehead. It's not good for anyone's faith to tie it closely to an individual."

"You're not a figurehead, you're an example." She gestured to him to join her. "And everyone's faith has to start somewhere. Eventually it either breaks, or it stands on its own, and neither of us can do anything about that."

"They look to you, too."

"They do." Ginnevra kicked at the last of the fallen leaves, which were sodden and lumpy. "Nothing I can do about that, either."

Giulliomocte's breath hissed out of him in a long, thin stream. "I fear falling back into bad habits if I am honored for myself and not for the Goddess I represent."

"That fear will stop that from happening. I promise." Ginnevra stopped and faced the Revered. "The Goddess demands much of Her servants. I don't know what it's like to be an anointed, but I know so long as I care more about Her challenges than I do about how others treat me, I remain Her servant and not some privilege-blinded autocrat. I can't imagine it's much different for you."

Giulliomocte lowered his head. "I feel the weight of having disappointed so many. Hallowed Riccobene risked much in supporting me, given how many people believed my appointment was political."

"And now you're just wallowing in guilt," Ginnevra snapped. "Stop that. It's unattractive in anyone, let alone an anointed. Look. You made mistakes, and you were fooled, and maybe that means your path isn't what you thought it was three weeks ago. But I've seen you work miracles, and I can't believe your spiritual life is as over as you seem to think. Hell, you came back from the dead! The Blessed will have something to say about *that*, at any rate."

She saw his lips curve in a smile, though his face was still in shadow. "So I should behave like an anointed and stop conjuring an immutable future, is that it?"

"That's a very poetic way of saying get your head out of your ass, but yes."

The Revered laughed. "Very well, prime. I'll remember this. I think I understand why you have the calling you do."

"I still don't, so that makes one of us," Ginnevra said.

TWENTY-SIX

J ust over a week later, they rode into the outskirts of Abraciabene, banners snapping in the brisk winter air. It would have been a more triumphal entry if their caravan hadn't come up against a wagon train also heading for the holy city. Its wagons, more ponderous than theirs, moved slowly and were clearly incapable of moving aside for anyone, even servants of the Goddess.

Buonnane scowled at the wagon driver just ahead. His back was impervious to her irritation. "We're going to take as long getting from here to the Citadel as we did the whole way from Lake Salvectus."

"I'm sure they'd make way if they could," Ginnevra said. "But it's hard not to wonder if they've slowed down on purpose. To gawk at us, naturally."

"If they're gawking, they're doing it secretly." Buonnane slid a finger beneath her coif to scratch an itch. "Goddess save me, but I want a *bath*."

"Oh, now I'm thinking about it." Ginnevra mentally went over the inns she'd stayed at in the outer city, considering the amenities of each. Eodan couldn't enter the Citadel, monster or not, but Ginnevra had experienced the lackluster accommodations the Citadel provided paladins and was just as happy to stay elsewhere.

Hoofbeats faster and louder than her own alerted her to Eodan's approach from behind. "The wagon drivers say to head for the New Moon Inn," he said, reining in Ginger to match Dauntless' pace. "They have an arrangement with the owner."

"I was afraid we'd have them trailing us through the city," Ginnevra said. "Are the anointed prepared to walk?"

"The Dedicates say they are looking forward to stretching their legs." Eodan squinted at the head of the wagon train before them. "Is it just me, or have they slowed down?"

"I'm tempted to ride ahead and ask, but that would be inconsiderate." Ginnevra tugged on Dauntless' reins so he wouldn't ride up the rear of the last wagon. Boxes and barrels made up its anonymous cargo. "I can be patient."

"You're really bad at patience," Eodan pointed out.

"Which is no doubt why the Goddess has provided you an excellent opportunity to practice," Buonnane said with a straight face.

Ginnevra watched the city gate approaching, far too slowly. "Sometimes the Goddess has a terrible sense of humor."

Traffic slowed even more the closer they drew to the iron-banded doors of the gates. Though travelers on foot passed through without being stopped, the guards questioned anyone driving a wagon. Ginnevra wasn't sure why they cared. Abraciabene's primary purpose for existing wasn't commerce, and anyone entering with goods for sale probably wasn't there to make a fortune or undercut local businesses. She stifled a bored yawn and inched closer.

Finally, they stopped in front of the guards, whose own bored expressions gave way to stunned awe. "Your name, my lady?" one asked, his voice trembling.

"Ginnevra Cassaline, prime of the Blessed, escorting Revered Domenico Giulliomocte," Ginnevra said with her most neutral expression.

"We had word of your coming," the other guard said. "My lady Cassaline and the Revered are to report directly to the Blessed. Your companions will handle the disposition of your wagons and follow in due time."

Ginnevra wished she dared ask how they knew to expect her, but she held on to the mystique of her office and said, "Very well. Thank you for your service."

Once they were past the gate, Eodan said, "That wasn't predicting the future, was it?"

"More likely scrying," Buonnane said. "It's not perfect, because humans have too much free will to permit seeing far into their futures, but I'm sure the Blessed has ways of seeing what's happening in the present." She turned to Ginnevra. "If we don't meet again—it's been a pleasure riding with you, prime."

"Likewise, captain," Ginnevra said, clasping Buonnane's gloved hand in farewell.

The New Moon Inn lay a short distance down Abraciabene's wide main street, and when they saw it, Eodan said, "I think I'll stay here and help with the unloading, then get us a room."

"I'll be back soon." Ginnevra kissed him and rode back along the line of march to where Giulliomocte rode flanked by Zana and Pia. "Revered, we're summoned," she said. "Come with me."

Giulliomocte saluted the paladins and turned his mount to follow Ginnevra. "So soon," he said. "I suppose that was to be expected."

"Are you nervous?" Ginnevra asked.

Giulliomocte's eyes focused on something in the far distance. "I'm not, actually. Whatever comes next, I trust I will be able to endure."

Ginnevra nodded. "I have so much to tell the Blessed I don't have room in me for fear. Though I wonder sometimes what she thinks of my visits. I always seem to have something unusual to describe. Maybe all primes are like that."

"Or maybe it's just you, and the Blessed expects the extraordinary when you arrive," Giulliomocte said with a smile.

Ginnevra shuddered. "I'd rather just be one of many, thanks."

She was used to passing through the gate to the inner city with no comment, but to her surprise, when they dismounted at the gate to the Bastion, last ring of the city before reaching the Citadel, the guards there also let them by without stopping them. Both women bowed low, not to Ginnevra, but to Giulliomocte, and took their horses without comment. The Revered managed not to show his astonishment until they were out of earshot, surrounded by the black basalt houses of the Bastion. "What was that?"

"All right, now I'm a little nervous," Ginnevra said. "I dislike not knowing what other people expect, and that certainly looked like they knew who you are and why you're here."

"I suppose they can't know what's happened." Giulliomocte wiped his forehead, which was beaded with sweat despite the freezing air. "I feel terrible accepting their respect when I don't deserve it."

"You don't know that yet." Ginnevra quickened her pace. "Let's hurry and find out the truth."

Despite her words, she didn't want to run within the Bastion, and not only because there were anointed at some of the black marble shrines circling the inner wall. She was struck, as she was every time, with how peaceful and calming the black basalt stones were. There was only one road, and it circled the Bastion without deviation, so the anointed who lived in Abraciabene could walk the path in an endless circle, praying or meditating or just drinking in the quiet peace. Ginnevra had only ever been to Abraciabene on business, but the idea of walking this sacred space appealed to her.

She examined the single-story basalt houses and reflected on how much they resembled the cabins on the shore of Lake Salvectus, in size at least. For once, her memory of that place didn't hurt or infuriate her. Those people had died horribly, and she hadn't been able to prevent it, but where mortal justice ended, the Goddess took over. She didn't feel comfortable praying for their souls—she didn't have any idea what they deserved—so she silently thanked the Dark Lady for giving her a small part in sending those souls to whatever rest the Goddess had in mind.

There were no guards at the Citadel gate, which was a short low-ceilinged arched passage of stone. Ginnevra and Giulliomocte crossed the vast courtyard without drawing attention from the paladins and anointed going about their own business there. Ginnevra's gaze was drawn from the stony battlements of the Citadel to the flag flying atop its tallest tower. Because the Citadel looked like a castle and not a sanctuary, the flag might have been that of a great lord, but it was the same banner that had flown above their wagons the whole four weeks of travel.

For the first time, Ginnevra considered whether the Blessed ever thought of herself as a power to be reckoned with, like a queen or elector. If she did, that made Ginnevra the representative of that power. She shivered in the cold air and pulled her cloak close about her. It was a frightening but ultimately irrelevant thought.

She led Giulliomocte to the iron-banded doors that were the Citadel's entrance and pulled one open. Within, darkness shrouded the hall that led deeper into the Citadel. Her eyes instantly adjusted to the dimness, lit only by a single torch halfway down the hall.

The rapid patter of footsteps drew her attention to a young woman in the night-black surcoat with the dark moon emblazoned on it. "My lady, are you summoned?" the girl said.

"Prime Ginnevra Cassaline escorting Revered Domenico Giulliomocte," Ginnevra replied.

The girl's mouth fell open, and her gaze settled immediately on Giulliomocte. "Revered," she said, her voice faint, then she visibly collected herself and said, "Follow me, please."

Ginnevra didn't need a guide to the Blessed's chambers, but after the first turn she realized that wasn't where they were going. The girl led them through dark corridors into a great hall that might have been lifted from some lord's castle, complete with a long fireplace that was currently unlit and a couple of trestle tables lined with benches. Ginnevra cast a glance at the great dais with its high table before their guide hurried them through the hall to an arched opening.

Beyond the opening lay a vast circular chamber, windowless and lit by lamps burning with magical fire. The fires made bright splotches on the gray-streaked black marble facing the walls, glimmering like pools of molten brass. The girl came to an abrupt stop and bowed. "My lady, Revered," she said, her voice muffled by the hair that fell down around her face.

Ginnevra had stopped too, but not because of the girl; she was surprised to find the room occupied, it was so silent. Women in the black robes of Hallowed stood in a semi-circle with their backs to the wall and their hands concealed within their enveloping sleeves. All of them wore their hair loose, something Ginnevra had never seen a Hallowed do before. Their eyes were fixed, not on Ginnevra or Giulliomocte, but on the Blessed, who sat in a low-backed chair carved of a single block of basalt. It was rough-hewn, not polished, and soaked up the fiery light like a pool of shadow. The Blessed also wore her hair loose, framing her pale face and making her solid black eyes seem fathomless.

Ginnevra hesitated. Surely this was none of her business. But Giulliomocte walked forward until he faced the Blessed at the center of the chamber. "Blessed," he said, inclining his head.

"Domenico," the Blessed said, her voice low and musical so his name sounded like a tune plucked on a lyre. "Welcome to the Citadel."

"Thank you for your welcome," Giulliomocte said. "I apologize for wasting your time."

No one spoke or moved, not even to whisper a question to a neighbor. The Blessed's eyebrows raised like a couple of black wings. "Wasting our time? Why would you believe that?"

"Because I intend to request that you not make me Hallowed," Giulliomocte said.

Still, the assembled Hallowed made no sign of surprise. Ginnevra's tension wound her so tight she was sure she would snap. She returned her gaze to the Blessed as the woman said, "Then you do not believe you are worthy?"

"The Bright One deceived me, and I believed I was listening to the Goddess." Giulliomocte sounded far calmer than Ginnevra believed was reasonable. "This led me to prideful and sinful acts, and nearly cost me my soul. I am too weak a vessel to hold the highest rank of the anointed. Please accept my apology for failing you—all of you."

The Blessed rose, a graceful movement like a reed blowing in the wind. "Then you admit to having been deceived. Do you mean you are deceived no longer?"

"Thanks to the patience and endurance of another of the Dark Lady's servants, I saw the truth and rejected the Bright One's command." Giulliomocte's voice trembled slightly, but only for a moment. "But my failure to see the truth immediately makes me unworthy."

"I see." The Blessed turned her dark gaze on Ginnevra, who straightened in surprise. "Prime Cassaline, what is your witness?"

Her phrasing told Ginnevra what to say. "Revered Giulliomocte was deceived, but he accepted my word as truth and ultimately rejected the Bright One. He gave his life rather than follow her."

That, she expected to cause a stir if nothing else did. But the Hallowed lining the walls remained so still Ginnevra started to wonder if they were alive. The Blessed didn't so much as blink. "Died, and was restored by the Dark Lady's grace," she said, with the same calm inflection.

"In the person of a monokeros, yes, Holy One." This time, she didn't bother being amazed at what the Blessed knew.

"Another creature we believed lost." The Blessed walked forward until she was standing next to Giulliomocte. They were the same height, Ginnevra noted.

When she next spoke, the Blessed raised her voice so her words echoed off the walls. "Do you who gather here today bear witness?"

"*Aye*," said the circle of women, their faces unchanging.

"Hallowed Puliese," the Blessed said, still in that ringing, carrying voice, "do you have something to say?" Her eyes never left Giulliomocte's. Ginnevra saw him close one hand into a fist.

One of the women twitched as if she wanted to step forward, but she remained where she was. "I do not, Holy One."

"Nothing about this man's elevation, perhaps?" The Blessed's lips quirked in a half-smile. Ginnevra, facing her, did not think it was a friendly smile.

"No, Holy One. I have nothing to say." Hallowed Puliese's jaw tightened.

"Very well. Kneel, Revered Domenico Giulliomocte, and receive our Lady's blessing."

Giulliomocte's shoulders were shaking. "Holy One," he said.

"Kneel before you fall over, Domenico." The Blessed's smile became amused.

Slowly, using one hand for balance, Giulliomocte knelt. The Blessed rested her left hand on the top of his head and raised her right hand above her head.

"Dark Lady," she said, "we Your servants gather in witness of Your will. Let this man be Hallowed to Your service for the rest of his days. Grant him Your blessing, and grant him, as he asks in holiness, the desires of his heart as he turns his heart to You. Ever in Your name."

The earth shook, drowning out the responses the rest of the Hallowed made, and a streak of golden light flashed across Giulliomocte and the Blessed. Ginnevra flinched and flung up an arm to cover her eyes, but the light was gone as fast as it had appeared.

The Blessed removed her hand from Giulliomocte's head and extended it to him, helping him rise. "Hallowed Giulliomocte," she said, "welcome."

"Holy One," Giulliomocte said, his voice shaking, "I don't understand. I failed so completely—"

"You are not the first to hear the Bright One's voice and mistake it for that of our Dark Lady," the Blessed said. "You are, however, the first to reject the Bright One's command and the first to redeem yourself from that path. We honor your faith and courage."

"But—" Giulliomocte turned to face Ginnevra. His wide, astonished eyes pleaded with her. "I didn't—it was Prime

Cassaline, she was the one who convinced me I was wrong. I had no faith at all."

"Sometimes faith means leaning on the belief of another." The Blessed put her hand on Giulliomocte's shoulder and turned him to face her. She tilted her head back and said, "Is that not true?"

A voice like thunderous silk filled the chamber. *You all come to your faith in different ways,* the Goddess said. *Domenico, you leaned only upon your own understanding and it left you open to corruption. Remember.*

Giulliomocte nodded. He looked dazed. "I will, Goddess. I swear it."

Swearing is unnecessary when your whole heart is given to the truth. The Goddess sounded amused. *But I understand. Cristinna, spread the word.*

"Of course," the Blessed said.

Ginnevra.

Ginnevra startled. A low hum of laughter ran through the room, but she was too surprised to care. "Yes, Goddess?"

You need not fear. You are one of many for whom I intend great service to Me. But I imagine I can thank you for restoring My creation to Me without sending you into giddy raptures of pride.

Ginnevra blushed so hard she was afraid her head might pop. "No, Goddess. Never that. Is the monokeros—will we see them again?"

I never tell you the future. But to answer your true question—the monokeroi may serve Me freely once more, and for that, I am grateful.

Ginnevra bowed her head. "Thank you."

My blessing upon all present, and My love. Golden light swirled like motes of dust in a breeze, brushing against each of them, and then the room's silence was once more an ordinary one.

The Blessed released Giulliomocte and drew in a deep breath.

"That was less inscrutable than usual," she said in a normal voice. "Domenico, are you satisfied?"

"If I said no, I would be the most ungrateful man alive," Giulliomocte said with a rueful smile.

The Blessed nodded. "Come, greet your newest associate," she said to the others.

Ginnevra stepped back to allow the other Hallowed to throng Giulliomocte. She kept an eye on Hallowed Puliese, just in case, but the woman showed no sign of dissatisfaction with the first male Hallowed. Ginnevra had a good idea why the Blessed had asked Puliese for her comments. The Goddess's approval probably meant Giulliomocte wouldn't face outright challenges, but that didn't mean there weren't more like Puliese, watching for him to misstep. Ginnevra closed her eyes briefly and prayed for the newest Hallowed's faith and conviction to carry him through.

Warmth touched her heart, making her smile.

THAT EVENING, she sat in the tap room of the New Moon Inn with Eodan's arm around her waist and her head on his shoulder, soaking in the heat of the blazing fire. "I finally feel warm," she murmured.

"We can head south tomorrow, if you like," Eodan said. "Far south, even."

"I don't mind staying here a few days. I want to see Serenna settled. Maybe even until her father arrives." Ginnevra stretched out her long legs and sighed with pleasure.

"She seemed confident in her decision," Eodan said. "And that's one more paladin for the Goddess."

Ginnevra nodded. "Captain Buonnane's company sets out on

the return journey in a week, and by then Serenna will have made new friends and gotten a taste of life in training."

"Do you miss it? Being part of a company?"

She tilted her head to look at him. "Not really. Not in the sense of wishing my life were different. Sometimes I look back on those days, but it's never with regret." That made her think of something else. "Have you spoken to Revered Pratese recently?"

Eodan didn't comment on the abrupt change of subject. "I've talked to her now and then. Her heart's broken, and that's never easy to overcome." He smiled then. "She came close to asking me to sleep with her."

"*What?*"

"She wanted comfort from someone who wasn't going to break her heart more. I steered her away from the subject and nobody was embarrassed."

"That's brave of her, considering she has to know what I would do to her if she made a move on you." Ginnevra snuggled closer. "I hope she finds peace."

"So do I."

They sat in silence for a while, watching the flames. Ginnevra listened to the low hum of conversations without trying to pick out individual words. Her mind drifted, unmoored from her body, touching on memories from the last four weeks without settling in to remember more deeply. It felt like falling asleep, except that she was aware of her body, of Eodan's closeness—and with that, she recognized the fey feeling she'd experienced twice before.

She stood, jostling Eodan, who had fallen asleep. "Come with me," she whispered, tugging on his hand.

They walked outside to stand in the innyard. Snow had started falling some time before, and a light dusting clung to the hard-packed earth and the posts supporting the short fence circling the yard. For once, Ginnevra didn't miss her cloak. She took Eodan's hand and said, "There."

In the street, scant yards from the door, a monokeros stood in a pool of light that came from nowhere Ginnevra could see. Its midnight flanks gleamed in the mysterious light, as did its silver scimitar horn. Deep blue eyes regarded Ginnevra. It said nothing, but Ginnevra felt it was waiting.

"You do see it, right?" she asked

Eodan nodded. "It's astonishing. So beautiful."

Ginnevra let go of Eodan's hand and walked to meet the monokeros. "Are you the one I spoke to, or another?"

The monokeros restlessly scuffed the ground with one hoof. "Yes, and no," it said. "We are all one, and we are all unique. If not, we couldn't have been freed."

"I think I understand." Ginnevra raised a hand, tentatively. "May I?"

The creature bowed its head. Ginnevra laid her palm against its nose and gasped. "It's like touching running water. You're so alive."

"It is our Lady's gift," the monokeros said. It raised its head and looked at Eodan. "Not something you are entitled to."

Ginnevra snatched her hand away and turned to look at Eodan, whose jaw was set tight with anger. "That's cruel." she told the monokeros. "Someday—"

"I do not speak of his race," the monokeros said. "You have sins to atone for, and a past to reconcile. There is nowhere you can run to escape the truth."

"That sounds like prophecy," Ginnevra retorted. "Shouldn't you be afraid of falling back into captivity?"

The monokeros turned its blue-eyed gaze on her. "That is a glimpse of what was, not what will be. We do not prophesy. But it does not take a prophet to know that no one is whole who leaves his heart in the wrong hands." It turned and trotted away, then broke into a run that carried it down the street toward the gate and out of sight.

Ginnevra hurried to Eodan's side. "What was that about? It can't possibly—Eodan, stop looking like that!"

"Like what?" Eodan's voice sounded dull, as if he were remembering something awful.

"Like you've been cursed. You know that's not how things work. The monokeros didn't mean you were helpless in the hands of fate!" But her memory of how certain the monokeros had sounded made her words feel weak.

Eodan let out a deep sigh. "It wasn't wrong."

"What do you mean?" Fear struck her, a nameless horror that she was about to lose the person she loved most in the world.

Eodan shook his head, slowly. "Ginnevra," he said, "do you trust me?"

"You know I do."

"And I will never do anything to hurt you."

Ginnevra clenched her hands to keep them from shaking. "You're scaring me."

"I'm sorry." He put one hand over hers. "I need you to trust me a while longer. There are things I haven't told you, things about who I used to be—no dangerous secrets, at least I don't think they're dangerous, but things I'm ashamed of. Things I'd like to forget. Things you might not forgive me for."

Ginnevra covered their linked hands with her free hand. "Putting off a serious conversation never ends well," she said. "You know you can tell me anything, and I won't hate you."

Eodan smiled. "Soon, beloved. I promise. I just need a little time, that's all."

It wasn't a satisfying answer, but Ginnevra couldn't think how to change his mind short of forcing the issue, and she didn't want

PATH OF THE PALADIN

to do that. So instead, she put her arms around him and kissed him. "I can wait."

Eodan's arms went around her waist, and he drew her close. The warmth of his body reminded her that it was cold outside and she didn't have her cloak. "Let's go upstairs," she suggested.

"The room doesn't have a fire," Eodan said.

"Then we'll have to keep each other warm," she replied.

She cast one glance over her shoulder as they walked back into the inn. Far down the road, she saw the glint of light on silver, a moving shadow, and then it was gone.

About the Author

In addition to The Books of the Dark Goddess, Melissa McShane is the author of many fantasy novels, including the novels of Tremontane, the first of which is *Servant of the Crown;* The Extraordinaries series, beginning with *Burning Bright;* and *The Book of Secrets,* first book in The Last Oracle series.

While her home remains in the mountains out West with her family and two very needy cats, she currently lives in Kerala, India. She wrote reviews and critical essays for many years before turning to fiction, which is much more fun than anyone ought to be allowed to have.

You can visit her at her website
   www.melissamcshanewrites.com
   for more information on other books and upcoming releases.

To subscribe to her newsletter, which is published monthly, visit **www.melissamcshanewrites.com/contact-me-2/join-my-mailing-list**

ALSO BY MELISSA MCSHANE

Sands of Memory

Call of Wizardry

THE DRAGONS OF MOTHER STONE

Spark the Fire

Faith in Flames

Ember in Shadow

Skies Will Burn

THE CONVERGENCE TRILOGY

The Summoned Mage

The Wandering Mage

The Unconquered Mage

THE BOOKS OF DALANINE

The Smoke-Scented Girl

The God-Touched Man

Emissary

Warts and All: The Deluxe Expanded Edition (forthcoming)

The View from Castle Always

Winter Across Worlds: A Holiday Collection

www.ingramcontent.com/pod-product-compliance
Lightning Source LLC
Chambersburg PA
CBHW070912260626
47162CB00007B/2642